Henry Hendrickson

Out from the Darkness

An Autobiography unfolding the Life Story and Singular Vicissitudes of a

Scandinavian Bartimaeus

Henry Hendrickson

Out from the Darkness
An Autobiography unfolding the Life Story and Singular Vicissitudes of a Scandinavian Bartimaeus

ISBN/EAN: 9783337121556

Printed in Europe, USA, Canada, Australia, Japan

Cover: Foto ©Raphael Reischuk / pixelio.de

More available books at **www.hansebooks.com**

OUT FROM THE
·········· DARKNESS.

AN AUTOBIOGRAPHY

*UNFOLDING THE LIFE STORY AND SINGULAR
VICISSITUDES*

OF A

SCANDINAVIAN BARTIMÆUS.

By HENRY HENDRICKSON.

WITH A PORTRAIT OF THE AUTHOR.

H. J. SMITH & CO.,
CHICAGO, PHILADELPHIA, KANSAS CITY, OAKLAND, CAL.
1890.

TO MY GENEROUS FRIEND,

MONS ANDERSON,

OF LA CROSSE, WIS.,

THIS VOLUME IS RESPECTFULLY DEDICATED,

AS A SLIGHT TOKEN OF THE APPRECIATION IN WHICH HE
IS HELD BY THE AUTHOR.

FOR NOBLE QUALITIES AND GENEROUS DEEDS WHICH HAVE WON THE
RESPECT AND ESTEEM OF ALL CLASSES IN THE NORTHWEST.

PREFACE.

Custom, which is all but inexorable, demands from the author of a book, a few prefatory words to introduce his bantling to the world; and it would be ungracious to regret the opportunity to say a few last words by way of a beginning. The preface to a book, like the prologue to a play, must be written after the work is otherwise complete; and it is pleasant to realize that the promises of long ago are within a few days of fulfillment in the publication of this volume. The story of a blind man's life will not, I trust, be found dull and uninteresting, for as Tennyson says, "I am a part of all that I have seen;" and that may be supplemented with the words of Hamlet, "In my mind's eye, Horatio."

The gold fields of Australia and the peculiarities of its population; the perils of Chinese navigation, the great fire in Chicago in some of its phases, some of the dangers from American monopolists and "ratteners," and many questions of social importance which more or less immediately affect the blind, have been woven into the web of this tale. Beyond the hackneyed round of autobiography I have ventured to give brief sketches of the history

IX.

of the Scandinavian peoples all over the world, and following to its ultimatum in this country the growth of liberal institutions, have presented to my readers some few ideas as to parliamentary government as developed by the Anglo-Saxons in England. The Scandinavians as a people, are interested in every fact that shows how freedom has become the rule among the favored nations of the earth; and the blind of every race cannot fail to assist in the diffusion of a work from the hands of one of their own number.

THE AUTHOR.

TABLE OF CONTENTS.

CHAPTER I.

INTRODUCTORY MATTER.

CHAPTER II.

"LET THERE BE LIGHT".

CHAPTER III.

I EXPLORE.

XI.

CHAPTER IV.

SCHOOL DAYS IN EARNEST.

CHAPTER V.

CHARACTER STUDIES.

CHAPTER VI.

WARNING.

CHAPTER VII.

IN WAR TIME.

CHAPTER VIII.

SEEKING AND FINDING.

CHAPTER IX.

BUSINESS EXPERIENCES.

CHAPTER X.

I SEE THE SIGHTS.

CHAPTER XI.

EXCITEMENT IN BADGERDOM.

CHAPTER XII.

FREE ADVERTISING AND PROSPEROUS BUSINESS.

CHAPTER XIII.

PROSPECTING.

CHAPTER XIV.

PARTINGS AND REUNIONS.

CHAPTER XV.

THE AFFLICTIONS OF JOB.

CHAPTER XXIV.

MAY THEIR FAME ENDURE.

CHAPTER XXV.

NOT YET THE END.

Out From The Darkness.

CHAPTER I.

INTRODUCTORY MATTER.

Born in Valders, Norway—Scope for Blind Man's Narrative—
Charms of Fatherland—Peasant Class in Norway—Sketch of my
Parents—My Grandfather's Favoritism—Primogeniture—Mysterious
Sympathy—Trance-like Vision—News of Death—Purport of Warn-
ings—I become Blind—What is Sight Worth?—Burial During Trance
—My Return to Life—Blessings that Remain—Education of Blind.

> "This life is but a sleep, and a forgetting
> The soul that rises with us; our life's star
> Hath had elsewhere its setting, and cometh from afar—
> Not in entire forgetfulness, nor yet in utter nakedness,
> But trailing clouds of glory do we come
> From God who is our home."—*Wordsworth.*

THE sublime mystery of life, fraught with
joys for the saddest of mankind, and with sorrows for even those most aloof from the meaner
cares of earth, dawned upon me in Norway, in the
farming district of Valders, on the 16th day of
December, 1843; and, although an environment of
anxiety has been my lot, I have yet realized enough
felicity on this green globe to enable me to thank
my Creator for the boon of existence. I am content with the mercies which have been allotted to

2

me, with the compensations which are inseparable from my lot; and out from the darkness would raise my voice, in the hope that the lessons from my experienece may prove of service to my fellows— as well to those who are blessed with the capacity to see the blue o'er-arching firmament, the emerald footstool adorned with flowers, and that emblem of eternity, the ocean, as to those who are bereft of the faculty of vision.

My autobiography shall be faithfully written, and dulness shall be avoided, if that be possible, by omitting the record of prosy details, such as are common to every career. There are no pet theories to be advanced in my pages; no self-laudations to sicken my readers, and alienate their regard; and there shall be no distortions of fact and experience, if the pen will obey the impulse of the mind. Sensationalism is the vice of the day, and, according to some authorities, the writer who will not resort to its attractions must suffer the pangs of neglect; but at all risks, I'll none of it; my trust shall be in the best feelings and strong mentality of manhood and womanhood.

The adventures of a blind man, if truly told, can not be made picturesque by glowing delineations of wood, mountain, river and sea; that is a charm denied. The yielding sod beneath my feet lacks the emerald beauties which I find descanted on by others, and I would fain feel what others may de-

scribe in deathless words; but there are worlds of
thought and action into which the landscape does
not enter, which the mind alone may grasp; and
the seals of that vast library are open alike to the
sightless and the seeing. There is ample scope
and verge enough for all my powers of description,
but I shall avoid trespassing beyond the bounds of
patience; a grace that is not always exemplified by
able writers.

It has often seemed to me that there are regions
of concentrated thought and vivid imagination,
which can compensate the thousands who are bereft
of vision for all the glories of architectural excellence, for the exquisite colors of the rainbow, for the
never-to-be-forgotten tints of sunset and sunrise, for
the hues of flowers, for the brightness of the human
face; and in that consciousness I find cause for unspeakable joy in the goodness of my Creator. A very
large proportion of all the men with whom I come
in contact in my travels, are careless about, or at
the best not diligent in, the cultivation of their
mental powers; are even negligent as to the preservation of their senses; as though the boons of
heaven might be safely buried in the earth, as the
timid steward in the scripture parable did with his
master's treasure enfolded in a napkin.

The facts of my infant life are necessarily known
to me only by report; and in that respect the blind
are on the same plane with the most favored of our

race. My birthplace, and the time at which the mysteries of this form of existence first began to affect me, have been already told; and I was yet a child when my father transplanted the whole of his family to this great Republic; hence, I cannot describe, except from rumor and common report, the charms which for every true Scandinavian must ever cling to the land of Fjords and Fjells.

I often find myself repeating that line from the genial poet, Goldsmith, author of "The Vicar of Wakefield," "The Deserted Village," and other works that will long live in the minds of men:

"A bold peasantry, their country's pride,
Which, once destroyed, can never be supplied;

because those lines aptly describe the status of the class to which my father belonged, although it might be claimed that he was rather a yeoman than a peasant. The two names describe the more and less wealthy members of the same great class, the noble army of industry, by whose conquests the earth is subdued to the purposes of man, and the prosperity of nations is builded upon a basis ten thousand times more to be relied upon than war, and upon whose successes in the humbler arts of life the triumphs of science, literature and art —advanced fruits of civilization—alone, become possible.

My father was one of the most energetic and

muscular men of his class in Valders, and his extraordinary powers of body were matched by a will power seldom equalled, a constancy of mind that could hardly be excelled. He had been wise or fortunate in the selection of a partner, for my mother was dear, not only to her children, but, as it seemed, to all persons with whom she came in contact. The sweetness of her disposition carried her through ceaseless trials and vexations which might well have exhausted her patience, and still there was always a smile in the tone of her voice which gladdened my soul like heavenly sunshine, whenever the kind fates brought her across my path. Her life knew no idleness, and but little rest in all the long years that I can remember; she was industrious, almost to a fault, in providing for the wants of her seven daughters and four sons.

I was the fourth child born of that happy marriage, but the first son, and therefore my position under the law and custom of primogeniture which then obtained in Norway made me a personage of some importance. Had we remained in Valders, and no change come over the customs of the country, the estate held by my father would upon his demise have descended to me as my birthright, subject only to minor claims on the part of my sisters and brothers. My earliest recollections are engrossed with acts of favoritism showered upon me by my grandfather, who loved in that way to

distinguish the first boy, his lineal male descendant
and namesake, successor to the paternal acres and
to numberless traditions of the greatness and honor
which in the earlier centuries of the Christian era
belonged to the fighting race of sailors and naviga-
tors from which we sprung. Children have quick
perceptions, but they are seldom able to divine remote causation; hence, while immediately conscious
of this kindness as a special manifestation in my
favor, I did not comprehend that my grandfather's
love for me was a consequence of my relation to the
estate as heir at law. I can distinctly recall, however, that on many occasions I felt proud that I was
not one of my sisters, a feeling that has not yet
been totally eradicated.

There must have been singular ties of sympathy
between my grandfather and myself, although I was
so young when I last felt the pressure of his hand
upon my head. My parents left Valders for this
country in 1847, when I was a little more than
three years old, and of course I was brought with
them; but his image is deeply engraved upon my
mind, and, had my fingers the skill to express
the yearnings of my soul, the picture of the venerable Norseman, perhaps in some degree idealized,
should illustrate this portion of my reminiscences.

Twenty-eight years ago, when I was just eighteen years of age, and nearly fifteen years had
elapsed since the last sounds of his benediction had

died on my ears, I lay one day on my bed in a kind
of waking trance, as sometimes happens to me
even now; most assuredly I was not sleeping; my
thoughts were pleasantly turned towards dear old
Norway, and one by one the images of old times
and my younger days were floating across my field
of mental vision, without volition on my part—
although the tender associations of the days that
are gone by forever are choice food for my soul —
when I heard the heavy and peculiar steps of that
old man upon my stairway, approaching the bedroom door. The sounds struck me with wonderful
distinctness, and I could locate them beyond a
peradventure, for in the era of my reign as his
favorite I had watched and waited for the first
tokens of his accustomed visits, and my heart
danced then as it was dancing once again. Nearer
and yet nearer came the home-like and welcome
sounds; the door did not seem to have been opened,
but he was standing by my bedside, and in the
natural sequence of events I felt the pressure of his
hand, with a grasp slightly tremulous, more so than
of yore—a sensation just as palpable as was ever
communicated by one human being to another, yet
in some mysterious degree still differing. Then the
tones of his well remembered voice, softened as it
might have been by age or distance, filled my soul
with emotions which are still indescribable, as he
said: "I have come to bid you good-bye, my child;

I shall never see you again. May God bless you!"

When the voice ceased I was as vividly conscious to all external impressions as I am now; but there was no appearance that could account for my mental condition—no touch, no sound of retreating foot-steps—and I was alone. There were no signs of trepidation, such as we are accustomed to connect with the remotest approaches of the supernatural, when in the long evenings our friends recount the links by which in every family the unseen world is drawn vividly towards this actual moving panorama. But I have no theory, cut and dried, by which the phenomena of my experience could be made plain as the school-book to a child; and I therefore simply state the fact, as it was recorded in my consciousness at that moment to be retained as long as memory holds a seat.

I have tried to reason the matter to some possible conclusion, but my powers fail me in determining whether the mind was reached through the instrumentality of the senses, by some process of which we are normally unconscious, or whether, by some means just as full of the unknowable, unconscious cerebration was the spring from whence the phenomena arose, stimulating the sense to an abnormal activity, in which the unreal and remote became tangible and immediate for a season. On any hypothesis the mystery remains, and I can throw no new light upon its causes. All the signs indicated

A TYPICAL NORSEMAN.

a visit from my grandfather—his voice, his footsteps, the pressure of his hand; and if his house
had been near our own, as it was in Valders, instead
of being severed from us by thousands of miles of
storm-lashed ocean, not to mention the travel from
the seaboard to our new domicile, it would have
demanded very powerful testimony, from witnesses
of known veracity, to prove that the dear old man
was not present unless the absence of sound and
touch, and the apparent vacuity of the room, in my
first moments of awakening from the trance, had
suggested to my judgment that the appearance had
been spiritual rather than physical; yet it may be
true, as some of my friends believe, that the phenomena arose purely from delusion of the senses.

It will be seen that the ties of mutual regard between my grandfather and myself must have been
very close and intimate, when my mind could go out
towards him in the singular manner which I have
endeavored to describe; but the most curious portion of the story remains yet to be told, unless the
laws of coincidence may be cited to account for all
that is wonderful in our life on earth. At about the
moment when that interview occurred, it was afterwards ascertained that my grandfather had passed
away from this scene of being; and about two
months later the information reached the family in
due course of post. Unfortunately for the exactness
of my narrative—and I am aware that it militates

against its scientific value in no small degree—I did not record the exact moment, hour and day of that waking trance as I should have done. Life and not death was in my mind at the time, notwithstanding the purport of the solemn message which I undoubtedly received.

One-half of all that is said to us, when we seem to be fully alive to every earthly influence, fails to convey its true purport to the mind, until subsequent reflection or unlooked-for developments have become interpreters. The first whisperings of love, the warnings of destiny in a thousand forms, the words of the priests, the monitions of circumstances, the shadows of coming events of which seers tell us, which a readier and more highly cultivated mental being might enable humanity to read as the master perceives the melody in the cramped lines on the pages before him, are all in vain offered to us by the kind, ministering, unseen hands that would warn us on our way from the cradle to the grave. Many incidents just as remarkable have written themselves into my eventful life, and they stand out in ,bold relief among my memories of things, clearly defined at this moment, linked more or less with the trance condition; but I advance no claims to be considered a clairvoyant, because it has frequently happened that I have not comprehended until long afterwards the significancy of my vision; hence it would be absurd to vaunt myself as a clairvoyant—as the French describe one who can see clearly.

I have no desire to build theories, but it is necessary, for the faithfulness of my narrative, that all these strange experiences should be presented in the order of their occurrence, and the explanations which may reduce them to the rank of the ordinary phenomena of life must be relegated to the ingenuity and attainments of my courteous readers.

My blindness overtook me when I was only six months old, at which age I seem to have passed through the valley of the shadow of death, and to have been snatched thence only at the cost of being shut in forever, or as long as this earthly tenement endures, from all the physical beauties by which we are surrounded. Imagination sometimes portrays the actual in robes which may transcend the loveliness of nature; but I have no standard whereby I might determine what is true, and my ideal is preserved from rude shocks such as the seeing world must realize. I have heard my favored friends enthusiastically praise some charm or treasure promised to their vision, and have read the tones of their voices as they described their disappointments; in my case, the dream of beauty remains unchallenged, a living entity.

The word-painting, by which I am dimly permitted to see the actual, would poorly serve my purpose, for want of a common medium between the seeing world and myself, unless my imagination came to my aid. I have heard of a blind man, who said that touching scarlet cloth reminded him of the blare of a trumpet; but that explanatory statement, to my mind, makes a volume of explanation necessary. No words can make clear to me the lovely tints of the simple flower, whose fragrance and whose structure I can comprehend through other senses; but the deprivation which robs speech of half its excellence will be atoned for fully in the more perfect communion of souls toward which we are daily drawing near.

My deprivation occurred after a long siege of wasting sickness, which had reduced my vital powers to zero. I was supposed dead; and, but for the custom of deferring the funerals for many days, which obtains in Norway, I might have been heard of never more until the graves are opened at the sound of the last trump. Thousands of human beings come to their end in that way, and only rouse from their lethargy to find that they are shrouded in the cerements of the tomb, enclosed within the narrow tenement to which all must come at last. Who has not heard of, read of, or may be even seen, the evidences of mute agony which are sometimes revealed when the opened coffin shows the loved sister, brother, husband or wife to have turned around in the last resting place, and to have struggled for an impossible relief? The thought is terrible, but it is borne in upon me by this incident in my own career.

The trance condition is not more mysterious than sleep itself—a coma of the brain and nervous system, longer continued than the nightly rests to which we are accustomed, and wrapping the heart and respiratory organism in repose. We are inured to sleep and its phenomena in some degree, but there are features in that portion of our lives which few have thought of, and none have fully mastered. The simulation of death, called trance, in which the spent forces of body and soul seek renewal in perfect rest for a time, is a field of inquiry at which we have barely glanced; yet therein lies many a loved Lazarus between two worlds, awaiting the fiat of the Eternal to recall him to this sphere of our being.

But let me return to the circumstance of my supposed death. Thirty-six hours elapsed from the time of my apparent demise, as I am informed, before there were any signs of returning animation. So settled was the conviction that I had gone to my final rest, that no mirror was held before my nostrils to be removed undimmed as a proof of my decease. My death was considered certain, and the coffin was tenanted by me for more than a day, my grandmother performing for me the last sad offices, sorrowfully closing the eyes which have never since opened to the light of day. The loving fingers which did for me that melancholy task would

gladly have restored to me the blessing of sight, but
to restore vision to the blind is a divine gift which
has not been exercised since the first days of the
Christian Era.

It seemed probable that the disease, which left
me maimed and darkened, had done its work before
her services were invoked, and in any case the affliction was irremediable. The story of my return to
life has been told so often in my presence, from the
first moments to which memory will carry me, that I
almost seem to remember the circumstances myself.
That is an admitted impossibility, although I certainly can recall physical appearances which could
only have reached my brain as objects of vision in
my early infancy, seeing that I have been blind
since the early age of six months. The agonized
suspense which waited on my second birth, in the
minds of my parents, it is impossible for me to describe; none but parental hearts can fathom the
depths of tenderness which such an awakening from
death to life must have called forth, and to the imaginations of such of my readers I must leave the
subject. I have been told that as I lay in the coffin
my eyeballs seemed to quiver beneath the lids, but
the eyes were never opened voluntarily, and for
hours my friends waited upon nature.

I was removed from the narrow bed with tremulous joy, but it was a source of much anxiety that
my eyes remained closed as though the lids had be-

come paralyzed. At length the lids were raised
with kind solicitude, and then a small white spot,
no larger than a pin's point, was discovered on each
eyeball. That blemish increased so rapidly that
within twenty-four hours the eyeballs were com
pletely covered, and on the morning next ensuing
the eyes burst, discharging their humors. Thus I
have been sightless almost all my life, unless there
is a power, as I sometimes believe, in the brain or
soul, by which we may see and comprehend immediately without the intervention of organs of vision.
It is not possible for me to exactly formulate my
faith in this respect, but the mere enunciation of
this crude idea may call out the views of other and
abler men to whom the same thought must have occurred.

The blind are not necessarily despondent under
their deprivation, for nature abounds in compensations, as various as the changing conditions of mankind. We are comforted by tones of sympathy,
oftentimes more precious than sight, when those
who express their kindly regard are thoughtful
enough to avoid an appearance of patronizing us in
our affliction. Kind voices reach us at brief intervals from out of the darkness, and loving hands are
stretched forth to help us everywhere; but there
have been times when I could almost endorse the
sayings of a quaint friend, who expressed his regret
that the expenditure incurred for my tiny coffin

should have been made in vain. Certainly we have
come to a country where expenditures are much
more lavish than in frugal Norway, and my dimensions are much greater than they were; but I trust
that, all things considered, there are no reasons
why I should be other than thankful for my preservation from being buried alive.

I would not have it imagined for one moment
that I am unmindful of the blessings which our
Father has permitted me to enjoy. The mind of
man is many-sided, and every facet receives light
from heaven or earth, out of which happiness in some
degree may come. Every thought in the busy,
teeming brain, every fact presented to us for acceptance from out the laboratory of nature, extending
our knowledge of the material universe, every additional evidence of man's goodness vouchsafed in
the struggle for life, wherein it is our privilege to
lend some aid of greater or less value to our fellow-
men, every proof of the advancing intelligence of
the race, and above all else, every new industrial
pursuit brought within the compass of our faculties,
by which they may attain a riper development in
the service of humanity and in the better protection
of our families and ourselves from the approach of
want and suffering, is a contribution to our pleas-
ures of no mean order. Our joys are, in a great
measure, proportioned to our fitness and energy in
the discharge of the multifarious duties of life; and

within the current century there have been wonderful advances made in the instruction of the blind ;—
an item of large importance to the nation, seeing
that the numbers enduring the affliction of partial or
utter darkness and isolation in this respect average
about one in two thousand in the United States.
The gainful employment of so great an aggregate is
of vast importance to the community.

3

CHAPTER II.

"LET THERE BE LIGHT".

There is an idea in many well informed minds
that the blind are cooped up in perpetual and complete darkness, and some of my own expressions have
that bearing when I consider them critically; yet
nothing could be further from the truth than that
impression.   Egyptian darkness, such as may be
felt, does apparently wall in and entomb some
sufferers, bearing them down body and soul with a
terrible sadness, which we must hope will find its
complement of joy in realms beyond the grave; but
in my own case, although there is a complete an-
nihilation of the organs of vision, I seem to live in
unvarying brightness.   38

I cannot pretend to say under what optical law this peculiarity arises, but the fact is just as I have stated, and some of the *savants* among my numerous friends may be able to help us out with a theory. Explanations have been frequently volunteered, but none of them, so far, have completely covered the ground.

One attempt at an interpretation of the phenomenon, which comes nearest to a solution to my mind, was recently offered by an ingenious friend. He says that, inasmuch as my supposed death and actual blindness fell upon me during the daytime, in our bright Norwegian climate, where the air is brilliant and clear, and the ground, even during winter, covered with virgin snow, undimmed by traffic and the smoke of great cities, the brilliant whiteness of that light must have impressed upon my retina just that strong sense of day which has lived in my optical memory from that moment until now. His suggestion would make what is to me a physical condition dependent upon memory, and it may be that he is right, but I want for evidence. Memory, then, or some physical condition, or possibly both combined (for no man has yet clearly defined to my satisfaction in what manner memory does its work so that the distant past can be recalled in many cases more vividly than the affairs of yesterday) have aided in the preservation of this luminous appear-

ance, which never fails me in my waking hours by
day or night.

My earliest remembrances are permeated with that
consciousness of light, and to that fact, rightfully
or not, I attribute the cheerfulness and constancy
with which I have been enabled to endure and sometimes conquer severe reverses. It would be to me
a source of much pleasure could some of my more
learned readers supplement my narrative with a lu-
cid interpretation of the circumstances which it is
my duty to chronicle. The humblest human being,
who will truthfully record exceptional facts, can
contribute some few grains of sand toward the mountain of knowledge from which the masters of science, philosophy and religion may unfold the laws of
being. I have striven honestly to do all that de-
volves upon me in the premises, in my exceptional
condition.

The childish reminiscences which were at one time
of grave importance to myself, have sunken into in-
significance when viewed through the media of advancing years, and I shall not allow them to burthen
these pages, unless in the few instances where they
point toward important epochs in my career. I distinctly remember that in my third year my parents
were engaged in preparations to emigrate to this
country, and the even tenor of my young life seemed
to have been broken adrift from all moorings, with
the unsettling of our former condition. It may be

that some of the incidents of that time, which seem to date from actual observation of occurrences as they transpired, were actually impressed upon my mind by subsequent narrations and reminders which, when we attempt to carry ourselves back toward childhood, surround every fact with misty uncertainty, or with seeming certainties, which reason assures us must be ofttimes fabulous.

Voyages across the Atlantic, which had few terrors for my remote ancestors, had become much more formidable with advancing civilization to the Norsemen of the nineteenth century. Higher standards of comfort at home and better estimates of the value of time had much to do with the changed condition. It would be difficult to convince me that there has been any falling off in the courage of the Scandinavian races, or in their peculiar fitness to encounter the perils of the ocean.

In the year 1847, rapid sailing and steaming were in their infancy; clipper ships were only dreamed of by a few men, and the working out of the idea waited for such events as the discoveries of gold in California, and still later in Australia, to make extraordinarily expeditious voyages an object. The modern improvements which have made the ocean a most convenient highway, such as our ancestors, Vikings though they were, could not foresee, had not yet begun to affect navigation from Norwegian ports in any material degree; and our transit from Europe to America was terribly slow, estimated according to the calculations of to-day.

I suppose that my health was not very good on board ship, and my younger brother died; but whether this arose from constitutional weakness, an unsuitable dietary scale, or defective ventilation, this deponent saith not. It must be patent to all observers that the deaths of children indicate some infraction of nature's laws more significantly, by far, than deaths in advancing age. As a rule, on shipboard, when the vessels are well constructed and well handled, "the toddlin', wee things" that can keep the deck are better able to weather the vicissitudes of the voyage than the old people.

It was no easy thing, even to get started on our way; passengers in sailing vessels were comparatively uncommon; they have since entered largely into the calculations of shipmasters; but we were detained at Dramman no less than three weeks, before we could procure a passage in a vessel bound for a port from which our final departure for this country could be arranged.

At Hamburg, our little family was detained five weeks. Travelers who seek pleasure in a luxurious transit from one country to another, content to kill time with sport, or to be toted around in search of curiosities, expending competencies for which others have toiled, may have some difficulty in comprehending the hardships to which my parents were subjected by that detention—adrift, as it were, between two continents, losing sight of the ancient landmarks, and yet uncertain as to the new home toward which we had set our faces. We were pioneers in a new course, having been the first party of emigrants for America that ever in our day had left the farming districts of Valders; hence the delays to which we were subjected, with all the attendant losses, were quite natural.

Our experiences, hard and unsatisfactory as they were, may have helped to smooth the way for thousands who have since followed us across the trackless deep; but that consideration does not seem to have presented itself to my father as a possibility, and if it had he would still have been inconvenienced in no small degree by the discomforts and the cost incidental to such long waiting. Steam voyages across the Atlantic are now often accomplished in less than as many days as we occupied weeks in the sailing vessel, and still we were expeditious, by comparison with the first Norsemen that visited this continent centuries before Columbus brought modern civilization to its shores.

I should be far less Scandinavian than I am, and much less sensitive to the claims of historic truth, could I omit, on any suitable occasion, to assert the prior discovery and temporary colonization of this vast country by the Norsemen in the eleventh century. The facts are open to every student, and Long-

fellow has presented some of the incidents of that
eventful time, begemmed with the jewels of his imagination, in deathless verse; but I must remember
that a child of three years, rocked by the billows of
earth's stormiest ocean, is not expected to wax eloquent in defining the labors of Leif Eriksson, so for
the present the laurels of Columbus shall rest undisturbed while we complete our transit from the old
world to the new.

By the way, there was one incident connected with
our detention at Dramman which it would be wrong
to pass without comment, as it serves to indicate a
condition of mind which then existed among the so-
called educated class in Norway, but which is probably now lost sight of by modern thinkers. I allude
to the sturdy opposition and manifest alarm with
which the clergy of my native land met the slowly
rising tide of emigration. No sooner was it known
in the neighborhood that my father meant to abandon
the place of his nativity, than he was beset by the
slow-moving, conservative element in his own class,
with warnings urgent and innumerable against the
rash step which he contemplated. Chimeras dire
were hurled at his devoted head without ceasing.
The young man who carried a banner with a quaint
device, and said "Excelsior" when well-meaning people troubled him with their counsel, had an easy
time compared with the plague of remonstrance that
was endured by the first emigrants from Valders,

and the fact that all the warnings were given in kindness rendered the task of replying more difficult.

As the time for departure drew near, the members of the congregation to which my father belonged devolved upon their pastor the task of convincing my father that it was a sin to remove his family from the Christianizing influences of Norwegian life, and to carry them away to a heathen and barbarous land. With many prayers and arduous studies the good old man fitted himself for the momentous struggle in which he was to engage, and, while we waited for sailing orders, at Dramman, the amiable controversialist came down upon us, with the earnestness, though not with the fell intent, with which "The Assyrians came down like a wolf on the fold." Nearly all the old neighbors were on hand when the exhortation commenced, and the horrors of the jungle in India were freely used to people this country with wild beasts, so that there seemed to be no option for the emigrant, in the description that was given, but to die of storm and famine on the voyage, of fever and ague, or some other malarial disease on the strange shore, or to be eaten alive by nameless monsters that held an unquestioned reign in the dense forests of this continent.

The oracle spake, and, when his lips had closed, silence fell upon the little assembly. My father could not attempt to controvert the statements by which the other auditors had been overwhelmed, but he was not convinced that the Merciful Creator by whom he had been girt about with love in his old home would fail to protect him and his in the new. His purpose was unshaken, but he was puzzled to render his determination into words, without failing in the courtesy that was due to one whose blameless life and loving intent made his long recognized authority almost omnipotent.

"Are the diseases always fatal there?" queried my father. "Almost always," was the answer; and an unconditional surrender was considererd inevitable.

"Do the people die more than once?" There was no response from the dear old pastor, who had never dreamed of such a question, and, while the neighbors laughed uproariously at the strange suggestion, the dominie retired to another room to fight the battle over again in his own mind.

Since that day hundreds of thousands of Scandinavians have made their homes in America; pastors and their flocks have crossed the seas together; innumerable churches have been built to Almighty God by Norsemen, from Maine to the Golden Gate, and experience has proved that, with care and foresight, disease and famine can be warded off as well in the new world as in the old, while the savage beasts, by which the early emigrants were to have been intimidated withal, are distanced in cruelty and hate by man himself in the very centres of civilization on either continent.

The Blue Peter at the fore, the signal for sailing came at last. Dramman was left behind us with many a heart-breaking sob, and we looked out upon the immeasurable deep. The reflections of the old people have been recounted so often in my presence, from that day to this, that it almost seems as though I had passed through all the emotions and had seen all the sights which they realized. Hamburg was an unknown land to me when we left, as on our day of landing; but, looking back from to-day, it seems as though the busy streets were quite familiar to my sight.

I can recall the bustling quays and wharves, the Bourse, the Botanical and Zoological Gardens, just as clearly as though standing on Elbe Hill I had literally seen them. The old city, more than a thousand years old, probably having its origin in one of the fortresses built by Charlemagne to repel the nomadic tribes and give fixity to European society, has taken a new lease of life in our day, under the ægis of steam and rapid transit, and bids fair to eclipse its Hanseatic greatness completely. But there is an end to every thing, and so at last we bade adieu to Hamburg, where we had stayed long enough to form many enduring friendships.

Traveling by land is relieved by an almost infinite variety in the prospect, but the ever-changing sea presents a sameness which only the poetic soul can fill with a sufficing joy. True enough, there may be

no two billows precisely alike, but the family resem
blance strikes every beholder, and, when day after
day you look out upon seven miles of sea with a
circumference of firmament coming down to embrace
it on every hand, it is impossible to avoid praying
for a change. No wonder the ignorant mariners
that sailed under Christopher Columbus grew weary
of their voyage into the unknown, and became muti-
nous. They had no chance of excitement from the
cry, "A Sail! A Sail!" as we had; no other keels but
theirs had plowed the waters where they stood for
four hundred years, and the canvas pendent from
a strange mast would have been a cause for terror,
unless the size of the craft permitted a hope of conquest. Passing vessels were not very numerous in
our time, until we drew nigh our destination; but I
can remember more than once the hurry that there
was at sea when the chance offered to send back a
few words of greeting to the dear old home. Those
who were not writing crowded to the ship's side, as
though every line in the strange hull was dear to their
hearts, and, when the boat was lowered from the davits
to carry the mail bag to the other ship, and effect some
exchanges in provisions, every sailor that manned an
oar seemed to deserve the homage of those he left behind because he was facing a peril of death to stretch
out a hand to our friends in Norway.

Quebec was our desired haven, but before we
touched that port the news had reached Valders that

we had foundered at sea, all hands perishing, and my father, the last survivor, making a manful recantation of his heresy in leaving Norway in opposition to the advice of his pastor. The completeness of the narrative might have suggested its fabulous character, but my grandfather, never doubting the tale, became delirious with grief. In his rhapsodies of sorrow, the fond old man would hold converse with his lost ones, as we arose weird and ghost-like from the briny bed to which lying rumor had consigned us; and when, months later, the fact of our safe arrival at our destination reached him through the mail, it required much persuasion, besides the testimony of the well remembered writing, to combat the effects of his long continued phantasy.

Arrived at Quebec, we made our way through Montreal to Buffalo without noticeable incidents, and we there took passage by steamer to Milwaukee. I suppose my puny appearance attracted some attention on the boat, as I can recall the wistful looks with which kind eyes regarded me. The dietary provision made in Valders for our passage across the Atlantic was not well calculated to sustain a weakly child, and my ailing appearance was largely due to that circumstance. Perhaps that possibility was divined by the head steward of the steamer, and his kind heart, yearning for some child that he had loved and lost, found comfort in showing attention to the writer. Certain it is that I was made free of the

steward's pantry, with all the hereditaments thereto
belonging, and, while I reveled in sweets and cloy-
ing delicacies which would have afflicted one-half the
grown people on board with nausea, I was the envy
of every child.

These lines may never meet the eyes of my unknown benefactor, who has probably joined the innumerable caravan many years ago; even though
alive, the good man may not have thought of his
kindly acts in any such way as they affected me,
for generous natures forget the services they render
just as readily as the stream loses track of the shadow
which was mirrored in its depths; but somehow I
could not refer even cursorily to that brief voyage on
the lakes without mentioning my sense of the loving
kindness which was bestowed upon me, unless I would
stand self-accused of black ingratitude.

Col. Solomon Juneau, a French fur trader, generous
to a fault, was the first white settler in Milwaukee, and
when our family landed in that city he was the richest
and most influential man in that locality. The site of
Milwaukee was occupied by a Pottawatomie village at
the time when the adventurous trader took up his
abode in what is now called the Cream City. He had
been a resident there twenty-two years when my
father landed in Wisconsin, in 1847, and the population was over ten thousand, rapidly increasing.
The lake bluff, and the lands rising from the river
quite abruptly in many parts, were not occupied,

THE BARREL IN POLITICS.

and nearly the whole population had located itself on the swampy lowlands, where business is still largely transacted. The Colonel, who was Mayor, proprietor of much of the city lands, and a flourishing storekeeper, offered many advantages to my father to induce him to stay where he was, but my progenitor had an abiding sense of the value of health, and to all the suggestions of this generous friend he replied, "If I can find nothing better than a swamp in this country, I will go back to Norway, where at all events we are solid." The site of Milwaukee has been the home of many races at various times. The Pottawatomies had a village there when the first official record was made as to the river and harbor in 1817, and the ineffaceable records of the Mound Builders, which may date from thousands of years before, are on hand in many directions to show that an industrious and partly civilized people with some knowledge of manufactures and art continued for a long term of centuries to enjoy life upon the margins of its lake and streams.

Some curious ideas as to popular government were begotten in my father's mind, during the stay that we made in Milwaukee. There was an election to some office, local or general, and Col. Juneau's store was, as usual, the headquarters of the winning party. There was no lack of stirring eloquence, for the tongues of some men will wag as long as the river flows; but the main reliance of the astute Solomon was placed on a barrel of whisky, which stood near the entrance to the store. Voters were expected to help themselves to as much as they cared for of the contents of the barrel, and then, as the "spirit" of the occasion entered into them they saw their way to deposit their ballots in favor of the Colonel and his friends. The barrel was certainly on the winning side, but my father did not admire the process.

There were other ways besides handling the barrel in which Juneau was always to be reckoned upon for he never failed to respond in a liberal manner to any proposal which had for its purpose the improvement of Milwaukee. None of the old residents ever mentioned him without recognizing the generosity of his nature but for which he might have become a millionaire.

CHAPTER III.

I EXPLORE.

Oakland Farm—Truth Lies in a Well—Maternal Impulse—The Long Sleep—Childish Isolation—Sister Rachel—Schools of the Period—Unthinking Visitors—Gideon Ives—Prejudices to Combat—Institution for Blind—Pursuit of Knowledge—Result of Investigation—Mr. Miltimore—Sister Mary—*Esprit de Corps*—Recent Discoveries—Science is of God—Ambition a Virtue—Among Playfellows—Indian Summer—Degrees of Blindness—Rock River—School Life Out-doors—Railroad Surprises—Daltonism—Cheselden's Operations—Site of Institution—Philanthrophic Efforts—Perkins Institute—New York—Philadelphia—Columbus—Stanton—Louisville—Nashville — Raleigh — Indianapolis — Jacksonville— Janesville—St. Louis — Macon — Jackson— Baltimore — Vinton —Jackson—Flint—Austin—Talladega—Little Rock—Faribault— Oakland — Batavia—Kansas — Cedar Springs—Romney—Baton Rouge—Institutions in Europe—Liverpool—Edinburg — London — Vienna — Prague — St. Petersburg—Berlin—Paris—Amsterdam--Zurich—Dresden—Dublin Copenhagen—Stockholm—Koenigsburg—Breslau— Barcelona—Naples--Gmund—Lintz—Pesth—Manchester—Glasgow—Freisingen — Bruchal — Hamburg — York — Cork — Munich — Lausanne—Laura Bridgeman—Dr. Howe.

————

Notwithstanding all the inducements held out by the Colonel, my father resolved to continue a farmer, and after many slips succeeded in purchasing about two hundred acres of excellent land at Oakland in Jefferson county, seventy miles west from Milwaukee, to which place we traveled by team, over roads which reminded us continually of the ups and downs of existence. Upon the newly purchased land was a makeshift dwelling and a well around and over which was no fence nor screen to prevent accidents.

Providence, in blessing me with an inquiring mind, has, on many occasions, led me to the very verge of great disasters; but always hitherto some circumstance has intervened in my favor, so that I have escaped the worst consequences which seemed for a time inevitable.

That unfenced well was jealously guarded by my father and friends as long as they were around, and words of caution were strewn around me as thick as leaves in Vallambrosa; but the only result was that I grew more and more impatient to pursue knowledge under difficulties. One day my father was absent and my mother so busy in household matters that I was for a time forgotten, so that the chances favored an exploration. The well was speedily reached, and the rude windlass, which had often inflamed my curiosity, was hastily overhauled. I was congratulating myself on an undreamed-of sagacity, which could touch pitch, handle fire and hang over a well without risk, when the bucket unshipped from its resting-place, ran down with a crash, and I followed it head-foremost for forty feet into the bowels of the earth. Luckily the water in the well was deep enough to protect my cervical vertebrae, and after sprawling around a few seconds I found my way to the coping of the stone work, about six inches above high-water mark, where I could sit, half dazed but secure, until help arrived.

Truth lies at the bottom of a well, and I was very near the place; but it was not until long afterwards that I thought of our near contact, and about the same time it occurred to me as regretable that truth should *lie* anywhere.

An hour must have elapsed, when a neighbor, coming to draw water, discovered me on my modest perch, and her cries speedily attracted every woman in the locality, my good mother among the rest. The first impulse of maternity was to share the trouble which she could not alleviate, and it required the combined srength of all her friends to prevent the dear soul throwing herself down into the water to sustain me until more serviceable help should come. Happily her design was frustrated, or I should almost certainly have been made an orphan. After a prolonged delay, which seemed an age, and was possibly an hour after my discovery in the well, a male neighbor was found, who was able and willing to descend to my rescue; and the rope, securely fastened about my waist and shoulders, brought me to the surface of the green earth again. That I had sustained some severe if not fatal fracture was a matter fully determined among the neighbors, but my mother, finding me inclined to sleep, left me to the influence of tired nature's sweet restorer; and for nearly eighteen hours after my restoration to the paternal sod I slept the sleep of the just. When Morpheus at last abdicated his empire over me, I was hungry enough to have eaten the fatted calf, and, failing to obtain just such sustenance, my appetite has ever been a standing menace to my friends, although they have fenced their wells about ever since securely.

From the time named until I was eleven years old, the days hung heavily upon my hands, as my deprivation of sight cut me off from such tuition and work as other children of similar ages could avail themselves of, and in the thinly settled neighborhood where we lived there were no little companions to join me in boyish games. Only children, and the very, very few grown people who can remember when they were children, have an idea how much of solace there is in mud pies and such like amuesments for the youthful intellect, and the mud pie-ist wants an audience, just as inexorably as the orator.

My only refuge under the circumstances named was my dear sister Rachel, several years my senior, who constituted herself my guardian, and, so far as the difference in age would allow, entered into my pursuits. Advancing years have erased many things from my memory, which were at one time stamped there, as I believed to last forever, but the maturity of my faculties has only made more clear to me the debt of gratitude I owe to Rachel for her tender solicitude, and I cannot imagine that any lapse of time will cause me to forget my obligation.

I would gladly have attended the district school, but the distance from our house was an obstacle, two miles and a half being a weary pilgrimage for a blind child to attempt alone, twice every day, more especially when it is remembered that companionship was all that I could obtain as the result of my travel. The teachers had no means at their disposal, nor any skill generally, which would adapt them for the schooling of a blind boy; and, unfortunately for my welcome, on the few occasions on which I visited the establishment my presence and peculiar condition called off the attention of the pupils generally from their studies. Could I have spoken English, oral instruction would have been possible to some extent, but that language was then as dead to me as Sanskrit is now.

From all these considerations it will be seen that my circle of life was narrow in the extreme, and my chances for improvement small. At home, where all that the exigencies of a new settler's life would allow was gladly attempted on my behalf, my feelings were lacerated by almost every visitor commiserating my parents on the burden which they had to carry in the person of their sightless son. The barbed arrows of their well intended sympathy rankled in new wounds for many years, and added incalculably to my suffering.

There are but few men and women who undertsand how quickly a little child can grasp the meaning of a word half spoken, and apply to his own condition ,the seamy side of their very natural reflections; yet their own memories might help almost every one, in some degree, to master the idea, if nature had not provided, in mercy to the race, for a speedy forgetfulness of all painful experiences. Where there are peculiar conditions of suffering, as in the blind, the feelings become more acutely, even morbidly sensitive, as in my own case. I could not close my ears against the talk, in which I was too often the subject, and molten lead could hardly have been more agonizing than some of the sentences uttered by good people who never dreamed that they were inflicting unmerited punishment. The sorrows of that day might have gone with me to my grave, however, but for the possibility that these few words, kindly spoken, may save some other tiny sufferer, blind or crippled in some other way, from being wounded in the house of his friends by ill considered speech. In that spirit I leave the subject thus introduced to be elaborated by the ingenious minds of my cultivated readers.

Relief was long coming, but it came at last. A friendly neighbor, since dead, Mr. Gideon Ives, a man of more than average intelligence, and almost unbounded kindness, whose name was a household word in our Scandinavian settlement, repeatedly urged my parents to send me to the Collegiate Institution for the Blind, at Janesville, Wisconsin. Old Joe Willett, proprietor of the Maypole, in Dickens' novel, Barnaby Rudge, hated to come upon the county to repair the damages inflicted by the No-Popery mob, because there was, he thought, a savor of pauperism in the process, as though he came upon the parish under the Poor Law; and just such an idea so entirely possessed the mind of my father, that every reference to the Institution was frowned down for nearly two years. Mr. Ives would not be silenced, because he saw in education my only chance for development into usefulness.

I was nine years old when the idea was first broached, and eleven when it was carried into operation, the interval being necessary to overcome the scruples of my parents. They had been told that children were half starved and almost wholly neglected by the managers, so that minds and bodies became stunted under the discipline, or want of discipline, which prevailed in the State Institution; and that idea weighed upon them long after the thought as to semi-pauperism had been cast to the winds by inquiry. Similar doubts and fears obtain even now in many localities, and they operate with terrible effect against the welfare of many blind children; so that there cannot fail to be some advantage in referring to the subject here. Not long since, in La Crosse, Wisconsin, I found a promising little fellow who was cooped up at home because of such prejudices on the part of his parents, and it afforded me much pleasure to disabuse their minds by narrating my own experiences as a pupil for several years and subsequently as a visitor to the Institution. He was sent soon afterwards to commence his career as a pupil; and, unless my skill in augury is entirely at fault, he will add largely to the credit and esteem which has been fairly earned by the management.

I owe it to the Institution to speak in the very highest terms of its usefulness, and shall not readily forget how much I am indebted to Gideon Ives for his perseverance in urging the matter upon the old folks at home. When admitted, at the commencement of the term, October 1, 1854, I was the first pupil presented; and the loneliness which had been experienced at home was cheerful companionship by comparison with the sound of my own footsteps, echoing unanswered through the vacant rooms of the second story, where I had been put away for safe keeping while the Superintendent went into Janesville City, about one and one-half miles distant, on some business that demanded attention.

After a time, having exhausted my devices within the class rooms, I started out to perambulate the halls, and was not long in discovering their metes and bounds. Only one wing of the structure, since burned, had then been erected; but the doorways which were to connect the first wing with the remainder had been boarded across loosely to prevent accidents. Of course the loose boards and the doorway had a charm for me, which soon became irresistible, and my wandering footsteps returned to the point again and again. Why was it boarded? What was there concealed beyond the aperture? The adventure was worth prosecuting, and a minute later I was at work forcing my way under the lowest plank with some considerable ingenuity, only to fall head-first into the excavation for the basement of the body of the building, a depth of more than twenty-five feet. Much shaken up as I was by my speedy descent, no bones were broken, and my voyage of discovery was extended in the hope that I might find means of escape from my cell.

Happily for my peace of mind, my fall had not been unheeded; the contractor for stone for the building, Mr. Miltimore, saw the result of my tour of investigation, from a distance, and hastened to fish me out from my dungeon. His arrival was so timed that I had just realized my own helplessness in the premises, when the sound of a friendly and most musical voice, although in a tongue unknown to me, brought me assurance of help. I have many times since then met Mr. Miltimore, and found him always a good friend, but his voice was sweeter when I

first heard it than it has ever sounded since to my
ears.

My sister Mary, since dead, attended me to the Institution, and, after I had been duly installed, made
her home for the winter in the Bower City—as
Janesville is called—so that she might be at hand
to hear and investigate any complaints, should my
treatment prove unsatisfactory. My accident was
unknown to her until her next visit, a few days
later, and then she had demonstrative evidence that
I was uninjured.

There were quite a large number of pupils in the
establishment when my sister came again to see me,
and, surrounded by companions in misfortune, I was
inspired by the *esprit de corps*, which forbade any
tendency to magnify our loss. The blind, as a rule,
endeavor to make it appear that they find compensations in the cultivation of the other senses, which
largely counterbalance their deprivation of sight.
Certainly it is better to bear up against loss bravely
than to whine over what cannot be changed. Un-
questionably it is wiser to thank God for what remains to us of all His mercies, than to grieve as
beings without hope because one sense has been ob-
literated, or perhaps only impaired.

I say perhaps only impaired, and the expression
is used advisedly. Who can say how soon some
Edison, equipped for discovery and invention, by
means of scientific research and mechanical adap-

tation, may enable the sightless to see? The optic
nerves remain, and experiments innumerable have
proven that some persons can decipher with their eyes
closed and bandaged as readily as others with the
aid of their natural organs of vision. We may yet
learn under the blessing of our Creator, through
the inspirations which come to this earth by means
of faithful investigation and insight, how to reach
and inform the brain as to the phenomena of visible
nature after the eyes have ceased their function.
Not long ago it was believed that the deaf were beyond the reach of sound because of defects in their
ears, although their auditory nerves remained intact; but science and discovery have revealed to us
that by means of a very simple fan, allowed to rest
against one of the teeth of the patient, sounds just
as minute as the faintest whisper can be conveyed to
the brain, and deaf mutes are being enabled to comprehend and speak the languages from which they
were supposed shut off forever.

When an inexpensive diaphragm of gutta percha,
expanded on a fan, touching a tooth set in the jaw,
whether the tooth be natural or artificial, can instruct the nervous system, and remedy so many of
the evil consequences of defective ears, can we imagine that the obstacles which prevent a similar action upon the brain through the optic nerves are insuperable?

Faith will remedy ten thousand ills, when by its

means the scientist is inspired to search with more
diligence into the arcana of the unknown, for God-
appointed means of relief.   Meantime it is well that
the class which suffers bereavement should cheerfully bear their burden, and wait for the evangel.
Our boys and girls were not possessed by any such
ideas as I have here set down, but they had borne
enough in their several households, in the form of
implied reproach, or repining over their misfortunes, to be ready to grasp at the consolation of
companionship with persons of their own class, and,
thus reinforced, to set up an *imperium in imperio* which
made it an offense against the community for any one
of the number to solicit the pity of visitors, or even
to receive its expression without resenting the suppo-
sition of superiority which pity necessarily conveys.

   My own condition of mind rendered the unlicensed
training which was thus indulged peculiarly pleasant, as it filled my soul with a laudable ambition
to be and to do something which should wipe out
the stigma of helplessness from my existence, and
at some time, not far distant, as it seemed, enable
me to challenge the respect and esteem of the little
circle upon which I had so long felt myself a burden.   That ambition, which entered into my childish mind at the very beginning of my school days,
has never ceased to animate my subsequent career;
and when I am confronted by some half instructed
zealot with denunciations of ambition *per se* as a vice,

JANESVILLE INSTITUTION FOR THE BLIND.

I feel impelled to cry out that next to and akin with hope it is our Almighty Father's choicest blessing.

I could no longer complain of a lack of playfellows, and our diversions were sufficiently numerous to render the old habit of moping, to which nearly all of the pupils had become more or less accustomed, an impossibility. I gave a wide berth to that loosely boarded doorway through which I fell *sans ceremonie* on the day of my arrival; but I learned from my companions, to whom my adventure was well known, that the aperture had been securely guarded immediately after my mishap. The weather outdoors was still pleasant and inviting, and, although we could not see the variegated colors of the leaves which adorn the woods of autumn, the balmy atmosphere of the Indian summer was peculiarly grateful to our feelings, now that we could roam at large in the grounds in which the Institution stood.

We were not all absolutely blind; some of my classmates could see just enough to act as guides in our impromptu excursions, and we detailed them for special duty as a matter of course. There is an adage that, "among the blind a man with one eye is king," and our conduct verified the saying; but the leader won his spurs by being the servant of his subjects. There is a sublime mystery in the fact that our Saviour washed the feet of his disciples; all the rulers of mankind who actually govern, must serve before they can command.

There is still a pleasure, although time has dimmed the lustre of the light, in recalling the *al fresco* sports of my Janesville days. We could descend the somewhat declivitous banks of Rock River, and whip its stream with flies of our own manufacture, when more costly equipments were impracticable, and sometimes our piscatorial labors were rewarded with a bite. When the weather was not too chilly, the water tempted us to venture on a swim, although none of our little party could have been considered dangerous rivals by Paul Boynton or Captain Webb; and some of my *escapades* in and upon Rock River will tend to show that my constitutional rashness was not easily chastened; but of such matters we can speak in due time. There was very little limit to our enjoyment during our school terms, after the tasks of the classrooms were accomplished, unless for some reason needful discipline had been imposed upon evil doers. There is not a boy living and in good health at this moment, and it is likely that there never has been, who went through a course of tuition without deserving correction; and woe to the unhappy wight who by escaping punishment in his tender years, heaps up severer misfortunes for later life. There is deep truth in the proverb, "If you won't be ruled by the rudder, you will by the rock." Perhaps there was an overdose of "rudder" in my case, for certainly up to this time I have experienced but very few "rocks."

The management of the Institution was not unnec-
essarily severe, and the course of study was not ex-
haustive; but the pleasantest part of our school
lives was that which we spent in rambling the
grounds between whiles, when all the boys were
teachers and pupils in the various fields of their respective excellencies. In almost every educational establishment the same fact may be noted in some
degree, but with us the load of restraint which had
been endured at home made a semi-masterless condition especially enjoyable. Circumstances so far
favored us during the terms of my attendance, that
no serious accidents befell any of the pupils, although
I can see now that we ran some terrible risks, which
might have had fatal endings.

One instance of misplaced ingenuity may be mentioned, which will give the gentle reader an inkling
of the dangers which the boys daily dared in the
prosecution of a practical joke. The Chicago & Northwestern Railroad passed near the Institution, through
a deep cutting, which was in process of being
bridged over, a few rude beams having been placed
in position across the chasm in the roadway. Upon that very risky perch a troop of blind boys might
have been seen with clock-like regularity about train
time, whenever the classes were not in session, taking soundings as to the depth below them. A number of clothes-lines, joined, with a big stone as a
plummet, constituted the simple but effective ap-

paratus for our operations. A few visits to the dangerous spot gave to each member of the party remarkable facility in scrambling along the beams; and, once in position, we waited patiently the arrival of the cars. The plummet was then sent down just far enough to reach the roof of the cars, along which it was dragged, bumping at every coupling, to the no small dismay of the uninitiated passengers within, who believed themselves on the verge of some disastrous, inexplicable accident.

This curious experiment was continued day after day with monotonous regularity until the officers of the road became aware of the true inwardness of the phenomena, and then a special messenger to the Institution made prisoners of us all for an extended term, until we had satisfied the superintendent of our contrition, and pledged our words never more to offend the railroad company. The chances of death which we all ran in that foolhardy series of adventures never seemed to occur to the minds of the participants.

I have mentioned that there were differences in the degrees of blindness to which the different pupils were subject. Some could distinguish between day and night, or could realize the passage of an opaque body between themselves and the lamp; while others, but for the sense of feeling, might have walked against a brick wall, expecting to pass uninterrupted. Daltonism or color blindness is ex-

tremely common among persons who have no idea
that they endure any defect of vision. The famous
John C. Dalton, whose name has been given to the
defect in question, could not distingush between red,
blue and green, and other members of his family
were similarly afflicted. Railroad companies have
become aware that the incapacity to distinguish colors is a fatal defect among railway men, to whom the
danger signal only appeals by the substitution of
one colored light for another. Numerous examina-
tions have established the commonness of this peculiarity, and it is probable that many otherwise preventable accidents have been precipitated, on land
and sea, by unsuspected color blindness. The eye
does not apparently differ from perfect organs of
vision, and for the average of work it may be just
as serviceable, but there must necessarily be a de-
ficiency in the capacity to enjoy a feast of coloring,
such as some of the modern painters love to display in
the galleries of their patrons.

Some of the lads were afflicted with cataract only,
others with opacity of the cornea, and happily, the
daily increasing skill and knowledge of the medical
profession have given sight to thousands whose cases
would have been pronounced hopeless half a generation ago.

A boy who was restored to sight by Cheselden,
was unable for fully two months to discover that
pictures resembled solid bodies; the coloring had no

5

meaning and but little delight for him, in spite of all that could be said in the way of tuition; but when at last the truth began to dawn upon his part- ly educated eyes, he persisted in touching the can- vas, expecting to find actual trees, castles and cat- tle upon the landscape.

Night blindness affects some who can see with tolerable clearness during the day, the incapacity be- coming gradually developed as the shades of even- ing fall, and becoming more or less complete in different persons after nightfall. Day blindness is another form of deprivation of sight. The patient sees as well as other persons in some cases, and in other instances much better than the average, during the night; but with the return of day comes total blindness or some less degree of incapacity. This kind of affliction prevails largely among Albinos.

None of our boys suffered from hemeralopia or nyctalopia, as night blindness and day blindness are respectively called, because, their deprivation of sight being only temporary and intermittent, such persons could be taught by ordinary means at inter- vals. We had in our little companionship some who were not totally in the dark, but who were gradually approaching total blindness from what seemed to be decay of the optic nerve or disease of the brain immediately connected therewith; some who were born blind and had consequently never seen the light of day; some whose affliction could

PERKINS' INSTITUTE.

be traced to eruptive fever, scarlet fever, small-pox and other diseases incidental to childhood; but with all my inquiries I could find no one among my schoolfellows whose case in any degree resembled my own, and in that fact I seemed to discover a mournful satisfaction. The mind of a child is even more remarkable than that of a man, in the strange contrarieties and illogical reasonings which it submits for our consideration.

The Janesville Institution for the Blind was founded by the State of Wisconsin in 1850, so that it was only four years old, and still incomplete, when my connection with it began. Built on high ground, a little distance from the populous city of Janesville, it became the most interesting architectural feature of that neighborhood, where there is much that is beautiful.

Before Wisconsin undertook the philanthropic and eminently sagacious work of providing for the mental and physical culture of the blind, ten institutions similar had been established in various parts of the Union, commencing in 1829 with the Perkins Institute, and Massachusetts Asylum, in Boston. New York followed two years later with an institution for the blind, in 1831, and the City of Brotherly Love, Philadelphia, made similar provision in 1833. Four years then elapsed without any new foundations, but work was being urged in several States. Columbus, Ohio, had the honor of being the first to follow

the lead of the Quaker City, and its institution for the
blind in 1837 was succeeded in 1839 by a similar
establishment in Stanton, Virginia.   The South then
took a hand in, and for several years most of the new
foundations for the blind were in that part of the
Union, including that at Louisville, Kentucky, in
1842, one at Nashville, Tennessee, 1844, and one at
Raleigh, North Carolina, 1846.   Indianapolis, Indi-
ana, started an institution in 1847; Jacksonville, Illinois, took up the running in 1849; and then Janesville
was selected by Wisconsin, as the site for its great
work in 1850.

Since that time the labors of wisdom and benevolence have not been allowed to flag.   In the year
1851 St. Louis, Missouri, founded an institution; in
1853 Macon, Georgia; Jackson, Michigan; Baltimore,
Maryland; Vinton, Iowa; and Jackson, Mississippi;
each began to make provision for their blind, and so
the good work went on until the oriflamme of civil
war flung to the breeze, temporarily stayed works of
mercy, or found new fields for their action.   Flint,
Michigan, founded an institution in 1854, Austin,
Texas, in 1856, Talladega, Alabama, in 1858, and in
the following year Little Rock, Arkansas, was similarly honored, after which there was no new foundation for four years, until Faribault, Minnesota, away
from the centers of warlike operations, began to
make provision for the blind in 1863.

As soon as the pacification of the Union began to

be realized, old activities were resumed in all directions. California established an Institution at Oakland, 1866; New York founded its State Institution at Batavia, 1867; Kansas made provision for the sightless in 1868; South Carolina built the Institution at Cedar Springs in 1869, and in 1870 West Virginia at Romney, and Louisiana at Baton Rouge, testified that although their lands had been deluged with patriotic blood, and their houses and fortunes destroyed by intestine commotion, they would still remember and assist the poor and helpless within their borders. The work goes bravely on in all directions, and the Union has already nearly as many institutions for the blind as Europe, although, of course, they are not yet as well appointed nor as rich as those established by our ancestors in the older nations, which were already wealthy when the Pilgrim Fathers sought freedom to worship God on Plymouth Rock.

Europe has thirty principal schools for the blind, besides many of local celebrity which are accomplishing beneficent work. The first school of any note was that founded at Paris in 1784, five years before the Bastile fell in the first upheavings of the great revolution. Liverpool established its school in 1791, followed by Edinburgh in the same year, and in 1800 by London. Vienna and Prague built schools for their blind in 1804, St. Petersburg and Berlin in 1806, Amsterdam in 1808, Zurich and Dresden in 1809, Dublin in 1810, Copenhagen in 1811, and then there was a lull in the benevolent activities of the nations for a season, until the wars of combined Europe against the Napoleonic dynasty had ended in the expatriation of the world conqueror to St. Helena. Stockholm was the first city to establish a school for the blind after the capitulation of Paris in 1815, and that event dates from 1817. Koenigsburg, Breslau and Barcelona founded schools in 1818, 1819 and 1820, Naples in 1822, Gmund in 1823, Lintz in 1824, Pesth in 1825, Manchester and Glasgow in 1827, Freisinge and Bruchal in 1828, and Hamburg in 1830.

Hamburg, York, Cork, Munich, and Lausanne in 1830, 1838, 1840 and 1844, respectively, have been the only great schools established in Europe for the blind since America began its philanthropic labors in the same direction; and it cannot fail to appear to any well constituted mind that our work compares favorably with the labors of the old world, especially when it is borne in mind that during that brief interval we have fought to its bitter end, at Appomattox, the greatest civil war the world ever knew, and solved a problem which caused the noblest minds to totter. It is not claimed that the benevolent institutions of this country are as well endowed as those of the continent from whence we came; but it is absolutely certain that, all things considered, they bear as unmistakable testimony to the Christian philanthropy of the people as the world can furnish elsewhere; and some of the results attained are as worthy of admiration as any of the triumphs of education under similar limitations that have ever been realized.

The case of Laura Bridgeman, an inmate of the Perkins Institution at Boston, illustrates in a peculiar degree the amount of relief that can be given to suffering humanity, under circumstances which seemed almost to deny philanthropy and science a foothold. Blind, deaf and dumb, without the sense of smell, and almost devoid of the power to taste, she seemed cut off from the race at every point save the avenue of feeling, through which alone her intellect could be instructed and her soul awakened. She might as well have been entombed, for all the solace that could reach her through the voices of her family, or the cheerful laughter which does so much to render the average home a place of happiness. Following her mother from place to place, she felt her arms and hands, as she pursued the daily work of the house, and imitating the motions so observed, learned in that laborious way to sew and knit, and discharge some other simple duties.

Her temper suffered in no small measure from her privations. Her moral sense could not be appealed to. There was no way by which the lessons which we find in our spoken and written language could be conveyed to her mind, at the time of her entering the institution, although her intellect eventually proved itself to possess powers beyond the average. Dr. Howe, the superintendent of the Perkins Institute, described her as having a large and beautifully formed head, with a strongly marked nervous sanguine temperament.

The first care was to give her a knowledge of arbitrary signs, by which she might be taught to interchange thoughts with others, and with almost unceasing care that end was accomplished. What seemed at first a mechanical trick dawned at last upon her intelligence as a means of conversing with an unknown world, and obtaining thence sympathy, knowledge and esteem, from a host of human beings who had been to her scarcely more than the domestic animals with which she came in contact. The wrecked mariner, signaled from the shore that help will be afforded him, and assured that rescue is at hand, could not experience a more solemn joy than was evinced by that poor child as she grasped the value of her education. From that moment she was more plastic than clay in the hands of the potter, for the brightness that was within enabled her to perceive the bearings of a thought, almost as soon as the work of communication began. The manual alphabet used by deaf mutes was mastered by feeling the hands of those with whom she conversed, and imitating every movement, success in delineation being announced by an approving touch on her head. To connect the letters, formed into a word, with the object so described, to change the signs of letters into letters themselves, in type placed at her disposal, to read the raised and sunken letters on the printed page, and to comprehend their import, must have seemed to those immediately concerned akin to raising a soul from out the cerements of death.

Her facility in such intercourse became wonderful, and she could speedily distinguish degrees of intellect in others, treating the weak minded with absolute contempt. Her mother, visiting the Institution unannounced, hoped that her child would recognize her presence by filial instinct; but it was only when after several attempts to awaken her memories of home the mother kissed her with that fervor which only parent and child can understand, that poor Laura learned who was with her, and she would not lightly leave her side again.

Dr. Howe, whose patient perseverance wrought these wonders in Laura Bridgeman's life, deserves to be remembered with esteem in every household, and his work must plead for him unceasingly before that throne where every work of mercy takes its rise. He who gave sight to Bartimaeus, and to Lazarus life itself, had a worthy and faithful follower in the good man whose soul has carried happiness into so many homes.

CHAPTER IV.

SCHOOL DAYS IN EARNEST.

Mr. Woodruff—Superintendent Lane—Severe Frost—Unexpec-
ted Vacation—Starting for Oakland—Off the Track—Good Samaritan
—Unknown Friend—Mr. Churchman—*Uriah Heep* Whipped—Im-
provements — My Store Clothes — Scandinavia Avenged — Currant
Wine—Hired Man—The Confession—Penalties—Snow—Sister Mary
Dies—Two Days' Sleighride—Cure for Somnolency—Patient Norse-
man—Gymnastic Exercise—School Resumed—Tree Diversions—I am
Suspended — Lucky Escape — Boat Building — Special Training—
Morris Jones—Our Voyage—The Wreck—Tne Whirlpool.

"I hold it true with him who sings
To one clear harp with many tones,
That man may rise on stepping stones
Of their dead selves to higher things.—*Tennyson.*

School days had commenced with me in earnest,
but the means at the disposal of the Superintendent,
Mr. Woodruff, were so limited that there was little
benefit to be obtained in the Institution, beyond
companionship with youngsters of my own age and
condition. Certainly there were opportunities to
make brooms and brushes under a moderately competent instructor, and to the facility then attained
I have since that time owed many a pleasant and
profitable hour. Acquaintance with the English
tongue was also something, and that grew apace, in
my case, with almost every boy for my teacher out-
of-doors, and the tutors in the several classes all
speaking that language.

The superintendent was a well-meaning, pleasant man, who did not know what was required at his hand, and who never made any serious endeavors to discharge the higher duties. He was careful as a janitor, and his salary, three hundred dollars per annum, may well have begotten in him the idea that there were no other functions imposed upon him. The boys treated him with consideration on account of his kindly demeanor, but nobody could imagine for one moment that the poor man was in his proper place; and when he took his departure, in 1855, there was a sense of relief in our minds, and a consciousness that he could not be paid less in any other vocation, however perfect his unfitness might be.

Our next principal was Superintendent Lane, a good man, who came from Jackson, Mississippi, in 1855, and remained six months. He has since become a minister of the gospel, and, in whatever walk of life he may be called to act his part, he will never fail to carry a kindly heart into his labors. He left a salary of one thousand three hundred dollars per annum, to accept less than half that amount in Wisconsin; and, finding an institution poorly appointed, instead of one fully equipped for the work, he became entirely disgusted with the change. Everything conspired to render him dissatisfied with his new location. The winter of 1855-6 was unusually severe; for more than a month in our

unfinished building—only a wing at the best, and
that, too, a wing that never beat the wind—the ther-
mometer ranged from twenty to thirty-two degrees
below zero, and hardly one nose could be found that
had not been tweaked by Father Frost.

Mr. Lane, accustomed to the milder airs of the
South, saw no pleasure in such extremes, so he
merely remained until the weather moderated, and
then in April gave his benediction to the Institution
in the form of "a big, big D," by way of a parting
salute to the boys. We regretted him much, for he
was kind to us always, treated every one generously,
displayed no administrative rigor, enforced no discipline, assumed that every boy was a gentleman, and
never questioned his attainments, leaving each to be
a law unto himself.

The youngsters, who are much more observant
everywhere than their elders are inclined to believe,
thought Mr. Lane a marvel of scholarly accomplish-
ments; and that tradition will remain with us to
the end. We were naturally sorry when he left us,
for his departure was the signal to break up school
four months before the usual time, and the institution had grown to be a home to most of us.

I shall not readily forget the commencement of
that long vacation, because, inasmuch as the *finale*
was not looked for, my friends had made no provision for my return, and it devolved upon me to take
my journey with the mail man, who carried the let-

ters at stated intervals to Christiana, Wisconsin, the post town nearest my father's farm. When we reached the office at Albion, Wisconsin, the carrier left me on the box seat of the vehicle, while he went inside to hand over the mail to the postmaster, and to exchange his budget of news from Janesville for the petty scandal that abounds in villages. I thought we had reached Christiana, our destination, and no sooner was my custodian in the office than I started for home. One village street is so like another that nothing warned me of my mistake until I found myself out upon the prairie, having walked far enough, according to my calculation, to have reached home, and being yet unable to discover any of the familiar landmarks. I had traveled at least two miles further away from my destination, and at last, becoming painfully conscious of my blunder, I reluctantly turned my steps toward a cottage by the roadside, to ask for direction.

Blind boys are very sensitive as to such mistakes, and would generally walk a long way around rather than confess incapacity; but I was at sea completely, without a compass, and I did not know which course to steer for my port. Before I reached the door, the voice of a stranger and the sound of buggy wheels attracted my attention. The gentleman who hailed me had seen some time before that I was a stranger in a strange land, and had followed

me, curious to know whether I was actually lost.
My evident uncertainty, as I paused near the gate-
way, determined him to come to my help. I told
him who I was, and where I was trying to find my
way, and within a minute was sitting beside the
stranger, who generously became my pilot in the
emergency. The wheels were as musical as a well
tuned instrument, and the thousand and one questions of my friend were as welcome as daylight to
the belated traveler. When we reached Edgerton
there was a bountiful dinner to which the good
Samaritan made me welcome, and then he carried
me nine miles further, away from his own road, to
deliver me into the hands of my friends at home.

I say it with shame, because it is my duty to tell
the truth, even although it may not be creditable
to the narrator, that on my arrival at my destination
I was so overjoyed to find the familiar spot, that I
rushed in to greet my mother, and forgot to ascertain the name of my benefactor. One fact only
could be recalled by me when I found on my return
to the gate that he had departed; his residence
was about four miles west of Cambridge. From
that day to this I have never met him, and now,
possibly, I never shall; but the service that was rendered me will never be forgotten.

The fall of 1856 saw me once more an inmate of
the institution, which was now to be a school in reality, under the supervision of Mr. Churchman, an

excellent superintendent. That gentleman, whose ability was recognized by the allotment of a salary of one thousand dollars, a large sum for Wisconsin in those days, continued in office until 1861, and the good results of his administrative skill remain until this hour. I say this with a clear conscience, as my conviction, although, as the outcome of many circumstances unfortunate for me, Mr. Churchman looked upon the narrator with disfavor nearly all the time that he reigned. There are some boys in every school who delight to carry tales, and assume a false humility, after the pattern of *Uriah Heep*, to ingratiate themselves with the principal. Such fellows are not universal favorites. Their hands are against every one, and they suffer the recognized penalty, every one's hand is against them. The tale bearer *par excellence* in our institution, a bigger fellow than myself, by far, forced a quarrel upon me one day, and was well whipped.

I suppose good fortune favored me in one sense, but in another that schoolboy victory was the bane of my life. The tattler reported me every day if he could, as a kind of Heenan and Tom Sayers rolled into one; and, because I would not recriminate on my accuser, there came to be a hard feeling against me in the mind of the superintendent, which might have had most serious consequences. For the smallest offence the boys were called up and reprimanded before the whole school, and the hardening effects of that method could be seen in every child. My own share of such lectures was away beyond the average, but I cannot remember that any of these exercises ever left me in an amiable mood; for there was a rankling sense of injustice, and uncalled-for humiliation, in the methods employed, as well as in the way in which the charges were held to be sustained. It is easy to see now that Mr. Churchman was imposed upon, but at that time it was very hard to find any palliation for his conduct. However, we have something else on hand besides discussing schoolboy grudges, and, with your permission, we will go on to speak of the new superintendent as an administrative officer, taking hold of an institution which was only a school in name and converting it into a reality of which Wisconsin might be proud.

The plans of the partly finished building were reconstructed, and improved by the process, so that the edifice actually served the purpose for which it was intended. The legislature was persuaded by him to vote larger sums, year by year, than had ever been appropriated before by the same body for like purpose, and, the money being available, the work was rushed through as rapidly as a due regard to its fitness would permit. Apparatus of all kinds, such as had been conspicuous by their absence in the former history of our school days, began to be used in the work of tuition. Maps, globes, scientific and philosophic mechanisms adapted to meet the wants of the blind, awakened a new interest in our studies, and better teachers than were ever before employed there were called into requisition. The discipline introduced was sometimes harsh, and ill-judged as harshness usually is, but it was better than the entire absence of discipline, which would eventually have made the Institution little better than a bear garden. Like many another wise king, our ruler lent his ear to unworthy favorites, but for which his career would have reached the pinnacle of excellence.

One day a remittance was sent to me by my father to purchase clothes, and Mr. Churchman took me with him into Janesville to make an investment. If ever in all my experience I felt my oats, that day was the occasion. There was a large sum of money actually in my keeping. I had been honored with a drive in the superintendent's carriage, was to be dressed for the first time in a suit of town-made apparel, so that the eye of the civilized world would be upon me, and already I could feel that the merchant tailor deemed me a patron worthy his best attention. Of course, I was nothing if not critical, and the best was hardly good enough material to encase me, so I was examining the whole stock with as much energy as though the clothing for an army of dandies was to have been chosen. With all these ideas and a few more of the same class, inflating the sense of my importance, imagine the shock that was endured when the deep, sonorous voice of the superintendent

6

grated upon my ear, in an audible aside: "I think this is good enough for a Scandinavian."

Shades of the Vikings! could such insolence be endured, and the perpetrator live? Was there no Valhalla in which the skull of such an enemy could be used as a drinking vessel, with his ensanguined life-stream as the feast? Come what come might, there had to be a terrible revenge for such contumely, if the *manes* of our ancestors were to be placated; and, though my anger was silent, it was deep. Man delighted me not. I was in the same case with *Hamlet*, and as undecided, as we drove back to the Intstitution, but my purposes were never forgotten for one moment.

An Irish lad, my companion in many a hair-breadth 'scape by flood and field, was made my confidant, and invited not only to stand with me in the imminent and deadly breach, but also to devise means for making such breach. He was like *Yorick*, a fellow of infinite jest, fitted to keep the table in a roar, but we did not roar worth a cent on that occasion; we gave the silent watches of the night to deliberation. His plan fell short of manslaughter, but it went into the depths, and in a certain sense it promised satisfaction. The venerable Churchman, like many another of his class, had in the cellar, for his own particular delight and consolation, a ten-gallon keg of wine—currant wine. That must be reached and tapped with straws, must be drained until nothing but emptiness and the aroma should remain, and then in the mystery, which we never doubted would enshadow our action to the last, we would contemplate the consequences of our revenge upon that insolent foe.

The scheme went merrily as a marriage bell. Our success equaled the most sanguine anticipations. The straws were inserted night after night, and, although we suffered agonizingly every day, being compelled to keep our beds and take medicine, we never failed to resume our self-imposed duty at night, with a constancy worthy of a better cause. To this day I hate currant wine, beacuse of that long-drawn-out vengeance upon the contemner of our race; but that remote ancestry from which we take our inspiration must have smiled at my devotion.

The keg at last was empty, but the developments for which we waited and hoped, came in a form that defeated our anticipations. The hired man, who alone had been entrusted with the key of the cellar, was deemed guilty of our sin, and was discharged for our transgression. His offence and his punishment were published, and already the poor fellow, overwhelmed by his unmerited misfortunes, was at the gate waiting for a conveyance to carry him and his boxes away. There was not a moment to be lost, if we possessed an adequate sense of justice, and my companion chivalrously agreed with me that we had no option but to confess our folly at once.

and face the music, even though it should involve
our dismissal from the Institution.

The *Jackdaw of Rheims*, who was cursed with all
the accessories of Bell, Book and Candle, for having
stolen My Lord Cardinal's ring, was an embodiment
of innocence, when he hopped and croaked in the
sacred presence with every feather reversed, by comparison with the guilty things that stood in the office
of the superintendent to own the misdeed for which
the hired man was condemned.

Mr. Churchman treated us better than we had any
right to expect. We were punished, but not dismissed. One month without dessert, and, during
the same term, enforced retirement to the dormitory
at seven every evening, was a kind of discipline that
spoke of a generous heart in the man before whom
we appeared self-accused. Had the charge been
preferred by some other accuser, and proved by testimony other than our admission, of course the penalty would have assumed widely differing proportions. Thus ended my thoughts of revenge for a
fancied insult, in my better appreciation of the man
who was less injured by our midnight escapades
than were the silly offenders.

The loss of my dear sister and friend, whose
name was mentioned as living in Janesville to protect me, in connection with my first appearance in
the Institution, occurred in December, 1856; and
shortly before Christmas I was taken home, to attend

her funeral, by one of the neighbors, who drove over for me in his sleigh.

My clothing was too light for a long ride at that season of the year, and the weather was very severe. The snow lay deep on the ground, and shovels were provided to enable the rest of the sleigh load to dig a path whenever the obstruction became otherwise insurmountable; but my puny proportions and general unfitness for work to which I was unaccustomed, prevented them allotting me a shovel. The drive of only twenty-two miles occupied almost two days, and exposure without exercise told upon me with great effect. During the second day, it seemed as though the cold had moderated considerably, and an inclination to sleep overpowered my faculties. The friendly driver, my custodian, must have noticed my somnolency, as he plied me with many questions, until I imparted to him my conviction that the weather was much warmer. As soon as that fact was mentioned he ceased to talk, but, handing the reins to another, he took me from the bottom of the sleigh, and dumped me into a snow-drift.

My lines had fallen into unpleasant places, and I could not understand the rigorous treatment to which I was subjected for the next hour. The driver, descending, picked me up and rolled me over in the crisp snow, without the least regard for my remonstrances.

His patience was unbounded, for he did not show a
scintilla of temper, although I said to him all the
meanest things that could be uttered in the Norwegian tongue. Perseverance was as marked in his
composition as patience, for, during all the time
that I was pouring out upon him my ineffectual
volume of abuse, he never ceased to drag me along,
running or walking, with difficulty, by the side of
the sleigh, until the lethargy which had been su-
perinduced by the cold had entirely disappeared.
The pains in my extremities, which were then ascribed to his unchristian conduct in handing me
from the sleigh with so little ceremony, can now be
understood as the efforts of nature to throw off the
dangerous effects of frost-bite; and I can understand the possibility, also, that but for the gymnastic exercises through which I was put, with an energy of which Ling never dreamed, that slumber
might have ended in the sleep that knows no waking on this earth.

My family thanked the driver friend for his care,
and taught me to bless him for the precaution, which
had probably, under the Divine favor, saved my
life. The sorrowful occasion of my coming home
filled the house with solemnity, for this was the first
inroad of the angel of death on our little circle since
our arrival in Wisconsin; and my sister who had
gone to her account was a special favorite with
every member of the family, because of the gentle-

SUSPENDED.

ness and loving kindness with which she had added
grace to every action in her energetic career. It
seemed to me that the sunshine had gone out of
my life entirely when the sods fell upon her coffin,
for she had been in a peculiar sense my guardian,
and I loved her with an affection which still endures.

My school career was speedily resumed, and, as a
matter of course, my melancholy disappeared in the
midst of my accustomed exercises and sports.

One of our most popular forms of enjoyment was
to swing in a rope suspended from the overhang-
ing branch of a great tree, on the grounds of the Institution. The tree was about five feet in diam-
eter, and the first branch was twenty-five feet from
the ground, ·so, inasmuch as we had not learned
tree climbing from the Australian savages, who stick
their grasping fingers and toes into the bark when
they are in pursuit of the opossum that must be had
for dinner, we had to look around for extraneous
aid. We used the second branch for suspending our
swing, but to reach that elevation was easy after
we gained the first. The preliminary stage in our
enterprise required some ingenuity and daring. A sapling with a forked branch broken off, so that only
about a foot remained as a kind of staging, came so
near to the first limb of the great tree that some of
our tallest lads, steadying themselves carefully by
the slender upperworks of the sapling, and biding
their time as the support swayed to and fro, could

grasp the desired limb and raise or lower themselves at pleasure. Only the tallest fellows of our little community attempted this delicate operation for some time, but familiarity with danger breeds contempt at last, and some of the smaller boys soon discovered that they could accomplish the same feat by springing just a little way upward at the right moment. Generally at the outset the boys that could see a little were on hand to direct the course of action, but by-and-by their services were deemed nonessential, and a group of youngsters would follow one the other up into the great tree and down again, as recklessly as other lads play leap-frog.

One day in the spring of 1857 it occurred to me that I would make the ascent alone, and the impulse was followed unhesitatingly. To climb the sapling was easy, and I was soon standing on the accustomed rest, ready to jump. Whether I sprang too early or too late I cannot say, but it is certain that I missed the branch, and in my fall, fortunately for me, my pants became entangled with the short arm of the sapling, so that I remained head downwards, hanging by the leg of my unmentionables until help arrived. I dared not make much noise to attract attention, lest my presence and condition, my head bowed to the earth in humility to atone for that "vaulting ambition which overleaps itself and falls on the other side," should lead to punishment; so I hung there in silent wonderment until the fruit—

rich, ripe and ready to fall, as it is said in the story books—should find appreciative observers, willing to pluck it from its unwonted abiding place, and say nothing. Perhaps it would have been possible for me to have sprung upwards and have clasped the sapling, but in those days of shoddy and devil's dust you could not reckon with absolute confidence upon the durability of cloth; so it was prudent to leave well alone.

James Russell Lowell, in The Bigelow Papers, satirizing the pretensions of the evolution theory, says:

> "The fears of a monkey whose holt chanced to fail,
> Drew the vertebræ out to a prehensile tail."

but there was no case on record in which pantaloons had obeyed the law of development; so that the passage in question, of which, by-the-by, I knew nothing at the time, afforded me no comfort whatever. Ten minutes or more elapsed before I was seen by my companions, and then they came trooping towards the spot in high glee over my ridiculous appearance. The sapling bending with my weight, just as the fishing rod of Izack Walton might have been deflected by a worm more than usually ponderous, held me about nine feet from the ground, and at that height I was compelled to remain until an impromptu staging could be erected for my relief. There came to me no words of sympathy from the crowd; people who occupy the high places in life are almost of necessity alone; but I could not see anything so very laughable in my predicament as that any of the fellows need roll on the grass with noisy merriment, intsead of lending a hand for my rescue.

In Albert Smith's veracious narrative, *The Adventures of Jack Johnson and Mr. Ledbury*, a volume full of mirth and humorous provocations, which every lover of fun should read, there is a description of Mr. Ledbury's anxiety as he hung from a wall, with his toes almost touching the ground, while his wicked friend Johnson urged him to hold on for his life until he could procure assistance. Perhaps that comical illustration may have occurred to some of their minds, but the cases were not parallel, as my fall, could I have cleared myeslf, might have been sufficient to break my neck, and I could not accomplish that end without damaging the clothes which Mr. Churchman helped me to select in Janesville. Well, thank goodness! I was relieved at last, after about twenty minutes of unsought distinction; but the duress under which I labored seemed to have lasted a whole day. The boys did not allow me to forget my dilemma in a hurry, but the secret was so well guarded from the tale bearers that Mr. Churchman never knew how near he had been to losing his *bete noir*, and I was spared a lecture before the whole of the classes in chapel, setting forth the enormity of my conduct.

The superintendent was a good man in every sense of the word, but he could not remember that he haa ever been a boy, or he would have varied some of his lectures with a brilliant flash of silence.

The only thing that surprises me in my school career is that I lived through it, when I try to recall the singular accidents which in our blind confidence we encountered.

The boys had all of them more or less pocket money, and in the workshops we were encouraged to use tools of almost every description; so we determined to build a boat. The lines of that structure may not have been such as would have passed muster with the Admiralty, but they were more ambitious, if not more successful, than those of the coracle, the boat of wicker work, covered on the outside with skins sewed together, in which the Britons ventured to skirt the stormy Atlantic, before the Romans, under Cæsar, landed. With what patient impatience we labored on our new enterprise! Had there been a prospect of our becoming successful mariners, going down to the great sea in ships and bringing wealth from far Cathay, we could not have been more deeply interested than we were in the construction of our little vessel. Cleopatra, reclining on the perfumed deck of that gorgeous pleasure boat in which she delighted to woo Pompey in the days when Rome did not think he had an equal in generalship, statecraft or patriotism, was not more proud of her silken sails, and of the music or costly dishes with which she regaled her guest

on the bosom of the mysterious Nile, than were we
of our humble pinnace, which was destined to carry
us for a brief term upon the placid stream of Rock
River.   Every spare hour—nay, every minute that
could be spared from our class work, we spent upon that model of naval architecture, until one day
she was ready for launching.

The water ran through her at first as if she had
been built as a colander or sieve, but by the time the
oars were finished, ready for use, the timbers had
become seasoned and staunch, so that a small quantity of oakum and tar, with a skillful application of
caulking tools, made her perfectly seaworthy.

There was a great deal of education for all concerned in our boat enterprise, but the lessons were
not yet closed.   Some day there will be a change
in our school policy, and the constitutional predilections of each individual will have their fullest and
best development under competent masters: the
predestined artisan being thoroughly instructed in
the laws of mechanics, the medical man of the future grounded in the mysteries of physiology, the
engineer, the architect, the painter, 'the sculptor and
the cook, being each fitted, so far as rudimentary
training can assist, to attain the highest excellence
in their respective lines of industry.   Now, unfortunately for the national welfare, every boy and
girl must pass through the same course of instruction, without regard to individual qualifications, and

in the best sense of the term there are none educated.   The best and most gainful industries, the mechanic arts, the skill of the artificer, and all others, the most truly dignified occupations, are looked down upon, or left to be supplied by foreigners and their immediate descendants, while the graduates of our school system qualify themselves to be clerks, and nothing more, crowding the market with an excessive supply, which must descend at last to the ranks of the laborer.

We had no cause to complain on that score, or at any rate very little.   Within the limited range available to the blind there was an earnest endeavor made to discover personal fitness, and usually the best qualities of the pupil were aided toward successful development.   There were exceptions, certainly, but these were faults of administration, not inherent vices of the system.   An idle music-teacher, whose name need not be mentioned, had placed under his care a boy named Jones, whose friends thought they had found in him a decided taste for music, which might be cultivated with advantage. The teacher, well paid and pampered, for he was a favorite, would not be at the pains to fairly test the capacity of the lad; after a probation, all too brief, he was cast aside as an unpromising pupil, upon whom instruction would be thrown away, and for two years his time was absolutely wasted as a consequence of that conclusion.   Jones was then

sent by special effort to Philadelphia, to the State
Institute, if I mistake not, where many pupils have
attained wonderful proficiency; and within a short
time evinced such taste and talent as a musician, as
entitled him to the position of musical professor in
the Janesville Institute, where his conscientiousness,
no less than his tact and skill, made him eminently
successful. The ability of Professor Jones is known
throughout the northwest, and in Janesville, where
he is more particularly known, his amiable qualities,
as well as his critical acumen and executive power,
have given him a very high place in the esteem of
his fellow citizens.

But I have wandered away from the boat, to talk
about my school fellows, and it is certainly time to
return, if we are ever to begin our long-looked-for
excursion. Every boy that could make good his
claim presented himself to us as a passenger, or as
a rower, or indeed in any capacity from midship-
mán upward, that afternoon, when we started on our
voyage; and when every inch of sitting room had
been appropriated, without encroaching on the seats
for the rowers, there were still many sorrowful faces
on the bank. But, "Yo! Heave, Yo!" that is what
seamen are supposed to say when sailing into remote
seas, and of course we said as much, or words to
that effect. Away flew the light barque over the
silvery spray, or she would have done so, but she
was not light enough to fly in any sense of the

term; there was no spray worth mentioning, and
what was there was not silvery, for Rock River is
not a rapid, brilliant stream.   But, youth at the prow
and pleasure at the helm, we were off on our cruise.
At first we felt our way, as it were, timidly, on the
new element, and caution diminished the muscular
force of the rowers; but courage grew with immuni-
ty, and, as the French say, "nothing succeeds like
success."   So we gradually increased our speed until we were carrying a full head of steam along the
middle of the current.

The sensation was truly glorious.   We had found
an element on which we could disport ourselves with
perfect safety, where the blind were the equals of
those with the blessing of sight, where no carriage
could endanger our lives, and where, with our boat
fully equipped and well manned, we could enjoy
all the advantages of healthful exercise in the fresh
air, without cost, as long as the timbers held together.   A song, a song, was demanded, and the
Canadian boat song, "Row, Brothers, Row!" was
trolled with admirable effect, waking the echoes
most joyously as we sped along, every line seeming
to accelerate our speed; when, crash! we had reached
our destination.   The navy had encountered a fatal
snag, and its timbers were literally rent in twain by
the impact.   It seems now that we were almost instantly in the water, swimming for our lives; but in
reality there must have been some delay, as the

boat, although broken, still held upon the snag, and
we were able to take to the stream without undue
haste.   All the boys could swim tolerably well, except one little fellow, who was taken into the boat
because no one could refuse him a pleasure, and
he became my special charge in this instance.   I
made him understand that there was no cause for
fear, so long as he did not convulsively grasp my
arms in the water, and he behaved like a little hero.
A very few minutes found us all ashore on the river
bank, not much the worse for our unexpected bath,
for the weather was decidedly warm, and we
reached the Institute in good time for supper, after
an afternoon of adventure, which gave to every one
of the boys a truly invincible appetite.

That was the end of our boat building, and our
enthusiasm has never prompted us to become compet-
itors for the honors which the leading universities
annually contest. The lesson brought to an end was
not spent in vain upon our faculties.

That was not the end of my river experiences, for
the water had an irresistible charm for me. I could
swim passably well, and never lost a chance to
plunge into the stream, whether I could take company with me or not. One day I had gone swimming alone, and, in my ignorance of the exact locality to which I had floated, found myself in a kind of
eddy or whirlpool, on the far side of the stream from
the Institute, between an island and the bank.

There were traditions about that eddy having sucked down strong men to destruction, and all the boys were cautioned to give a wide berth to the miniature mælstrom. There is no use attempting to conceal the fact, I was alarmed, and my fear magnified all the dangers that surrounded me. I tried to break through the charmed circle by vigorous swimming, but in spite of my will found every time that my course went with the circling current. As I was swept around, I knew that there was one point at which the water was shallow enough to permit my feet to touch bottom, but every attempt to wade ashore was defeated by the strong eddy, which bore me away. Once, when I repeated that effort, my foot struck a boulder of considerable size, and that circumstance inspired me with hope. After that incident I dived for the boulder every time that I seemed to be near the spot, and, the third or fourth time being successful, seized it, and carrying the mass of stone as ballast was able to escape the dangerous environment. I need hardly say that in recrossing the river I was careful to avoid the eddy, and after that time I knew, as it were by instinct, how to keep clear of the troubled waters.

7

CHAPTER V.

CHARACTER STUDIES.

One of the music teachers in our institution, and for many reasons not one of the popular instructors, albeit an able man in his profession, and painstaking in many ways which did not endear him to the boys, was a Mr. Campbell, from Boston, who has since established an institution for the blind in London, which has been described by competent visitors, themselves engaged in like tasks, as one of the best of its kind in Europe. Mr. Churchman was not only an able administrator, but he had the faculty, in which many good men utterly fail, to select from a crowd of applicants for appointment the men best adapted for their respective duties. Sometimes, in consequence of favoritism, he allowed practices to grow up afterwards, which in some degree marred their usefulness; but all his predilections were in favor of able men.

Superintendents of institutions for the blind in this country, and other instructors, have made spe-

cial visits of inspection to Mr. Campbell's Institution
in London, and have been amply rewarded in wit-
nessing the results of his assiduous application.
The wealthiest class of patrons in the United
Kingdom has been reached by the skillful manipu-
lations of the principal, and rich endowments have
almost rained upon the establishment, which is fitted
and supplied with all the latest appliances for the
tuition of the blind.   His stay with us was very
limited, and sickness in his family absorbed much
of his time; but the occasional lessons with which
we were favored, at considerable intervals, were of
such a character as to impress the advanced pupils
very favorably.   After less than two terms of little
more than nominal service, Mr. Campbell left the
Institute, and was heard of no more by the boys,
until the news came that he had taken London by
storm; had the press, the clergy and the aristocracy
loud in praise of his system, and could command all
the aid he desired in prosecuting his enterprise.

Professor Bischoff was one of the pupils in the
Janesville Institution during my stay, and from the
first his aptitude for music commanded the esteem of every teacher.   Other branches of study
were touched by him in a light and perfunctory
way, just sufficient to enable him to pass muster on
the score of general training and information; but
when his attention was directed to his favorite
theme, his whole soul seemed to leap into the pur-

suit.   As a teacher and composer he has won great
distinction, and his power as an executant secured for
him years since an appointment of great value, as or-
ganist in the city of Washington, D. C.

It is the custom of a certain class of writers to assert that the blind seldom attain anything beyond a
pleasing mediocrity in their several pursuits, including music.   Perhaps the critical acumen which per-
vades their strictures on the sightless will enable
them to perceive that humanity in the aggregate
does not attain even that moderate level.   There has
been but one Shakespeare, one blind Homer, one Virgil and one blind Milton for all the nations; and there
are millions to-day, among the so-called civilizing
races, that possess too little of the divine spark of
genius to be able to appreciate the works which the
masters have left for our instruction.   The well at-
tuned souls that have risen to eminence in music, are
so few that they may be counted on our fiingers; and
one of them, Handel, has left it on record that he
had been charmed by the executive skill of blind
players.   He did not ascribe to the class a pleasing
mediocrity, and he instanced individuals who approached excellence.   While the race generally can
show so few instances of supreme endowment, there
is no reason for the expectation that every sightless
man should, because of his deprivation, excel the
average of mankind; especially when we consider
that less than a century has elapsed since the first

institute for the education of the blind was established in Europe.

Professor Bischoff is one of many who have risen
far above the level which unjust as well as unfriend-
ly critics have assigned as the limit which the blind
can reach; and, for that reason, as well as on account
of kindly reminiscences connected with our intercourse in the classroom and elsewhere, it is a pleasure to mention his attainments and his genius.

Mr. Churchman's connection with the Institution
ceased in 1861, when he went to Indianapolis, Indi-
ana, to take charge of the Institution for the blind
in that city, at a much more liberal salary. His fitness for command had been amply demonstrated during the many years that he presided over the desti-
nies of our Institution, and there were none to question his capacity. For my own part, I have un-
grudgingly stated my conviction as to his merits in
every respect; and nothing but a desire to tell "the
truth, the whole truth, and nothing but the truth," as
they say in the courts, has compelled me to hint
that the good man was not without his weaknesses.
Favoritism, which has blurred the greatness of kings
and conquerors, asserted its power over him, and at
times betrayed him into overt acts, which his better
judgment, fully informed, must cause him to regret;
but in stating so much by way of censure on his
career, we are only vindicating for him the common
lot of mankind. In the palmiest days of old Rome,

when great and wealthy citizens were being buried
with all the honors which had been won in the public service, it was the custom to assign the most
prominent place in the funeral procession to a professional satirist and jester, attired in the garb of his
calling, and to require from him a rehash of all the
charges that had ever been preferred against the
man who was then being honored. We have been
much less severe than such a satirist might have
been.

Mr. Churchman found the Institution a shell, partly constructed on a faulty plan, and he changed its
character completely, leaving the building almost
entire, well furnished, and supplied with modern
equipments. He found only fifteen pupils in the
establishment, and these untrained beyond what
might be expected from every person obeying the impulses of his own untutored mind, or submitting himself to the influence of associates; and he left the Institution with sixty pupils, many of whom have attained excellence in their respective careers, and all
of whom were under firm discipline. I am glad
that Mr. Churchman left, because his departure left
an opening for a superior man, full of the best impulses, whose influence upon my mind and character
was in every sense beneficial; but my love for the
superintendent who succeeded him must not make
me unjust to the former *regime*.

We come now to speak of Superintendent Little,

who was the successor of Mr. Churchman, and who
died in harness, loved and respected by all classes
with whom he came in contact. To recount some
few of the merits of that gentleman is one of the
pleasantest duties devolving upon me in this little
history. He found the Institution in a much better
condition than prevailed at the time when Mr.
Churchman assumed control; but happily he introduced changes in administration, which proved
most beneficent. The rigorous discipline, tempered
by favoritism for some, and exaggerated into harshness and mistrust for others, was replaced by an
equable rule, which bore alike upon every person
in our little community, and brought out all that
there was of the best in every nature. There were
many changes made in the official staff under the new
superintendent, and we had reason to be well pleased
in that respect; but of course we could only speculate and surmise as to the cause for the removals.
One circumstance was very grateful to our feelings:
there was an end to the system of spying and tale-
bearing; and it seemed as though a father, confident
of love and obedience in his circle, would avail
himself of no petty scheme of *surveillance* in carrying out his determinate system of government.

Another change was immediately noticed. When
any of the pupils transgressed the rules, there was no
ponderous lecture in the chapel, to punish the innocent as well as the guilty; the offender was taken

apart from his fellows, and, without any special endeavor to humiliate, was made to see the enormity
of his conduct in a way which almost necessitated
reform. There was a special burden taken from my
shoulders, in the knowledge that all old accounts
were squared, and that my record for the future would
depend upon my own conduct.

The kindly demeanor of Mr. Little made even the
youngest child in the Institution feel easy in his
presence, as the inmates had never felt under his
predecessor, but at the same time, it is only fair to
say, that the dignity properly belonging to his position and his character was never compromised.
The old proverb says that "familiarity breeds contempt," and another gem compacted of the world's
wisdom is uttered in the words, "no man is a hero
to his valet;" but no boy dreamed of being familiar
with the superintendent; you might as readily imagine that one of the soldiers of the old guard
would forget the rank of Napoleon. He was a hero
and a philosopher in our esteem, always—that worthy
superintendent of ours—and it was a subtle influence, the very essence of the nature of his rule,
which, without the aid of a spoken word, always
seemed to inform the pupil that there were limits
that must be fully understood and respected by
him in his intercourse with the principal. He was
the friend of every inmate of the Institution, but such

a friend as even the most forward could not approach
without respect.

When Mr. Little came to Janesville as Superintendent of the Institution, he brought with him, as
his good genius and our best friend, and as
matron of that establishment, Mrs. Whiting. She is
a lady of medium size, not strictly beautiful, but
she possesses an even temper and pleasant expression
of countenance, indicative of a generous and loving
soul, which made her more than beautiful to us all.
Boys and girls alike were participants in her kindness, and never was a case known, after the commencement of her *regime*, during my stay in the
Institute, when sickness or sorrow overtook any of
the inmates without the motherly solicitude of our
good friend being manifested on behalf of the sufferer. There had never been a time during Mr.
Churchman's rule when a sick boy or girl was neglected or left in want of needful sustenance; but
the food of the heart, that home-like affection for
which every true soul hungers, could not be sent to
the sick chamber in the sufficient array of dishes
which carried actual diet; and it was just precisely
in that respect that we found our most wonderful
change for the better.

Good health was the rule in the Institution, but
sickness prostrated us all at some time or another,
though the care of our matron protected us from
many serious attacks, otherwise, humanly speaking,

inevitable; and then the youngster alone in the
dormitory found his sickly palate studied in the
dainty but simple nick-nacks that tempted his appetite, while they spoke of a love far dearer than all
the delights of sense. Hardly one could be found
in the Institution who did not know, from actual
observation or experience, that the silent watches
of the night witnessed her devotion to the duty
which she had accepted, not in the spirit of official
routine, but as a sacred trust. Moist eyes and quiver-
ing lips were eloquent in her praise, for it was known
and felt that she noiselessly visited the couches of
her sightless invalids to ascertain beyond question
whether the attendants had followed her instructions in the spirit as well as in the letter, and to assure herself that there were no symptoms more dangerous than those with which she had already become
familiar.

There was no parade of affection in her manner,
no pomp and circumstance of watching by our bed-
sides, but we were conscious always that we were
being cared for by one who wisely comprehended
our wants, and was prompt to relieve each ailment
that admitted of amelioration. Mrs. Whiting was
truly a mother to us all, and advancing years have
in no degree changed her attitude. What Florence
Nightingale was to the wounded and sick soldiery
during the Crimean war, Mrs. Whiting was to the
inmates of that institution; and if Scutari called

for administrative ability on a grander scale, the loving kindness of our matron brought her nearer to the individual heart, because, thanks be to the Great God above us, boys and girls are less indurated by the cares and anxieties of the work-a-day world than the disciplined and hardened soldier who has become a veteran in the trenches and on the battle-fields of the world.

Mr. Little knew the value of the acquisition that he brought with him to the Institute, even before we did, because circumstances had permitted him to see elsewhere that faithfulness and zeal which we experienced later; but it is not to be imagined that he fully comprehended the manifold tender relations and responsibilities of counsellor and friend outside the routine of duty, which that good woman assumed whenever the interests of her youthful charge urgently demanded her interposition. Her care was not limited to mere words of counsel, such as are often perfunctorily uttered by the comforters that sit around us echoing the words of Job's friends when afflictions come upon us, nor even to personal attention to the invalid confined to his sick chamber.

An array of names might easily be given of boys and girls, since arrived at maturity, on whose behalf her financial means were used without ostentation to ward off disaster, or to assist toward new departures, when the facilities furnished by the insti-

tute did not suffice for the educational requirements
of her young friends. We knew that such deeds on
her part were by no means uncommon, for the full
hearts of those whom she had benefited could not
restrain utterance; but the noble soul of our bene-
factress and friend carried to the farthest verge the
time honored maixm, "Let not thy left hand know
what thy right hand doeth." Grateful expressions,
often monosyllabic, on the part of those whom she
befriended, said as much as volumes might have conveyed, as to her simple but effective kindness.

This necessarily brief narration cannot do full
justice to the merits of the ladies and gentlemen
whose names are mentioned in our round, unvarnished
tale, but I have been impelled to speak of the chief
traits in the character of Mrs. Whiting, because her
influence on my own life has been peculiarly pleasant
and beneficial, and because she is one of the very
few ties that personally connect the present Institution with the past. Mr. Little, the much beloved
superintendent, died at the post of duty, striving to
restore the establishment to its pristine beauty and
vigor; his subordinates, with whom long use had
made me familiar, have nearly all been removed to
other spheres of activity. The building destroyed
by fire is now replaced by another edifice larger
and more suitable for its purpose; so that
change has been the rule. But Mrs. Whiting remained to preserve the identity of the old time with

the new, and whenever favoring circumstances permitted former scholars to revisit the loved spot, the warm welcome of that true-hearted friend was the brightest charm of the occasion.

The new structure seems strange, of course, to those who were among the earliest participants in the benefits which the Institute has conferred and is conferring; but there are some features which are as delightful as ever, and it is difficult to believe that there is not some good genius presiding over that old swing-tree, for instance, under whose umbrageous, wide-spreading branches our happy hours were often spent, and can still be readily recalled. Still it is a higher delight to think aloud, as it were, about the people who have been solicitous for our welfare, and their names are always dear to our memories; but our limits compel us reluctantly to end this section of our little book, and say adieu to Mrs. Whiting.

Mrs. Little, who is now the superintendent of the Institution, having been wisely called to that position after the death of her husband, came to the establishment as a teacher at the beginning of Mr. Little's administration as superintendent, and performed her duties with exemplary care. Successful leaders in any walk of life are usually remarkable for the skill and prescience with which they select their colleagues. Napoleon probably owed his statecraft, until after the victory at Tilsit, to Talleyrand, and even

his victories, on many occasions, to well chosen
marshals.   Mr. Little surrounded himself with men
and women admirably adapted to their respective
vocations; and the lady now under review, whose
recent appointment was due to the merits and self-
sacrificing devotion of her late husband, as well as
to her own eminent qualifications, is a case in point.

Ability to teach was not the only good quality that
commanded the esteem of the superintendent, and
thus it came to pass that, before the end of the in-
itiatory term, the amiable teacher was induced to accept a still more responsible position.   The marriage
occurred in the first vacation, and was in every
sense an occasion of much happiness until the reap-
er Death garnered the loved husband for the eternal
harvest.

Under the supervision of Mrs. Little, the Institution maintains the high status which it attained under the care of her husband, and it would be difficult to find an inmate who would complain as to the
management.   For some years her presence in the
establishment was marked by no incidents of note;
her duties were domestic, not public, but she was
none the less felicitous in her endeavors to promote
the welfare of the pupils.   There is a philosophical
axiom, "Happy is the nation that has no history,"
which was certainly true when history depended
for its chiefest charm on wars of aggression or defence; and in a large degree the same apothegm ap-

plies to institutions and to persons. Until the fire came to destroy the first Institution building, and to abridge the life of her dear partner, the career of the present superintendent may be said to have been devoid of historic interest; but the event which robbed her of happiness called upon her to assume a grave responsibility which will write her name in the annals of the State.

During Mr. Little's career at the Institute, his wife threw her whole soul with ungrudging effort into the Sunday-School movement, and she was the means of giving to that enterprise an undreamed-of prominence. Some time has elapsed since it was my privilege to visit Janesville, and then it was a pleasure of no common order to observe that the fair superintendent has completely justified her legion of friends in the confidence which was manifested by her appointment, and her success adds another to the long list of evidences that the intellectual and administrative faculties of the sex cannot easily be overtaxed. It is hardly necessary to remark how many have been the bright examples which have challenged the attention of mankind to woman's capacity to rule, yet there are some few names in the category which demand notice. The most brilliant epochs in European history are identified with the reigns of queens such as Isabella of Castile, under whose prestige Columbus re-discovered this continent, Elizabeth of England, under whom the globe was, probably for the first time, circumnavigated, and the Spanish armada destroyed, and yet others, hardly in any sense less glorious, whose names might crowd our pages, but could not render more apparent the fitness of the fair sex, in some conditions of society, to rule and direct mankind, begetting an emulation of a most beneficial character in the mass.

CHAPTER VI.

EFFECTUAL WARNING.

Overtime in Shop—Milwaukee Revisited—Boys in Blue—Strong Drink—Diseased Craving—Singular Dream—My Rescue.

But I am leaping before I come to the stile, and must return to my school days under Mr. Little's administration. We were expected to do a certain amount of work in the shops after having been instructed, and any over-time made by each boy was to his personal advantage. In the exercise of my privilege, working over-time, using, and of course paying for, the material furnished by the Institute, I had accumulated sixteen dozen brooms, with which I set out for Milwaukee, shortly before Christmas, 1861, and, partly on account of business, partly in pursuit of pleasure, spent my vacation in that city.

Usually, when, after years of absence, the child, advanced into youth or manhood, returns to a place with which he had been once familiar, all the old impressions of greatness or splendor are so shocked and belittled by the visit, that you almost doubt whether there may not have been some change made in the cradle of the city, or in your own, so that

8

the ill-matching memories have fallen upon the wrong spot.

The changes made in Milwaukee were in another direction entirely. The place had grown into metropolitan proportions. Its commerce had distanced all my anticipations. The streets were full of the bustle of a prosperous trade, and on every hand men moved with energy and activity, as though fortunes depended upon their decision of character at any moment. My delight was unbounded, as new experiences dawned upon me continually, and I looked forward with impatience to the time when my lines should be cast entirely in such a nerve plexus of enterprise as the ever expanding city presented. The old swampy streets in the lower section, which had been my only experiences when my father left the place determined to return to Norway if he could not otherwise find solid ground for his home, had put on an entirely different aspect, and the Milwaukee in which I found myself, away up toward the lake front, beyond Astor street, offered sites for dwellings never surpassed in the world.

Many of the residences that were visited by me during my stay seemed to be almost palatial in their dimensions and appointments, although I have of course seen much grander and handsomer homes since, in that city and elsewhere. The luxurious hotel buildings which now command the admiration of travelers had not then an existence, and if they had, probably my narrow means would have precluded my remaining in either of them as a guest during the Christmas time.

The Milwaukee house was my temporary home, and there were about one hundred and fifty boys in blue in the establisment, with all of whom I was immediately "hail fellow, well met." I would not like to say how much liquor, of the more expensive kinds, was consumed by me that Christmas, but I know, to my sorrow, that when the time arrived for me to resume my studies and work at the Institution, I carried with me an almost insatiable appetite for strong drink. Never since that time have I heard the drunkard denounced for his vice, by some vigorous-minded moralist who had been spared the allurements which carry millions to destruction, but I have felt that there may be a merciful judgment pronounced upon the fallen and depraved by our All-Seeing-Father, who knows by what insidious approaches the boat of life drifts into the stream which whirls, at the last, the bewildered victim over Niagara.

The money in my possession would not have gone far in paying for costly wines and liquors, but the truth was that during all the time of my stay in Milwaukee, I was not allowed to spend one cent by my generous entertainers, except in the liquidation of my board bill, and even that item would have

been attended to for me had I not resorted to strat-
egem.   Poor boys! many of them were as young,
and some younger than myself, but in the *abandon*
of that season while they were waiting to be mus-
tered in, they drank and sang with the merriment of
old soldiers hardened by a score of campaigns, and
scattered their money as recklessly as if Uncle Sam's
resources would never fail them to the end of their
lives.   With more than a few of that goodly company that anticipation was realized, for death found
them on their first battle-field, fighting gallantly
against their Southern brethren, who were as confident as they that the cause which had been appealed
to the bloody arbitrament of war was smiled upon
by the Supreme Being as a struggle for the inalienable rights of a brave and noble people.

I shall never forget my intercourse with the boys
in blue, for it came near costing me all that is dear
in life; but, notwithstanding the glamour of association with which it drew me toward the Circean
cup, which might have wrecked my career for both
lives and brought down the gray hairs of my father
and mother with sorrow to the grave, I have a
grateful remembrance of the unspoken sympathy
which was breathed every moment in their fraternal
solicitude.   Alone in my sleeping-room in the Institution, or in the midst of my companions in class-
room and workshop, the craving for stimulants never left me, and I never ceased to devise schemes for

the gratification of my insane desire. Money was plentiful with me, by comparison with what it had been in former times when I depended on scanty remittances from Oakland for almost every cent; but liquor could not be smuggled into the Institute without breaking through the letter and the spirit of the regulations, and it cost me a terrible pang even to think of rebelling against the rules which Mr. Little supported by his priceless example.

I do not say that the discipline wisely established by the superintendent was never evaded; the passion was growing too strong for conscience to control; but the limitations of my condition and the fear of discovery kept me within bounds, and it was only when an excuse could be made for a visit to Janesville, that I dared indulge to any considerable extent. The difficulties under which I labored all this time inflamed my desire continually, and my thoughts were ever directed toward Milwaukee, with a craving for the renewal of the joys of that companionship which first opened my mind to the world outside our almost cloistered seclusion.

One afternoon in the following May, as I was lying on my bed—not sleeping, for my thoughts were busy with my dear old grandfather, long since asleep under the sod in Valders, but still often present to my mind in spiritual communion,—the diseased craving for drink was upon me with more than its wonted force, and at the same time my

better self was in arms against the destroyer of my
peace.   My mental and moral nature warred unceasingly against the dominion of appetite, and had
so done at intervals for many months; but just now
there seemed to be a reinforcement of the better
influence, as though some unseen beneficent power,
surrounded and protected me from evil.

I was in dreamland, although my senses were not
lulled in slumber, for the old scenes in Valders
were blended with the more recent impressions on
my brain; and when I entered the cars to return, it
was with a consciousness more and less distinct at
times, that the Atlantic had to be traversed before I
could revisit my old haunts.   At Dramman, instead
of the faces and scenes which dimly haunt me
when the mysterious realms of memory are ran-
sacked to recall the past in Norway, I was astonished, and yet not surprised, by the recognition of
men, women and children whom I knew in Janesville, and could remember as having seen at the railroad depot, when, some months before, I had taken
my departure for Milwaukee.   The *vraisemblance* of
my former journey along that line was perfect, and
yet there were differences, as in the two sides of a
stereoscopic picture, and the minutest detail stood
out with almost painful distinctness.   I was going
to Milwaukee once more, but, as it seemed, was only
a passenger in spiritual essence, for none of the people that I knew ever recognized me by either word

UPSALA CATHEDRAL.

or sign. They spoke and jested with each other, but my presence was unsuspected, and the cars sped onward to station after station with the regularity of clockwork. Every feature of the different stopping places impressed me as it had done before, but I was piqued by the silence or unconcern of old friends, and was yet too proud to challenge attention by a direct appeal. Once I was on the point of speaking; it seemed as if I must speak, or perish in my silence, but some power restrained me, and although my lips moved, I could feel that my tongue uttered no sound.

Onward, still onward! I could distinguish the throbs of the steam power by which we traveled, and could reckon with absolute certainty upon the recurrence of a sound which told me that one of the wheels under our carriage was broken; and I wondered why no person in the throng besides myself observed the peculiar intonation of that fractured wheel. We reached Milwaukee, but the depot seemed to have undergone some change, and I was glad when my place had been secured in the old-time omnibus which was to convey me to the hotel.

Arrived at the familiar spot, I had no reason to complain of want of recogniiton. The old house was ablaze with light and merriment from basement to roof-tree, and from every door streamed forth a joyous crowd, with my name upon their. lips. I was welcomed as though my coming had long been an

object of desire, yet as though it had been feared I
should never fulfill that expectation.   Thoughts of
a carouse, in which seas of liquor should minister
to our merriment, almost maddened me with delight,
and yet at the same instant my better angel whis-
pered, "To drink is to die."

I looked again, and behold, the boys in blue
were not the dear fellows who once made me their
comrade, but hateful simulacra of my friends; and
there was a ringing dissonance in their voices,
which warned me to beware.   I entered the building by doors which were new and strange, and at
every step discovered some added splendor, which
could not compensate for the absence of that honest
and manly regard which had made my former visit so
entrancingly pleasant.   I was urged to drink at every
step, with every accent of entreaty and command,
but, alarmed by my surroundings, the appetite
which was once all powerful had died away, and I
would not have sipped one glass to win a kingdom.
There was a banquet more than regal in its magnificence, and for me the place of honor had been
reserved; but, as I looked a second time at every dish
of burnished gold, I saw beneath the show of delicate viands that every particular charm had drink
for its base, and, without the action of my will, I
found myself presently away from the table and the
room, wandering alone in dimly lighted passages.
Then again, I was once more surrounded by the boys,

but they mocked and jeered me when I refused to join them in their orgies, and it was a pleasure to escape from their boisterous mirth.

There are parts of that dream which evade my every attempt at description. I feel that my words are inadequate to convey even a faint impression of the agony of soul which covered me with beaded drops of perspiration as I lay upon my bed, but I must leave unsaid the horrors of that vision. I stood at last by the door of the banquet hall, a looker-on upon the scene from which I had escaped, and in the place which had been mine a being of majestic figure and malignant aspect spoke of me as a soul that must be captured. It was terrible to hear him blame his followers for having heaped contumely upon me, because in so doing they had armed me against their solicitations.

I was awake, broad awake, but dazed and stupefied by my dream. I had seen the vice and hate which drink engenders, and the fearful ingenuity of the depraved to win converts to their abhorrent system, presented in that vision as my waking hours had never pictured them, and a bonanza would not have tempted me to drink again.

Many years have passed since then; my friends often joke with me now about the silver threads, which are, I suppose, usurping dominion on my brow; but the influence of that dream has never died out; and somehow, whenever the scenes of that fantastic panorama have been recalled, the kindly gaze of my grandfather has seemed to rest upon me as it did at the time of our parting in Valders, when I was a child. The power which has been wielded for good over my life, by the memory of my grandfather, whom I have never seen save in dreams and visions since I was three years old, has often been a subject for wonderment in my maturer years, but the mysteries that subsist between the material and the spiritual natures blended in mankind are inscrutable. It is a blessing for us all that we are capable with the laureate Tennyson of "Believing where we cannot prove."

CHAPTER VII.

IN WAR TIME.

Hard at Work—Self Supporting—Blind Leaders—Bearings of the War—Anson Rogers—Broom Making—Professor Von Cleve—Value of Labor—Idle Boys' Amusements—Snake in the Grass—My Arab Steed—The Festive Cow—Miles Standish—The Alden Family —Priscilla Mullens—The Puritans—More Employments for Blind— I Graduate.

My labors in the Institution were now resumed with more energy than ever. I sought, in assiduous study or in continuous occupation in the work· shop, to drown the yearning for excitement which had recently asserted itself as a new feature in my life. My resolution to launch out into the busy world assumed absolute sway over me, and I became impatient as I had never been before in the same degree, of the idea which prevailed at home in Oakland, that I must remain to the end of the chapter a non-producer, dependent on the generosity of others even for my sustenance.

That man, young or old, is far gone on the downward grade, who can contemplate with contentment the condition of a pauper as his own. The coarsest bread and scantiest raiment won by one's own exertion satisfies the demand of the soul better than

the most luxurious provision which charity may furnish to-day and caprice may withhold to-morrow.
I had no thought then, and never have had, that
my friends would grudge me that portion of their
substance which might be needed to sustain me in
comfort.   Self-denial in many particulars had been
exercised by them in order to gain for me the advantages which I was even then enjoying, and there
was no uncertain tone in their words of assurance
that I should never want as long as the old farm
sufficed to supply the daily needs of the family; but
the more I saw and knew of the generous natures
which my unfortunate condition had so severely
taxed in the past, the more determined did I become that my own right arm, favored with the training wihch had been afforded me, should win my
bread in the future.

This impulse made me a more assiduous workman.   Over-time was improved to its fullest limit,
and broom-making, the only handicraft with which
I had become practically familiar, offered at that
time better remuneration than has since ruled in
that calling.   It was war time, and all industries
were well rewarded, so that there need be no fear
that willing hands would fail to procure bread.
We were exempt from the demands for new levies
which emanated from the executive at Washington
with significant frequency, for nature had made us
non-combatants; but one of my classmates, a young

man fearless in word and deed, predicted shortly after the affair at Fredericksburg, that we should all be wanted for high commands because of the predilection for blind leaders which had been exemplified in costly and destructive operations in the prosecution of the war up to that date.

I had little relish for satire, and too little knowledge of the state of parties to pronounce on the great questions which were agitating the nation, but my sympathies were with the boys in blue, first, last and all the time the war lasted. It was not until many years later that I learned how chivalrous and disinterested, however much mistaken, had been the motives and the deeds of the boys in gray. The nation that could man and equip two such immense armies, to fight for an idea, even though the war itself was fratricidal, need never fear the arms of European kingdoms, provided, always, that the quarrel should be of such a character as would fuse North and South into patriotic unity aginst the invader.

Party feeling ran high in Wisconsin, as well as in other States which were faithful to the Union. There were terribly exciting scenes sometimes, even in the usually peaceful city of Janesville. I had gone into the city one day on business of a personal nature, and was detained later than usual, when, toward evening, I found myself in the midst of a throng of exasperated men, evidently supporters of Abraham Lincoln, who were lashed almost to madness

by a supporter of the other side, a man named
Rogers, a well known resident, whose disloyalty
was considerd treasonable enough to entitle him to
a short shrift and a shorter rope attached to the
nearest lamp post. The words and bearing of Mr.
Rogers were such as few crowds would have endured
at such a time, but he was evidently unacquainted
with fear, and his self-possession won him respect
even in the minds of his enemies.

Years afterwards I heard of him as mayor of the
city in which he came so near being hung. His style
of eloquence had undergone few changes, and I have
many times, while listening to his speeches, wondered
what was the magic that saved him from death
that evening. He has a tongue as bitter as gall,
and a memory that never loses an item or a phrase
that will embarrass an opponent. The civilization
of the North-west was severely tried by men of that
type all through the war, and it is creditable to
those concerned that Judge Lynch was so seldom
invoked.

I speedily acquired great proficiency as a maker
of brooms, being able to turn them out of hand rapidly and well; and the results of my over-time work
kept me well supplied with clothing and other requirements, so that the resources of Oakland ceased
to be taxed in any degree for my maintenance. My
father did not like the idea of his eldest son depending on the manufacture of brooms for a livelihood,

but I found an independence that was intensely delightful in the prosecution of my calling, and was anxious for the time to arrive that would set me free to make a fortune by my simple craft. Had the superintendent been less deserving of the regard of the inmates, many of the boys who were of the same mind with myself would have taken French leave; but such an unceremonious departure could not be dreamed of under the kindly rule of Mr. Little.

We had learned to trust our own powers perhaps too much, for I have since that time found that there are limits to my nervous energy, an idea which had not dawned upon me when my days at the Institution were being numbered. It was a common belief among us that the nerve force which in normal conditions is distributed over all the senses, is in the abnormal state of the blind concentrated upon the remaining senses; so that within our limitations we were invincible. That faith has been severely tried and chastened by suffering, so that it has been modified in general application considerably; but in a few individual cases it still has the full assent of my faculties.

One of the professors of music, whose term at the Institution commenced long after my time, is perhaps the most extraordinary man it has ever been my good fortune to meet. His power as a musician was truly charming, and his company was sought by

the *elite* of the neighboring cities. Sitting down
to the instrument, he commenced every exercise of
his powers in instrumentation by describing in well
chosen words the purpose of the composer, and his
methods illustrated in the piece; and, having thus
prepared the minds of his hearers, he went on
to fulfill the programme with marvelous success.

Professor Von Cleve, the gentleman to whom I
have referred, was not only a musician; his powers as a literary man have been tested by some of
the most competent critics in the Northwest, to
my knowledge, and he was never found at fault,
as I have been assured, save in trivial details purely verbal. One of the best read men associated
with the press in Chicago, a gentleman in his fifth
decade, and a student from his boyhood, told me
that during a visit of many days' duration he pur-
posely varied the conversation with Mr. Von Cleve,
from poetry to philosophy, science and history, with
all the advantages of a well stocked library within
arm's length; yet he never referred to any passage
of marked beauty, precision or force in modern
writers within that wide range, without finding the
professor able to complete the sentence or paragraph
just as though the book lay open before a man
blessed with every sense in well cultured vigor.

His memory was truly wonderful, and it was frequently exercised in such a way as to convince every
beholder that it could be relied upon, without spe-

cial preparation or "cramming" for an occasion. As one of the leading members of a literary society connected with All Souls' Church in Janesville, in which every member had allotted to him or her some branch of the subject set for discussion—say, for instance, the life and works of Dante, Petrarch, Shakespeare, Milton, Dryden, Virgil, Longfellow, Bryant and others;—the task by common consent assigned to the Professor was to sum up and dissect the papers submitted by the other members of the club; his exegesis, without the aid of one note, being always the most enjoyable part of the evening's work.

His mode of study was addressed necessarily to the cultivation of memory. Average students are readers merely, and they read too much, just as everybody eats more than can be assimilated. The man who devotes himself, for instance, to newspaper reading, cultivates an omnivorous appetite, which devours with equal facility the dimensions of the last great gooseberry, the phenomena of solar eclipses, the latest scandals in church and state, proposals for phonetic spelling, additional particulars as to the death of the Prince Imperial among the Zulus, the drunken vagaries of the King of Burmah, and the exploits of Mexican Greasers, until he is not sure whether the spots on the sun are caused by the Zulu assegai, and his ideas become mixed in inexplicable confusion.

9

Von Cleve worked by system towards the best
ends. The book upon which he had entered was
entitled to so many hours per day and at the appointed time the reader regularly employed for the
service began the literary exercises none of which
were ever omitted save in the last extremity. It is
doubtful whether there is a man in the United
States of his age better qualified than my friend
Von Cleve for the professor's chair in a first-class
institution in which literary culture is the main purpose. He has of late been connected with one of the
leading journals in Cincinnati as literary critic; and
it needs no prophet to predict that if his life is
spared to the ordinary span of existence his attainments will command for him the highest honors
possible within his lines of study irrespective of the
peculiar claims which the *consensus* of mankind has
allowed to inhere in the mental labors of the blind.

Continuous and remunerative work which exercised
all the powers of mind and body did me much service. When a sick man laden down with wealth,
called upon that eccentric physician, Dr. Abernethy,
in London, to procure advice as to the treatment of
his dyspepsia, the apostle of health brusquely recommended him to "live upon twelve cents per day
and earn it." We actually earned all the food we
consumed and enough besides to pay for the accommodation that was afforded; so that our appetites
were not an affliction to the State although the cook's

arms must have been tired some days before we had completed our evening meal.

To this day the habits of industry which were formed in the Institute have never been lost; and it is still a pleasure to work irrespective of the fact that it is only by labor of body and brain that I can live and supply the needs of my family. In continuous toil, provided that it is not carried beyond the powers of physical endurance, which vary with every being, there is a balm which enables us to forget those shortcomings and defects which cannot be remedied by personal effort; and therein is an additional reason, if any could be wanted, why the system of industrial training among the blind should be carried as far as circumstances will permit. My own condition at home before my introduction to the Institute may be taken as an indication of the consequences of inaction generally, and almost every blind boy and girl has passed through a somewhat similar experience more or less extended. The faculties unused during many years longer would have become dwarfed, but there is a large spice of truth in the line of the old hymn, "Satan will find mischief still for idle hands to do."

I was at home during part of every year but I have not mentioned my goings and comings on such occasions unless there happened to be some incident worthy of note in my travels. One season

I was at home when the steam threshing machine was at work in our yard, and of course all the neighbors were on hand to help, each in his turn giving and taking just such aid from every farmer within a radius of some miles. One of the neighbors was very cross-grained, and whenever I happened in his way, no matter how good were my motives, he was sure to let drop some word or phrase which stung me to the quick. Such conduct on his part could not go unrewarded and my ingenuity was sufficient for the occasion. The straw as it fell from the machine was heaped up loosely in an immense pile covering an extensive area of ground. The hurry and systematic confusion of the times permitted me to come and go just as I pleased, unless I ran against my enemy, so I avoided him with laborious circumspection. Any of the others in the yard were my friends, and would have done much to spare me pain or sorrow. Availing myself of my opportunities, I was soon the unsuspected possessor of a ferocious darning-needle, and burrowing under the straw, towards the point where the grumbling tones of that disagreeable voice told me that my adversary was at work. I could move from place to place under the straw with nearly as much ease as if no straw had been there. There was no difficulty as to breathing, and no weight to carry.

The movement under the surface did not disturb the mass perceptibly, I suppose; or if it did, there

was such a continuous action of the machine and
fall of new material, that no one noticed the tiny
upheaval. Arrived at the desired spot, I had no
difficulty in thrusting that bloodthirsty darning-
needle into the calf of the grumbler's leg, and of
course I retired immediately, taking the weapon
with me.

The amazed cry of that man as he fell to the
ground, assuring every one that a snake had bitten
him, was a wonderful satisfaction to me, but I had
to restrain my laughter and make tracks, as more
than a dozen hands were busy in pursuit of the
snake, and it would not do for me to be found assuming the *role* of that *anguis in herba*. I was far
enough from the scene of disturbance to have no
difficulty in evading detection, and after a little
while all the men commenced to jest the surly
neighbor about the noise he made without cause.
He could feel that he was unjustly doubted, and
there was the puncture plain enough to be seen,
but the rest of the men resolved to doubt their own
eyes, since they could not find the snake.

Work was resumed after some whisky, prescribed
for the snake bite, had been freely partaken by almost
every one on the ground, and before long the surly
philosopher was as oblivious to his foregone agony
as any man in the party. Made more daring than
ever by impunity, I inserted my darning-needle once
more, and the former scene of confusion was re-en-

acted with similar results, The cry "a snake! a snake!" raised a third time, provoked a boisterous peal of laughter, in which, regardless of all risks, my voice joined, and my adversary recognized the sound. Luckily for me the others were all laughing, so that none corroborated his assertion. The charge against me was not believed, but I found it prudent to change my location, as the straw was once more wildly scattered, as well by those who asserted my innocence as by the grumbler and his friends.

The game had been carried far enough, and I lay there still as a mouse until the investigation terminated. Soon after, when all hands were busy with the machine once more, I stole away unperceived, and, creeping into the adjacent woods, did not appear until supper was nearly consumed. My innocent, unsuspecting way, and the fact that I came from a distance, and from a direction remote from the barnyard, saved me from interrogation; but my censor was a strong believer in my guilt, and he obstreperously asserted that the father of all evil did the mischief if I was not the perpetrator.

I must not omit to mention here and now my good horse, the companion I could always trust to carry me to accustomed haunts without the slightest direction from my hand. Coming to the sound of my voice whenever I was near enough to make him hear me, he would stand like a statue until I was on his back and gave him the word. If I want-

ed to go anywhere else instead of to the nearest
town (Christiana), it was necessary for me to turn
him in the direction I wished to travel when the
bend in the road was reached, and he would strike
off across lots without compunction.

Customarily my journey was to the post town and
back again; and the faithful creature would pull up at
the door of the postoffice store as steadily as though
he knew that he was trusted. It was unnecessary
to make him a fixture at the door, because he understood the business quite as well as I did, and that
precaution would have seemed like a deliberate insult to his sagacity. I have heard of men who liked
to claim for themselves horse sense, but have never
met any of that type of mankind who could be trust
ed by me as implicitly as my quadrupedal friend.
Shortly after the war broke out, and while I was
away at the Institute, the noble fellow was purchased,
with many other horses in the neighborhood, for
Uncle Sam's service.

When I learned, some time after the sale, that he
was gone, my grief was uncontrollable. But there
was no use in crying after spilled milk, as the proverb says, and I eventually sought consolation elsewhere. Once, when an opportunity offered, one of
our cows lying in my path asleep, so that I stum-
bled over her, I seated myself on her back, confident
that I could tame Bucephalus. The poor creature
was wild with fright, and my efforts to soothe or con-

trol her were abortive. Away she went on a mad gallop, and I had sense enough to know that a comfortable seat on the sod would be an admirable exchange for the distinction I was then enjoying, but my knowledge of the locality was so much disturbed by her gyrations, that to save my life I could not tell in what direction we were heading.

The pace was killing, and I strongly suspect that my attitude on cowback was not captivating; but it is always better to bear the ills you have than fly to others that you know not of; so I stuck to my dangerous elevation for all that it was worth. Rather more than a mile from the house was a deep gravel pit, some distance off the road, and for that unpleasant jumping-off place the alarmed steed ran with always increasing impetus. I knew nothing of the pitfall until her ladyship made the plunge, and I was sent plowing into the gravel on the opposite slope, my mouth full of the produce of the pit, my face, hands and knees excoriated, and my mind made up, beyond all likelihood of change, against embracing any more such opportunities as dreaming cows. There were great dilapidations to be repaired in my apparel before I could present myself again in society, but my physical damages saved me from censure on the clothes' account.

Longfellow, in his exquisite poem, "Miles Standish," describes the pride of a bovine steed fitly caparisoned, and provided by John Alden to carry his

TAMING THE HORNED BUCEPHALUS.

bride from the church to her home after the marriage; but perhaps the cow that ran away with me made comparisons to my disadvantage, as certainly my appearance is not nearly so prepossessing as it may be supposed that of "Priscilla, the Puritan maiden," was. The poet has cast such a glamour of genius around Priscilla, that she lives in my mind as almost an impersonation of the line from Keats,

"A thing of beauty is a joy forever."

Speaking of "Miles Standish" reminds me that the Alden family is well represented in Wisconsin by men and women of high culture and good lives. It was my fortune to be thrown into association with that distinguished line on several occasions, and it was easy to ascertain that the vigor and the tone of the Mayflower still survives. I used to feel very glad that Priscilla did not accept the offer of that doughty fighting man, who deputed his friend Alden to make his proposal in due form, and I have always admired the courage which prompted the maiden to say to the matrimonial ambassador, "Why don't you speak for yourself, John?"

The Alden family in Wisconsin, some branches of which are in Janesville and some in Madison, treasure among their heirlooms a silver brooch said to have been the property of Priscilla, and to have been worn by her as a fastening for some portion of her clothing when the Pilgrims were facing the icy winds of the Christmas season on the Atlantic coast. I handled the tiny jewel with reverence, as, although its argentiferous value might not be great, I could not disassociate the gem from the wearer, and I know that if it were mine it should not be parted with for twenty times its weight in virgin gold. Certainly the present owners would not be easily induced to sell that patent of nobility, which indicates their direct descent from ancestors whose names will live in the minds of men long after the roll of Battle Abbey shall have been forgotten.

In reading "Miles Standish," or rather in having it read for me—for I always find myself speaking of what I have read and what I have seen as though my power to see were as good as that of any of my neighbors—there were two or three facts that seemed to me singular, and as soon as I had the opportunity to dive into the living traditions of the Alden family, these problems were brought out for solution. The magnanimity of that brave little soldier, Miles Standish, in blessing the bride whom he supposed to have been stolen from him by John Alden, turns out to have been a poetic charm, lent by the genius of Longfellow. Standish, generalissimo and field marshal though he was, of the New England forces, sulked nearly all his lifetime with Priscilla, and was never reconciled to John. There is more beauty and moral grandeur in the ideal Standish, but the natural man seldom rises to such heights as

might enable him to look down with pleasure upon
the union of his lady-love with another.

The second point upon which I found myself seeking enlightenment was the surname of the Puritan
maiden. My curiosity was piqued by the studied
silence of Longfellow in that particular, and, therefore, almost my first inquiry was put in this form:
"Why was the beautiful young woman described
as 'Priscilla, the Puritan maiden,' and nothing more?
Surely, her father and mother bore some name."
The patronymic was then revealed to me, and I
thought that it never could pass from my memory,
but somehow I cannot recall the name now.   It was
of the same class with Muggins or Buggins; not
the "Mogyns de Mogyns" of which Thackeray made
fun, but the plainest, homeliest kind of Anglo-Saxon
surname, serving only in her case to illustrate the
line,

> "The rose by any other name would smell as sweet."

The Puritans were not usually possessed of aris-
tocratic surnames, although some of the aristocracy
took hold upon the movement, and lent to it in its
early days the nobility of their characters. Sir
John Eliot, the founder of the noble family of St.
Germains, was a Puritan of the noblest type. So
also were Hampden, and John Pym, and Cromwell,
and Sir Harry Vane, and John Milton, with a host
of others, when the nation was drifting toward the
war, which first shattered for the Stuart family in

England the idea of the divine right of kings; but
in the beginning of Puritanism, if we leave out of
account, as I suppose we must, the origin of the
Lollard movement in the preachings and translations
of John Wycliffe, under the patronage of John of
Gaunt, Duke of Lancaster, the seed fell in the
highways and byways, among farmers and their servants, among humble workmen in towns, among enthusiastic students in colleges and universities; and
when the converts to the living faith came in with
their lives in their hands, willing to die the death
rather than forfeit their hold on Christ by denying him, the name of the faithful man was of no
moment.

Praise-God Barebones has been made the laugh-
ing-stock of royalist writers and readers for many
generations, because of his patronymic and given
names; but the facts that he sat in one of Cromwell's parliaments, and that he had the courage,
after Cromwell's death and the failure of the son
Richard to hold the reins of power, to head a procession of the people which remonstrated with General Monk against the restoration of the Stuart
dynasty, will satisfy most men of our day that
there was good in him, although his ancestors may
have been hungry and in rags, as well as enthusiastic in the faith. For all these reasons, and many
more which might fatigue my readers should I attempt their enumeration, I do not regret that the

surname of Priscilla placed beyond doubt the low-
liness of her birth; but I have placed on record my
admiration of the artistic skill which covered the
unpoetic appellation of that heroic Mrs. John Alden.

A hero with only one eye must needs have a
picture, so that posterity might not be at a loss to
recall his features; the first painter that was called
in gave two eyes to the sitter, and tried to justify
the act of flattery; but the second, wiser and more
successful, painted only the bright side of the face
of his noble subject. Longfellow chose the better
part in describing the loveliness of the woman as she
lived in that New Englnad colony, alone, her parents having died of the hardships that beset the Pilgrims, and an object of solicitude to most men, married as well as single. Had John Alden, the cooper,
taken passage back to Europe in the good old ship,
there would have been a little volume of beautiful
poetry torn out of the early history of our civilization.

By the way, my memory has just enabled me to recall Priscilla's surname; it was Mullens. The poet
could make music of Rene Le Blanc, and of the
other names that figure in *Evangeline*, but one line
about Miss Mullens would have been fatal to Miles
Standish, and Longfellow exercised a wise discretion in handing her loveliness down to posterity in
the delightful sentence, "Priscilla, the Puritan
maiden."

The Aldens are public property, in a certain sense; the name is conspicuous in the records of the public service; the revolutionary army had its Aldens, some of whom were commissioned officers; the civil war had its Aldens, one of whom rose to high rank in the navy of the United States; the church has had its Aldens in important pastorates; the press has had its Aldens, vigorous vindicators of free thought, worthy to have descended from that John Alden that was a magistrate in Plymouth colony for more than fifty years; so that I cannot hold myself blamable in thus ransacking the archives of the family to ventilate its honors.

In speaking of Miles Standish as a man of small stature, I would not be understood to cast a reflection upon the commander-in-chief of the New England forces in the early days of the colony. The greatest soldiers of the ages have not been physically great; Washington is one of the very few exceptions to this rule. Napoleon was known among his troops as the Little Corporal. Wellington was only of moderate stature. Grant was a small man in all but the genius that made him invincible, and the list might be indefinitely extended, including Sheridan, Sherman, and a mighty host besides. The *amende honorable* has now been made to our departed friend, Miles Standish, and the *manes* of the hardy warrior are, we earnestly hope, placated.

Apropos to that adventure with the cow, we have

wandered away from the main purpose of this history, and must now return to the Institution, where the time was drawing near for departure. My impatience set me thinking of many employments not yet available for the blind who are taught in the establishment at Janesville, but which are taught to the inmates of institutions of a similar kind elsewhere. Mattrass-making, for instance, is an occupation which the sightless, if otherwise qualified, can prosecute almost as successfully as other persons. They might not prove as rapid in execution, but they certainly turn out as good and as sightly an article as ordinary mattrass makers possessing all their faculties. There is no reason why Janesville should not acclimate that industry for the blind, and many other such branches of employment are equally suitable. In many of the Eastern institutions for the blind, piano tuning and repairing have been so admirably taught, under competent masters, that graduates so fitted are now earning large salaries in many parts of this country, and in Europe; special qualifications are of course demanded for the attainment of eminent success in any avocation, but, wherever such qualifications are found, the absence of sight is not an insuperable objection.

Society has a manifest interest in the conversion of the blind into productive workmen, in the several lines of industry to which they are adapted. As organists in churches, and elsewhere, the blind can be

employed extensively, and in many churches, to my
certain knowledge, blind men and women are hu-
manely preferred in such labors.   Blind organists,
acquiring proficiency in their art by continuous practice, find advantages beyond the salaries paid, in the
facilities for procuring pupils; and the management
at Janesville will not take amiss at my hands the
few hints thus offered for the increase of the usefulness of the Institution.   I have so freely and gladly
acknowledged my obligations to its training, that
no one will accuse me of speaking in a carping and
ungrateful spirit; my motive is purely and simply
an earnest desire to make the machinery of benevolence more effective in its mission.

I was the first graduate under Mr. Little's administration, and unusual facilities were offered me in
the early part of 1863, as I desired to leave before
the end of the term.   On the second day of Febru-
ary, in the year named, having graduated with some
credit, I took my final leave as a pupil, and went
home to Oakland to commence my career as a workman.   The kindness extended to me by every officer
in the Institute sank deep into my heart, and I
would name each act of grace with much pleasure,
but I must avoid giving my pages the appearance
of a catalogue or directory, and therefore I embody
every person in authority there when I express, in
words too feeble for their task, my gratitude to good
Mr. Little.

CHAPTER VIII.

SEEKING AND FINDING.

Cultivating Broom Corn—Untimely Frost—Visiting Schools—Rowing on Koshkonong—The Mounds Opened—Literary Exercises—Renewed Friendship—Skepticism—Arguing for Conquest—Quaker Guns—Terribly in Earnest—The Cross of Christ—Conversion—Dreamland—Visions Realized.

My object in quitting the Institution before the end of the term was my anxiety, very natural under the circumstances already detailed, to induce my father and other farmers to plant a large area of land with broom corn. I had already called my father's attention to that crop as likely to prove remunerative, and I knew that some of his land would be planted; but my own presence and assistance in the work induced a much larger outlay in that line. Fifteen acres were planted successfully by several farmers, but, owing to damages from frost, the profit was not so great as I had led my father to anticipate. Other men greater than myself by far have found their calculations turned awry by severe frosts. Napoleon at Moscow dreamed he was the master of the world until he found the Kremlin in flames, and was forced from his canton-

10

ments out into the severest winter that Europe had
experienced in his day. It was not Kutuzoff, so
surely as General Frost, that defeated the invincible
conqueror. That instance is cited out of many,
lest any of my readers should be inclined to blame
me for the untimely frost which diminshed my father's profits and those of his neighbors on that broom-
corn investment.

Before going entirely into my business enterprises,
there are a few topics that have been omitted during my school career, which I would fain mention.
My visits during vacation time at the Institute to
the district schools within a wide radius from home,
were exceedingly pleasant, as the fullest privileges
were kindly allowed me by the teachers, and with
some of them enduring friendships were contracted. Spelling, geography and grammar were my
strong points, and in many an exhibition I was allowed to participate. My acquaintance with the
English tongue was then as nearly perfect as it has
ever become, and I could reap many advantages from
conversation with the more advanced pupils, and
with the teachers, whom I found generally well informed and cultivated. One of the teachers, resident
near Lake Koshkonong, was peculiarly kind to me,
and my visits to that locality on Saturdays, when
school was not kept, continued, from 1860 to 1863,
to be the most delightful seasons in my life. The
poet who wrote, with exquisite insight, of
"The sweet sessions of silent thought,"

was a seer as well as a sweet singer. One-half, at least, of all the joys of civilized life are found in silent thought; and he who cannot realize that fact is shut off from the depths of his own nature, as well as from the major felicities of communion with other souls.

During all the working-week I looked forward to that Saturday vacation by the banks of Lake Koshkonong, where the exercises of our day commenced with a ramble over the ancient mounds left by the primitive inhabitants of the Mississippi Valley. Since that time many of the mounds in question have been opened by explorers, under the direction of President Whitford, of Milton College, Milton, Wisconsin, and many valuable remains of the mound builders there exhumed to enrich the museum at Milton College.

My mind was not then as much alive to the value of such contributions to history as it has since become, so that the mounds were more thought of as protectors from cold winds, or as convenient resting-places in our rambles, than as the repositories of an almost extinct civilization.

Choice books were our main resource in our weekly holiday, the best passages of leading writers being selected and read by my companion for my instruction and culture; and we seldom rose from that feast of reason and flow of soul without having

reaped mutual advantages. When memory had
been stored with such food, our appetites for other
sustenance were, as a rule, fully up to the standard
established by hospitality, so that the inner man
did not fail of proper attention. Then, if the weather was at all pleasant, and oftentimes when it was
more than boisterous, we betook ourselves to the
boat belonging to the family, and went joyously
away over the bosom of the lake.

My companion held the tiller ropes and laid out
our course, so that I had only to handle the pair
of paddles which propelled us with celerity. It
was good to feel that there was one direction—
muscular power—in which I was the more than
equal of my companion, for the puny and weak proportions which have been frequently referred to in
describing my young days had now rounded into fair
proportions and considerable vigor. That boat
which we handled was not an outrigger of fragile
composition, such as Hanlan, the champion rower,
would demand, but a substantial structure, in which
a misstep would not be fatal, and which required
muscle and sinew even to move.

We could travel fast, as it seemed, but of course
we had no standard by which to determine our
speed, and there was as much ozone in the air to
fill our lungs with the breath of life in one part of
the open lake as in another. Conversation was our
delight; and the ideas which had been awakened

by reading afforded many topics upon which I sought further information from the well-stored intellect of my companion.

The intimacy thus established and cultivated was a solace to me for many years, during which our correspondence lasted, but, in course of time, responsibilities on both sides, which had not been anticipated, rendered it impracticable to continue the interchange of letters. After a long interval we met again, and I found the same kindness of soul actuating the nature of my old-time friend, from whom no lapse of time can ever cause my utter estrangement while we remain on this footstool.

There was another experience which elaborated itself in my young manhood, which must be mentioned here, because all my life has been tinctured by its influence. I had never realized Christ and Him crucified. Skepticism was strong in me, as it is apt to be at some period in every youthful mind. The shortcomigs of professing Christians weighed unduly upon my judgment, and made me conclude that there was no solid foundation for the claims of the churches. This condition of mind was really terrible in the eyes of my friends, who were timid and conservative in matters of faith; and I was reasoned with and exhorted, to no purpose, almost incessantly. Love of conquest was a part of my nature, and I was determined not to be taken at a dis-

advantage in any of the discussions that were at times
incessant.   The Bible became my companion; and
whenever there was an opportunity, I induced some
friend to read it for my edification.   The passages
most likely to be of service in a controversial sense
were mainly sought, and every line of promise was
scrutinized with eager attention.

Sometimes one person read for me, and sometimes
another, but none of them were fully aware that
my animating motive was zeal as a disputant.   The
passages upon which I relied to demolish my assailants, failed me in my extremity, and I renewed
the search again and again.   I procured the works
of notorious skeptics and read them by proxy, at
rare intervals, as there were few in the immediate
neighborhood whom I could ask to lend me their
eyes for such a purpose.   The critical acumen which
had been trained and strengthened in my endeavors
to discredit the sacred word found no difficulty
whatever in discovering the fallacies of its oppo-
nents; but I was unable to procure rest and comfort
for my soul in the contemplation of their feebleness.
Again and again I pursued my study, but always
with the same result, so that, although I still fought
as vigorously as I knew how, my guns were little
more serviceable than those of Magruder at York-
town, which made McClellan pause, as he ever loved
to do, even though the semblance of an enemy was
only a shadow.   My Quaker guns were continually

in position, but behind them was a mind harassed terribly by doubts about doubting, and seeking for finality in faith.

Three passages recurred to my mind always, as though in them lay the key to the relief which was sought. I can quote them from memory, and shall do so without presenting the chapters and verses, with which every Christian is familiar: "If ye obey the word, ye shall know whether the doctrine be of God, or whether I speak of myself;" "The Holy Spirit shall bear witness with our spirits if we are the children of God;" and, lastly, "The peace of God, which passeth all understanding." The promise seemed literally to glow in these words; and I repeated them to myself when alone, as though in the mere sound might come the "open sesame" out of my restlessness. "The peace of God, which passeth all understanding," was not mine, most assuredly; and when, by dint of audacity in argument, I had routed some weak-kneed brother, my conscience gave me no abiding-place.

At length it was borne in upon me that obedience was the condition precedent upon which the Holy Spirit insisted; and I found myself saying to my perturbed soul, "If ye obey the word ye shall know." I would strive, then, to yield an unquestioning obedience, because I felt that the proposition had a personal bearing, which must be solved in every man's life for good or for evil. The promise conveyed in that passage must be tested by me, and by that rule salvation must be worked out, or the scheme be put aside as valueless. I was now terribly in earnest, even in my doubts. Until that stage of inquiry was reached, I had attended church in a formal and perfunctory manner, seeking nothing, and finding less than I sought. The mischievous spirit had predominated in me, and nothing that was said passed beyond the portals of my understanding. Earnestness. if not devoutness, took hold upon me, as when a scientist is prosecuting his searches into the mysteries of nature, his faculties are all alive to chronicle the result. Perhaps the want of a prayerful condition warred against my peace. That state of mind was not unphilosophical. Somewhere in Tennyson I had found the lines:

"Prone on the great world's altar stairs,
Which slant through darkness up to God."

I would pray aloud before the whole of the people there assembled, and so settle the question beyond dispute. My prayer, carefully conned and corrected, sought to carry the Throne of Grace by assault of rhetoric and choice language; but when I fell upon my knees the resources of philosophy were as nothing. Words would not come at my bidding. Sentences which should have fallen from my tongue trippingly, halted in sorrow and humiliation, and I was as helpless as clay in the hands of the potter.

Still there were no results, and my doubts came back upon me with increasing power. Were not these sentences, after all, the words of men, without warranty for divine significance? Full of that conviction, or impression, I know not which to call it, I attended class-meeting, determined at all hazards to take the brethren into my confidence—to ask their aid, if one human being could help another in such a strait.

At the proper time I rose in my place to tell of my failure, and as before, the amplest preparation was inoperative; the picturesque expressions which would have illustrated my mental state lurked in my memory, confusing but not assisting my speech; and, when words came, they were as sounding brass and tinkling cymbals, powerless to interpret my soul. Standing thus in sorrow and agony, wrestling for deliverance, all the aids of frail humanity cast aside, the cross of Christ invited me to cling to its foot and bow myself down to the earth beneath the suffering form which bore our sins that we might be reconciled to the Father. The promises were verified in that moment. The change that came over my life may never be uttered in words, but every soul that has found grace knows the joy which wells up from eternal fountains, giving freedom to the tongue-tied sinner, so that he may venture to speak his thoughts without taking heed to shape his language.

The Holy Spirit bore witness with our spirits in very truth, and that night was blessed to many in the Pentecostal fervor of that outpouring. Peace, which no system of philosophy could disturb, found ingress to my soul, and abode there. In the ecstasy which attaches to conversion, I could have gone singing to a martyr's doom, and for a prolonged season my life traversed the earth on a higher plane of being than I had ever before imagined possible to humanity. I have since that time known periods of depression and gloom, during which I have seemed to cry aloud out of the depths, but the old doubts are gone forever. Continuous ecstasy may not be realized; perhaps the limits of reason would not endure the perpetual strain, but it comes again and again when the clouds of misfortune are lowering around us, so that despair of divine help never submerges the soul that has taken hold on Jesus.

Standing on the narrow neck of land which is called to-day, between the two extremities of the past and the future—which we shall yet learn is but the one eternal reality of which time is the shadow —we are approached on every hand by glimpses of what has been and what shall be. Shakespeare says:

"There's a divinity doth hedge a king."

And yet again the thought appears:

"There's a divinity doth shape our ends,
Rough hew them as we may."

So that not the royal personage alone, but the man is in some sense divine.

One night, during the time of great anxiety which I have attempted to describe, a dream, which has been many times repeated, passed before me like a wondrous panorama. I could see myself, in that vision of the night, as though there had been two on-lookers, between whom there was a curious, inexplicable bond of sympathy. Every material incident in a career which I have since learned was my own, up to and beyond the present hour, was presented in that singular phantasmagoria. There were periods of sunshine and melody, in which all was gladness, such as Longfellow has sung:

> "The nights shall be filled with music,
> And the cares that affect the day
> Shall fold their tents like the Arabs,
> And as silently steal away."

Then came times of deep sorrow, and sickness on the verge of death, with troubles innumerable, barring the road against advancement, so that leaden despair was master; and, while the belief in that ending was triumphant, the difficulties were not removed, but a way was found winding around the insuperable obstacles, and coming out into the open, sun-illumined life once more. The scenes and acts in that mystery have been interpreted by time itself with such particularity of fulfilment that I look with fear and trembling to the end, scarcely daring to hope—what yet I dare, for the sake of my little ones and their mother —that the phantasm may be realized. Every life comes to this earth freighted with the cares which are destined to develop its true worth, and even what we call evil is but a lesser good, which, in some degree, works into the infinite design. Dust are we, of a truth; but the dust is more precious than the sparks of the diamond, for the soul has an ever-living splendor, compared with which the sun's brilliancy is darkness.

CHAPTER IX.

BUSINESS EXPERIENCES.

Decline Offer of Home—J. O. Johnson, Northfield—Business in Fort Atkinson—Balance in the Bank—My Wheels Kellogg'd—Ruined by Rashness—Mr. Hovey's Counsel—Friends Assist Me—Johnson of Stoughton—Mons Anderson—Uphill Work—Leaving Fort Atkinson—Andrew Johnson—Seeking Work in Chicago—Rev. Oscar Shogrin—Factory in Chicago—End of War—All my Eggs in One Basket—Kinzie St. Bridge.

> " Between the acting of a dreadful thing
> And the first motion, all the interim is
> Like a phantasma or a hideous dream."—*Shakespeare.*

Business now began to absorb me. The new light from above only increased my sense of responsibility, so that I could not listen to the kind proposals made to me by my father to remain on the farm, have a workshop erected for me, work when I pleased, be idle when I would, and so make my life a kind of holiday.

When Napoleon was associated with Sieyes and Cambaceres in the consulate of France, the abbe hoped to persuade the first consul that he should leave the task of governing to his colleagues, contenting himself with wealth, splendor and idleness; but the future Emperor answered, in substance: "I am not a hog that I should be content to feed

luxuriously in this golden sty." The task of pacify-
ing France, consolidating its industries and commerce, codifying its laws and giving to the nation
its due prominence in Europe, seemed to him more
worthy of a man; and it was not his fault that the
allied powers made it necessary to enter on a career
of conquest. My designs were much less ambitious than those of the first consul, as my conquests
have been infinitesimal. I could not be satisfied
with any thing less than the fullest exercise of my
faculties. ·

In arriving at that conclusion I was much assisted by my cousin, J. O. Johnson, who is now largely
engaged in real estate and insurance at Northfield,
Minnesota. He was a very few years my senior,
smart as a whip, and sound to the core on all questions. He had lived with our family ever since his
arrival in this country from Norway, only leaving
the farm when his collegiate duties called him
away. His many personal advantages and excellent
address won access to the best society wherever he
went, and intercourse with the best trained men in
the business circles of the Northwest assisted him
to become the competent manager and financier
that I have ever known him to be from before he
left college. I sought his counsel as to the well
meant suggestions of my father, and he did justice
to the fullest extent to the loving motives of my
family; but he none the less pointed out to me

that to hybernate in such a manner when the world teemed with opportunities for a more adventurous and useful life, would be to sink into the condition of a poor dependent upon others, to lose ambition, and eventually to lose all mental vigor.

It made me sad to be obliged to cross the kind purposes of my father by striking out for myself, but the task devolved upon me in what I conceived to be the line of duty, and of course I obeyed the governing impulse. When my supplies of broom-corn were ready to commence the manufacture of brooms, I engaged premises for myself at Fort Atkinson, Wisconsin, and my father, with many of the neighbors, rendered valuable assistance in giving me a send-off. I was proud beyond measure of my enterprise; but, having borrowed the capital with which my outfit of tools was purchased, there was no time for strutting around in vain glory. Every day found me at work, early and late, and the best assistance that could be hired was steadily employed in preparing my wares for market. Before many months had gone by, all my little obligations had been canceled, and several hundred dollars in the bank vindicated my capacity for commercial transactions. Almost everybody could earn money then, but I placed my success to my individual credit, and was never tired of quoting my own case as a conclusive answer to all the croakers who had thought me rash and presumptuous in turning a deaf ear to the kind solicitudes of Oakland.

I had not then read Oliver Goldsmith's " Vicar of Wakefield," but if I had, no person could have induced me to believe that there was any likeness in life between honest Moses, the Vicar's son, and myself, the successful manufacturer and man of business, who had visited so many fairs without being induced to purchase a load of green spectacles with the price of my merchandise.

My load of green spectacles came in good time. A man named Kellogg, glib-tongued as a mountebank, came to our town selling patent rights for an improvement in broom-making, which would enable every man to make brooms enough to supply his family and the whole neighborhood for years together, in less time than was occupied by me in preparing my materials for a moderate order. I listened to the promises of the deceiver all the more readily because he recognized my business capacity, and could see that I was fit for something better than to superintend the making of brooms, as I was then doing, for a profit less than $2000 per annum. He raked in my little pile in less than no time, and in addition to that amount I borrowed largely among my friends, to pay for a county right, out of which I might soon clear enough money to purchase the fee simple of Jefferson county. Acting upon the advice of my false counselor, I en-

THE PATENT BROOM FIEND.

gaged a number of his colleagues to sell family rights
among the farmers, and it was not long before my
expenses, added to my original outlay, landed me
in debt nearly two thousand dollars.

I went out as a canvasser myself, as it became
evident that many of my agents were living upon
me without making any attempt to earn their salaries, and within a very short time succeeded in
selling about one thousand dollars worth of family
rights, all of which were delivered by me, with the
mechanism necessary for the work, and a package
of broomcorn seed, so that every man could be his
own broomist.

About that time, and before my returns had been
collected, I became aware that the wonderful improvement was a fraud of the first water. The
shrinkage of material, which in the old process
could be allowed for, made the patented method
absolutely worthless; and as a man of principle, I
had no option but to abandon all my claims and
shoulder the crushing load of debt which had been
incurred in my unfortunate speculation. The worst
part of all the business was the sneering laughter that
had to be endured from many who called themselves
my friends. I dreaded to go out of doors or to see
anybody anywhere, lest the covert sarcasm which
was so painful should reach me, as usual, under the
guise of sympathy and condolence. I thought myself smarter than my neighbors, and they were not

11

inclined to let me off without rubbing in the lesson that I deserved. At times I found myself almost despairing, although I would not tell the extent of my disaster to a living soul.

One day I was going to my workshop, when Mr. Hovey, one of the leading merchants of Fort Atkinson, who had been kind to me when things were moving prosperously, took me aside, and I felt sure that a new Jeremiad upon my want of wisdom was to be poured out upon my suffering head. To my surprise and delight there was not one word of the "I-told-you-so" order. He merely showed me how I could repair all my damages by sitting down to regular work as I had done before the swindle began, and comforted me by saying that with all his advantages he had not escaped the machinations of astute scoundrels. If my friend had given me a thousand dollars he would not have rendered me a service so valuable as he did in showing that my own right arm was my bonanza. My troubles shrank away from me under the *regime* which commenced at that moment, and, although it was nearly three years before the last cent of my Kellogg-swindle indebtedness was paid to the friends who kindly trusted me with their money or goods, yet I was soon able to show to all concerned that I was once more prosperous. The originator of my downfall has since ornamented the States prison, and well deserved the distinction that was bestowed upon him by society.

My friend, Mr. Hovey, was not merely my friend in matters of counsel. He stood by me materially on more than one occasion, when small creditors were pressing in their demands, and my appeal was never slighted when it became necessary to ask him for help. There were many others among the leading merchants in Fort Atkinson who lent me a helping hand, and without their assistance my task would have been much more difficult than I found it. Many, whose names I do not mention, were ready at all times to further my endeavors at self help; but there are some who will, I believe, excuse me for mentioning their names in this connection. Mr. Winslow, Mr. McPherson and Mr. Manning responded to my calls so often and so promptly, that the temptation is irresistible to quote them, as representing the enlightened benevolence of the little community in which I was located.

It was not only at Fort Atkinson that my friends were found, the little reputation that I had won was widely scattered, and I thank God most sincerely that He had permitted me in all my adversity to preserve my integrity unimpaired, so that my word was considered sufficient warranty for whatever was undertaken if the work was within the scope of my powers. I had a good friend at Stoughton, Mr. Johnson—not my cousin of that name—whose purse

never failed me at a pinch, and from that time until
his death I found him a true and fast friend,
never varying in times of calamity, except to become
more solicitous for my welfare.   There were many
who showed their solicitude whenever occasion
offered, by counseling me to abandon all attempts
at being self-supporting, as it was well known that my
father would give me an asylum on the farm for the
asking; but the gentlemen whom I have taken the liberty to name encouraged me in the manlier course,
which I have consistently endeavored to follow.

There was one friend at a still greater distance,
Mons Anderson, of La Crosse, to whom I had re-
course when things were looking at their worst, and
his response to my application was most generous.
When our family came from Norway to Milwaukee,
Mons Anderson accompanied us, and his circumstances were none too prosperous when he landed in
the State of Wisconsin.   When we removed to Oakland, he remained in the city, and by the aid of his
remarkable capacity he succeeded eventually in building up a considerable fortune in La Crosse, to which
place he had removed.   His name was a household
word all through the Scandinavian communities of
the West, but with us there were special ties of affection as well as respect.   I went to him as to an older
brother, and told him frankly how I was placed.
He entered into my troubles more fully than some
brethren would dream of, showed me in a consider-

ate way where I had blundered, pointed out the manner in which I could most readily recuperate, and gave me an earnest of his true-heartedness in the premises by loaning me two hundred dollars with which to carry out the plans he had suggested.

Thus fortified by my friends, I should have been indeed a craven could I have doubted that the dark clouds would break overhead and permit me another sunburst. I left La Crosse with my heart too full for utterance; and the prosecution of my business to profitable ends became easier every day. I should have been wiser in my business arrangements, no doubt, if I had called my creditors together, showed them my position and my prospects, and sought an extension of time, so that my immediate earnings would have been available as capital for further enterprise, until the day came when I could pay each man *pro rata* without leaving myself entirely bare. But my pride and my sensitiveness revolted from such an unfolding of my circumstances to all concerned; so I kept along all the time paying away the last cent upon old debts, and leaving myself often dependent upon my friends for the means to make purchases and employ labor under circumstances which promised liberal returns. Under the better system I should have paid off all my debts much sooner, but under that which I adopted I am happy to state that all were paid at last. I shall have occasion once again in this history to speak of my good friend, Mons Anderson, and for that reason I can leave him here with this brief notice of his discriminating kindness.

I continued at Fort Atkinson until the summer of 1864, when, having finished up all the broom-corn in the neighborhood, I found that it would be unprofitable and therefore irksome to remain longer. I could have procured any quantity of material from Chicago, but at such prices as would have left me no margin for labor and outlay, and as usual I had paid away every dollar as soon as it was earned, so that there remained no capital with which to operate. An opportunity was now offered me to make up a quantity of broom-corn at Christiana, for my good friend and neighbor in old times, Andrew Johnson. There was not a great deal to be done for Mr. Johnson, only one hundred dozen of brooms, but that offered me a fair margin of profit, which was applied at once to the liquidation of old debts.

Arrived at the end of that engagement, and hating idleness, I used the little money remaining in my possession to convey me to Chicago, a center of business about which I had often heard, but never set foot in, up to that date.

I found the metropolis of the Northwest all that it had been pictured to my mind, and even more—a very whirlpool of activity and enterprise—but knowing no person in the vast concourse of men, it was not easy to convince anybody that a blind man was capable of earning a livelihood. A dog, a string, and an inverted hat, were considered the insignia of a blind man's calling, and when I presented myself at the different factories, asking for employment, it was not easy to convince the persons to whom I applied that there was no scheme of mendicancy concealed beneath my offer. Day after day I made the round of the broom factories in the city of Chicago, and the sounds of work and traffic told me that there should be no difficulty in giving me the chance to earn my bread; but always the answer came in various forms, that there was no opening for me. I was asking my fellow-men for leave to toil, and nothing more. I sought no charity—sought nothing, in fact, but what an honest man might ask with dignity—sought it in deep earnestness of spirit and speech, because my bread depended on my success, yet on every hand was met with an embarrassing refusal, until I could say with Robert Burns:

> "Man's inhumanity to man
> Makes countless thousands mourn."

I have said that I knew no person in Chicago, and that was the actual truth; but as a church member in good standing, I could look for sympathy to the pastor of the Illinois Street Scandinavian M. E. Church, and to his residence I bent my steps as a matter of duty before leaving the city in absolute despair.

The Rev. Oscar Shogrin was a man of fine appearance, not massive, but well proportioned, and I could feel that he regarded me during my visit with much interest. My story was soon told; indeed, I might have said with Canning's Needy Knife Grinder, "Story, sir? Lord bless you! I have none to tell;" but my despondent face may have possessed an eloquence upon which I had not learned to calculate. I had taken more negatives during my few days in the city. than the most successful photographic artist. I was leaving, having answered the questions of my friend, and broken my fast with him (I had not thought it necessary to say it had been some time unbroken), when, much to my surprise, he inquired whether eighty dollars would be of service.

Eighty dollars? Why, a perfect paradise of a broom factory could be started with eighty dollars, but where could such a sum be found for me without security, and in a city where no man would trust me even to make a broom? There was a great deal of energy in my declaration beyond a doubt, for I felt that the time was gone by for jesting about sums of money. Eighty dollars was not a light matter. But further surprises were in store for me. The dear old pastor had eighty dollars of his own (the wonder was that such a man had one cent), and he made me take it from him as a loan, to commence my career in Chicago. When Samson found a

beehive in the lion's carcase, he was not more as-
tounded than I was at finding a Methodist pastor
with eighty dollars. Before I left the house of the
good man that night, he made me accept the loan,
and I sent next day to Wisconsin for all my tools
to commence broom-making.

A shop was soon rented in which a blind man
could find work, materials were purchased, willing
labor was freely expended in making ready, and my
success was speedily assured. Within a few weeks
several men were working in my factory. I denied
no man an opportnity to try. My profits were larger
than I had imagined possible in the country, and
my capital was enough for every conceivable purpose. With some difficulty I made my banker-pas-
tor take interest upon his advance when the principal was repaid, and that was the only occasion I
remember in which our sentiments ever differed.
Years afterwards an opportunity offered itself to me
to render him a service, and the old gentleman was
as generous in acceptance as he had been in be-
stowal. He has built up many church societies to
very large congregations from very small beginnings,
and the sterling trustfulness of his nature has won
for him high appreciation from all classes. An
age of such men would be almost millennial, and to
speak of him is a delight.

I was now once more careering along at high
pressure, and money came in with unexampled rap-

idity. Every venture seemed to have been touched
with the finger of Midas, as it turned to gold, or at
any rate, into greenbacks, which served all purposes for me just as well. In the spring of 1865 I
could have gone out of business with two thousand
dollars, and should have acted wisely in so doing,
but it was not my good fortune to be able to read
coming events, although they sometimes cast their
shadows across my path. I worked by wit, and
not by witchcraft, as the phrase runs in Shakespeare,
and perhaps some of my readers will not credit me
with much wit.

The war was coming to an end. That was known
to all men long before the actual surrender at Appomattox; but I could see no reason why the termi-
nation of the too-long-continued fratiicidal strife
should bring about a collapse in values. People
would want brooms, although the besom of destruction ceased to sweep the land; so I went right ahead
with my work, expending every cent of my capital
in materials and labor, when nearly every factory
was closing out at a sacrifice. The end can be
readily divined. The war closed, and brooms came
down with a rush, but I would not be warned by the
first fall. I continued to pack all my eggs in one
basket, worked with the diligence of a beaver building his habitation, although my brooms, when made,
were of less value in the continually-falling market
than was the material of which they were made be-

fore I had expended labor and capital upon it. When idleness and a tour of observation would have been wisdom, my industry and perseverance on the wrong track proved my ruin. I shut up my factory, at last, because the factory would have shut me up otherwise, and there was hardly a cent left in my treasury when all my debts were paid. Talk about being as bare as a robin—my case was worse, for I had not a feather to fly with.

There was one incident in my Chicago career that ought to be mentioned before I bid adieu, for a time, to the vast metropolis. I had gotten pretty familiar with the streets in my peregrinations on business, and, although I had sometimes unceremoniously ventured into a coal-cellar, or some other subterranean storehouse, through an open trap, my confidence in my own resources was almost unbounded. One evening early in the spring of 1865, I was hurrying homeward along Kinzie street, having just made a large purchase which I was anxious to have made up, when I stepped off from the roadway just as the bridge was beginning to swing around. Perhaps the bystanders had never noticed that I was blind, as they were unprepared for the false step that I unfortunately made; certain it is that, until I was just plunging into the river, there was no sound of warning as to the danger that threatened my life.

Quicker than thought itself my arm swung instinctively towards the retreating bridge as I fell, and my left arm, the nearest to that structure, grasped the lower rail. It was not an instant before my right arm reinforced the left, and the gymnastic exercises incidental to tree-climbing were life itself in that energy which enabled me to mount to the roadway as the bridge swung towards midstream. There was noise enough then on both sides of the river, cheering and clapping of hands, for some moments, as though the interested spectators wished to *encore* the performance, on which I would not willingly enter for a fortune; but, as I descended from the railing over which I had clambered, I fell on my knees silently to give thanks to Almighty God for my almost miraculous escape.

FALL FROM KINZIE STREET BRIDGE.

CHAPTER X.

I SEE THE SIGHTS.

Off to New York—Roped in—Country-Made Boots—Knicker-
bocker Mansion—Barnum's Museum—Menagerie in Flames—Incidents of the Fire—New York *Herald*—Murder Under My Window.

Before my return to Wisconsin, which seemed to
be inevitable after business in Chicago had petered
out in my line, I determined to visit New York, in
the *Micawber*-like hope that something would turn
up for me in that vaster emporium of trade and
commerce. I could not say why there was such a
hope, but somehow if I had ventured back to my old
home without going East, I should have felt that a
chance had been thrown away. Acting upon that
will-o'-the-wisp intuition, I secured my tickets for
New York, and was soon on my way, rushing with
hardly any means towards a city where I knew no
person. It would not have astonished me in the
least if Commodore Vanderbilt had come to meet
me in Jersey City, and propose that we should combine our resources to get up a corner on brooms;
but I did not ask for him on my arrival at the depot.

Crossing by the ferry-boat to New York, some cas-
ual words of politeness from another passenger, whom

I found well acquainted with the course of travel, induced me to ask for directions which would enable me to find a comfortable hotel, where a person of very moderate means could be accommodated for a time. Unfortunately for me I had been accosted by one of those "ropers in" that disgrace our great cities; but I supposed he was dealing with me in singleness of heart, when he said that he was a "runner" for just such a hostelry as I described, and that he would convey me direct to that haven. I can now understand, that as "a young man from the country," it was supposed that some money could be made out of me, and before many minutes had elapsed I was introduced with scanty preface to a den of infamy, in which there must have been nearly a score of unfortunate women, some far advanced in liquor, and all more or less under its influence.

It was of no use my assuring them persoanlly and collectively that I had no money to spend in drink, none whatever; if I had no money, why should I have visited that establishment, a place well known, the proprietors of which made a fortune almost every year by selling liquor to the dupes and victims of vice by whom I was surrounded? I was in the worst crowd that ever embarrassed me in my life; and from what I had heard about the police force in New York City, it seemed quite possible that if any disturbance arose out of my adventure, my name would figure in the newspapers as a frequenter of a place that I utterly loathed. This thought warned me that I must be as wise as a serpent, but I could not inspire as much terror as a serpent would have done under the circumstances, otherwise I might have glided out with little opposition.

Bad as my surroundings were, the unfortunates were not all equally vile; two of the party who pretended to be asking me to come up to the bar to purchase whisky, availed themselves of the chance to give me directions as to the doorway and stairs, and begged me to escape for God's sake. That hint was all I wanted, for I had been whirled around so many times since entering the room that my way out had been a conundrum until that moment. The unlovely sirens by whom I had been assaulted at first, cursed my unhappy counselors for their failure to make me produce my money, and I was roughly handled for some minutes, but at every step I was nearer the place of egress, from which neither force nor solicitation could turn my face. I tried to prophesy smooth things for peace sake, but it seemed as if that door had been a mile from me, so slow were my steps in retreat. When some of the more obstreperous insisted upon my standing drinks around and caught hold upon me to enforce that decision, my awkward feet, first one and then another, would come heels first, with crushing emphasis, upon the favorite bunions of my tormentors, and when they howled with pain, I was always sure to lift the wrong foot first, so that the agony was prolonged. In that way, owing to my deplorable stupidity, and my country-made boots, my only weapons, the worst of my enemies got stamped out of my way; and while their pains were winning them sympathy my hesitating footsteps found the top stair, verifying the instructions of the friendly Magdalens, so that I need hesitate no longer as to making my escape.

Curses loud and deep followed me as I ran; but I was soon out again in the streets of New York, and comparatively safe. It is a terrible reflection that so many thousands of fair and beautiful women should descend from their primitive purity every year to recruit the armies of sin in our great cities. I had never until now realized how abhorrent was that form of vice, but alas! I have discovered also that the most shocking sins that were known to old Rome, when criminal practices were at their worst, are aped in the great city of New York, by creatures bearing the form of womanhood, who surrender themselves to lives of prostitution. The subject is so repugnant to goodness that I hasten to purge my pen of all reference to such abominations.

I found myself in Greenwich Street soon after leaving the house I have mentioned; and, fearing to accost wayfarers, who might mislead me, I entered a large dry goods store to seek information. The proprietor was as kind and considerate as if I

had made a large purchase in his establishment,
and, acting on his advice, I stayed that night and
afterwards in an old-established hotel, which engrossed the upper floors of the block of which his
store was a part. The building was very old-fashioned, with broad staircases and halls, such as
might have accommodated a dozen Hollanders, with
all their apparel, without any fear of overcrowding. The structure was of Holland bricks, and
considerably more than two hundred years old, as
I was informed, having been originally constructed
for a Van Renssellaer, or some other Dutch dig-
nitary accustomed to style and comfort, in the
early days of New Amsterdam, before the Duke of
York changed the ownership of the city and territory, as well as the name.

I could not see all that there was of old and curious in that singular edifice, but my hands were
passed to and fro over the massive doors of cherry
wood, with old-fashioned brass door-locks and
knobs, and I paced the old-time fireplaces until I
knew their dimensions perfectly. My room, in the
front of the hotel, and on the third story, was large
and comfortable; but, having entered on my inves-
tigations with a desire to know all that the circumstances of the time permitted, and being favored by
my host, my rambles and inspections were extended over a large part of each floor. Some of the old-
fashioned mantelpieces might have been designed

for church porches, slightly dwarfed and changed
in outline, to permit of the massive shelf which
was indispensable to housekeepers two centuries
ago.   It seemed as if I should never tire of my sur-
vey, but fatigue at last began to tell upon me, and
I was glad to stretch my weary limbs on that bed,
big enough for a whole family of Dutchmen.

In my dreams that night, the troubles through
which I had come were passed in review; but, instead
of my boots descending upon tender bunions, the contemptible runner received the punishment, and my
heel bruised the serpent's head.   During my stay
in the city it was my purpose to visit Barnum's
Museum, if I should be so fortunate as to procure
employment, but, to my astonishment, the vast collection of wonders from all parts of the world was
burned down two days after my arrival, and my
natural curiosity was disappointed and gratified in
ways that had never entered into my calculations.
We knew enough about fires in Chicago to dull my
interest in ordinary conflagrations, although Chicago
had not then eclipsed the greatest fires in former
historic times; but, when the rumor was circulated
that Barnum's Museum was in flames, I could
not resist the impulse to join the hurrying throng,
which made a perfect tide of men and women,
bound for that scene of brilliant ruin.

My pace could not compete with that of the
crowd, for I did not know what obstacle might be-

BARNUM'S MUSEUM AFTER THE FIRE.

See page 700.

set my path; so that I was content, as usual, to be
passed in the race.   To many of my readers it may
seem strange that a blind man should hasten to a
fire, which, of course, he could not see, and could
hardly wish to feel; but the idea will suggest itself to most ingenious minds that, in a crowd, men
see and hear, to a very great extent, by the organs
of other people. When the great orator and agitator
of Ireland, Daniel O'Connell, addressed immense
concourses of his fellow-countrymen on the repeal
of the Union, it was not possible for all the listening
mass to hear the melodious, organ-toned voice of
the speaker; yet the last man in the remotest line of
the monster meeting shouted as enthusiastically as
the nearest and most favored hearer.   I was but little worse off than he, and the eyes of all around
me were involuntarily placed at my service; my
ears answered all purposes.

I was told by the exclamations of almost all my
seeing neighbors of every material incident in the
drama.   My memory of that exciting time is wonderfully distinct at this hour, but of course any description that I might attempt would savor of the
imagination, because I could not in any other way
than by mental effort of that kind connect events
which passed before the eyes of the multitude, and
were printed upon my brain by their words, and
the terrible noises from within the building.

The reader may, perhaps, conjure up before him

the horrors which for a time kept New York on tip-
toe. Lions, lionesses, tigers, elephants, bears, kan-
garoos, boa constrictors, anacondas, rattle-snakes,
and deadly serpents of all kinds were struggling in
their madness of terror to find egress from the burning structure, and their noises were at intervals
appalling. The whales and alligators, which had
been for some time on view in the museum, were
being gradually scalded to death, until the glass
sides of their tanks suddenly broke, under the
influence of fervent heat, and they were dispatched
by the hissing flames.

I heard that an orang-outang, escaping from the
fire, found his way into the editorial sanctum of
the New York *Herald*, where Mr. James Gordon
Bennett was then sitting at work, and, although the
intruder could have been perfectly at home there, the
employes of the establishment, fearing that another
of that stripe would be an overdose, rushed upon
the new comer before he realized his fitnesses and .
overpowered him. That story was, I think, told to
me some days later, but all the incidents range
themselves in my sensorium with equal authority.

Several times there were stampedes in the tremendous crowd of forty thousand people when some
of the more dangerous living curiosities made their
escape out into the streets, and at such moments I
wished myself at home; but as soon as the possibility of being trampled to death passed from my mind,

I congratulated myself on being near enough to the mighty conflagration to experience its heat. It would be something for me to tell my neighbors in the country in the dull days which make conversation delightful, even though it may not be of the best quality, that, on the 13th day of July, 1865, I had been one of the crowded concourse that witnessed the destruction of Barnum's Museum, and had narrowly escaped with my life, in the manner already described.

I remained in the surging throng until evening, too excited to know that I was hungry and thirsty, and I must say, for the credit of the city of whose worst sides I have already given some hint, that no person said an uncivil word to me, and that many tendered me personal assistance.

Accepting the kindness of an elderly gentleman, who told me that his name was Compton, I was piloted out of the struggling mass, just when darkness was falling upon the earth, and directed towards my hotel, where I found rest, peace, and a good supper, all of which I could appreciate. I had now been several days in New York, and all my peregrinations had not opened up one avenue of employment, so I knew that I must not continue in that city, away from all who knew me and might give me their aid.

That night I was aroused from my sleep by sounds of an altercation in the street, just under my window, which was in the third story, and wide open, for it was in the heated term, when fresh air is a great desideratum. For some time I remained in my bed and listened, until it became clear to me that one man under the influence of liquor, and supposed to have money, was engaged in a fracas with a knot of scoundrels, who were determined, at all hazards, to carry away the plunder. I hastened then to the casement, and looking out—if a man who cannot see may be supposed to look—added my voice to the clamor below, shouting "murder!" and "help!" as loudly as I could. Since that time I have reflected that perhaps my well-meant interference changed what might have been robbery, with violence, into murder, as the events in the fearful drama were certainly precipitated by my alarm.

I heard every sound with terrific distinctness. The cries of the struggling man, who had evidently hurt one of his assailants, made me shudder, for he knew that his life was in danger. "Knife him!" said a hoarse and brutal voice, and immediately after, the sounds from the murdered man told me that his head had been almost severed from his body; his moans and sobs were inarticulate; and there was a fearful gurgling in his throat, which will never pass from my memory. I redoubled my cries for assistance, until the other inmates of the hotel were roused, and I could hear the sounds of the patrol

hastening to the spot. There was a hurried consultation among the murderers, but whether divid-
ing the spoils of that abhorrent deed, or appointing
a rendezvous, I cannot tell; certain it is that I
heard their hushed and stealthy footfalls as they
departed to their lurking-places, just before the police came up and found the murdered man in the
very article of death on the pavement.

I had supped full of horrors. Modern Babylon
had no charms for me. Misfortune threatened to
dog my steps in New York city; and, do what I
would, that impression could not be erased from
my mind, so that long before morning came I had
resolved to return to Wisconsin, where I did not
doubt of my ability to earn a subsistence, even at
the worst.

It is useless to say anything as to my journey. I
was rejoiced to escape from Sodom, and, unlike
Lot's wife, I did not look back upon the city from
which I was retreating.

CHAPTER XI.

EXCITEMENT IN BADGERDOM.

Home Again—Christiana Friends—Feast of Reason—Oakland Farm—Deacon Smith—Settle in La Crosse—Professor Anderson—Prairie du Chien—Dousman House—That Wallet—Removal to Strange Hotel—Midnight Marauder—Police Unable to Assist—Returning Penniless to Oakland—Singular Discovery—Significance of Dreams.

———

At Christiana I found a welcome to the home of my old friend, Andrew Johnson, and a quantity of broom-corn that he wished me to convert into brooms. There were six hundred dozen brooms made and sold during my stay; and, as before, I partook of the hospitality of the family on the pleasantest possible terms. If I had been at Oakland, my status could not have been more assured, nor more profitable in every sense. I was one of the family, and the rule observed there was truly excellent. The father, mother, son and daughter were all fond of reading, and choice works, the best obtainable in that neighborhood, were read aloud by the several members of the group alternately, and the suggestive facts and passages were afterwards considered more fully in our conversations; so that much of the matter was fully assimilated.

Charlemagne, at the height of his power, resting

in his career of conquest and organization, used to surround himself with the wisest and best men of his day, in the palace where his heterogeneous family made their home, and become a pupil for the time at the feet of Alcuin, or some other of the group of sages that he had attracted from Britain, Ireland and Germany. His feasts of reason may have been more select than ours, in such choice company, but they were not more enjoyable; for we could call upon authors to furnish such glorious floods of thought on matters of supremest human interest, as in his day had never been dreamed of in Europe. My intercourse with the Johnsons has always been tinctured with the associations of that visit, and I remained there at work until the summer of 1866, at which time I found myself clear of debt, with a small margin available for other operations. Times were good then, if we compare them with the dull seasons with which we have been familiar in later years, but they were so far below the level that we had grown accustomed to during the war, that we had no hesitation in saying they could not be worse.

For two years from that time my home was at Oakland, with my family, and my industry enabled me to feel that I was not a drone in the little hive. Fifteen hours per day, steadily applied in gainful labor, will supply almost any young man's wants; and, whenever the materials were to be had, that

was my average, unless, as sometimes happened, I
struck a quantity of material made up, and was able
to drive a profitable business peddling my merchandise. In April, 1868, it became necessary once more
to strike out away from home, where there was not
room to employ much help.

My father rendered me all the aid in his power,
and was never tired of assisting my enterprise, but
I wanted the more profitable scope which can only
be found in town life. So I went to La Crosse to
consult my excellent friend Mons Anderson once
more, and make preparations for business, either in
that locality or elsewhere. My capital not yet very
large, was still enough to enable me to feel that I
could stand alone, and the fact that under all my
series of reverses I had defrauded no man of a cent,
was a valuable property among men of business.
In the spring of that year I engaged to take the
crops of broom-corn from thirty acres of land near
La Crosse, several farmers having planted areas
for me, amounting to that in the aggregate. While
on my travels to determine where I should locate,
it was my good fortune to find a friend in the person of Deacon Smith, in one of the little towns on
my list. My guide was at a loss to find the house
of the Deacon, but acting upon my own idea, I
stopped at a house near that occupied by him, and
my guide waiting at the gate, I mounted the steps
of the dwelling. To my inquiry, "Is the Deacon

in?" came the answer from two ladies, that he
was up-stairs; and I was about to ascend under
their guidance, when some flippancy of manner on
the part of my guides, warned me that I was in
bad company. I had strayed into a den, of whose
vileness the better class of people knew nothing,
and but little time was lost before my friend, the
Deacon, relieved himself from such neighbors.

After the fullest consideration of all the advantages which were offered me in many towns, I
could find no place better adapted for my business
than La Crosse. Many of the most flourishing
business men in the Northwest have made this place
the centre of their operations, and circumstances
daily demonstrate their wisdom in that choice as
well as in other particulars. My broom-corn venture turned out first-rate. General Frost did not
visit the country that year until my supplies were
housed. The crop being new among the farmers, I
was greatly in demand at threshing-time, as nobody
else in that neighborhood was competent to direct
the operation, and the machine for the purpose was
made under my inspection. I was more than a little proud of that circumstance, although I could not
claim credit as an inventor.

One of the consequences of my removal from
Oakland which I most regretted, was the necessary
separation from a gentleman whose mind had already given promise of the ripe excellence which

the world of letters has since that time liberally acknowledged. Prof. R. B. Anderson, a Norseman
by descent, was known to me when both of us were
children, but it was not until my last two years at
home that our intercourse ripened into intimacy
and friendship. He was then one of the faculty at
Albion College, but his eminent abilities entitled
him to a wider field, such as he has since enjoyed
as professor in the State University at Madison, as
U. S. minister to Denmark, and as a lecturer and
historian in high repute in both hemispheres. While
I remained at Oakland the pleasure of his society was
one of my most felicitous means of mental culture, as
he possessed a fund of patience as well as scholarship, which rendered his visit supremely delightful.

The first book that was published by him, "America Not Discovered by Columbus," exercised the editorial mind all over the civilized world as few
works in our day have done, and prepared the way,
pioneer fashion, for the very acceptable series of
works which have won for him the friendship and
esteem of such men as Longfellow, Max Muller, and
a whole host besides, the poets and *litterati* of our
day. I recall him now, not as the brilliant writer
and translator, but as the amiable and faithful companion who devoted whole days to me, when I
could afford him no return, reading and writing for
me and unfolding the powers of my mind in a thousand ways, which none but the highly gifted could
have imagined possible.

Naturally it was a deprivation to be removed from intimate association with such as Prof. Anderson; but circumstances have often since that time enabled us to foregather, as the Scotch would say, and I have found but little change in him, notwithstanding his successes.

As my business increased, it became necessary for me to travel over a wide radius and to handle large sums of money, often returning from a trip with more than $2,000 as the outcome of my transactions. I was away on one occasion during my residence at Oakland, and on my return arrived at Prairie du Chien with more than $1,500 in my wallet, which it was my custom to carry concealed from prying eyes. I had often stopped at the Dousman House, and was so well known there that, if I had wished, my bill could have stood over from one trip to another. New proprietors had just taken possession, and they knew nothing of me, so that when after dinner I was about to quit the office without paying for my accommodation, my action caused the new host some surprise. I had only some very small amount in loose change in my pocket, and I did not want to go beyond my fractional currency while there was almost a room-full of strangers to see my mysterious wallet. Greatly to my chagrin the proprietor assumed that I wanted to dead-beat my dinner and then was about to vamoose the ranch, so instead of speaking to me quietly as one

with more intellect might have done, he spoke aloud
in a very insolent manner.

All ideas of prudence took flight immediately;
the old Adam was roused—nay, Cain himself was
uppermost; my wallet was used first to smack his
impudent face and then flauntingly opened to pay
his demand and prove him the blockhead that he
was. All this was very stupid, but there are many
good Christians that could not meekly endure to be
treated as dead beats. As soon as my bills were
opened out on the counter, reflection told me how
rash and inconsiderate I had been; but there was
no use in lamentations. I thought of the Italian
proverb *che sara sara*, and resolved to see it
through, as "what is to be will be" any way.
There was much excitement in the room, the landlord apologized until his civility was more oppressive than his insolence, and disliking to meet him
any more I removed my few effects and myself
to another house to await the train next morning.
I can't recall the name of that other hotel, although
I ought to remember it surely.

All that evening my conscience chided me for
my impatience; and my wisdom, coming as usual
too late to be made useful, revealed the possible
consequences of my action. My best course would
have been to have handed, over my wallet and contents for safe keeping to the hotel proprietor, but I
did not know him personally, and for that reason

I trusted my own sagacity.   My anxiety haunted
me all the evening, and even after I was in bed
sleep seemed impossible.   It was useless to exam-
ine and re-examine the door, which I had securely
locked before retiring.   My fears were insurmountable.   At last sleep fell upon me, but such a sleep
as that which breeds nightmare.   There was no rest
in it.   The soldier sleeping beside his cannon in
the embrasure which he must defend with his life
before daybreak might sleep sweetly by comparison.

I might have been asleep about an hour, or may
be less, for I had no means of knowing exactly,
when some tingling sensation all over me heralded
the approach of evil.   Had I jumped out of bed at
once, or even shouted, all might have been well;
but my faculties were in a torpor such as I never
remember in all my waking life.   I lay there without uttering one word, hardly daring to breathe,
while the stealthy, cat-like footsteps came along the
hall and paused in front of my bedroom door.   I
would have given all the money in the wallet, which
I had hidden in my pillow inside the pillowslip, for
a loaded revolver, or even a knife, but the courage
which never before utterly failed me was at so low
an ebb that I doubt if I could have used arms.
I thought of that poor fellow beneath my window
in New York, and absolutely trembled.   The door
would not open easily, as my key was left in the lock,

but that was dropped silently after a few seconds,
I heard it swing against the door as though suspended by a wire, and then within a minute the door
slowly opened. The worst countenance that ever
libeled the human face divine might have been considered humane by the side of that vulpine visage,
in which greed and cruelty contested empire with an
almost devilish cunning.

At the first glance I knew that my childish subter-
fuge of putting my wallet in the pillowslip would
avail me nothing; that wretch could have found my
treasure though it had been buried beneath the fires
of Hecla. That lantern in his hand seemed hardly
necessary to guide him, he was so familiar with
the place, but he stepped cautiously, though he was
slow in his movements no longer. He was armed;
I could see the handle of a revolver protruding
from his pocket, but the weapon that horrified me
most was a long-bladed, glistening knife, which
would be called into requisition a dozen times before the noisier instrument of death would be employed. Now that my enemy was almost upon me,
within a few feet of my bed, my terror was natural; but why should I have been so unnerved before
he entered the room? It was a momentary respite
when he took up my garments one by one, exam-
ined them and noiselessly replaced them with careless ease; but he stood over me now, and feigned
sleep was my only chance for escape. Surely he

knew that I was blind, and he could not dread recognition. To hold my breath now would reveal my secret wakefulness; I must breathe with laborious regularity, or die. The pillow drawn from beneath my head did not arouse me; but I feared that I must cry out, so intense was my need for that money, when the wallet was drawn from its hiding-place.

Within one minute from that time he had left the room, replacing the key in the lock, withdrawing the wire, and locking the door from the outside, the better to conceal his depredation. Fain would I have cried out now, before he could escape with my hard earnings, to conceal them with his matchless ingenuity; but I dared not until his footsteps died away in whispering echoes, I knew not where. Then my courage returned, the glamour had lost its power, I shrieked unceasingly, holding my door the while, clamoring until every person in the house was awake. I would not unlock the door at first, when a crowd assembled in the hall, but when the proprietor demanded admittance his voice gave me assurance, and I called everyone into the room, to hear the story of my loss. There was no one in the hotel answering the description, no guest nor servant except those present, and my bewilderment was as complete as theirs. Sleep was out of the question for me and for everyone else that night. What to do without the money I knew

13

not. My own portion I could lose, but how could I face my creditors? Would they believe a story so wild? The desperate depression under which I now labored was worse than the agony of fear.

Morning dawned at last, and the gray light was never more welcome. The police were as little able as ourselves to suggest any clue; they could find no trace of the lock having been tampered with, and a professional so acute would leave no chance for detection. With what a loathing I sat down to the table, to rise again without breaking my fast! I was full of the terrible disappointment that it was my misfortune to carry to Oakland, yet impatient to get away from the scene of my peril and my disaster. The sympathy that was freely given me by my fellow-travelers fell upon deaf ears. My sorrow filled every sense. The cars arrived, the time for departure was at hand, but before quitting Prairie du Chien for the last time in my life, I would look once more at the bedroom. There was the pillow upon which my head had rested, with the impression undisturbed! Why was that so, when the robber had drawn it away from under me? I took the pillow in my hands, and a fainting sensation came over me as the wallet dropped upon the bed. Every greenback was there, as I had left it over night. My robbery had been a nightmare, and all the incidents a dream up to the moment of my shrieking and jumping out of bed to arouse the inmates. The blood rushed anew to my heart, my brain reeled, but I returned to Oakland a happy man.

Dreams are as various as the characteristics of human life, and they have figured in all history, sacred as well as secular: sometimes projected from unknown heights, for the noblest purposes; sometimes welling up from the depths of human consciousness, so remote from the daily event as to resemble prophecy; and yet again sometimes offering nothing to our view but the distorted picture of our own hopes and fears. There was nothing, probably, in the character of the shepherd king Pharaoh that could account for the dream with which that monarch was favored as to years of scarcity following upon seasons of exceptional plenty; yet that dream and its interpretation changed the destiny of Joseph, so that, instead of languishing in prison, where he might have died under the shadow of a false accusation, he was removed to the palace, and became the chief counsellor and prime minister of the king. The influence of that dream did not end there; it brought home to the brethren of Joseph the enormity of their crime against him, while they were succored in their extremity, because they had spared his life.

The children of Israel went down into bondage because of the sins of their fathers; but that time of tribulation was not all darkness. The culture of Egypt was then hardly surpassed on the earth, and Moses was the natural exponent of the Divine will in the mighty scheme of deliverance, conquest and development, which gave to the Jewish nation lawgivers, literature, and a line of kings through whom has come salvation for the race. The dream of Pharaoh has been a reality for all mankind, and it grates cruelly upon my inner consciousness when people say, "it was only a dream." An overworked professor, defeated by a problem, rose in his sleep, and attained the solution which was denied to his waking hours. My dream bore in upon my mind, in enduring form, lessons of great moment to my happiness, which all the anxieties of the day might have failed to render permanent.

CHAPTER XII.

My days at Oakland were ended, and the steady pull of much more exciting business at La Crosse engrossed my faculties. One amiable old man, Knut Knutson, an old and wealthy resident of that town, took much interest in my enterprise, and never wearied of well doing. Many busybodies gave me their advice every day, and, as soon as their tongues were silent, my ears hastened to forget their garrulity. It was not so when my friend Knutson spoke. His words were weighed with scrupulous care, and his promises were precious. His introduction and recommend made me a wel-

come customer in any store that carried such materials as I required; and, if any special bargains
could be secured for my business by prompt cash,
the old man was ready with his never-failing pock·
etbook or bank account. Once, in an emergency
of that kind, he gave me his endorsement for nine
hundred dollars, and he rendered the service with
such grace as greatly enhanced the benefit. The
venerable old man, then nearly seventy years of
age, suffered severely afterwards from his too great
facility in believing the words of needy strangers, and
others, but for my own part I rejoice that his disinterested benevolence in my case never cost him one
hour's solicitude nor one cent of loss.

When moving from Oakland to La Crosse, I was
confident that my small capital, in addition to the
tools and machinery that had been retained ever
since my first start as a manufacturer in Fort Atkinson, would be enough for all purposes; but no sooner was I fully embarked in my venture than the
great difference between my former locations in
Wisconsin and that in which I was then engaged
began to dawn upon me. I could command almost
any number of orders, at reasonable profits, and my
chances for obtaining materials were much better.

Except during my stay in Chicago, which was in
the last year of the war, I had found no place so
entirely up with the times as La Crosse; and the
business men were so earnest in the spirit of good-

fellowship with which they took hold of a new
comer, that my La Crosse experiences are among
the brightest that I can reckon in my town life.
My esteemed friend, Knutson, was my banker in
many a profitable undertaking which his own wisdom had suggested, and his good nature made his
voice full and melodious at an age when piping
treble prdominates with most men. I could not see
his face, but out of his voice and the grasp of his
hand I could draw a picture, in my own mind,
of his personal appearance, which came very near
a resemblance; albeit, it would, perhaps, have
stood as well for a faithful resemblance of the other
Knut, or Canute, who gave to his courtiers in England so apt a rebuke as to their flattery. Whenever
an hour's leisure enabled me to do so, I enjoyed to
sit down with the old man, or to work near him on
any silent task, and listen to his stories of the Norsemen of old, with which his mind was stored in the
long winters in Norway, when he was much younger.
The scenes of his childhood and young manhood
had for him a charm which flowed into the minds of
his audience, and it was delightful to hear him expatiate upon the beauties of our fatherland.

I am not among those who would advocate the
maintenance of national rivalries in this new and
vigorous commonwealth, where our children will
be known as Americans, but I should be ashamed
of myself if the day could ever come when I would
cease to be proud of being a Scandinavian.

Returning, as my sojourn in La Crosse requires that I should do, to my friend, Mons Anderson, whose kindness to me at all times makes the subject peculiarly pleasant, I can recall him to my mind's eye as he first came to this country, his land of promise and performance. He landed in the state of Wisconsin, in the city of Milwaukee, at the same time that our family arrived, in 1847, as I have said elsewhere, being only a boy in his teens. For the first two or three years of his life in America, he was in the employ of a gentleman in Milwaukee, afterwards eminent as a banker; and it is just possible that his association with the financier tinctured his whole life with a wise regard for money, which has always been used by him as a master in the science of finance, directing its action towards worthy ends. He was not a rich man when he removed to La Crosse, unless his native energies and skill may be counted as wealth. Many men commencing an independent career with untold thousands, are practically poorer than was my friend, with only five dollars in his pocket, and that was I believe, the whole of the floating capital with which Mr. Anderson began his La Crosse experiences. Twelve months spent as a clerk showed his capacity as a salesman, and won him the respect of a wide circle of friends, who were pleased to find him at the end of that time ready to commence business on his own account. The enter-

prise upon which he had entered grew steadily under
his hands, and his trade, wholesale as well as retail,
had assumed large proportions before the opening of
the war, in 1860-61. He was a sagacious buyer before high prices ruled, and was able coolly to anticipate and provide for contingencies in the presence
of which less capable men embarked in business
were utterly lost. His profits were immense, and
yet he was able to undersell his neighbors, so that
he attracted purchasers from a vast area of the
Northwest.

It is not my intention to give a detailed description of his various successes; suffice it, that the end
of the war found him a millionaire. Thousands of
shrewd traders, keen at buying and selling, who
had built up piles of money during the "onpleas-
antness," made shipwreck of their fortunes when
Lee surrendered, by continuing to purchase on the
war basis; but there was no foolishness of that kind
noticeable in my friend. With him there was an
instinctive knowledge as to what should be done, and
what left undone; beyond instinct, indeed, it was
insight, the best attribute of intelligence. That he
should amass a great fortune and retain it, was
quite in the natural order of things. His business
premises are now the largest in La Crosse, and
they are not surpassed by any in Wisconsin. Hundreds of families depend upon his undertakings for
good homes and comfortable positions in society,

and he is one of the rare exceptions among merchants in this age of "smart men," whose word is his bond.

On my arrival in La Crosse in the spring of 1868, to consult Mr. Anderson, that gentleman suggested that I should start a shop for broom-making in that city. My arrangements had already been made for a few months in advance, but the advice so earnestly given was sustained by such unanswerable arguments that in the fall of that year I was domiciled in La Crosse. I had long before that time experienced his kindness, and become his debtor for many substantial proofs of his confidence and regard, and my faith in his counsel was unbounded.

My business prospered as he had foretold, and my three years' experience in that city was among the happiest and most evenly prosperous of my life. Oftentimes I was the recipient of kindnesses from utter strangers, which were to me at that time mysterious, but which I have since learned were due to the widespreading influence of Mons Anderson, exerted without ostentation, producing results which were to me and to many others most gratifying. Some time during the seventies Mr. Anderson went to Europe, revisiting Norway, and traveling through all the principal cities of the continent, accompanied by several members of his family. The change which time and energy had worked in the fortunes of the once penniless boy were doubtless highly appreciated by the merchant prince; but his manners were as unassuming, and as far from the pretensions of the shoddy *parvenu* as can well be imagined. His return to La Crosse in the summer of 1877 was an occasion for great rejoicing in his wide. circle of friends, who gave him a generous welcome home. I am very proud to be permitted to claim Mons Anderson as one of my best friends outside my own family.

I have, I think, mentioned elsewhere, that many others in La Crosse besides Mons Anderson and Mr. Knutson befriended me, and in that respect I must not omit to mention a gentleman who was then prominent in the public life of La Crosse. He was a storekeeper on a very large scale, with responsibilities enough on his shoulders to have warranted him in refusing attention to anything outside his own wholesale and retail stores; but, as is oftentimes the case, the very multiplicity of his affairs gave herculean energies to the man, and he found leisure to render to many others as well as to myself essential services.

One incident, among many, will illustrate the character of my friend. Soon after my arrival in La Crosse, almost a stranger, I found myself in a peculiarly awkward strait, and my natural sensitiveness disinclined me to impose on the good nature of my friend Anderson, or on my more recent friend Knutson, by informing them how I was situated.

Circumstances made Mr. Solberg acquainted with
my position, and he rendered me a series of unlooked-for disinterested aids, which were invalua-
ble.

It will be seen that my venture in La Crosse was
entered upon under circumstances full of excellent
augury.   My brooms had a good name, and I tried
to make them worthy of their reputation. "Good
wine needs no bush," said the ancient proverb; but
good brooms were all the better appreciated because
the leading men in the town said their best things
in my behalf. Wherever in my travels I found a
man that dealt with any of the first-class houses in
La Crosse, I could reckon with confidence upon a
customer, and I could ascertain without difficulty
the business character of any person that wanted
credit in my round.   That was no small advantage
to a young beginner, as usually such persons as myself have to run the gauntlet of all the dead beats in
a community before arriving at the basis of substantial success.

I was the best advertised broom-maker in America, although my outlays in that direction had been
very trivial. On my arrival in La Crosse from
Prairie du Chien by boat, my trunk, containing
nearly two hundred dollars worth of goods, was put
ashore from the boat and the check collected. I
supposed as a matter of course that my valuables
were stored, and in my misplaced confidence went

off into the country to look after my broom-corn interest.   On my return from the rural districts,
many days having elapsed, the results of my carelessness duly appeared; the trunk was nowhere to
be found.   No blame attached to the steamboat
people; the fault was my own and that of the thieves
who had forgotten the commandment.   Just at that
time there was a fierce war between rival steamboat
companies, and their rights were espoused in all but
sanguinary manner by their respective newspapers.
Mr. Pomeroy, widely known as "Brick" Pomeroy, was
editor and proprietor of the La Crosse Democrat,
the paper which was opposed to the company in
whose boat I had traveled, and no sooner was the
loss of my trunk made known than editorial articles, letters, paragraphs, and indeed every form of
missile known to the press, was hurled at the peccant
company.

It was assumed for the purposes of warfare that
the steamboat company had actually stolen my trunk
to compensate them for the low prices which prevailed on the river.   The Republican opened fire
immediately upon the Democrat, and the fun grew
fast and furious. My part in the strife was almost
purely passive, except when demanded for the purposes of interviewers.   In common honesty I was
bound to admit that the fault was my own, but that
had little or no effect upon the controversy.   For
ten weeks the campaign raged on both sides.   The

company accused of theft went to an expense more
than twice the value of my property, in trying,
without avail, to trace it; and their organ in the
press published weekly bulletins as to the status
of the investigation; but the enemy, though van-
quished in that way, could not be silenced, and all
his guns were double shotted.

The immediate consequence of all this newspaper
conflict was that I was the best advertised broom-
maker in the West. The people sent their orders
for miles around, to recuperate my losses. At the
end of ten weeks from the commencement of hostilities, my trunk was found one morning on the front
steps of the International Hotel, La Crosse, having
been left there by some of the Arabs, who silently
stole away during the night; and although my
trunk had sustained some damage, the bottom having been knocked out by the marauders, the contents were uninjured, complete as on the day of the
loss. Both of the newspapers used me well, as I
was advertised in each of them for twelve months
free of cost, and the thieves allowed their con-
sciences to luxuriate for my benefit, as probably they
had never luxuriated before, since their first entry
on criminal practices.

At the end of the first year I had made clear about
fifteen hundred dollars out of my business, besides
living in good style, covering considerable outlay in fitting up my premises, and traveling in the

establishment of my trade. Broom-corn had been easily obtained in sufficient quantity and at moderate rates, while profits on the manufactured article had ruled high. Workmen were sufficiently numerous to enable me to select efficient and steady hands, and I paid the best wages known to the trade, so that my manufactures did not suffer by comparison with any others in the same line offered in the market.

The prosperous beginning thus made, acclimated the new industry, and there was no necessity for special inducements the following season; farmers were quite willing to plant broom-corn in reasonable quantity. Seventy-five acres were engaged in the spring of 1869, an advance of one hundred and fifty per cent in amount over the area engaged in the spring of 1868, and still the quantity was inadequate to meet the demand, nearly one hundred acres of broom-corn being actually made up in my factory. I extended my travels as far as St. Paul, Minnesota, and did a very prosperous business in that city, in the summer and fall of 1869.

My first patron in St. Paul was Mr. McQuellin, and subsequently Mr. Kelly, the leading partner in another large grocery firm, not only bought largely himself on liberal terms but induced other merchants to favor me with orders, which kept me working my hands at high pressure until the rivers no longer admitted of navigation. The railroads, which now give so many benefits, were then beyond our reach, so that traffic was attended with many difficulties. Mr. Kelly, who is still in business in St. Paul, has been my friend ever since, as he is, and he deserves to be, a very prosperous gentleman. In the spring of 1870 I did not engage broom-corn, as there were enough farmers interested in the crop to supply the demand without any such action on my part, and I had procured facilities for purchasing supplies in St. Louis, Missouri, much better in quality than I had ever seen raised in Wisconsin.

My business continuing to increase, I built a shop of my own in the summer of 1870, the place theretofore occupied by me having been rented. My own premises were very much better than those I had rented, having been constructed expressly to meet my wants, and my facilities were better than ever. I was master of the situation for a time; my shop was my own property, and paid for, no man having a lien upon it; and my stock and materials, tools, machinery, brooms and money made me feel wealthy.

In my travels I was frequently called upon by my friends to assist them in the selection of musical instruments. My training in the Institute at Janesville aided me felicitously in the thorough education of my ear, so that a false note in music, or a reedy and metallic tone in instrumentation, strikes me like a cold blast. I could have wished for a better insight and more practice as a player, but the few advantages which have fallen in my path have been of much value in my career. Sometimes the instruments of the best makers fall far below their reputation, and it is of considerable importance to purchasers that they should have the advantage of the judgment of a reliable expert before investing their money. Occasionally a new name is introduced among manufacturers, heralding the very best class of instruments, but skilled analysis of the claims of such aspirants for fame and emolument will alone guard against imposition. To pass by on the other side because a maker is new in his profession, is a course which cannot be justified. Stradivarius was once only a beginner. A dozen manufacturers may be only pretentious frauds, and that is the case sometimes when great names are used, but a worthy percentage can always be found, to whom honor and repute are verities.

The reputation of the Story and Clark organs is such as hardly to need any words from me; but I cannot refrain from speaking of the delight afforded in my home by the full rich tones of an organ purchased from this firm, as my family gather about it to practice for their Sunday concert, or in merrier mood the older children train the younger in the songs last learned at school. For sustaining and

14

accompanying the voice, or for rendering instrumental music, these organs are equally and admirably adapted; and from the many varieties of case made by this firm, ranging from "Doric," "Ionic," "Chateau" and "Romanesque," to the "Mozart" and the "Monarch," with their powerful registers, various qualities of tone, combinations and orchestral effects, there is nothing in the whole range of artistic taste, as it appeals to eye or ear, that may not be abundantly satisfied in a choice made from among these instruments. We treasure ours as a thing of beauty and sweet sound—a double joy.

My social circle extended itself every day, and my friends were friends indeed. A very few words will give an idea of the manner in which my interests were cared for in that city by men upon whom I had no claim save what their good nature granted. Because of my blindness, correspondence and accounts were beyond my powers, except with much labor and under great difficulties, and to employ an accountant and secretary could not be ventured upon, as, setting aside the cost, my affairs would have been entirely at his mercy. Two gentlemen, who were then assistants in leading businesses in La Crosse, earning large salaries—Mr. O. C. Erexrude, now a prosperous business man in Blue Earth City, Minnesota, and Mr. Shape, bookkeeper in a wholesale grocery store, and now in a large way of business on his own account in Milwaukee—undertook my bookkeeping and correspondence, without an atom of remuneration except my gratitude; and to their disinterested help, in the manner indicated, I owe much of my temporary prosperity. There were several other gentlemen who extended to me numberless courtesies, including Mr. Konant, Mr. Haugan, and the Rev. Mr. Rye, who contributed in no small degree to my happiness by expanding my ideas and adding to my fund of knowledge.

As soon as I found that any man was better informed than his neighbors, generally or specially, it was the habit of my mind to attach myself to him, just as a syphon dips into a reservoir, and my receptive intellect, thirsty always for such treasure, was not content until it had drawn off the results of his mental experience. There was no sordid motive in this. I became the disciple of every man of superior attainments who would allow me to learn from him what he could gather, as it were, with a glance. Kepler was not sordid when he attached himself to the service of Tycho Brahe, from whom he may be said to have inherited, as his pupil and fellow-worker, the Rudolphian Tables.

CHAPTER XIII.

PROSPECTING.

———

"Love took up the harp of life, and smote on all the chords with
      might ;
Smote the chord of self, that, trembling, passed in music out of
      sight."—*Tennyson's Locksley Hall.*

Only in the way I have set forth was it possible for me to continue my studies until the time to which I ambitiously looked forward, when I should win the affectionate regard of a lady willing and able to become my better self in all my pursuits.

Already I had centered my hopes upon the dear woman who is now my wife, but I dreaded the possibility of some reverse in my prospects, which might render it impossible for me to provide ade-

WALBORG HENDRICKSON,
Wife of the Author.

quately for one so self-sacrificing and faithful. Men are, in too many cases, unmindful as to the future in contracting matrimonial engagements, and I knew of many instances in which lovely women—I speak of mental and moral beauty as the only loveliness which I could fully appreciate—had been induced to leave the circles in which they had been reared amid all the requirements of social enjoyment, and had, within a few years, been reduced to penury and toil, unless they would accept refuge with their own families from the storms of adversity which the husbands of their choice could not escape. Such misfortunes will befall the wisest and best, under some circumstances; but it is the duty of every man who aspires to become a husband, to use all the circumspection in his power to guard his home circle from preventable suffering. Woes must come, at the best. There is no family exempt from the common lot. Longfellow has said, with much beauty, and in sorrowful truth:

"There is no flock, however watched and tended,
But one dead lamb is there ;
There is no fireside, howsoe'er defended,
But has one vacant chair."

I went to St. Louis in the summer of 1870, with a large quantity of my manufactures, but found the market very much depressed, and was obliged to close out my stock at low figures. This was the commencement of many misfortunes, but I looked upon it as only one of the petty oscillations to which the most prosperous enterprises are subject. My mind was less buoyant than it had been when my visit to St. Louis was concluded, and I suppose that my tell-tale face, as usual, revealed my mental condition when I returned home.

Visiting the International Bank to make my customary deposit, soon after my arrival in La Crosse, I found the manager as conversant with the general tenor of my recent experiences as if I had, in so many words, made him my confidant—a course I never scrupled to adopt in any circumstances that called for counsel—and, full of the kindliest motives, that gentleman advised me to change my methods of procedure. A grocery establishment, much more extensive than any already existent in La Crosse, was to be started immediately by a new customer of the bank, a Mr. Weaver, and that gentleman wished to handle, as one branch of his business, all the brooms I could manufacture. The proposition bristled all over with advantages. Instead of traveling through the country making sales, and leaving my factory to run itself in my absence, I could remain all the time on the spot, giving the impetus of personal supervision to every branch, and securing the highest efficiency.

Impressed thus favorably by the counsels of my banker, and influenced as he was, by the idea that Mr. Weaver, the new-comer, was in every sense competent and reliable as a man of business, I listened to the proposals gladly, and lived out my dream of prosperity in a very few months. Mr. Weaver was remarkable as a theorist, but almost an utter failure as an executant. The supplies, which under my own management would have been converted into prompt cash, less the moderate traveling expenses which could not be avoided, now lodged in his store and warehouse month after month, until navigation closed, and we were comparatively frozen in, so that all my best markets were beyond my reach. It is the fault of my sanguine nature that, despite some unahppy experiences I am prone to believe that men will do all that they say and can do all that they undertake.

Mr. Weaver covenanted with me that he should advance upon all my brooms one dollar per dozen as soon as they passed into his hands, and within thirty days pay the balance of the full market value less ten per cent commission for handling them. I ought to have held him squarely to his bargain, and have ceased to deliver my manufactures as soon as he ceased to fill the bill, but just there my constitutional trustfulness was my undoing. His words were so full of promise that the brooms continued to be deposited, although he failed in almost every particular.

At the end of the navigation season, when my chances were apparently played out for that year, he had on hand six hundred dozen brooms upon which only three hundred dollars had been advanced and the term was long gone by when under his agreement every broom should have been paid for less the commission at market rates. I had reduced my trouble and responsibility only to increase both beyond measure, but somehow I would not despair of a favorable outcome. There were many small towns within easy reach in which sales could be effected by personal effort, and I was off on the road once more attending to my own business as soon as I could arrange with Mr. Weaver to free me from the proviso that he should handle all my goods. There was warmth and sunshine in the thought that I was once more my own master and own man although the weather was cold enough to remind me of the freezing sleigh-ride between the Institution and Oakland at the time of my sister's funeral; and a number of small transactions enabled me to touch ready cash once more, enough for all needs except the repayment of Mr. Weaver's advance.

While buying and selling that winter, I was assured by many travelers with whom I came in friendly conatct, that I could readily sell out all my stock in New York, on terms that would leave a liberal margin. So I hurried back to La Crosse, saw Mr. Weaver as to the likelihood of my enterprise succeeding, and in a few days afterwards

was in New York, ready to close out all my surplus
stock, including the brooms in Mr. Weaver's hands,
subject to his claim of three hundred dollars. The
foreman of the workshop in the New York Institution for the blind gave me letters of introduction to
merchants who could take all my brooms, then and
thereafter, with a mutual advantage; and within a
few hours I had sold out all that there were to dispose of at really excellent prices, the firm to pay
freight, one hundred dollars per car load, and three
dollars per dozen to me.

I was overjoyed with my success. My misfortune had forced me out into a broader market, in
which my beaver-like industry would have full scope,
and the few debts which had been crowding me
would be but as rain-drops in a river. I was in
La Crosse just as rapidly as the cars could bear a
merchant of so much importance, and my shipments
were made without delay, cars were chartered at
the agreed price, one hundred dollars per load, and
I went in to obtain my bills of lading from Captain
Moulton, the freight agent, a gentleman from whom
I had received many kindnesses. Unfortunately
that was one of his busiest days, and, instead of
concluding the affair at once, the Captain asked me
to come in again for the bill of lading the next
day, or anytime; they should be made ready as
soon as the rush was over. A better manager under
such conditions would have stuck right there and

seen the transaction completed, but I saw no reason to hurry; next day or the next afterwards would answer all purposes, as the shipment was really dispatched.

Just as I was leaving the depot, news reached me of a considerable sum due me in one of the outlying towns being in danger unless it was looked after at once. My losses had been heavy enough to make me vigilant, and I started within the hour. Engrossed with my collections and looking after new business, thirty days had elapsed before I landed in La Crosse, and then to my surprise I found that the brooms, instead of being billed at per carload, were billed at per dozen, making a difference of two hundred dollars per car load. The merchant in New York refused to take delivery paying such charges, and my prospects in that direction were petering out completely. The railroad companies could not be induced to admit that any mistake had been made on their part, although ultimately one of the companies gave me one hundred dollars off my loss, and a commission merchant in New York, in whose hands the business was put for settlement, let them out of the difficulty by paying all the freight demanded.

My troubles came upon me like a cyclone suddenly streaming through a sky until that moment all but cloudless. Expenses, commissions, interest, advertising, and sales by auction at last, left

me only about three hundred and seventy-five dollars to my credit, in the hands of the New York
agent; and Mr. Weaver, going to that city in the
prosecution of his own business, volunteered as my
friend to collect that amount subject to his little de-
duction of three hundred dollars for advances.   The
money was duly paid to my very dear friend, my
altogether too dear friend, my atrociously expensive friend, Mr. Weaver, who charged me the whole
of my seventy-five dollars for the trouble of collect-
ing his three hundred dollars, and so ended my interest in the brooms.

That Weaver spoiled the web of my life, warp and
woof, for some years; but I suppose that in the
end his injustice and incapacity injured himself
more than me, and for my poor part I try to forgive
him, notwithstanding all that I suffered at his
hands.   The explanation offered in these few lines
as to the causes of my embarrassment in La Crosse,
could not set me right with my friends, unless the
round, unvarnished tale was fairly unfolded.   I
have not excused myself at the expense of any person, friend, or foe; no man living can see the faults
in my career more readily than myself; but unfortunately my ready wit comes after the event.   I
have nothing extenuated, nor set down aught in
malice, and it was no light thought that after all my
years of prevision, I had involved another for
whom I cared a thousand times more than for my-

self in the load of disaster which from that time onward had to be carried.

After my arrangements had been made in New York, and my shipments had been actually made, opening up a business which seemed certain to prove enduring and profitable, so that whether the river was frozen over or not I could find an outlet for annually increasing supplies, there was no apparent reason for my continuing the life—the very unsatisfactory life—of an unmarried man. Consultations with eminent medical men had satisfied me that inasmuch as my blindness was not a congenital defect, there was no good ground for fearing that my children would inherit my calamity; and that reasonable conclusion has been borne out by the fact. I daily, aye, I may say hourly, return thanks to Almighty God for the blessing of sight which my darlings enjoy. The gloom of misfortune would be, I fear, insupportable if my marriage had been the cause of their entering upon lives of darkness.

My beloved partner, who has never uttered one word of repining during our years of toil, sometimes on the verge of want, was fully aware of all my reasons for hope, as she had long been my most trusted counsellor, and she agreed with me that the time was opportune for our long contemplated union. I have heard of a laggard lover in his seventeenth year of sparking, who was urged to greater

speed by his lady-love gently saying, "I could be
content, John, with your company in a garret,
though we lived upon bread and water;" but I am at
a loss to know of what mettle John was compounded
when he could say, "Well, my dear, if you can manage the bread and the garret, I think I might
scratch around and find the water." The dream of
my life was a home for my wife and little ones,
in which poverty in mind, body and estate should
be alike unknown; where friends might ever find a
welcome, and where intellect, irradiated by the
moral tone which religion alone can assure, should
reign supreme; and if some of my brightest hopes
have been dimmed by suffering, we have still never
experienced the cold and darkness which prevail in
those households where love has ceased to rule.

The family into which it was my good fortune to
marry had seen many vicissitudes within a comparatively few years. Mr. Boyer was one of the
most extensive dry goods merchants in Christiania,
Norway, and, until the very evening of his life, had
met with no reverses. Socially his position was all
that could be desired, and his capital sufficed for
all the demands of his business, while his income
was so liberal as to permit the indulgence of his
generous impulses whenever the relief of indigence
or the patronage of art challenged the exercise of
his means. Among the various brotherhoods which
in Norway, as well as elsewhere within the range

of civilization, come in as co-operating bodies in works of benevolence, co-ordinate even with the churches, Mr. Boyer had filled all the chairs in succession in Lodge, Chapter and Grand Lodge, so that it goes without saying, or *sans phrase*, as the French have it, that he was a worthy member of society, always ready to respond when called upon to fulfill the points of fellowship. Many men struggling against adversity found in his well timed and wisely given aid the means by which they rose to fortune, and the luxury of doing good was the only recompense that the good old man desired.

In the crisis of 1857, which struck Norway very heavily, his means were severely taxed by his endeavors to sustain deserving men whom he had previously assisted, and a succession of heavy failures among his agents and business connections made it impossible for him to meet his engagements. There are thousands of smart men in this country who would have gone through his ordeal, going through their creditors at the same time, without moulting a feather; but the old man, punctilious as to the value of an unsullied name, could not endure the humiliation of even a partial failure and remain in the city, where every incident reminded him of his changed conditions. He sequestrated his estate and handed it over to assignees for realization in the interest of his creditors, and, refusing every

CARL JOHAN'S STREET, CHRISTIANIA, NORWAY.

proffer of assistnace, set sail for Australia, where he
did not doubt that he should be able to rebuild his
shattered fortunes.

His wife, three sons, and three daughters, remained in Christiania, hoping against hope, month
after month, and then year after year, that, on the
gold fields in the British colony of Victoria, he
would find a *succedanœum* for his material losses.
He was heard from as a gold-digger on Ballarat,
one of the greatest gold-fields in the world, where
men all but starving, faint with hunger, and unable
to procure another meal by cash or credit, had
driven the ill-aimed pick into a "nugget" of gold
too heavy for one man to lift, and there was, of
course, a possibility that some such fate was in
store for him. Hope deferred, which maketh the
heart sick, told upon him, and his letters, more
rare than ever in the atmosphere of misfortune,
came freighted with bad news. He was sick in
the lonely hut which he had erected near the Buninyong road, and strangers—rude, rough miners,
none too prosperous themselves—were ministering
to him. Months passed before other letters were
received, and then it appeared that he had recovered from the disease, thanks to the bracing airs of
Mount Buninyong, but that his strength was steadily failing. His son Frederick, who had embraced
a seafaring life as a means of helping his mother
and sisters, determined now to follow him to Aus-

tralia, but it was not easy to ship for Melbourne.

A vessel bound for India was first obtained, and from Calcutta he shipped for Melbourne by way of China. At the port of Amoy it became known that the trading vessel Amazon was but half manned and practically unarmed, a few boarding pikes, pistols and cutlasses being the entire armament, and the Island of Amoy, although taken by the British in 1841, and two years later thrown open to the trade of all the world, was the resort of as cruel a set of pirates as ever disgraced Algiers.

Soon after quitting the port of Amoy, the Amazon was attacked by a little fleet of piratical junks, and although the brave skipper was backed by the desperate courage of his crew, every man of whom was equal in fighting capacity to three of his almond-eyed assailants, the paucity of numbers and arms on the side of the British made their defeat unavoidable.

The ship was captured, the valuable parts of the cargo transferred to the robber junks, and the vessel scuttled so that she sank out at sea and was supposed to have foundered in a storm. Fred was stunned by a blow on the head from some weapon or missile while the fight was hottest, and remained insensible for many days, apparently, as when he recovered consciousness there were no traces of the conflict which had raged so fiercely, and the pirates were many miles from the coast, with a number of

like craft within hailing distance, lying in wait for
unarmed merchantmen.   The fates of the remainder
of the officers and crew long remained a matter for
conjecture; but from many hints and half sentences
in "Pigeon English," or business English, such as is
used in Chinese ports, which the poor boy could
speculate upon rather than understand, it became
evident at last that every man speaking English on
board the vessel had been killed

Fred could never understand exactly why his life
had been spared, and proceeding on the maxim,
"Let sleeping dogs lie," he did not ask questions,
which might have renewed dangerous debates of
policy.

The Bucephalus, hailing from Boston, United
States, was attacked by the fleet of junks during the
boy's captivity, and he was compelled to take his
trick at the wheel during the attack, as the pirates
would not trust him with arms, perhaps fearing that
he would fight on the side of the defenders; but the
Yankees had guns that were not Quakers, and their
assailants sought safety in flight.   Fred would have
given one of his arms to have been able to ask the
protection of the stars and stripes, but his deliverance came in another way.   A great storm arose, a
kind of fierce simoon, and the unsailor-like conduct
of the Chinamen gave the junk no chance to weather it out.   The latteen sails, poorly reefed, would
not blow out of their bolt ropes as canvas might

have done, the main mast went by the board, and the vessel, on her beam ends, seemed certain to go down at sea, when, to the surprise of all hands she struck on sunken rocks, and soon after went down within half a mile of high and inhospitable looking cliffs. When the fog cleared away there were no Chinamen visible, and the after part of the ship was under water, her back having been broken on the reefs.

One day and night the boy clung to his slippery holdfast on the bowsprit of the junk, and then he was taken off by a trader bound for Foo Chow, which had been driven out of her course by the destructive simoon and detained for some time in the shelter of a well wooded, sparsely inhabited island, repairing damages. At Foo Chow he found that the great tea shipping firm of Russell & Co. was about to send a cargo of tea to Melbourne, Australia, and as a special favor he was allowed to work his passage as assistant to the supercargo, an American of the very highest character and connections, from Batavia, New York.

While waiting at Foo Chow, an opportunity occurred to communicate with Amoy, and from that port letters from Norway, which in the ordinary course of events would have been lost, were obtained, informing Fred of the death of his mother. His sisters wrote that she had died of a broken heart. His elder brother, assistant to the chief of a bureau in the Department of the Interior, wrote that her death had been hastened by grief.

There were no further noticeable incidents before his arrival in the great gold-mining colony of Victoria, as the vessels chartered by Russell & Co. were too formidable to be attacked by junks. Many of the pirates were seen, but they were harmless river craft and coasters, engaged in reputable traffic in the presence of superior metal, so that there was no chance to sink them as a punishment for the past and a preventive for the future. A few ships, apparently unarmed, but really carrying heavy guns and small arms, with men enough to work them, might have saved thousands of valuable lives every year, and millions of dollars worth of cargo, by enticing the pirate junks in the China seas to reveal their true character, and then capturing the crews in *flagrant delicto.*

Arrived at Melbourne, Fred was astonished to find a city of metropolitan proportions, where he had expected to see a primitive settlement, dependent on sheep-farming and gold-digging, with perhaps a little kangaroo-hunting and fishing thrown in to make weight. Melbourne now has a population of more than two hundred thousand souls, and the prosperity of the colony is exceptional. Criminals expatriated from England, formed the rough ashlar course of several of the Australian colonies of Great Britain, but Victoria steadfastly refused to be made a

convict settlement, so that when the better class of
Englishmen sought places of resort for themselves
and families, away from the grinding competition
of the older countries, yet under the British flag,
the colony of Victoria, with Melbourne as its capital, offered advantages which could hardly be excelled, coupled with a delightful climate.

There came a time in the history of Victoria when
all the influence of the mother country was exerted
to change the policy of the colonies so that the
criminal classes, dangerous to England, might be
transported there, and the attempt proved a failure,
much to the credit of the people. Gold was discovered in paying quantities in Buninyong, near
Ballarat—then a sheep station or squatter's run—
near the end of 1851, and all kinds of labor, skilled
or not, was immediately appreciated almost ten to
one. The roads to the several diggings, varying on
different routes, were from sixty to one hundred
miles of dust, at all depths in summer, and almost
impassable quagmire every winter. This state of
things could not be readily improved, because free
labor could hardly be induced to work at road-mak-
ing for high wages, when every man that passed
along the route, "humping his swag" to the mines,
could tell some wonderful story about a fortunate
digger who started with barely enough money to
buy a pick, and had returned after only a few
weeks' absence, with enough gold to make him a

KING WILLIAM STREET.

millionaire. The least sanguine of the road-makers
was apt to see analogies in such narratives closely
answering to his own case; and on the strength of
his having just money enough to purchase his outfit, he would try his luck as soon as he could draw
his pay.

In the year 1854 there were wagons on the road
to the diggings, which had been bogged and dug
out again so many times that more than three weeks
had been consumed in traveling with half a ton of
merchandise in each load, less than a hundred
miles. The English government sent out a ship load
of convicted criminals, five hundred in all, on board
the John Hashemy, to be employed in making and
mending roads, or any other work that the colonists
saw fit to direct, free of cost, beyond housing, feeding and guarding the prisoners until their respective sentences had expired; and a similar load of
cheap labor, male and female, would be transmitted
to the colony, in never-ending succession, every
month. It was known that the convict settlement in
Van Dieman's Land had made metaled roads from
one side of the island to the other, in all directions,
and had constructed other public works, without
taxing the free colonists one cent, as the British
government actually paid the salaries and wages of
the warders and other officers necessary to the safe
custody of the convicts; and moreover, many of the
settlers had grown wealthy by employing convicts

as assigned servants without wages, on their farms
and in their houses.

With such marked results observable within easy
reach, it must have seemed to the government of
England impossible to doubt that the Melbourne
people would jump mast-high to secure a continuous
supply of slave labor, the color-line being convict-
ism.

The three daily papers, the *Argus*, *Age*, and *Herald*, contained one morning the announcement of the
ship's arrival in Hobson's Bay, the harbor, road-
stead and anchorage of Melbourne, and the same
sheets invited the people to suspend their business
by common consent that day, so that a meeting of
all the citizens might be held at noon, after fullest
deliberation, to consider the proposed deluge of
criminality. A committee, hastily convened, distributed through all the offices, ware-houses, banks,
stores and shops, placards saying that all hands in
each establishment had gone to the anti-convict
meeting; and when the time arrived to call the assemblage to order, there were not less than fifty
thousand men on the ground, breathing the wholesome sentiment that England should not send her
criminal classes here to poison the young colony
almost in its inception.

The talk that day from the rostrum as hastily
constructed as a Parisian barricade, was wonderfully
to the purpose; the convicts were not allowed to

land, and England never sent another ship-load to
the colony.   That incident serves to illustrate the
kind of community in which Fred found himself
when he landed in Melbourne. Rebellion against
wrong, and, if necessary, revolution, were cherished
as sacred and inalienable rights, to be used only in
the last extremity; but lynch law, too often the
shame of this country, was not known in Victoria.

Ballarat was the objective point, to reach which
Fred had traveled over thirty thousand miles, and
he found his father altered in almost every particular
except as to the gentleness and manly integrity of
his bearing. With some circumlocution the boy
was about to tell his father that his mother was
dead, but the old man anticipated his purpose,
saying on such a day "she appeared to me to say
that she had gone before me, and laid her hand upon my head; the spot she touched has been white as
her own robe from that moment." Sure enough there
were the marks indicated, but whence came the coincidence no man can say. The date given by him
corresponded exactly with that in the letter which
he had never seen and the contents of which were
never communicated until much later.

The old man toiled unceasingly in his laborious
calling as a miner, and his son did all in his power
to assist the enterprise with money earned in other
employment, and with the labor of his own hands
when other work happened to be scarce; but the

fact is, that putting aside exceptional instances in
which individuals have become suddenly rich, gold-
mining is a wasteful industry.   An ounce of gold is
worth about twenty dollars, putting fractions out of
our reckoning, and every ounce of gold put upon
the market by gold diggers, from the first outbreak
of the gold fever in Sacramento Valley, California,
has cost, in the labor and capital necessary to produce it, very nearly twenty-seven dollars.

The pursuit is like gambling in some respects, or
like book-writing; the people who enter upon it
seem to be bewitched, and continue to the bitter
end in nine hundred and ninety-nine cases out of a
thousand; but the thousandth man coming out
ahead with a little fortune, is talked of to the exclu-
sion of the whole army of failures, so that his success
serves like a wrecker's light upon a rockbound coast
to draw thousands to destruction. The fortunate
man made his pile perhaps on a small outlay of
money or labor, but in estimating the cost of gold
to the community we must place to the debit all
the labor and capital expended in the search, and
to the credit the net results of every find.   Careful
analysis carried through by competent statists in
California and Australia, show a wonderful uniform-
ity of figures illustrating the wastefulness of mining
in both hemispheres.

The *ignis fatuus* hope, without which life is unen-
durable, lured both father and son for four years

longer, and then one day the old man failed to respond to the son's morning salutation.   There was
a smile upon his lips which seemed to light up the
whole face even in death, and it might be imagined
that as he passed away the beckoning finger of one
who had joined the angelic host called him to that
better home of the soul, where God our Father
wipes away all tears, and sorrows are unknown.
He had never known actual want, and his character draping him in dignity, which asserts its power
through homespun as surely as through rich apparel, had won him recognitions, honors and attentions for which many of his rich neighbors would
have paid highly. "The light that never was on
sea or land" shone upon him at the last, and when
his bones were laid to rest in the little churchyard,
there was a noble concourse of men and women
who had recognized the righteousness of his life,
and to whom it was indeed a sacrament to see him
laid in the earth in the sure and certain hope of a
glorious resurrection.

Sir William Jones has translated from the Persian
a very beautiful verse which always occurs to my
mind whenever I think of that old man's death, so
far from his kindred and his old-time friends, yet
so near to the hearts of the discriminating few to
whom rank is but the guinea stamp.   The thought

of the Persian poet runs in this wise, and   the lesson may be good for us all:

> "On parent knees a naked, new-born child,
>   Weeping thou sat'st when all around thee smiled ;
>   So live that, sinking in thy last long sleep,
>   Calm thou may'st smile when all around thee weep."

CHAPTER XIV.

PARTINGS AND REUNIONS.

Fred goes Home—Reunion and Separation—Masonic Benevolence—Mrs. Boyer's Struggle—Martin Boyer in Chicago—*Skandinaven* Newspaper—Walborg Boyer Joins Martin—Removal to La Crosse—The *Fatherland*—Walborg Hendrickson—Perils of the Atlantic—Fred and Sisters Wrecked—De Bruce and the Spider.

The gold fields of Ballarat had no longer any attraction for Fred Boyer beyond the limits of God's Acre, where the bones of his father had consecrated the earth, so he turned towards that home in Norway, where loved and loving ones awaited his return, and where the account of his stewardship must needs inflict pain, although it might be that sorrow such as he was bearing into their lives could not fail to sanctify and elevate the moral nature. The colony of Victoria was not less lovely than when he first saw it. Melbourne was certainly growing in wealth and beauty every year; its university, its public library, its parliament houses, town hall, postoffice, churches, theaters, and other public buildings, decked the city with splendor to which the bright and warm, yet bracing air, added new beauty; and the club-houses, places of business and private residences kept pace with the increasing importance

of a city destined, at no distant day, to become the
capital of Australia. Still, Melbourne, like all else,
seemed changed to him—had a message in every fea·
ture to hurry him away. There is a sadness about
every accomplished duty which warns us of the
end, and from every scene in life, even the most
joyous, wells up a tiny rivulet of sorrow such as was
hinted at by Longfellow in the line: "I fear to
think how glad I am."

There was yet another reason why the young man
fondly dreamed of the Fjords of Norway. He could
attach a peculiar and personal meaning to the poet's
words:

> " 'Tis sweet to know there is an eye doth mark our coming,
>   And look brighter when we come."

The busy city could have found him profitable
employment, for as an artist he wielded a pencil
which few could excel; but he waited no longer
than was necessary to find a ship that would take
him home again to his family and friends with a
minimum of delay. A ship bound to Christiania
was out of the question, but there were prospects
of a passage to Copenhagen, upon which he spent
some days. Eventually he was glad to take ship
for Hamburg, and so reached his desired haven by
a course a little more circuitous. The joy to which
he had looked forward in his day dreams as to that
welcome home extended, in some degree, even to
the dear soil of his fatherland; but in the moment of

BOTANICAL GARDENS, UPSALA, SWEDEN.

realization, when the dimmed, cloud-like outline
began to unfold its beauties to the eager eyes of
the young man, so long a stranger in strange lands,
it seemed as though a sorrow's crown of sorrow in
remembering happier things would rob his return of
all the enchantment which imagination had decked
it withal. Tennyson, who contests with our own Longfellow the supreme faculty for reading the heart of
humanity, says, in his exquisite poem, "The Princess:"

> "Tears, idle tears, I know not what they mean ;
> Tears from the depth of some divine despair
> Rise in the heart, and gather to the eyes,
> In looking on the happy autumn fields,
> And thinking of the days that are no more."

Suddenly as the hand of death had fallen on their
father, the little group in Christiania were not unprepared for the melancholy tidings. There is a
prescience in some families which outruns the course
of post, and can divine the message which has
never been shaped in words. Every lineament of
that well remembered face was dear to them all—
dear as remembered kisses after death; but they did
not sorrow as those without hope. There was for
them a sweet augury in the smile with which he
turned his face toward the better shore. In their
orphaned condition the brothers and sisters had remained together, aided, in no small degree, by the
brotherhoods and associations to the prosperity of
which their father had largely contributed, and,

when unmerited misfortune fell upon them all, the
Masonic fraternity would have provided for all the
family. The aid which the father declined for his
own sake, was in his absence rained down upon his
children and their mother until death removed her
from the scene.

The death of Mrs. Boyer was precipitated, if
not caused, by disquietude on account of the long
continued absence and failing health of her husband. That was to her the worst consequence of
their fallen fortunes. Could he have remained by
her side, adversity would have been deprived of
its sting; not that she desired to cast the burden of
her sorrow upon him—that was no part of her purpose in life; but that she hoped and believed that
she could lighten the load which he must carry,
by her kindly word and smile. Their two lives had
grown together until it was death to tear asunder
the tendrils by which they had been mutually sustaining and sustained. She knew that he would
suffer excruciatingly in the absence of the tender
claims and attentions which had been the salt of
his life; but, as was usual in her generous nature,
she underestimated the sacrifices daily looked for at
her hands as head of the family, providing for the
household out of an income so small that her customary allowance for petty personal expenses had,
for nearly all her married life, been much larger.

At first, when her husband went to the gold

fields, she was buoyed up by her faith that a man so good, and until now so successful, seeking wealth for others at the utter sacrifice of his own comfort, must necessarily be favored in his enterprise; but that misdirected confidence died out when months became years, and his labors were unblessed with the prayed-for competency.

Her sons were as good and as earnest in their endeavors to mitigate her burden as their circumstances would permit. The assistant in the Department of the Interior placed his salary entirely at his mother's disposal, and was happy in the fact that he could in some degree atone for the many acts of self-denial on her part that he daily witnessed. The youngest son, Fred, we have already traced around the globe, going to the succor of his father, but his first idea in becoming a sailor was that he would become self-supporting at once, and should be able, within a few months at furthest, to add his mite to the scanty store of the household. The other brother inherited from his father a business faculty, which he applied to the best purpose possible in Christiania, but his eyes were always bent on the Atlantic as the highway that should lead him to fortune, although he never contemplated emigrating until his sailor-brother should come back to relieve him from his immediate duty.

The girls had fewer resources than their brothers, but within their limitations they were assiduous in

their efforts to make their mother forget the freight
age of anxiety and disappointment that was bearin,,
her down to the tomb.   When the news of that
fit of sickness reached Norway, at first from the pen
of a stranger countryman, who wished to prepare
them for the worst, her natural impulse was to
follow him at all hazards, but, alas! necessity has
no law.   She could not leave her family uncared for
without feeling that she was recreant to her gravest
responsibility, nor could she, by any alchemy within her power, procure the means for such a voyage
without appealing, as her soul shrank from doing,
to the generosity of her friends.   She suffered almost in silence until the end, carrying her troubles
as a sacred chastisement, which, for some inscrutable purpose, was necessary; but the fibre which
had borne so much snapped asunder in the midst of
her daily duties, and she died with the name of her
husband, coupled with that of her Redeemer, on
her lips.   She had been ailing for some months, but
none thought the end so near.   The even tenor of
her life had been scrupulously patterned upon the
maxim: "Whatsoever ye would that others should
do unto you, do ye even so unto them," and, under
saving grace, we cannot doubt that she was prepared for the change upon which at last all mankind must enter.

Martin, the second son , who had learned the business of a compositor, but found his earnings too

small in Christiania to enable him to provide as he would have wished for his sisters, thought the time had arrived for carrying out his plan of emigration to this country, and by dint of the most painful economies was at length able to accomplish his design. Landing in New York and being unable to find work at his trade in that city, he continued his journey to Chicago and there entered upon what proved to be steady employment in the office of the *Skandinaven* newspaper. Compositors do not usually trouble themselves as to the policy of the book or paper upon which they work; the number of ems that they have the opportunity to set up during the week, and the chances for "phat" that fall to their share, are far more important factors in their sum of happiness; but there was something so broadly Catholic in the management of the *Skandinaven*, as viewed from the standpoint of a young man newly arrived from Norway, that every day's work was a new contribution to the education of his faculties.

The paper was not on the fence as to either politics or religion, but the management wisely felt that what the reading public most required on all questions, ecclesiastical as well as civil, was an open arena in which without fear or favor every man might speak his mind. The great English poet and revolutionist, John Milton, uttered a grand sentence, which will be quoted for centuries

16

to come by enlightened men vindicating the right of unfettered debate, when he said: "Let truth and falsehood grapple. Who ever heard of truth being put to the worse in a fair and open encounter?" The same great authority, greater in his prose than even in his undying poetry, set forth the personal responsibility of every individual thinker in the words: "I am in the place where I am demanded of conscience to speak the truth, and therefore the truth I speak, impugn it whoso lists." No permanent danger can arise from fearless discussion. The truth is from the fountain of all goodness, and will flow on forever, though all the powers of darkness should combine to stay its course.

Martin's employment on the *Skandinaven* was pleasant as well as profitable. The circulation of that paper being larger than that of any other paper addressed to his compatriots in this country, the proprietor could employ the very best editorial talent available, and was under no necessity to cut down wages to the lowest fraction. Before many months had elapsed he was able to enter upon his long meditated scheme for the transfer of his sister to this country, and he spared no exertion to expedite the event. His sister Walborg was the first to respond to his offer of assistance, and his means were yet too restricted to allow of the three sisters being brought over at the same time.

A group of friends taking ship for New York included Walborg in their little circle, so that she was under the best of guardianship during the voyage and journey which landed her in Chicago under her brother's tender care. She was not content to sit idly down and see her brother toil for all the family while she had faculties which, properly employed, might hasten the reunion. She knew that the brother in Christiania cherished ambitious designs which were incompatible with the fullest discharge of his brotherly duties, and she wanted for his sake, as well as for her sisters', to relieve him from a responsibility which was felt to be burdensome; and being so fortunate as to find a clerkship which she could satisfactorily fill, her every hour was given to business during the work-a-day week. Sundays, holidays and almost every evening the brother and sister spent together, for until the circle was once more complete they felt that it would be a wrong to the absent ones to waste their substance in festivities; but they were happy in the consciousness that they were doing what their parents, could they see their sphere of labor and their motive, must of necessity approve. Every mail which brought them word from the old country told of the preparations that were being made in Christiania by the two girls who were left behind, eagerly waiting for the word to follow.

It was upon a circle so broken and diminished that Fred entered when he returned from Mel-

bourne; and he felt as he rejoined his sisters in
Christiania that the separation, which was now re·
alized for the first time, had been the hidden cause
of that sadness, which made his native land revisited seem to be draped in tears. His own tidings were
not cheering, but his coming home was of good augury, notwithstanding, and while his return was yet
new, letters came from Chicago full of the happiest
tidings; the way was prepared for the girls, and
they could not come too soon. Martin had been
offered an excellent situation upon the *Fatherland,*
a Scandinavian paper published in La Crosse, Wisconsin, and that more advantageous opening had
made it possible to provide for their speedy passage.
Martin removed immediately to La Crosse and entered upon his new duties, but Walborg remained
in Chicago for a time to fulfill her engagement as
well as to wait until she knew whether the arrangements made by Martin would prove permanent.

After a short interval of separation the brother
and sister were reunited in La Crosse, where Walborg found almost instanter a clerkship, even more
to her taste than that from which she had been excused. It was under such circumstances that I first
met the lady who is now my wife. Praises of her
sisterly faithfulness and care, of her womanly tact and
capacity, of her beauty, neatness, industry and gentleness, piqued my curiosty so far as to induce me to
make her acquaintance, in the many social gather-

ings which allowed of such a pleasure without the
appearance of particular attention on my part; and
for fully two years I went no further lest I might
find myself rebuffed, or still worse lest I might find
myself accepted by some Xantippe who would re-
pine over my sightless condition afterwards and
render my home-life a torture.

As my knowledge of her true worth increased,
my circumspection was yet more severely tried, because I would not by any solicitation commit Walborg to a promise to share my fortunes until I had a
reasonable certainty to submit to my fair country-
woman.   My want of success in St. Louis at the beginning of the last season, described in La Crosse,
depressed me all the more because of my hopes
and fears as to an early settlement in life, which
might be shipwrecked if the markets upon which I
had been accustomed to rely should fail. The
Weaver proposition was more readily accepted, perhaps, because under the circumstances it was pleasant as well as profitable to stay in La Crosse and
look after all my interests, and, in the greater permanency of my resources under the new arrangement
in which I had at the time the fullest confidence, I
saw no reason why I should not have a home of my
own in the best sense of the term.

I could not write a love story if I tried, and I
would not if I could, for wooing is like praying, a
sacred duty which should not be paraded before

the world. When sometimes I have heard young
people billing and cooing like turtle doves in the
presence of uninterested persons, I have been reminded of certain stores or *magazins* in Paris to
which my attention had been called, in which the
whole stock of the establishment is exhibited in the
plate-glass window; and I have been inclined to ask
whether it might not pay to place a little of the re-
dundant window-dressing upon the shelves, or in
boxes, where it could not be damaged by the garish
sunshine, and might prove valuable for future use.
My suit was accepted, with all my great drawbacks,
of the greatness of which I was not reminded by a
word nor a tone, and it only remained for us to watch
the course of events so that our venture in life
might be entered upon with the best auguries.

When the Weaver promises failed of fulfilment,
the probability of an early marriage was dimmed
almost to extinction, and the close of the river
against navigation with nearly all the industry of the
season locked up in the warehouse of my dear friend,
was as the sound of a death knell. Then came the
revival of my hopes as the chances for trade in the
smaller towns were suggested, and as the reader is
aware, my second visit to New York grew out of the
smaller enterprise. It would be mere surplusage to
reiterate the story of my journey and my success.

With the impetus of my good fortune fresh upon
me, my sales no longer depending upon a compara-

tively narrow and moneyless market, I saw no reason to postpone that happiness toward which
every human life should be directed; hence it
happened that when my palace of cards fell to the
ground through the blunders which have been detailed, I was not alone in my misfortunes. My
wife and myself did not sit down to indulge in the
expensive luxury of grief; there was too much work
to be accomplished for any such folly. Fred and
his sisters, attempting to cross the Atlantic, were
twice driven back to Queenstown, Ireland, the first
time so badly wrecked that the crew, passengers
and cargo had to be transhipped with great delay,
and the second time with the steamer in need of such
repairs as made it matter for rejoicing that their
lives were spared from the terrors of the deep, and
the voyage was not completed until six weeks from
the first departure. Thus we were entered upon married life at last, in spite of all our prevision, with
auguries such as might well have deterred us from
thinking of such a step, but we could not, and we
would not, retrace our steps for a fortune.

My first set-back in Fort Atkinson was but the
prelude to my greater success in Chicago, and my
most unprosperous ending there after a prolonged
term of money-making business did not mar my
prospects for a third start, which proved in every
sense so fortunate for me, in La Crosse. Why
should this reverse prove final? Robert the Bruce,

hunted from his kingdom a lurking fugitive, with a price upon his head, almost despairing of his power to redeem Scotland from the thrall of the Saxon, saw, as he lay on his poor pallet in an out-house, a spider engaged in its task of house-building, trying to swing by a thread of its own spinning, so that it might gain a foothold which was necessary for its work on a distant angle. Ten times the courageous creature tried and failed, but with the eleventh effort it succeeded. The lesson of perseverance was not lost, and the Bruce was bold enough to win his throne. Why, then, should I despair, with so much to encourage renewed exertion.

CHAPTER XV.

THE AFFLICTIONS OF JOB.

Closing out in La Crosse—Reasons for Leaving—Visit to Oakland—Departure for Chicago—The Great Fire—Evil Auguries Unheeded——That Awful Scene—Journey to St. Louis—Generous Treatment—Feeding the Hungry—Looking for Work—Friends Again—Mr. Dacus—Mr. Shepard—Mr. Cupples—Letters Home—St. Louis Ratteners—Six Months' Fight with Ruin—Frozen Out—Manufacturer and Mule—Broken Down at Last—Dr. Metcalf—The Ratteners' Victory—The Bitter End—The Spirit of the Association—Monopoly and Revolution.

_____

"I have been young, and now am old; yet have I not seen the righteous forsaken, nor his seed begging bread."—*Psalms xxxvii*, 25.

"Boast not thyself of to-morrow; for thou knowest not what a day may bring forth."—*Prov. xxvii*, 1.

The book of Job and the sorrows of the man of Uz rise before my mind's eye whenever I attempt to recall the events of the few years of my life immediately following my marriage, although I dare not compare myself with that ideal embodiment of patience under unmerited misfortune, and it would be unjust in the last degree to give currency to the idea that my wife deserved to rank with the most exasperating of Job's comforters.

We were married on the eighteenth day of May, 1871, and almost immediately after that event it

became apparent that every cent of my laboriously
earned capital had disappeared. Under all these
disadvantages, and pending a settlement of some
kind, we remained in business in La Crosse until
the fall of that year, working up the materials left
on hand from my once heavy stock, and striving
to reduce in a just and equitable way the load of
debt which should have been liquidated by my returns from the New York sale. I strove by solicitations, and eventually by threats of legal proceedings, to obtain concessions from the railroad companies, whose excessive charges, and the delays incident thereto, were my undoing; but, as one of
my friends remarked, there would have been a deal
more wisdom in saving my wind to cool my por-
ridge. I turned over to my creditors, in the last
resort, my house and furniture, which might have
been held against all claims, under the homestead
exemption in Wisconsin, and with a few items of
personal luggage, and the more portable articles
of household use, we prepared to leave La Crosse
without a dollar.

My friend, Mons Anderson, whose manifold kindnesses have been too scantily acknowledged, for
they were incessant, took me aside on my farewell
visit, and compelled me to acknowledge my penniless condition, as I intended to secure my passage
through to Chicago by pawning my effects until
money could be earned to redeem them. His gen-

erosity passed all bounds, but I will not wound
him by enlarging on his kindness. His words of
encouragement to my wife and myself put courage
into our hearts, which was worth more than the
money put in our pockets, or the many costly presents with which he prepared us for our next house-
keeping. It may seem strange that we should leave
the city endeared to us by so many tender associations, where friends so constant and counsellors so
faithful abounded; but the fact was, that the profits
of the broom business in that locality had fallen so
low, with so little prospect of its improvement for
at least a year, that there would have remained no
margin to pay for my labor, after providing for interest upon the borrowed capital upon which I must
proceed if my business was to be resumed. I could
have raised the capital readily enough, but my
wife concurring with me in the conclusion that we
had better begin at the foot of the ladder elsewhere,
we set out upon our travels, intending to seek our
fortunes in Chicago.

We went to Oakland on a visit to my old home
for a week, and once more had offered to us the
advantages which I had so many times personally
declined; but the reasons which weighed with me
in my younger days were incomparably more absolute now, when the responsibilities of my new condition were likely to make fresh demands on my
energy and enterprise. Our long deferred bridal

tour was somewhat sorrowful, although our friends
did all in their power to console and cheer us in
our uncertain prospects. Chicago seemed to me a
name to conjure with, but it was not easy to make
my father see it in that light, and my mother was
full of forebodings. The week came to an end at
last; the Sunday was spent in devotional exercises
in the little church in which I first found peace,
and our names and troubles were brought before the
great white throne by many loving souls who wres-
tled earnestly, as did Jacob of old with the Angel,
and if deliverance came not, we have faith to believe that it is because the ways of God are not as
our ways:

> " Not enjoyment and not sorrow is our destined end or way,
> But to live that each to-morrow finds us further than to-day."

When we arrived at the railroad depot on Monday
morning, to commence, or rather to re-commence,
our journey, the news was on everybody's lips that
Chicago was on fire; but, knowing the tendency to
exaggeration in every mind and on every tongue, I
discounted what was told me in a very liberal way.
The neighbors who had accompanied us so far
urged our return, to wait until some certainty
should be reached as to the continuance of the city
or its being litera'ly burned off the face of the
earth, but I would not listen to such suggestions,
not because a day or two just then was of any great
consequence, but rather because of my superstitious
dread about turning back.

CHICAGO FIRE. 1871.

The augurs whose business it was to foretell the
probable outcome of warlike expeditions in Rome,
by observing the flights of birds, by examining birds'
entrails, or by other means equally nonsensical,
could not look in each others' faces without laughing, so conversant were they with the absurdity of
their profession; but the fact remains notwithstanding, after eighteen hundred years of Christianizing
influence, that few men can be found who are absolutely without faith in omens. Few ship captains
will dare commence a voyage on Friday; the hardi-
est sailor turns pale at the sight of a shark following his vessel if there is any sick man on board;
the housekeeper who has upset the salt is doubtful
of the consequences unless she had the presence of
mind at the moment to throw a pinch of it over
the shoulder; and so on, through a long category of
omens in which even eminent men, such as the
first Napoleon, have been unquestioning believers.
I had not the heart to turn back at the beginning
of my journey, and I did not doubt that we should
find the conflagration extinguished by the time of
our arrival in the burning metropolis.

That idea was short-lived. Before we had passed
Milton Junction the news had been flashed over the
lines with awful particularity, how the fire, which
had been raging a very tempest of flame for more
than sixteen hours, had broken out, no one could
tell how nor where with any certainty, just as the

people were going home from church, and up to
that moment had defied all efforts to arrest its progress.   The wind, fresh at the beginning of that
cyclone of destruction, had grown stronger as the
tongues of flame leapt into the air, until the heart
of the doomed city glowed like a furnace.   The
water-works had been burned, so that there were
hardly any means available to fight the devouring
element, and flames floating in the atmosphere had
fallen upon buildings supposed to be fire-proof,
shriveling them as an ordinary fire might consume
paper.   There was no longer any room for doubt as
to the terrible reality, and in the presence of a calamity unparalleled in the world's history there was
no margin for exaggeration.   It was too evident
that we could find no home in Chicago, but we
must go on, as almost our last dollar had been expended in transportation to that point, and what to
do we knew not.

At every station now, men who had escaped from
the flaming dwellings and stores of the metropolis,
came on the cars to tell of the fearful sights they
had seen, of robbers plying their vocation in open
day, deaf to expostulations and entreaty; of men
narrowly escaping with their lives from stores in
which they had built up fortunes, remembering of
a sudden that they had left their valuables within
easy reach in the burning pile, and returning back
again into the jaws of death, to be seen no more

until the last trump shall sound; of men working hard against the flames, without food, nearly all night, drinking whisky as though it were water and finding no evil consequence in the awful excitement of the time; of others partaking freely of liquors broached in the streets, reeling into cellars and basements in their intoxication, and being found hours afterward, burned into cinders.

The stories which reached us became horrifying, and many passengers left the cars at intermediate stations, but there was no such option for us; and inasmuch as we did not choose to tell the simple but humiliating reason for stolidly pursuing our way, the strange obstinacy of the blind man and his wife rushing on, regardless of warning,

> "Into the jaws of death,
> Into the gates of hell,"

became a theme of common conversation.

The burning of Chicago was for us a calamity almost as great as that suffered by the hundreds of thousands burned out of house and home. The home on which we had counted in our extremity was swept from us, and we had no abiding city nor association, but were hastening on as fast as steam could carry us, into a city where one-half of the people were homeless and without bread. I felt hot tear-drops fall on my hand when we drew near our destination, and I knew that my poor wife realized

the despair of her blind leader. I was worked up
to desperation by her silent agony, and I resolved
that I would tell my story in brief to the first man
that accosted me manifesting a willingness to converse. It was not long before an opportunitiy occurred: a passenger taking Chicago on his way to
St. Louis, Missouri, moved perhaps by our discon-
solate appearance, asked if our home had been in
Chicago.

True to my purpose, I told him all that was necessary to enable him to grasp our situation without,
however, revealing to him fully our impoverished
condition, lest he might think us mendicants. He
gave us his counsel readily, and in few words:
"Go to St. Louis; the people are notional and narrow, but they are hospitable, and you will surely
find employment." That sentence determined me,
and from that moment St. Louis was my destination. I knew many merchants with whom I had
transacted business in that city, and once there I
could earn a home for us both.

The difficulties of transhipment were easily overcome, thanks to my newly-made friend, but the cost
of our passage was a problem of which I could not
guess the solution. We had in our pocketbook
enough money to pay for shelter and a meal, but
we were hurried off so rapidly that no thought of
refreshment was to be entertained until it was too
late to make inquiries. Excitement around us on

every hand was momentarily increasing; some men,
probably thieves, but suspected of being incendi-
aries, were said to have been hanged, and it was
argued that the fire would be renewed in every
quarter until vigilance committees took up the task
of self-defense by putting all suspicious characters
to death. The air was hot and stifling; one seemed
to breathe cinders and pulverized ashes. A man on
the cars said that cinders still hot from the consuming city had fallen on the Crib, two miles out
on the lake. Another asserted that in the very
worst portions of the fire the atmosphere itself had
become inflammable. The flames had defeated all
calculations, had sailed, as one man said, right in
the wind's eye, little less rapidly than where there
were favoring breezes, except in those localities
where the strength of the gale enabled the gusts of
flame to convert stone itself into fuel. Chicago, as
far as the eye could reach, showed nothing but
lines of blackened ruins, except in places where the
flames still raged.

It must be remembered that I was no longer utterly
blind; my wife was with me. The west side of
the city, where the blaze first arose, had sustained
much damage, but a part of that section had escaped
the fatal tongue of the destroyer. The bridges had
some of them been utterly burned, and all of them
more or less damaged within the radius of the conflagration; the tunnels even had not escaped. The

flames leaping from that side, had cleared the river
at a bound, sweeping the south side and the north
side into a lurid dream. So rapid had been the
march of the destroyer, that whole families fled
from their gorgeous dwellings, leaving furniture,
pictures, carpets, and all the insignia of wealth, to
feed the flames, without an effort to save them,
and coming back a few hours later, were unable
to recognize the sites of their own dwellings, so
complete had been the action of that whirlwind of
fire. Furniture saved from innumerable homes, and
piled up in the open squares remote from habita-
tions, took fire there and burned to ashes. Men
driving horses with wagon-loads of furniture and
goods, through the streets, were consumed, with all
that they were struggling to save.

It was a scene to shudder over, and it seemed as
though thousands in escaping from the flames must
inevitably perish of starvation. It did not appear
possible that a city so young and so completely
ravaged, just on the verge of winter, would rise
again from its ashes with such expedition as to
afford employment, during the inclement season
then imminent, to every builder in its own population, and to draw thousands of artificers from the sur-
roundnig country. Could we have only seen the
future but a few months ahead, perhaps our course
might have been changed, but no man knows what
a day may bring forth, and that provision has been

wisely ordered. That there was no danger of immediate famine we soon had convincing proof; but
who could imagine that a scene of destruction without parallel in the modern nations, would be followed by a display of recuperative energy almost
sublime, as soon as the ruins became cold eoungh
to permit the work to begin? In the midst of
our distress we found cause for thankfulness that
we had paid our visit to Oakland, but for which
we might have been not only homeless, but also
without clothes or furniture, out upon the prairies
or by the lake front, with thousands besides,
praying for rain. With thoughts innumerable and
anxieties absolutely sickening, we were trying not
so much to pierce the future as to deal with the
immediate need, a passage to St. Louis. The
French have expressed the helplessness of mankind
in their maxim, "*L'homme propose et Dieu dispose*" and
we proved its truth in our case most happily. Man
proposed and God disposed, most assuredly. The
railroad companies gave free transit to every person desiring such aid to fly from the city of flame,
and the cars were crowded with just such eager
throngs as we may imagine seeking safety by flight
when a sin-defiled universe shall realize the wrath
to come.

We were off on our way to St. Louis, and at
every station the fugitives from the fire were importuned by good Samaritans to eat and drink of

the choicest viands they could offer. Never was
there such an outpouring of generosity upon the
earth as that which ministered to the Chicago
sufferers in the era upon which we had now entered.
No man could despair of a world in which such loving kindness was possible. The Living Redeemer was
on the earth in the spirit which said, "A new commandment I give unto you, that ye love one another." The scanty means which were intended to
provide for our first wants in Chicago remained
still in our possession to answer a like purpose in
St. Louis. Provisions of all kinds were heaped up
with prodigal profusion in every car, and still at
every station we found sweet-voiced messengers
of mercy waiting with baskets and hampers laden
with fresh supplies, which they could not be persuaded to believe were unnecessary. Thus it continued all through the journey, and, but that I fear
my narrative might grow tiresome, a thousand and
one instances of special kindness and consideration for my dear wife and her blind partner might
be told as incidents of that singular time.

Arrived in St. Louis, there was enough provision
left in our car to have loaded a wagon, and I was told
that the whole train of cars was just as bountifully
provided. Some of the passengers were about to
select from the store of good things enough to carry
them over the next few days, while they might be
out of employment, but they desisted when word

was passed that all the principal hotels in the city were open free to Chicago sufferers. We were carried to the Planters' House, an admirable hotel, made welcome as princes, and when we tendered payment next morning assured that no money would be taken from us if we stayed a week, or until we could employ ourselves in the city. Such benevolence was sacred, but it must not be imposed upon, so we found other quarters that forenoon, and I sallied out to discover what were my chances in the way of work.

I was unable to hire myself out as a workman, although I wanted piece-work only, and was willing to forego my claims to remuneration if brooms were not properly turned out of hand. As a fugitive from Chicago, I could have been lodged, fed and clothed with pleasure; but as a blind man seeking employment there was apparently no opening in St. Louis. My only chance was to start a shop in the city, and commence the manufacture of brooms on my own account, and that was no chance at all, because no premises were obtainable without paying one month's rent in advance, and they might as well have demanded from me the moon and the seven stars as a deposit. Besides, even supposing that the sweet influences of Pleiades should procure me a workshop and a home, without money I should still have been powerless, being no longer possessed of the tools and machinery for my factory, which had been surrendered with my homestead and all its belongings at La Crosse.

A gentleman employed on the St. Louis *Republican* as a reporter, Mr. Dacus, became aware of my quandary, and, but that his means were no longer equal to the generous impulses which as a planter in better days he had nobly indulged, my difficulties would have been of brief duration. We were for a time a committee of ways and means, and I feared that our deliberations would be permanent, so small were the likelihoods of any profitable outcome; but Mr. Dacus, whose character was justly esteemed by his old friends, many of whom were wealthy, entertained different ideas. Mr. Dacus introduced us to an old associate of his, with whom he had spent months and years of joyous companionship before the war, when both were much richer; and Mr. Shepard advanced seventy-five dollars to enable us to secure premises and materials with the use of machinery; and when after a very few days he found me busily at work, he supplemented his first kindness by increasing the loan to two hundred and twenty-five dollars.

I was now fairly started on what seemed to be a prosperous career. With my sample brooms in hand, I went to the largest dealer in that line in St. Louis, Mr. Cupples, a merchant confining his attention mainly to willow and wooden ware, and he encouraged me with an order for one hundred dozen brooms per week. There was a service of praise and prayer in our little home that night, for, although we were working for small prices, there was a margin of two shillings per dozen after covering all expenses, and our home for the winter would be assured. Mr. Cupples was very kind to us in many ways, and came to be reckoned among our friends. Four pairs of hands in addition to my own were employed in the little factory within a few days, and before the first month came to a close there were six men earning good wages in my shop. There was good news to send to Oakland and La Crosse, and we were overjoyed at being able to write home.

All this time we were blissfully unaware that there was an inhospitable element in St. Louis life, which looked with cruel eyes upon our endeavors, and had determined to drive us out of the city. In the old cities of Europe there are guilds and corporations which rule with almost arbitrary power in all matters touching employment in the handicraft which they severally represent, and their powers used to be still more absolute than they are now. Some such combination has been established among the master broom-makers in St. Louis, with a capital which I have been told aggregates more than one million dollars, and the purpose of that organization was to prevent any new comer from running a factory there on any terms.

English "Ratteners" in Sheffield and elsewhere
had been known to warn away men who were striving to support their families by honest labor, outside the pale of the illegal combination, and, failing compliance with their tyrannical orders, the
"Ratteners" would throw deadly explosives down
cottage chimneys into the fires in the rooms where
the doomed men and their wives and little ones sat at
their meals; they had in numberless instances mixed
powder with the fuel which such workmen must
use, so that in the exercise of their needful industry
they met death; in ways too numerous to be
specified the "Ratteners" had compassed the ruin
of their victims; but surely such tyrannous proceedings in England, under coalitions disowned by
the law, and based on the ignorance, prejudices
and fears of workmen, could find no parallel in enlightened, liberty-loving America.

It was not long before I learned that "Rattening" is not confined to England, and if my perse-
cutors did not resort to such means as have been
used by the Molly Maguires in Pennsylvainia, or
the followers of the miscreant Brodhead in Sheffield, it is because the command of unlimited capital enables them to work the ruin upon which they
resolve, without damaging their status as master
manufacturers. I had been at work a little more
than a month, and, cheered by my moderate success, had purchased the tools and machinery which

at first had been only rented, when, the very day
after we had written home to tell of the progress
that had been made, I was waited upon in my little workshop by three well dressed, gentlemanly
appearing men, who told me they were a committee
appointed by the Broom-maker's Association to
inform me that I must quit the business on which I
had entered or leave St. Louis.

I tried in vain to argue my claim against the demands of the autocratic Association; as the committee had not been delegated to reason on the matter, it was their simple duty to say to me that if I
would go at once, making no fuss, they were au-
thorized to pay me the actual cost of my materials
and machinery; but in the event of my declining
that proposition, or even delaying acceptance, they
would run me out without one cent to buy a crust.
I pleaded with them to give us until spring so
that we might not be driven out penniless to face
the winter, offering them any guaranty in my power
that I would quit St. Louis then to return no more.
The eloquence of St. Paul, which moved the men
of Athens beyond the depths of Greek philosophy,
would have been powerless against that pitiless Association, and it only remained for me to try
whether my unceasing labor and the prayer for daily
bread might not avail in that high court of heaven,
which the malice and corruption of mankind cannot
warp nor circumvent.

That interview took place on Monday, and when the week drew on to Saturday without any overt act of antagonism, I began to hope that the Association was not so flinty-hearted as its representative committee would have me believe. My representations and deferred submission had worked some change in their ruinous programme; although I had scrupulously avoided any reference to my personal defect, it was possible that my sightless eyes had pleaded for me beyond the power of language, and although they would not in so many words consent to my invasion of their usurped domain, they had concluded to leave me alone severely for the winter.

My hopes interested and cheered me until Saturday, and then the completeness of my isolation became manifest. I was indeed to be left severely alone, but it was to be alone without a paying customer for my manufactures. Until that day my patron had sent his wagon every Saturday to fetch the quantity of brooms that had been contracted for as the weekly supply, and to save expressage was quite an important item when only twenty-five cents remained to me on every dozen brooms. That Saturday the wagon failed to visit my workshop, and after exhausting my ingenuity to account for that fact on any other theory than the dreaded one that Mr. Cupples did not want my brooms, I went to his establishment to ascertain the cause of the delay. I left his store that day with my brain loaded and throbbing under defeat; my enemies had triumphed. Naboth's vineyard had been carried by storm.

The Association, knowing that Mr. Cupples was my only customer, had engaged to supply him with all the brooms he would require at two shillings per dozen less than he had been paying me, and in consequence I was left out in the cold. Out of consideration for me, as I had depended upon his money to pay my workmen and other imperative demands, he consented to take from me the quantiity made that week at the Association price, so that I had worked all the week for nothing, and I was left alone with my despair. One week only had passed since we wrote home the glad tidings that we had commenced once more to climb the ladder of fortune, and before our modest congratulations had reached their destination our hopes had burst like a bubble.

The Sabbath, usually a blessed season in our little household, was a lenten feast that day. Spite of ourselves, the blackness of our environment domineered over our faith, and it was not possible either to dismiss the subject from our thoughts or to discover any practical outlet from our distressful condition. It was too late now to accept the terms offered by the committee in the beginning of the past week; the war had been entered upon, and was already ended, at our cost. But even assuming that there was a *locus penitentiæ*, and that we might capitulate, *sans phrase*, it would leave us homeless, without tools or materials, and without the means to remove ourselves to another city, where such another combination might permit us to remain. Every cent that the cruel Association offered in the first place would be necessary to satisfy our friendly creditors, and there were reasons of an urgent kind why my wife should have had peace and cheerfulness in her home that winter.

If there had been any other industry to which I could have turned, my course would have been clearly defined, but no such option was mine. The winter was a season of dread to me, and the resignation with which my wife met every fresh reverse was an additional reproach to my impatience under misfortune and injustice.

We could find no guidance under our troubles that would take us out of the battle, so we determined to continue the struggle, however unequal might be the forces engaged. My chances were gone completely, so far as the wholesale dealers were concerned, as the Association would not scruple to supply them all at a loss rather than permit me to gain a point; but there were many small traders scattered all over the city and suburbs who might be induced to buy their small parcels from

MANUFACTURER AND MULE.

me if my strength was equal to the task of distrib-
uting my wares without a conveyance of any kind,
after spending the major part of my time every
week in their manufacture. The small dealers
showed me innumerable kindnesses when I made
my rounds among them, but carrying three or four
dozen brooms on every journey at the outset was
a strain upon vital energies, never truly robust,
which could have but one ending. Month by
month that weary winter passed away, and the
same number of brooms seemed heavier every time
I started. One day, when I should have gone the
rounds as usual, a kind of vertigo seized me, and
I fell to the ground, as weak as a child.

It was now warm weather once more, and my continuous labor, never less than fifteen hours per day,
under loads, sometimes, that would have tried the
strength of a mule, had told on my constitution
just as might have been expected. For five weeks
I was unable to move from my bed, and Dr. Metcalf, the gentleman to whom I am indebted for
medical attendance, one of the leading men in the
profession in St. Louis, was astonished to find my
system rallying so soon. For some time before I
was actually prostrated, the doctor had noticed the
inroads of fatigue and disease upon me, and, out
of the largeness of his heart, had called repeatedly
at the workshop, ostensibly to observe me at my
work, and witness my processes of manipulation, but

really because he looked for a much more serious fit of sickness to supervene much earlier.

Helpless upon my bed for five weeks, I pondered, feebly at first, and later with more energy, the many problems of life which had been suggested by my own career; but all my speculations ended, somehow, every time in the practical question, "How could preparation be made for the new life that must soon be added to our household?" Clearly we could do nothing in St. Louis, enfeebled, as we were, by overwork and anxiety. Dr. Metcalf said, "Go North; it is your only chance. A summer here will kill you." The battle had been fought to its bitter end, and the Association had badly beaten the blind broom-maker. Perhaps in my extremity, and seeing the end of their machinations, the conquerors would treat their fallen foe with magnanimity. Thiers and some of his colleagues entertained some such hope as to Bismarck, when beleaguered and starving Paris was compelled to ask for terms of capitulation. Comparing small things with great, there were some elements of similarity in the two cases. The conquerors, small as well as great, were alike merciless. The wolf might as well have been asked to show compassion to Red Riding Hood.

Reduced almost to a skeleton, with hardly strength enough to crawl, I went to the men who had caused my misfortunes and asked them to close me out on their own terms. With much solicitation on my

part they consented to do so, on conditions which
left me nothing for my labor as broom-maker and
as mule, for the three months preceding my fit of
sickness, and, poor as we were when we stayed
our first night in the Planters' House, we were
wealthy at that time by comparison with the dire
poverty into which we were plunged when we engaged our passage on the steamboat to Prairie du
Chien, giving our furniture as security for ultimate
payment. We were in an incomparably worse
case than we had been in October, 1871, when we
landed in St. Louis from the smoke and lurid din
of the Chicago fire. Then we had money in our
pockets enough to pay for food and shelter, and our
effects, few though they were, were unincumbered;
but above all that and far beyond it in genuine
importance, my health and strength were unimpaired, so that any task seemed possible. Carrying a stiff upper lip, which had been my prescrip-
tion in many troubles, was almost too great a strain
on my emaciated body; and but for the necessity
which my wife realized to sustain me with her
courage, I believe she would have broken down
altogether, while we were saying good-by to our
few friends, almost as poor as ourselves.

I don't know whether the "Ratteners" maintain
their Broom Association still in St. Louis, but I
suppose they do, and I hope most sincerely that
this chapter passing under their notice may awaken

in their minds a salutary compunction for their abhorrent practices, which involved in the spirit of
their action both robbery and murder. *Shylock* uttered an unquestionable truth when, pleading for
restitution of his escheated fortune, he said to the
court, which had been won by the beauty, eloquence and wit of *Portia*:

> "You take my house when you do take the prop
> That doth sustain my house ; you take my life
> When you do take the means whereby I live."

"Rattening" antagonizes the free institutions under which life, liberty and the pursuit of happiness
are recognized as the inalienable rights of every
human being, and there should be some way of
bringing conspirators to justice when they say to
any man by word and deed, "we will compel you
to abandon your pursuit of a livelihood, or we will
worry you into the grave." Monopolies are hateful in every land, but they are specially detesta-
ble in the home of liberty. Striking through the
lives of men like myself, they aim at the spoliation
of the community by rendering honest and legiti-
mate competition impossible. The immediate means
used for my removal was a reduction in price below living rates, but in the natural order of things,
as soon as they had destroyed my feeble chance,
they taxed the public by advancing their prices until they had obtained full satisfaction for the temporary abatement.

In England in the days of the great Queen Elizabeth the Londoners mobbed her majesty's carriage on her way to Parliament because she had granted monopolies which were oppressive to the people. In Paris during the revolution of 1789, which began with the pinch of hunger and bread riots, the sufferers in the streets, failing satisfaction through their remonstrances, hanged and beheaded monopolists and tyrants as warnings to others of their class. "Let the people eat grass," said one of the horde of monopolists who had amassed enormous wealth by handling the taxes, squeezing from the people a hundred dollars to give twenty to the treasury; and his brutal saying was borne in mind by the desperate populace until the day of vengeance arrived. They had literally fed their families and themselves upon nettles and weeds as long as a green thing could be gathered, their oppressors meantime outraging the decencies of life by ostentatious extravagance, and when famine, bursting all bounds, drove them *sans culottes* from attics, cellars and hovels, out into the streets to seek revenge, they slaughtered their profane reviler as he was trying to escape from the city, and made his head a football having first filled his mouth with grass.

Monopolists will not have it always their own way in this country. It is sublime to suffer and be strong, but the strength must earlier or later mean demolition of the cause of suffering, if men are true

18

to their nature and their responsibilities. Humanity has duties which are inconsistent with the endurance of tyranny beyond limits, which are happily narrowing every day, and it is well for the race, for our children, and for theirs in the near future, if not for us, that society will not permit the continuance of the spectacle of

" Truth forever on the scaffold, Wrong forever on the throne."

CHAPTER XVI.

RETURNED TO OAKLAND.

Friends in Wisconsin—O. S. Loo—Sickness in Family—Ambrose Hall—Sun Stroke—Mr. Stewart's Treatment—The Sernsons—Removed to Fort Atkinson—Traveling Again—Second Sun Stroke—Again on the Road—Sun Stroke No. 3—Fortune Telling—Deceiver Deceived—Dr. Dee's Purse.

"Let not him that girdeth on his harness boast himself as he that putteth it off."—I. Kings, xx., 11.

"Canst thou bind the sweet influences of Pleiades, or loose the bands of Orion?"—Job xxxviii, 31.

Arrived at Prairie du Chien, my furniture remained in the hands of the steamboat company until it could be redeemed, and we took the cars for Edgerton ourselves, C. O. D. In that little town there were many friends upon whose intervention we could reckon with certainty and our confidence was justified. We were conveyed to Oakland; but, conscious of the very poor figure that we must cut on the farm if we went there after so many times declining the shelter that was proffered, I determined to rent a little cottage of which I knew, and to keep expenses at a minimum unitl I could recuperate. My friend, O. S. Loo, whose name I have several times been on the point of mentioning earlier in this little volume, sent the money to Prairie du

Chien, and my furniture was soon afterward brought by return wagons from Edgerton. There is no man living who has had more cause to be thankful for friends than myself; they have been raised up on every hand—not in the sunshine, where friends are supposed to abound, but in the very blackness of the storm. It is a satisfaction to myself to record their names occasionally, but usually, when an injury has been inflicted on me, I leave the names of the unfriends unwritten.

My strength did not come very rapidly, although every thing that could be done for me was accomplished by my friends, many of whom might have said, with Job, "I was eyes to the blind, and feet was I to the lame." Three weeks after we entered on cottage life, our first boy was born, in June 1872, but his troubled career ended in a few days— the natural result of his mother's terrible anxieties and sufferings. Over-exerting herself in that fearful time, struggling beyond her strength to save the boy, my wife fell sick, and for fully six months it seemed impossible that she could ever rally. For all that time it was impossible for me to earn one cent; my attendance in the sick chamber was an imperative duty, although my mother gave all the attention in her power, and our nearest neighbors, Mr. Ambrose Hall and his wife and family, never slighted an appeal.

Among tried friends as we were, the monetary

trouble was the smallest item in our calculation, as
when my powers were renewed, I could soon erase
every pecuniary obligation; but during that time
of affliction, it was an awful tax upon our strength
and patience to travel six miles to the nearest
drug store, and nine miles to the railroad station.
One day in July, the weather being fearfully warm,
my wife suffered a relapse, about midday, when
none of the neighbors nor their teams were on hand,
and I started for the drugstore afoot, running when
my lungs and my limbs would permit, and then
falling into a rapid walk, to rest and prepare for
another burst of speed. I had traveled the road so
often that I knew every foot of the way, and my
ears would warn me of the approach of a vehicle.
It was not like wandering around in a city, where
sidewalks yawn for our destruction; there were no
unusual excavations nor obstructions to be dreaded.

I remember reaching the drugstore, a distance of
six miles, in little more than an hour, and I hoped
to return in about ninety minutes, as I wanted to
husband my energies. There was no chance for a
lift on the road, and the sun was beating down upon me as I hastened on, until I lost consciousness
completely, and for four hours, as nearly as I can
estimate I must have lain there on the hot road,
hatless, for my head covering rolled away as I fell,
and, when I tried to move after my swoon, my
limbs and body were powerless and cold as ice.

With the return of consciousness I slowly realized
the situation. The first thought was the object of
my journey, the medicine, and, to my joy, the tiny
parcel was clutched in the palm of my hand. Ex-
ercising all my will power, which used to be considerable, I managed to rise to my hands and knees,
and felt around for some landmark that would tell
me where I was, and what direction I must pursue
to reach home. In that search I found my hat,
and, with much difficulty, succeeded in replacing
it on my head.

When means were at last discovered to determine
the locality in which I had fallen, I ascertained
that I was more than two miles from home, and
half a mile from the nearest house. That struggle
to reach Mr. Stewart's dwelling was the most agonizing effort of my life. With tremendous exertion
I could crawl only a few yards without pausing to
rest, and twice, when I tried to push on regardless of the sense of weariness, I fell, and remained
prone on the earth for many minutes. Antæus like,
I found myself strengthened by contact with mother
earth, but my absorbing dread was another loss of
consciousness, which might extend into the night,
and in the darkness some wagon returning from
Edgerton might end my life. Fully two hours of
intermittent effort, all that my enfeebled condition
could accomplish, were consumed in crawling to
Mr. Stewart's door, and then I had not the vigor to

summon assistance by knocking until after several minutes' rest. Luckily for me, Mr. Stewart had seen many cases of sunstroke, and he proceeded, *secundem artem.*

Before anything was done for me personally, a messenger was dispatched to Ambrose Hall's cottage with the requisite medicine for my wife, and then I resigned myself to treatment. I drank whiskey, glass after glass, thinking it only water, but the icy coldness was not broken for nearly half an hour. Then a profuse perspiration followed, and I was comforted with the assurance that the worst had passed. Far on in the evening I was conveyed home in Mr. Stewart's buggy, and there were two invalids in the house, neither capable of properly assisting the other.

I was not absolutely prostrated, as I had been after my attack of vertigo in St. Louis, but I was almost powerless for several days, and sleepless nights became the rule for months. There was a feeling of dullness in my head more intolerable than occasional acute pains, and from the time of my first sunstroke until this hour there has ceased to be that elasticity in my nerve fiber of which I had been more and less conscious until that attack. Disasters then ceased to follow us for a time; the neighbors divided the responsibility of caring for us until I could be about as usual. The Sernsons, the Halls, Mr. Loo and other neighbors near at hand, never omitted an opportunity to make us feel that we were among friends whose tender regards never ceased.

In November, 1872, my health was sufficiently established to permit of my starting business afresh, and although my wife was not strong, her condition admitted of removal from Oakland. We found suitable premises readily in Fort Atkinson, and, materials for broom making being abundant, our indebtedness of two hundred and fifty dollars was but a bagatelle. People to whom we owed small sums brought broom-corn to be made up, and with the sounds of the old industry once more filling our home my strength increased apace, although the rule of eight hours' labor, eight hours' recreation, and eight hours' rest had to be lost sight of. We could purchase all the materials we wanted on time, and some of the farmers employed me to manufacture on shares, so that, until the whole of the broom-corn within reach had been made up and sold, we thought ourselves in clover. By that time we were nearly out of debt, and we had a good reputation for making and handling first-class brooms, which made it easy to make arrangements with the proprietors of a large factory in Milwaukee to sell their brooms on commission. I had the pick of their stock all the time, and, having a prudent regard for the value of my name, I would not sell an inferior article.

My earnings were sufficiently liberal to leave a margin after all our little liabilities had been paid, for my wife was an excellent manager, knowing exactly how to make every dollar do its best. In the summer of 1873 I was again smitten down by sunstroke, and was sick until the fall of that year, consuming all my wife's savings, but that year we kept clear of debt. As soon as my strength returned, my old employers were glad to have me resume my sales, so I was once more on the road in the fall of 1873, continuing my sales with much profit until the following summer.

A third sunstroke in 1874 warned me by its increased severity that I could not travel during the heated term; and I have been told that but for a blood-vessel having burst in my brain, that third prostration under *coup de soleil* must have proved fatal. The hemorrhage from my nose and ears was copious and long continued, and the marvelous stories that were told me as to the amount of the discharge can only be accounted for on the principle that persons who are unaccustomed to the sight of blood lose their wits in its presence, and unconsciously fall into habits of exaggeration. By the fall of the year, as usual, my health was renewed, and my sales went on briskly, because nearly all over my district the storekeepers and merchants, knowing my ways and the times at which I might be looked for, kept their orders open until my visit.

That winter a very curious incident transpired in the town or city of Rockford, which was one of the places where I could always reckon on good orders. I was sitting down to dinner, when I became conscious that a person sitting opposite me on the other side of the table was regarding me with a fixed stare. It would be impossible for me to say why it is so, but I can always tell when I am being stared at, although no word may be said. From remarks made by others I knew that the person staring at me was of the other sex, and from my own sensation I knew well that she scarcely removed her gaze from me during the time we sat at the table. I was so old as to have outgrown boyish vanities, or I might have been foolish enough to imagine this a case of "inadvertent fascination," such as old *Tony Weller*, the father of *Samivel*, delighted to expatiate upon, when cautioning his son to beware of a widow. My diagnosis of the case was that the lady did not think me absolutely blind, and was trying to settle to her own satisfaction why I pretended blindness, and how the deception was maintained. My colored spectacles cover that portion of my face so entirely that I am not surprised when people assume that my defect of vision is only partial.

As soon as I rose from table and went into the office, I asked mine host who was the lady who sat opposite me at dinner, and what was her occupation. She was a fashionable fortune teller who made her rounds regularly at certain seasons of the year, to enlighten a very numerous class in every community as to the past and future. It was of course very natural for her to believe every man an imposter or an ass or an amalgam of the qualitiies of both, which might be used with advantage. No wonder she wanted to decipher my disguise and my reasons for resorting to deception. Talleyrand, the diplomatist par excellence, cut away the underpinning from an adept in the arts of diplomacy by frankly telling him the points he wished to gain in the business on which they were engaged. Human life abounds in evidence of the truth which Butler asserted in Hudibras:

> " Doubtless the pleasure is as great
> In being cheated as to cheat."

Having ascertained who and what the lady was, my interest in the matter died out. She was a well known professional, her name was quite familiar, her facilities in telling the secrets of the past and unrolling the mysterious scroll of the future had often been instanced in my hearing, and it was perhaps an honor to be stared at by one who had made so many stare. Changing the subject, I asked the landlord if there was any boy around that would earn a quarter by leading me to the postoffice and back during my stay. There was a boy then in the office, the son of the fortune teller, he said, who would do all that I wished in that way for less money, as his time hung heavy on his hands.

As we walked toward the office where I went for my letters, the boy told me all the story of his life, and it was a tale that might have been converted into gold in one of our periodicals. His father, a man in high repute in Auburn, New York, had been dead six years, and the bewitching widow, caught by the shows and pretenses of a dashing disciple of Count Cagliostro, who spent money with a lavish hand, bestowed upon him her affections, her hand, and what he cared most for, perhaps, her fortune. The stepfather was not nearly so kind to the boy as the lover had been, and the mother was gradually estranged from the truant husband on that account. His main dependence was fortune-telling by interpreting dreams, by cards, by palmistry; indeed, he was an adept in all the tricks of divination, and by the time her money had disappeared almost entirely, she had descended to his level in morals, or so nearly that she had no compunction about embracing the profession, while cutting adrift from the professor.

The boy said but a few words, and had no idea that in doing so he revealed the mystery of his mother's career, but two or three names and incidents supplied all the links that were necessary to fit it with a budget of facts that had fallen in my way some months before, and the whole chain of causation

TELLING THE FORTUNE TELLER'S FORTUNE.

was made clear. The stepfather was then in California, coining money in a leading theater, as a Wizard of the East, or of some other cardinal point, but spending it just as rapidly as it came, while the wife won a liberal competency by manipulating one branch of his many tricks. The boy did not want his mother to know that he employed his leisure in my service, and for my part it was in the last degree unlikely that I should ever exchange words with that lady.

At the postoffice, having taken good heed as to my course, so that I could return unattended from that point, aud having a few business calls to make, I relieved the boy from duty, and was soon doing a land-office business in brooms, which was only concluded in time for supper. At supper I was conscious of the same fixed regard as had been experienced at the dinner table, but not quite so persistent; and when I was on my way to my room soon afterward I was met at the head of the stairs by the fair necromancer, who wished to know if I had no curiosity as to the future. Intending only to play the game of bluff, I replied that I knew quite as much about the past and future as she did. That answer impressed Madame ―――― with the idea that I was in the same profession, and she suggested a conference, in which we should each tell the other the past and the future. Seeing at a glance how excellent was my opportunity, I assented to the proposal, and when she politely offered me precedence I went through a mummery of incantation extemporized for that occasion only, as they say in the theaters, regardless of expense, and then went on to tell her in brief, and in a fragmentary way, her maiden name, her first husband's name, the name she then should bear by virtue of her second marriage, the fortune she had allowed to be squandered, and some other items which she thought nobody could recount unless inspired by Mephistopheles himself.

The woman practiced in the arts of deception was utterly deceived by my ruse, and when I challenged her to show her skill in my case by a similar revelation, she fairly wilted. I could not reveal my source of inspiration without compromising the boy which of course was out of the question. So my skill as a mind-reader, or diviner, was established at a bound. I was urged by the successful fortune-teller to join her in the profession, with a guarantee of twenty dollars per day, but of course I declined to obtain money under false pretenses, and besides there was no certainty that I could always find the right boy to pump me full of the facts to meet the case immediately before the dupes came to be manipulated.

The fortune teller in the nineteenth century is just as full of superstition and ignorance as was his predecessor three centuries ago, and is, therefore

just as easily sold. The notorious Dr. Dee, alche-
mist and astrologer in the reign of good Queen Bess,
when Virginia was first named by Sir Walter Raleigh,
had the temerity to send to the queen an old copper
warming-pan, from which a piece had been cut, and
a piece of gold corresponding with the excision, as a
proof that he had transmuted copper into the more
precious metal. The wary daughter of Henry VIII.
and Anne Boleyn appropriated the gold for all that
it was worth; but, when Dee asked a reward for his
discovery, she sent him an empty purse, with the
message that a man who could change all the metals
into gold wanted nothing from his sovereign but a
purse in which to carry his wealth. Dee drew from
the wealthier classes in Europe enormous sums of
money by exhibiting a black crystal, probably a
piece of cannel coal, well rounded and polished, in
which he pretended to read all things that ever
had been or ever should be, for every victim that
was willing to pay for the imposition; and at last
the hoary-headed fraud became so completely a believer in that piece of coal and its pretended revela-
tions, that, under the management of a scoundrel col-
league of his, he was induced to part with his house,
his money, and his young wife, to his villainous partner, and so ended his days in absolute want.

I don't say there is no power in incantations, and
there never has been, because the story of the
Witch of Endor calling up Samuel at the demand of

Saul rises before me; but I must say, for my own part, that Madame ——, the fortune-teller, who was so easily fooled by my clumsy pretense at divining, was as good a witch as any that I have seen.

It is not easy to understand why ladies well educated and refined, conversant with ancient lore and modern science, and accustomed, in their daily intercourse, to discriminate against ignorance and vain pretenses, should be able and willing to listen with patience—not to say pleasure—to the charlatanry of the common fortune-teller, who is, for the most part, an ignoramus as well as a fraud. During the remainder of my stay in Rockford I was treated with marked respect by Madame ——, as a being possessed of supernatural gifts; and when, at the time of my leaving for fresh woods and pastures new, I finally declined the offer to enter on fortune-telling as a profession, I was urgently requested to retain her address in my pocketbook, so that if I ever changed my mind in that particular she might be allowed the opportunity to bring me out, for our mutual advantage.

WALDEMAR OBER.   LILY. THERESA.
MYRTLE ELMA.   CYRUS MELANCTHON.

CHAPTER XVII.

HARMONY.

Falling Through Sidewalk—Yankee Notion Wagon—Town Life —Among the Grangers—Primary and Caucus—Duties and Rights— Organs and Pianos—At Home with My Family—Amusements— Battle Creek Joy—Smith's Coat—Professor Griff..a—Society Blunders—Music Hath Charms.

In the spring of 1875 it was my misfortune to fall through an unguarded opening in a sidewalk, and the awkwardness of my descent dislocated my ankle, absolutely wrenching it, so that I suffered excruciating pain, and was disabled from following my avocation until far on in the fall. Even then my ankle was so weak that walking was a slow and painful process, and much to my sorrow, I was forced to abandon the occupation of traveling agent for the Milwaukee factory. To provide a conveyance and driver in every town I visited would have swallowed all my margins, and of course the occupation was useless to me if it would not supply bread for my family.

The word family reminds me to mention that our little girl was born in November, 1875; and, inasmuch as she was a very feeble child, the doctor in attendance upon my wife recommended our removal

19

into the country, as the less salubrious air of the town in which we lived gave little chance of her survival.

Just at that time it became necessary to find a new occupation, and, upon our removal from Milwaukee, I purchased a Yankee-notion wagon, with which I could have prospered very well indeed if my capital had been large enough to meet the wants of my customers. My life was very pleasantly passed, and the work was not actually laborious. I could lay out my day's work with tolerable certainty, and soon knew nearly all the people on my route with some degree of intimacy. Ascertaining on one journey any special requirements that could be supplied on my next round, I exchanged anything that could be sold on that occasion for farm produce, such as butter, eggs, cheese, or dairy-fed pork. I often, before my day's work was ended, had sold these for greenbacks, at prices that paid for both transactions. My bit and sup were never grudged wherever meal time or night found me, and there was always a comfortable bed at my disposal after the evening's conversation came to an end.

I would not ask for a more delightful life than that of a notion peddler among the grangers, when it has become known that the man means to treat his patrons fairly, and understands his business well enough to be able to give value in exchange for their surplus. The grangers are the salt of the earth in our civilization, and but for their influence it is plainly to be seen that this country would rapidly fall into decay. Pope said, "God made the country; man made the town;" but he was only half right in this statement. The town is the handiwork of the Creator, through human instrumentality, and the handsome marble block devoted to commerce and manufactures should conduce to His glory as much as the heavenward-pointing spire of the church. In all good works, whatever the objects of the directors, "Paul may plant and Apollos water, but God alone can give the increase."

The fault of our town life is that a horde of camp-followers, who have no particular callings, live a parasitic existence, just escaping the conditions which would call for police intervention, and make themselves indispensable as ward bummers in the local and general elections, which are almost always in order. They run the primaries in nine cases out of ten, are the power behind the throne in the caucus, to which they have sent representatives, and can often use their might, even in the convention, to the detriment of the better elements in society. In the country the same conditions do not exist in the same degree. The man who would be a ward bummer in the city has no foothold in the cleaner and more wholesome community, or his attempts are discounted in the counsels of a more leisurely class, which has the clear-sightedness to understand that the government, in their State capitol and in Washington, must be precisely what they make it by conscientious labor, or by disgraceful connivance.

In the city it is one of the rare events to find a merchant prince or man of established character in any walk of life brought out as a candidate for office, because such desirable persons will not condescend, by their agents or otherwise, to woo the most sweet voices of the bummer class. Of many such men in our great cities it may be said as truly as Shakespeare wrote the lines of Coriolanus:

> "IIis nature is too noble for the world:
> IIe would not flatter Neptune for his trident,
> Nor Jove for his power to thunder."

Precisely for that reason the best class of thinkers and men of action in city life are never brought to the front in civic rule, and are seldom seen in our Legislatures or in Congress, unless some exceptional era of corruption has compelled a crusade against bummer rule. Republican government, in which every citizen is sovereign, demands active virtue in the individual participating in every process in the election of men to fill the legislative and executive offices of the commonwealth; and it is precisely because those conditions of social and political life come nearer to realization in the country than in the cities, that I pin my faith to the farmers. I should despair of popular government if it depended entirely upon dwellers in towns, although the urban voter is generally quite as well educated and as well informed as his fellow elector in the rural districts; but the difficulty arises from the urgency of his engagements, which will not allow him to participate in the preliminary exercises which are necessary to the integrity of our electoral process; and in many instances men have become so disgusted with the ringboned and spavined candidates nominated on behalf of their party, that they have refused to cast a ballot.

I have no wish to talk politics here; but at the same time I would not have it imagined for one moment that I have lived until my hair is gray without forming political principles, and being ready to carry them into practice. The neutral tinted man, to whom all programmes and all men are alike, is not a creature that I could admire; but the noisy zealot that carries partisan violence into every action of his being is but little better than a nuisance. This book is not meant to disseminate the views of any party save that which says, "Render unto Caesar the things that are Caesar's, and unto God the things that are God's." We have no autocrat to rule over us; that deliverance was wrought by the founders of this republic more than one hundred years ago; and it would indeed be a shame upon our manhood if in mere supineness we should allow the duty and the right of self-government to fall into disuse. Our sons should inherit

from us the rights which were bequeathed under the
Declaration of Independence and the Constitution,
and if we should some day grow wise enough to
provide in a thorough and efficient way for the rights
of woman as well as the rights of man, so much
the better; but woe to the nation which fails to
broaden the base upon which the liberties of civilized man may some day be challenged to meet the
advancing forces of barbarism, which have always
hitherto submerged learning, arts and inventions,
when the people have become too weak or too listless to stand up in their defense.

He is lacking in the essentials of patriotism
who would not raise his voice at this hour to denounce the tendency to inaction in politics and morals which is spreading around us. The careful discharge of church duties in every relation will go far
toward keeping the life sweet and wholesome, but
we are and must be of the world as well as of the
spirit; and Milton was quite right in saying: "I
cannot praise a fugitive and cloistered virtue, unex-
ercised and unbreathed, that never sallies out and
seeks her adversary." The training of the church
and the class-room should make us more active,
because more fully alive to the duties of citizen-
ship. I see no reason why in the near future we
should not have a great political revival in our
community, lifting the body politic into the condition realized by the little aggregate of less than

three million souls, who sorrowfully but valiantly
bade defiance to the richest nation in Europe, when,
as Emerson has sung:

"The embattled farmers stood,
And fired the shot heard round the world."

So high was then the sense of responsibility that
men of worth stood out from every condition, not
only to become living targets for veteran soldiers,
but to dare the possibilities of death on the gal-
lows, should their brave efforts fail, for having taken
up arms against their tyrant sovereign. When
Washington and his fellow-soldiers in the revolutionary armies could dare so much for a nation only
in the gristle, which could offer only a few rewards
to bravery, and within its boundaries possessed little beyond the possibilities which we are making
tangible, what is there that we should not do for
that nation now in its young prime, with her flag
respected on all seas and in every country, her credit unquestioned in every mart, her words of counsel
and remonstrance heeded in every cabinet, her alliance sought by every government, her commerce a
prize for a world's ambition, her protection a tar-
get against the designs of tyranny, her literature
worthy to have descended from Chaucer, Spenser
and Shakespeare, and her free religion untrammeled
by one tie of State control, such as every man may

find for himself in the language and the life of our
Redeemer?

I find that, talking about the duties of citizen-
ship, I have wandered away from my friends, the
grangers, so I must return to them and to my wagon
loaded with Yankee notions. Loaded! Well, not
loaded, exactly; that was my trouble. If that
wagon had really been loaded I might not now have
found myself writing a book. My capital was too
small to allow me to carry a full stock. Sunstrokes,
falling through sidewalks, buying new materials
when I should have closed out my stocks, blundering or being blundered for, or swindled in business, being beaten without mercy or justice by that
"Rattening" Association in St. Louis, and other such
incidents which defy recapitulation, had made it
difficult at times even to live, and impossible to
save such an amount of capital as would carry a full
stock of Yankee notions, maintain my family and
myself, pay my driver-assistant, without whom I
could not travel, feed my horse, and keep my wagon in going order. I was compelled to make another change, and a chance occurred to utilize my old
associations. I have mentioned elsewhere that
oftentimes on my rounds when I was in business in
La Crosse, my attention was invited to the claims
of rival instruments which had been offered for sale
among my friends. My musical ear having been
partially educated, I found much pleasure in using

my semi-efficiency in the manner suggested, and by dint of much practice as an amateur, I found my powers of discrimination largely increased. I traveled now regularly selling organs and pianos, and the doors that were opened to me as a peddler of notions were not closed when I came in another calling which brought harmony to many homes. In this line but litle capital was demanded, and I was able to spend more time at home with my family.

Naturally domestic, it was a joy to me beyond what many fathers realize, to hold my little girl upon my knee and amuse her with tales of what I had met with in my travels, and then when my tongue was fairly going there were more than a few comical incidents which it seemed as though my wife would never tire of hearing.

Once, when on my travels in Michigan I was going to Battle Creek, some friends told me to let myself be introduced to a gentleman named Joy, a lawyer in practice in Battle Creek, and let him tell me his story. Fearful that it might be a story of a lifetime as long as my own, or as that of Coleridge's Ancient Mariner, I hesitated, but I found that Mr. Joy has only one story to tell; he tells it to every friend, and to every acquaintance every time it can be done; but he does it so well, having given his whole mind to that labor of love, that even though by the first symptoms men know all that

will come, there is hardly an instance on record of
any man saying "Don't."

Many of his friends bait their trap with the sentence, "'Tisn't everybody that can tell a good thing
even when they know it," and that never fails to
draw the story: "You may well say that. There
was a young fellow by name of Smith, rather uncommon name, a student in the college at ————,
and he was the hardest up young man you ever saw,
but as bright as a golden eagle. He was almost
out at elbows, his clothes glittered in a way that
no tailor could approve, and though his soul shone
through his bright eyes whenever a fellow-student
trembled on the verge of a joke, there was no sole
worth mentioning to keep his feet from the road.
Hard up was no word for it; he was quite run into
the ground. But for all his poverty, Smith was a
favorite with every man in the college, president,
professors and all. One day when Professor Griffin
was passing along the corridors on his way to the
usual meeting of the Faculty, he was surprised
and delighted to see Smith in a new rig, glossy and
fresh from the tailor's.

"New Mr. Griffin was not the heraldic, meta-
phorical Griffin, a fire-eater, but a genuine, kind-
hearted man; and acting upon his friendly impulse,
he stopped to chat with Smith. 'Quite glad, Mr.
Smith, to see you have some new clothes; and they
are nice clothes, too; they fit you well; but say,

isn't the coat too short?' 'All right, sir; thank you,' said Smith; 'It will be long enough before I get another.' The Professor saw the point in a minute; there was no difficulty about that. Many men see the lightning, but few can imitate its movements.

"He doubled up like a jack-knife and went off laughing like a man possessed. It was wonderful the way he laughed. The faculty was in session, and on such occasions dignity is in order, but Mr. Griffin could not stop laughing. He leaned on the table and laughed as if he must die of it. He sat down in his own particular chair, and almost rolled on the floor. He laughed until nearly all his colleagues were affected with the cachinatory disorder, and the President, unable to control his curiosity, asked the cause. 'Why, sir,' said Professor Griffin, and he burst out laughing again, 'I met young Smith in the corridor; you all know young Smith, but you would hardly know him now, for he has a handsome new suit of clothes. I was glad to see the change in his appearance, and I stopped to tell him so, but while speaking I noticed that his coat was disproportioned to his height, as you know he is a tall young man. 'Isn't your coat a little short?' said I. That was enough. It was wonderful how quick the answer came. He didn't hesitate one second. 'Short, sir? No! It will be a long time before I get another.'"

That was Mr. Joy's one story, and the way he laughed while he was telling it was enough to convulse any audience. I think his appearance must have been sometimes more comical than his words, but of course that was a matter for my imagination only. It was enough for me that I could delight my little household any time by telling Lawyer Joy's story, and in all my little *repertoire* that was the most effective. So, in my brief stay at home holidays, waiting for the word as to people likely to buy organs and pianos, I very often referred to Battle Creek, reciting the gentle dullness of Professor Griffin. My wife's acquaintance with English is sufficient to enable her to understand that story now, but there was a time, shortly after our marriage, when Norwegian was of necessity our vernacular, and we used to enjoy a joke at her expense, pretending she had made the mistake, of which a farmer named Ericcson, near La Crosse, was guilty, when asked how his potatoes had turned out. His answer was, "Good, but seldom."

That failure of Professor Griffin to convey to others the idea that had power to penetrate his own cranium, can be verified as a sample of the natural endowment of nearly three-fifths of all the people met with in society. Sit down with a dozen men, and whisper to your next neighbor any anecdote or *bon mot*, the most simple, and request him to pass it in a whisper to the next and so on, until it has made the circle of the room and returned to you; the story will have been changed so much in the dozen narrations that you won't see its relationship to the story you started, without tracing the blunder back through every link in the human chain. Horace Greeley, a writer whose caligraphy was a marvel, made a head-line of the words "No cross, no crown," when brave John Brown was awaiting his doom at Harper's Ferry, and the puzzled compositor, with some pride in his own sagacity, set up the words, "No cows, no cream."

I was delighted with my new avocation for its own sake, apart from the fact that it gave bread and a little more to my family. Music has often seemed to be my best earthly solace, although my skill as an executant is only moderate. The waters of misery have submerged me many times in my eventful career, and if in the very depths of my distress I could find an instrument on which I might play, or still better, if some capable performer would favor me with a spirit-stirring piece, I emerged from my dullness like a giant refreshed. I never tired of praising the restorative powers of music. The madness of King Saul was soothed when the Psalmist David, in his boyhood, struck the harp. That poor maniac, George III., whose tyrannical obstinacy severed the Colonies from the mother country, and in a sense built up these United States, used in his old age, when blindness fell upon him

in the decay of all his faculties, when deserted by
his children like King Lear in the fable, to find a
charm which pacified his soul in crooning sacred melodies.

There is a bliss unspeakable thrilling the heights
and depths of cultivated natures, when soul speaks
to soul, without the intervention of words, through
the compositions of the great masters, and when
circumstances favored me so far that, in my capacity as salesman for musical instruments, I could at
any time lay my hands upon a Steinway, a Knabe,
or a Chickering, there was no woe that could not be
driven away under the blessing of my Redeemer.
The genius of the *maestro* put to flight the petty
environments of trouble and disaster when things
seemed at their worst; and my soul, which had almost abdicated its powers, rose toward the empyr-
ean, finding rifts of golden promise in the dark
clouds which had shut in my sorrow-dimmed intellect. I cannot say that I ever saw the stars, so long
is it since the blessing of sight ceased to be mine,
but in my imagination they shine down upon me
out of the heavenly depths, as in the beginning of
our era the star shone for the wise men who came
from the East to the manger at Bethlehem, to discover the new-born child; and music aids me more
than spoken words to that exquisite delight.

Music is indeed God-given. The human
heart throbs responsive to its touch. The im-

agery of the poet pouring forth his inspiration, has no trope more beautiful than is contained in the language of Job: "When the morning stars sang together, and all the sons of God shouted for joy." The celestial harmony which used to be accepted as the utterance of a poet's rhapsody, is now known to science as a veritable truth; and it is not difficult to imagine that in the exaltation of sense which may come when this tenement of clay shall no longer clog our faculties, the music of the spheres shall swell into diviner strains, the anthems of the just made perfect. This earth can be made heaven-like by music. Give me only the instrument to which I am accustomed, and peace to translate into sounds the sweet and entrancing bequests of the masters whom I humbly follow, and I envy neither king nor kaiser; I can even forget that I am blind. Pillared porticos and sumptuous dwellings surround me, with delights that seem familiar, and even though but a few minutes earlier I might have tightened my belt to reduce the importunities of my epigastrium, there are in my mind the sensations of one bidden to a feast.

Having said so much about music and musical instruments, it is perhaps unnecessary for me to say that I am an enthusiast in my pursuit; and that when I have once discovered a taste for music in a family, and have learned that the means are available to indulge and cultivate the capacity, it is very difficult to convince me that the instruments I can sell are not the best adapted to the wants of that household. I do not make myself a bore by my persistency, or at any rate, I strive to avoid any such result. Having explained as briefly as possible what I can offer (and of course the best qualities of the best makers pass through my hands—the organs made by men whose names are household words, and every kind of first-class piano,) I strive to make it understood, not as a figure of speech, but as an actual verity, that I never use my reputation to push the sale of an instrument until I have made myself conversant with its value, and can give so much of a guarantee as my character affords, that it is worth the price demanded.

If, having gone so far as that, I find a hesitancy in the mind of the would-be purchaser, I accept that as an indication that, for some reason which it might not be convenient to name, the transaction must be deferred. I withdraw for the time, taking the precaution to name two or three well known families that can be consulted as to the genuineness of my protestations; and leave an address through which Henry Hendrickson can always be reached. In that way I avoid the very semblance of annoying my patrons, without abandoning the chance of business; and upon the first hint that another call will be acceptable, I hasten to my appointment wth a reasonable certainty that a sale will be effected.

I hold it beyond question that the home which does not contain an instrument capable of giving expression to the creations of Mendelssohn, Beethoven, Mozart, Handel and their compeers, is wanting in one of the great requisites for culture and delight. I would endure many privations cheerfully rather than allow my household to be bereft of the joy which they have found so often in the deep, rich, entrancing tones of my favorite instrument, interpreting the thoughts of long ago, with a sweetness which will, I hope, live in their minds until we gather by the river within the celestial portals, where the melodies of the angelic host shall utter, in perfect fulness, the praise and worship which have been fragmentary and incomplete upon this earth.

20

CHAPTER XVIII.

PRIDE OF ANCESTRY.

Talking to the Children—Icelandic and Scandinavian Voyagers—
Civilization in Iceland—Skalds and Eddas—Value of Sagas—Colum·
bus in Iceland—Scandinavian Narrations—Greece and Iceland—Intestinal Strife—Independence Lost—Vinland Colonized—The Crusades—Growth of Church—Scandinavian Origin—Old Rome and
Teutons—Norway of Old—Finns, Magyars and Mantchoos—Norsemen and Goths.

In my work in the sale of musical instruments I
have no cause to complain of want of success; but
I never reflect upon my mule-like drudgery in St.
Louis, when I was endeavoring to keep a home over
our heads in despite of the "Rattener's" Association, without thinking that, if the State Institution
for the Blind at Janesville, Wisconsin, had fitted
me at the outset of my career for handling musical
instruments of all kinds as I am now doing, my
health and vigor, and that of my family would have
been much greater, and we might have been spared
much misery. In saying this I have no wish to un-
dervalue what was effected in my case. My friend,
Mr. Ives, found me at home, almost useless for
any purpose, and rapidly cultivating despondent
habits of mind, with occasional bursts of mischiev-
ousness, which would have terminated in my becom-

ing a very unprofitable citizen. His strenuous solicitations changed the current of my life into useful
channels, enabled me as a broom-maker to become
self-supporting, and opened my mind to habits of
study which, if they have contributed nothing to the
literary and scientific knowledge of the age, have
enabled me to store my mind with the leading facts
of history, so that I can utilize my leisure by giving instruction to my children, with their mother's
aid, converting our home into a little college where
the lessons of patriotism are unceasingly enforced.

Earlier in this volume I glanced, and only
glanced, at the discovery of this continent by Icelandic and Scandinavian voyagers, many centuries
before Christopher Columbus procured from the
Court of Spain the means to venture into those seas.
It would amuse as well as astonish many of my
readers, could they hear the questions and exclamations of juvenile Scandinavian students with reference
to their mighty ancestors, the unquestioned masters
of the seas when Iceland was the home of learning
in Europe. They seem to know almost from their
cradles about the discovery of Iceland by the Norwegians, early in the ninth century, and the consol-
idation of a little republic on that island, which had
a brilliant existence from 928 A. D. to 1262, during
which time the Skalds visited the nobles and great
families on their estates, diffused a love of literature,
and built up a language, which, although closely

related to the Norwegian, has to this hour an independent existence.

The literary monuments of the Icelandic tongue
are many and various, commencing with the poet-
ical Edda, parts of which were almost certainly
written in the ninth century—many writers claim
for it an existence in the eighth century—although
it was not compiled by Saemund Sigfusson until
some time between 1054 and 1153, within which
dates the Norsemen had made themselves masters
of England. The prose Edda, possibly written by
Snorri Sturleson, but more probably compiled by
him, dates in the latter form from 1178 to 1241,
and the completeness of its statement of the pagan
faith of our ancestors, as well as its review of the
art of poetry as then understood, gives to the work
a peculiar significance.

The Skalds were in their day as celebrated as the
Kings and the Jarls, and the names of Egill Skal-
lagrimson, Eyvind Finsson, Thord Kolbeinsson,
Ivar Ingarmundarson, and others, suggest gigantic
attainments and authority far beyond all that their
literary remains appear to justify. It may well be
that their writings lack the fitness which would win
admiration in the nineteenth century, just as the
lubrications of Duns Scotus, the subtle doctor, as
he was called in his own time, have long ceased to
be praised, although in the thirteenth century, and
long after, England, Scotland and Ireland contested

the honor of having given him birth, and the friar professor was esteemed a very miracle of learning, philosophy, and religious fervor.

The Sagas are, however, the great triumphs of literary attainment upon which not only all Scandinavians, but all the scholarly men of every nation are agreed. Perfect in artistic form, they offer a reliable basis for the history of the Scandinavian races, and in a large degree for that of the civilization of Europe. To the Sagas, various in form and multifarious in the subjects of which they treated, Columbus was in all likelihood indebted for the hints which he improved in the re-discovery of this continent, as there seems to be no doubt that the great Genoese navigator, pursuing his calling as a maker of maps, visited Iceland before he began to importune the Courts of Europe to give him command of an expedition which was to sail west until it reached India.

The Scandinavian peoples still preserve in some degree the arts of narration by the domestic hearth, to which we are indebted for the Njalssaga, an epic which challenges comparison with the Iliad. Iceland was wondrously adapted to bring that faculty to perfection. The brief and dream-like summer into which all the operations of the husbandmen were of necessity crowded, was followed by a prolonged and severe winter, which made indoor amusements and work the mainstays of intellectual and social life.

The father was the intellectual center of his home, and he told the adventures of Njal to the listening groups, as his father had handed it down to him, from a remote antiquity, until the time arrived for the Saga to embody the story of all ages. Almost in the same way, allowing always for the differences of climate, the poets and reciters in the Grecian states preserved the spoken records of demi-gods and heroes, until blind Homer, master of them all, imprinted his name and genius upon their utterances.

I say, allowing for differences of climatic conditions—for in the Scandinavian and Icelandic home there were no Olympian and Isthmian games to tempt youth to enter arenas of display—the fireside was the theater of eloquence. The boisterous Fjords and freezing winds beyond the shelter of the Icelander's cottage, made every home a separate colony during the major part of the year, and when sons and daughters plied their sires with questions as to the great names that adorn their common history to-day, the venerable reciter of the glory of his nation and race burst into loftier strains of enthusiasm and reverence, which were remembered thereafter as the goal of that generation, until new combinations in language, fresh coinages in words, permitted a new mint-stamp to express the growing appreciation of the divine in manhood.

The Sagas are in this way the embodiment of the

history of souls as well as of nations and races, and as such they will grow in importance through time. The civilization of Iceland was phenomenal during the few centuries which have been indicated, but then the isolation and segregation of family groups, with the customs of enthusiastic recital at which we have glanced, produced in many of the leading families a determination to rule or ruin, such as we have often seen exemplified in the councils of other countries. Ruin and desolation, widespread, almost universal, were the natural consequences among a people too brave to be subdued into retainership, and at last the colony was so much weakened by dissensions that the island, no longer able to vindicate its right to self-government, became a dependency of Norway, and continued so to exist, subject to Denmark still later, until the one thousandth anniversary of the foundation of the colony, since which time its recognition of Danish supremacy is limited only to the headship of the same sovereign.

This story has charms for all Scandinavian peoples, because of the moral and political lessons with which it is fraught, telling, in a practical and convincing way, to every ambitious man in whom the lust for rule may become ripe with dangers for his fellow-citizens, that the outcome of misdirected energy aimed at the conquest of popular freedom will be more likely to reduce the threatened community to foreign domination than to induce the people to bear the yoke of a domestic oppressor. The poetry and the prose of Iceland, precious as they are, though they have been written amid the ice and snows of an almost perpetual winter, in low huts of lava blocks and moss, are not more to be considered than the philosophy which arises out of that experience which for so long a term deprived the people of their nationality.

The lesson belongs to all the Scandinavian races, and should be remembered by every man in his home, so that when he is called upon to speak of the Norsemen of old, he may impress upon his children, and their children after them, whether they live in monarchies or in republics, that there is no guarantee for the liberties of a nation, and the sterling independence of a people, save in the mutual regard with which every citizen feels called upon to defend the rights of his neighbor. The law which was given to the individual by Him "who spake as never man spake," applies with precisely similar force to the state, under whatever name it may be known. "Whatsoever ye would that others should do unto you, do ye even so unto them."

The Sagas leave no margin for reasonable doubt that this continent must have been well known to Norway in and after the ninth century, until the black death, as it was called, in the thirteenth century, so completely decimated and reduced the parent kingdom that its very existence was imperiled.

Thorwaldsen, the sculptor, in whose well-earned fame every Scandinavian finds cause for honorable pride, is said to have been the direct descendant from the only child born in the colony of Vinland.

The claims of the first discoverers upon European gratitude would have been largely enhanced had their knowledge been communicated to other nations; but just then the several governments were beginning to realize the idea of overcrowding which was felt by Abraham when he parted company with his kinsman, Lot, although the two families occupied a territory upon which subsequently kingdoms were reared; the necessity for an outlet for a superabundant population found an answer in the surplus-destroying crusades. Millions of men, and these the virile entities of their time, abandoned their homes within a few generations to pour out their life blood upon the sterile plains and deserts of the Holy Land, and, as well by their absence as by their destruction, the populous countries were deprived of their increase, and filled with ideas which were temporarily a death blow to national development.

The church alone grew until she could plant her haughty foot upon the necks of kings, and compel popular submission to almost any demand. Crowns were in her gift, sovereigns were her vassals, and when in some few cases monarchs were

brave enough to resist her aggressions, the anathemas
of the church followed by excommunication, seldom
failed to destroy the powers of the champions of
civil rights. Under the rule of the church, with occasional blood-lettings in the name of the Redeemer,
whose tomb was supposed to be desecrated by the
infidel reigning in Jerusalem, the interests of the
people were not considered, nor was there any necessity for the establishment of colonies abroad until literature, which had been in leading-strings,
stepped out from the control of the monks, and by
means of the printing press appealed to the thinking
powers of humanity.

Then the Sagas of Iceland revealed to Columbus
what the hardy Norsemen had done and discovered,
and he, full of that insight which is given only to
leading minds, comprehended and applied the
knowledge which was an enigma to less favored
mortals. His greatness was none the less great
because he used the knowledge which others had
built up, instead of sailing on a blind chance to discover an unknown country. Thus it is not from any
envy of the fame of Columbus that we insist upon
the claims to priority of Eric the Red and his son
Liefr, who not only knew the country, but actually
founded the colony already mentioned, in Vinland,
or southeastern New England.

But it is not enough to speak of Iceland and of
this country's earliest discoveries. The Scandina-

vian races have a past bright with the deeds of heroes, which carry us back to the time when the Roman Empire commenced its disintegration; and from
that time until the present, there has hardly been
one generation of mankind in Europe which has not
had occasion to remember the Norsemen. In my
fireside stories, and when I speak to larger audi-
ences, I am demanded of conscience to do homage
to the noble natures which triumphed by force of
arms and by mother wit over long-established dynasties in Europe, and wrote their names with em-
phatic splendor upon the spirit-stirring pages of
history.

That little population of Norway, aggregating less
than twenty million souls, occupying the western portion of the Scandinavian peninsula, with the Arctic
Ocean on the north, with Sweden and Russian Lap-
land on the east, on the south the Skager Rack, and
on the west the North Sea and the wild Atlantic,
was indeed a fit cradle for a line of sea kings.
From east to west the greatest breadth is only two
hundred and seventy-five miles, and from north to
south the length is only one thousand and eighty
miles; but when we consider what has been accomplished, under favoring circumstances, within and
from within that area, we are reminded of the will-
power of the man who said, "When I am mad I
weigh a ton."

The question who were the Finns has never been satisfactorily answered, although many facts connect them with the Magyars and Mantchoos. They were the primitive inabitants of Norway, the aborigines whom the Northmen displaced, as the greater waves oft scatter the *debris* which the lesser billows have planted on the coast line. The Gothic peoples, barbarians though they were to the effeminate Romans, had a rude, brave civilization of their own, which expressed itself in their respect for woman, and for personal freedom; and they came with the force of an avalanche, bearing down all obstacles to possess the land, and eventually to extend their empire beyond the margin of the mighty deep. The Finns were as nothing before the army of newcomers, but they were treated with some consideration, as when a giant sits in the presence of weaker mortals he is content to let them breathe the same air, and disport around his footstool. The conquering race can usually discover reasons why the conquered may live, though it be only as "hewers of wood and drawers of water."

CHAPTER XIX.

THE NATION'S DAY BROADENS.

Harald Harfagar—Erik the Cruel—Hako the Good—Hakon Jarl—St. Olaf—Norse Pagans—Canute the Great—Sweyn—Magnus I.—Harald II.—Olaf III.—Magnus Barefoot—Sigurd—Sverer—The Black Death—Union of Calmar—Margaret of Denmark—Aristocracy Displaced—Books in Dark Ages—Reformers and Church—Thirty Years War—Napoleon and Bernadotte.

The age of demigods passed away, as such eras pass in the infancy of every great people, and we step from the dim records of tradition to actual history with the reign of Harald Harfagar, or Harald the Fair-haired, from about 863 to 933. He was a greater man, dominating over great leaders, and when he had established his dominion they departed with thousands of their followers to harass the coasts of Europe, and make good a foothold elsewhere. From the nobleness and magnanimity of Harald Harfagar to the narrow and tyrannical disposition of Erik the Cruel, was a descent too rapid to be endured, and the people who had submitted joyfully to the father rose in rebellion against the son, and he was driven from the kingdom after a reign of only five years.

Hakon, or Hako the Good, another son of Har-

ald, who had been educated in the court of the
English king, Athelstane, and was known as his
foster son, was called to the throne which his father
had dignified, and thus the principle of hereditary
government was recognized even in the act of departure, just as the English, when determined to
endure no more of the obstinate folly of James II.,
transferred the sceptre to his eldest daughter, Mary,
and her husband William of Orange.

The hereditary principle in government, strictly
followed, has often been the ruin of a nation's prestige, because wisdom and courage do not descend to
the first-born invariably, and in many cases none of
the sons of great men have preserved the characteristics of their sires. The sterling worth of Hakon
the Good is attested by his title; he gave to his
kingdom a code of laws, and tried to introduce
Christianity, but the sturdy old pagans resisted his
entreaties, and it was not until three centuries
later that the nation was gathered into the fold.
The Danes repeatedly aided the sons of Erik the
Cruel to drive their uncle from the throne, but they
were unsuccessful until 963, when he was unfortunately slain in battle with them, and the realm was
divided between Erik Graafell and Hakon Jarl,
two cousins, until Hakon Jarl died, in 995. After
that the Norwegians revolted against the son of
Erik the Cruel, and Olaf came to the throne, filling
it with glory.

Olaf is to Norway what St. George is to England,
St. Andrew to Scotland, St. Patrick to old Ireland,
or St. Denis to France, but he is more real than
either of the other saints except maybe St. Patrick.
Before he was twelve years old he commanded a
Viking fleet, by virtue of his descent from Harald
the Fair-haired, and before he was nineteen there
was no warrior on the seas more dreaded. He was
installed on the throne of Norway on his return
from an expedition against France and Spain, and
but for zeal in the promotion of Christianity his
reign would have been peaceful at home as well as
glorious abroad, for his fame was the pride of the
nation. His father, the first Olaf, had been the
chosen theme of poets and romancers during all his
reign, and his honors survived him, although the
freedom of his native land did not. My children
can tell you how Olaf, being defeated in a naval
engagement by the Danes with overpowering numbers, leaped overboard with all his armor to avoid
capture by the enemies of his country, and so died
in the year 1000 of the Christian era, but before
his own countrymen had embraced the cross.

There was a fierce and ungovernable pagan spirit
among the nobles, as well as among their followers. When one of the princes was on the brink of
conversion, and the waters were ready for his baptism, the Christian father congratulated him on his
escaping the pit filled with fire and brimstone in

which his ancestors had suffered since their deaths, and must suffer to all eternity. "Are all my ancestors in hell, then?" quoth the implacable warrior. "They are," said the impolitic Father. "Then I will go there also. None of your baptism fcr me!" Among such stalwarts ordinary measures of persuasion were of no avail, and the Olafs, first and second, tried to rear the cross of the Redeemer in Norway by force of arms. The first, as we have seen, died at sea, after a brilliant career, which has kept his name alive to the present hour; and the second perished in his zeal for his religion. The subjects of the Saint, enraged because of his persistency for the new faith in season and out of season, rose in rebellion against him, with all the pagan forces available, strengthened by the enemy without, and the courage and strategic skill of the monarch availed nothing against the combination.

The great Canute, then King of England and Denmark, who claimed Norway as part of his possessions, landed near Droutheim in 1028, after the king, since canonized, had reigned fourteen years, and the incipient Saint was driven into Russia, where for two years he busied himself in preparing for the liberation of his kingdom. In furtherance of that enterprise, Olaf II. returned from Russia with a considerable force in which Sweden supplied a contingent, but he was slain in battle at

Stiklestad, in July, 1030, after his army had been routed.

Canute the Great conferred the government of Norway upon his son Sweyn, after the death of Olaf, but when Canute died the people would not endure Sweyn as their monarch, and the son of St. Olaf reigned as Magnus I. for twelve years, being killed in battle by the Danes in 1047. Harald II. was slain at Stamford Bridge, in England, in 1066, and his successful foe, Harold, the last of the Saxon Kings, was defeated and slain at Hastings immediately afterward by William the Norman, who established Norman succession.

Olaf III., son of Harald, strove to introduce among his subjects the civilization of Europe, and his name is justly held in reverence. Magnus Barefoot, his son, was a conqueror, and he carried the arms of Norway successfully to the Isle of Man, the Orkneys, the Shetland Isles, and the Hebrides, being slain in battle by the Irish in an attempt to conquer that kingdom. Ejsen, Olaf and Sigurd, sons of Magnus Barefoot, were now made joint kings, but the other two dying young, Sigurd remained alone until 1130, carrying Norwegian prowess to the Holy Land, joining Baldwin, King of Jerusalem, in a successful expedition against Sidon, fighting gloriously against the Moors, and winning for himself a name among the greatest heroes of a noble race.

21

The history of our nation and people is such as may be transmitted from sire to son with pride and advantage. For more than half a century Norway was torn by intestinal commotions after Sigurd's death, so many claimants for the throne being equally balanced, until the year 1184, when Sverer, who claimed to be the son of Sigurd II., established his dominion. The nation that would be powerful abroad must needs have peace at home, and Norway paid dear for her commotions. For many years the kingdom, which had been an important factor in the government of almost every European country whose coast-line could be harried, could hardly protect her own borders, but the courage of the people was unbroken.

The black death, which desolated nearly the whole of Europe at various times, so that it is estimated that twenty-five millions of people died of that malignant disease imported from Egypt and the Levant, fell upon Norway with absolutely crushing effect in 1348, and within two years two-thirds of the population had been absolutely swept away. Medical skill there was absolutely none, either in Norway or in any other land, competent even to mitigate the sufferings of the afflicted, and from the first attack to the death of the patient there was hardly any variation until the climatic or other unknown conditions which favored the spread of the destroying agency gradually abated. The overflow of the Nile is supposed to have been the starting-point, when the disease spread its ravages for the first time on record in 544, and the want of hygienic knowledge in Constantinople, then the center of civilization and of commerce, intensified, and diffused its malignity all over the world.

In Hecker's "Epidemics of the Middle Ages" this subject has been so completely analyzed and set forth that it would be folly to attempt more than the very briefest digest in our pages, and that only in the hope that the Scandinavian races, wherever located, will at all times co-operate with well defined purpose with all nations in promoting the laws of health, which, under the Divine blessing, must be in a physical sense the gospel of saving grace to every generation of all the nations.

The act of the union of Calmar became possible in 1397 only because the ravages of disease had destroyed the spirit and the natural resources of the nation; and although under that act there was no express provision for the abandonment of Norwegian liberties, yet the actual fact was that, under Margaret of Denmark, an able and politic monarch, the Danes became supreme in Norwegian affairs. Danish emigrants displaced the old Norwegian nobles, and their power as an order was utterly broken.

In the present day an aristocracy might be erased in any of the great countries of Europe without permanent injury to civilization or good government.

In England, even, where for many reasons the aristocracy is the highest in tone of such orders on the earth in any age, there would be no absolute loss to learning, arts and liberty, in the removal of the privileged class to another country, because the people generally have so completely taken into their own hands the science of government, the arts of defence, the means of industrial development and exchange, and all the detail of social advancement, that the welfare of the community could not be so imperiled for one moment.

In the fourteenth century it was otherwise. The learning and civilization of the time was mainly dependent upon privileged orders. The common people, accustomed to a continuous struggle for daily bread of the poorest quality, and unaware of the blessings of civilization, because of the absence of any endeavor to educate their children and themselves, suffered the direst neglect of their material resources in the destruction or degradation of the nobles. Books there were few of any class, because of the enormous expense of their reproduction by the pencils and pens of the monks immured in cells, and the nobles were almost the only persons that could afford to buy them. A manuscript volume, more or less illuminated by the use of colored inks and gold, was esteemed a present such as sovereigns might exchange, and, unfortunately, most of the works so perpetuated were of so low an intel-

lectual type that little injury would have accrued
to the world in their destruction. Learned men, to
whom the ignorant looked with reverential awe,
expended their powers of mind in debating how
many angels could dance upon the point of a needle, and all the vigor of their subtle brain was lav-
ishly used in sifting that undiscoverable essence.

There were some few rolls of papyrus, parchments
and other manuscripts, the destruction of which
might have been an almost irreparable loss, but
they were few and far between. Many of those who
possessed these costly treasures—the books of the
middle ages—were unable to read them, and their
lives were passed in such turmoil and fierce strife
that the inclination was as much lacking as the power. The nobles of England who forced King John
at Runnymede to grant to the nation the recognition of its liberties, known as Magna Charta, were
generally obliged to make their marks upon the ennobling document, being unable to sign their names,
and it need hardly be said that those who lacked
the clerkly ability to write their autographs were
wanting in the capacity to read. The cultivation of
scholarship, such as it was, remained in the hands
of the church, with few exceptions, until the end of
the fifteenth century, when printing presses and
movable types had given to the western nations the
art preservative of all arts—printing.

Norway had discovered America through the en-

terprise of Eric the Red, and had attempted its settlement through the agency of Liefr, son of Eric;
but, in the decadence which was now realized,
America was no longer an object worthy of an effort,
and the information gradually ceased to have a place
in the popular mind.   Happily, it was preserved in
the Icelandic records, at which we' have glanced,
and also in the Vatican at Rome, where historians
may yet unearth great wonders.

There was little worthy of note in Norwegian history pure and simple until the Reformation, which
had been attempted by John Wycliffe in England,
by John Huss, Jerome of Prague, and John Ziska
in Bohemia, by Savonarola in Florence, and others
innumerable in smaller degree, was consummated
in the sixteenth century by Luther, Melancthon,
Zuinglius and their compeers in Germany and Swit-
zerland, and then within twenty years from 1536 the
country became thoroughly Protestant.   National
thought occupied a higher plane from that era, and,
under the Lutheran Church, education of the
faculties began in a sense that had long been foreign
to the hierarchy of the kingdom.

It is perhaps wrong to speak of Norway as a kingdom, considering that the nation has long ceased to
enjoy a separate existence.   From the days of Margaret and the Union of Calmar, the interests of Norway came to be treated as of secondary importance
whenever they conflicted with Denmark, except dur-

ing the reign of Christian IV., from the latter part of
the sixteenth century to nearly the middle of the
seventeenth century, when the Danish king spent
much of his time in Norway, rebuilding Christiania
and founding Christiansand. This reign was an
oasis in a vast desert of oppression, and the king
was entirely in sympathy with the Protestantism
of his subjects.

We find him in 1625 assuming the command of
the Protestant armies, in the thirty years' war
against the forces of the Emperor of Austria, with
whom nearly the whole of Catholic Germany co-op-
erated in the endeavor to minimise and if possible
erase the more rational faith. The defeat sustained
by Christian at Lutter in 1626, at the hands of the
veteran general, Tilly, did not drive the Scandinavian races from the front in the war for freedom of
thought; for Lutzen, where Gustavus Adolphus fell
in the hour of victory which his matchless genius
as a warrior had organized, saw the great Wallenstein utterly defeated only six years later, and the
great peril of Protestantism averted by Scandinavian
courage and magnanimity.

Christian IV. was an able and wise monarch,
subtle in council, intrepid in the field and just to
the country which too many sovereigns of Denmark
before his time and since, until this century, have
persisted in treating as a conquered province. Denmark found in him a prince of exceptional quali-

ties.   Coming to the throne when only eleven years old, he reigned sixty years with honor and profit to his realm, and bequeathed to his successors union and strength.

Unhappily for all concerned, the wisdom that distinguished Christian the IV. was not the chief characteristic of those who came to the throne of Denmark after him, so that the eighteenth century was an era of great injustice and oppression to my native land.   Frederick VI. changed the tenor of events in some degree in 1808, when he came to the throne of Denmark after the Napoleonic wars had revolutionized the dominions of Europe, and it had become necessary to recognize the rights of every community.   The possession of Norway as an addition to the crown of Sweden was guaranteed to Bernadotte by England and Russia as an inducement to that general and marshal of France to join the coalition against his imperial master, and the story of shame is too well known to need recapitulation.

Norway was properly indignant at such a high-handed procedure as a reward of the treason of Bernadotte, but the strength of the community was not sufficient to ward off the blow, although a brave defence was attempted.   One good consequence arose from that endeavor in the recognition of the right of Norway to independent government by its own legislatures under the almost nominal leadership of the king of Sweden.

CHAPTER XX.

Sweden is not forgotten in our family circle, for its inhabitants are also Scandinavians, and the race is one. The Eastern part of the Scandinavian peninsula is the home of the Swedes, or Svea. Norway is north and west, the Baltic and the Gulf of Bothnia are to the east, Finland is to the northwest, the Baltic is to the south, and to the southwest the Skager Rack, the Cattegat and the Sound are natural boundaries. From north to south the greatest length is nine hundred and seventy miles, and from east to west the greatest width is two hundred miles at the utmost; the population being about four million five hundred thousand souls. The main chain of the Scandinavian range of mountains divides Sweden from Norway, and the Norwegians, jealous of their bounds, maintain a wide avenue along the range through the forest, with monuments of stone at regular intervals. The Laps and Finns, the aborigines of Sweden, were driven out by the Goths from the Southern portion of the country which they settled, giving thereto the name of Gothland. The god Odin is said to have led the Svea from Germany, and to have turned aside from the Gothic colony—as a kindred people—to drive the aborigines from their second home.

Odin occupies in Scandinavian mythology the place that is assigned to Zeus in the Greek as creator of the world, father of the gods, holding the supreme power and being possessed of all knowledge. The Valkyries were specially under his control, and in battles his decision gave victory irrespective of strong battalions.

The decision in councils of the gods, and the strategy to accomplish every end, emanated from Odin, to whose fame the German scientist, Baron Von Reichenbach did homage in calling a peculiar iridescence, which only some few people can see, about the arms of a magnet and in strongly magnetic persons, Odic force. The field was not fertile, in the faith of our ancestors, unless Odin gave his blessing, nor could the winds and waves be propitiated unless the ruler willed success to his worshipers. The vagueness that belongs to every mythology, separating with a broad line of demarcation the imaginings of men from revelation, can be found of course in the mythology of Scandinavia and Germany. Odin the supremely wise was indebted to

Mimer's fountain for his inspiration, having drunk
at the stream by special favor, and left one of his
eyes in pledge for the accommodation; so that
Odin is always represented with one eye.

In Egyptian mythology the several qualities and
functions of intellect were represented by different
animals, or by parts of animals, as, for instance,
the head of a bull, the wing of a bird, the serpent
swallowing its tail, to typify eternal duration, and
so on. Such a process was absolutely necessary
where arbitrary descriptive characters were unknown, as all minds, however barbarous, could
gather some ideas from images and pictures of living things; and so among the Scandinavian races,
the functions of the eternal mind were typified by
animal life. Two ravens sat perched on the shoulders of Odin: Huginn as the perceptive faculty,
and Muninn as memory. They were supposed to
fly every day through all the universe, and to return
to his shoulders, whispering in his ears the secret
things of which they had become possessed in their
flight. We, requiring no such machinery to convey a far grander thought, say only that the Creator
of the universe is all-seeing and everywhere present,
as well as all-wise and omnipotent.

Zeus was supposed by the Greeks to sit enthroned
in never varying brightness, an idea compatible
with the climatic character of the Grecian Archipel-
ago; but the more hardy Norseman could not be

satisfied with a listless and contented deity, hence
Odin, the god of the elements, holding the heavens
and the earth in the hollow of his hand, was represented in his mantle of cloud riding through illimit-
able space on a horse with eight feet, and holding
in his hands the lightning with which offenders
might be stricken in the moment of his wrath.

The mythology which would in time have equaled
that of the Greeks in beauty, as already it has
transcended the former in power, was, happily for
the race, dwarfed and arrested by early contact in
the superior minds with a purer faith in Christ;
hence the student of to-day can see in the learned
shadowings of these ancients of the earth, yet moist
with the dewy freshness of the world's morning,
the mental endeavors of untaught men to fashion a
First Great Cause equal to the wondrous works of
creation. The universality of such efforts among
all peoples, however remote from the true light,
and however crude and mysterious the outcome in
many instances, cannot be without significance for
the philosopher who trembles on the verge of
atheism.

It is very probable that the true Odin was not so
great a man as Moses, the law-giver, and certain that
he was far below him in that he lacked a mission from
on high; yet doubtless he was a warrior of such eminent powers and favored with so many successes that
his followers gave him credit for supernatural ability,

and as the myth-forming process advanced, raised him
by imperceptible degrees, until he filled their heavens as well as their earth. The Saxon god Wodin,
or Wotan, and the old German Wuotan, from whom
we have named Wodensday, or Wednesday, is clearly the same personage with the Scandinavian Odin;
and thus, if not otherwise, it would be easy to trace
through their mythologies the race relationship between the peoples on the shores of the Baltic and
those who remained in the forests of Germany or
migrated to Gaul and Britain to build up the enduring civilization in whose light Christianity is the
sunshine of warmth and brightness.

After the death of Odin, an event which might
have given a fatal blow to the pretensions of his
disciples, the government was administered in his
name by the high priests, who were in charge of
the temple at Sigtuna; and from that hierarchy came
a ruling class which in course of time lorded it alike
over Goth and Swede, taking the lead in all councils as great kings, while the lesser chiefs were regarded as *smaa Kongar*. Upp-sala, or the High
Halls, was built by Frey Yngve, son of the Pontiff
Njord, the immediate successor of Odin, on the
ruins of the first temple at Sigtuna, and he also was
placed by his admiring people among the gods when
death took him away. The royal line of Ynglingar
was founded by him, and is supposed to have ended
wih Ingjald Illraada, the Bad Ruler, some time be-

fore the eighth century. There is no absolute certainty in dealing with the traditions of a people, but there is always some seed of truth in folk lore, however ancient and however vague.

Olaf was called the Lap King, because, being an infant in arms when he first received the homage of the princes, that incident afforded a margin for a humorous allusion to the aborigines. With Olaf authentic history may be said to begin in Sweden, in 903. The interval from the death of the Bad Ruler has but little light even from tradition, but it is believed that Christianity was introduced into Sweden in 829, by a monk of Corbie, named Ansgar, who found the old paganism too firmly imbedded to be disturbed in any perceptible degree by his zeal and devotion. Nearly two centuries after his work began, Olaf embraced Christianity and founded a bishopric at Skara, but the people held firm to their old beliefs and practices nearly a century longer. Edmund the Old was the last king of the Uppsala line, and he died in 1055, having been mainly distinguished as a persecutor of the Christians.

The Goths made war upon the Swedes after the death of Edmund, and we may be sure that the conquerors had the assistance of the priests in their upheaval, as we find Stenkil, a Gothic chief and Christian, made king over both tribes as the outcome of the struggle. Anarchy ruled for nearly a century, while paganism contended for the mastery,

but the embattled hosts of heaven were on the side
of the cross, so that there was no possibility of ultimate victory on the part of the old faith.   Bryant
said with force:

> "Truth crushed to earth shall rise again ;
> The eternal years of God are hers ;
> But Error, wounded, writhes with pain
> And dies among his worshippers."

When the contest inclined to favor the Swedes, in
the twelfth century, we find a Christian prince coming to the front in person of Sverker I., in 1135.
He reigned twenty years, with honor to the nation,
and manifold advantages were reaped from his administration, restoring prosperity and order, estab-
lishing Christianity on a broad basis, and giving
corresponding development to law and justice.

Erik the ' Saint, and cousin of Sverker, was his
succsesor, and followed boldly in his footsteps.
The cross was firmly planted in all parts of his domain, the Finns were conquered and converted at
the sword's point, the laws were amended and better applied, and his reign of five years' duration
has left as deep a furrow for good as many able
monarchs have accomplished in three decades.
The rule of his immediate successors was uncvent-
ful, so completely had order been settled, and the
church grew in power every day.   This fact was
happy for the nation, for the monks were full of
zeal in good works at that time in Sweden, and in

the thirteenth century we find them not only ful-
minating the terrors of divine justice against evil
doers, repressing outrage and disorder by their influence and example, but becoming the teachers of the
people in useful arts and industries.

In many countries already, the monasteries had become sinks of iniquity, in which the lives of honest
abbots who dared demand faithfulness and labor
were unsafe, but in Sweden a better rule prevailed,
and when the best known methods of tilling the
ground were desiderated, or the people wished to
plant gardens, prepare salt for daily use and sale,
build roads and bridges to facilitate commerce and
travel, or to construct water mills that would utilize
the powers of the river and mountain stream in the
preparation of grain for food, the monks were the
great civilizers of the day, and their undertakings
conferred blessings as well as won them.

We are no monkish chroniclers, but while we do
not close our eyes against the excesses which in
many lands were too apparent to be gainsaid, it is
our duty to speak of the monasteries in Sweden at
the date indicated, as among the most valuable of all
the native institutions. The monks had traveled
from different parts of Europe, the habits of the order and their well known poverty being their safe-
guards against outrage and robbery, and their passports to the knowledge that had been developed in
all the fields of gainful industry. Indolent, luxuri-

ous creatures, desirous only to feed on fat things, found no temptation to leave their abodes in sunny Southern lands for the rigors of the North, and in that way Norway escaped from many plagues that were experienced in the more temperate climes, where reformers tried in vain to purify the lives of the so-called religious for more than a brief season.

It was fortunate for the kingdom that the monasteries in Sweden were centers of industry, and the monks willing teachers, skilled in the useful arts, competent to improve the *cuisine* of the humble cottage, to facilitate the operations of the workshops, to minister, in some degree, to diseased bodies with herbs and simples, as well as to exalt Christ before the eyes of those afflicted with spiritual maladies.

The Folkungar line commenced in 1250 with Valdemar, a powerful chief of that race, and he reigned vigorously for more than half a century. His brother Magnus succeeded him in 1302, augmenting the kingly power all through his reign for the protection of the people against the nobles. His added title, Ladu-Laas, or Barnlock, indicates that the granaries of needy husbandmen were not more safe against the rapacity of the privileged class in Sweden than in the rest of Europe until the monarch assumed his proper position as the defender of the weak against the strong. Could the history of feudalism in Europe be fully written with the completest

22

insight, it would be found that the downfall of feudal
power in every realm was mainly due to unscrupu-
lous exactions by the nobles, forcing the commons
into a good understanding with the sovereign, and
an increase of kingly power, until the spoilers were
made amenable to law or were erased from the
earth in rude attempts at civilization.

The king died in 1290, and for nearly thirty years
his three sons contested the crown of Sweden; but
at length, in 1319, the grandson of the last-named
king, Magnus Smek, ascended the throne, if this
is not too muscular a method of expressing the accession of a child three years old. Through his
mother he acceded to the throne of Norway in 1320.
Later, marrying his son to Margaret of Denmark,
he gave that son Hakon the throne of Norway.
Relying upon his dynastic strength in so many alliances, the king thought he could abolish the Swedish Senate, but much to his surprise that body deposed him and chose in his place Albert of Mecklen-
burg as king. Albert was defeated and expelled by
Margaret of Denmark, and the Union of Calmar
brought the three kingdoms under one sovereign in
1397.

This combination continued in force for more than
a century, but it was several times imperiled, and
more especially by the revolt of the Swedes under
Engelbrect Engelbrectson, who was only defeated
by the arm of an assassin, a Swedish noble. This

was in the reign of Erik of Pomerania, nephew and
successor of Margaret, who died in 1412, and three
years after the death of the illustrious rebel, Erik
was deposed, in 1439, and succeeded by his nephew
Carl Knudson. Anarchy was the rule in Sweden, if
misrule can be so dignified as to have rule, for more
than seventy years until Christian II. ascended the
Danish throne in 1513.

Anarchy was repressed with a strong hand by the
new king, but his severities drove the Swedes into
rebellion, led by Gustavus Vasa. The career of Gustavus Vasa might well have inspired the poet. Descended from the old Swedish kings of the Uppsala
line, he was the son of Eric, Duke of Gripsholm,
and was just twenty years old when called by cruel
circumstances into the service of his country as the
leader in a revolution. The Danish domination
was unpalatable to Sweden and long had been, but
the youth entered the public service in the joint
kingdom in 1514, was sent as a hostage for the safety of the King of Denmark four years later, and was
treacherously sent to Denmark loaded down with
irons. Escaping from that kingdom in 1519, he betook himself to Germany, where he listened to the
eloquence of Luther and became one of his enthusiastic adherents.

Immediately after the coronation of Christian II.
that monarch conceived the idea that his kingdom
might best be consolidated by an act of sanguinary

treachery, and he caused the assassination in cold blood of ninety-four nobles, including among them the father of Gustavus Vasa. This was in 1520, and the young reformer, fired with indignation in which patriotism was reinforced by filial love, roused the Dalecarlians to rise in revolt, and with their aid won the battle of Westeraas in 1521, became administrator of his native land, and soon afterwards king, founding the line from which sprung Gustavus Adolphus, the finest disciplinarian and military tactician of his age.

His coronation dates from 1523, and four years later he openly professed the Lutheran faith, making it the State religion in 1528. He was a man of fine qualities, but extremely severe, and there were many domestic wars in consequence of the antagonism which the reactionary party found latent among the peasantry. His wars with Russia were such as were forced upon him by the aggressive policy of the Muscovites, and in all his statecraft he was an upright and able ruler.

The reigns of the immediate descendants of Gustavus Vasa were unimportant. The good qualities of a sire will sometimes disappear for one or more generations, and then will reappear with potency through many successions. The eldest son, Erik XIV., reigned only eight years, and was hopelessly insane some years before his death, in 1568. His brother, Johann III., reigned twenty-four years, but

was not distinguished, and his son, Sigismund, King
of Poland since 1587, would have restored Roman
Catholicism when he came to the throne in 1592,
but that the people could not be manipulated by
the Jesuits, as he was. Having weaned the affections of his subjects by residing in Poland, he was
deposed by them, and the throne given to his uncle,
Charles IX., son of Gustavus Vasa, and a monarch
capable of great administration.

Gustavus Adolphus, son of Charles IX., and grandson of Gustavus Vasa, was only seventeen years old
when his father died, in 1611, but he had already
seen service. The nation was at war with Denmark, Russia and Poland when he came to the
throne. His genius turned every circumstance to
advantage. Denmark was detached from the warlike combination by a treaty, and then the more remote foes were chastised until Russia gladly made
a disadvantageous peace, and Polish Russia over-
run, called Wallenstein, and the Emperor Ferdinand to the rescue. The deeds of the great leader
in the thirty years' war sound like the story of the
seven champions of Christendom, so brave and yet
so wise, was every movement.

The cause of Protestantism seemed lost on the
continent of Europe when the King of Sweden, with
his little army of veterans, landed at Usedom in
1630. He did not expect to return alive, so, before
setting sail with his fifteen thousand warriors, he

settled the affairs of his kingdom, appointed a re-
gency, gave his daughter, four years old, in charge
to the estates and set out like a knight errant of
the highest order to peril his life for religion. He
was ridiculed by his enemies, called a "Snow King,"
as though he might be expected to melt away, and
the protestant leaders whom he had come to help
were cold as charity to his advances lest he should
be overwhelmingly defeated and they trampled under foot for having given him countenance and succor.

To the surprise of all classes that God-fearing
little band, perfect in faith and in discipline as
Cromwell's Ironsides, pushed on from victory to
victory, respecting every man's rights, and defeating their enemies at every blow. The battle of
Leipzig, in which the great General Tilly was defeated, showed the Protestant princes, and the Catholics, also, that there was no king of snow in command, unless the snow was an avalanche, capable of
overwhelming all opposition. Had the king been
ambitious of personal gains, he might have captured Vienna without another blow, as the army of
Tilly had been utterly routed, so that hardly two
thousand men remained in one body, and all the
material of war was in the hands of the heroic monarch; but his care was for religious freedom, so he
left the easier tasks to his tardy colleagues, and
drove on in search of other foemen worthy of his steel.

The movements of Gustavus Adolphus were rapid and decisive. Leaving Vienna as of no moment, he drove the Spaniards from the Palatinate, returned to Nuremburg, hailed there as the deliverer of Germany, crossed the Danube, driving Tilly, with another imperial army, before him; then passed the Lech, in spite of Tilly's force and generalship, compelled a general engagement, in which that commander was defeated and slain, advanced to and captured Munich, and became master of Bavaria.

The emperor Ferdinand, who had disgraced and dismissed Wallenstein because of his insolence, ambition and rapacity, felt himself now in danger of being annihilated by the Protestant hero, and, to save himself from that possibility, he submitted to the demands of the invincible Wallenstein. The Emperor conferred upon him supreme power over the army, consenting to abdicate his own right to command the troops in any matter and under any circumstances, in consideration of Wallenstein resuming control. The Emperor breathed again, having given to his commander-in-chief authority which the traitor had resolved to use for the undoing of his imperial master. The defeat of Gustavus Adolphus was now assured, as there was no commander alive the peer of Wallenstein. The tactics of the rival commanders—both brave, both able beyond compare, engrossed hourly attention from the world. Each knew the other to be master in the science of war, and they fought, the one for the gratification of his own ambition and greed, the other for an open Bible in Europe and freedom to worship God.

Gustavus might again have fallen upon Vienna, and postponed the deadly conflict, but he was the soldier of the cross, and could not turn aside to gain profit or renown. Lutzen was before his mind's eye, with Wallenstein strongly entrenched on the plain, so to that goal of his life work the Christian hero modestly addressed his steps. Wallenstein, confident in the strength of his position, awaited the attack of his antagonist, and was overwhelmingly defeated, as Tilly had been, although, unfortunately for Europe and the world, the protestant hero was slain, falling covered with wounds in leading a cavalry charge for the emancipation of humanity from the thralldom of priestcraft.

The affairs of Sweden were controlled by the Chancellor Oxenstiern in the absence of his royal master, and, after his death, until Christina, the daughter of Gustavus Adolphus, had arrived at years of discretion, if that indiscreet lady may be said to have ever arrived at years of discretion. At first she gave excellent promise that she would prove worthy of her sire, but her life was a disappointment to her friends; she resigned the cares of state to her cousin, Charles Augustus, wandered about Europe with a queenly retinue, living mainly for pleasure and dissipation, until in Rome she abjured the faith of her fathers, and died in the ancient fold in the old-time sacred city, at the age of sixty-three.

The wars of Charles X. were brilliant and successful, but they were wars of ambition, such as must in the end impoverish the conqueror. Sweden should be supreme in the Baltic; that was a noble resolve, but his genius for conquest stretched beyond that and compelled interference by other powers. He invaded Poland, and captured Warsaw in person, being recognized as King of Poland by the army and the greater part of the nation, but a coalition of the other powers, led by the Czar, the Emperor Leopold and the King of Denmark made his victories barren. He subdued the great elector, Duke of Brandenburg, and made him his vassal, but was compelled to abandon all his doubtful advantages by subsequent treaties. He overran Bremen, Holstein, and Schleswig, and held Copenhagen at his mercy, but France and England compelled him to make peace with no other gain than the sovereignty of the principal islands. Renewing the war on an unreasonable pretext, he was once again dictating terms to Copenhagen, when the Dutch sent a fleet to release the Danes; the Duke of Brandenburg drove the Swedes from Jutland, and the maritime powers were resolved to stop the war, when Charles died, in 1660.

Sweden under Charles XI. was despoiled of much
territory, but Louis XIV. intervened on behalf of
the kingdom, and compelled the restitution of the
conquered places; yet she came out of the war in
a dilapidated condition, her fleet destroyed, finances
ruined, and a doubt entertained also whether the
government could hold its position unless foreign
aid was obtained. Under such circumstances a
coup d' etat, as the French would call it, made the
power of the king despotic, and the outcome of a
series of wars for conquest was the loss of liberty
at home. Charles XI. was an able and very careful administrator, and under his statesmanship Swed-
en so largely recuperated that when he died, in
1697, the country was once more in a condition to
assert her supremacy in the Baltic.

The death of Charles XI. and the accession of his
son, Charles XII., a boy of fifteen, suggested to
many of the neighboring powers that the opportunity had arrived for depriving a weak monarch of
much of his territory. Poland, Saxony and Denmark
were the parties to the compact of spoliation and the
Duke of Holstein, brother-in law of Charles, was
the first person attacked. To the astonishment of
the confederates the young king strengthened himself by treaties with England and Holland, and
then making a descent on Denmark, compelled that
country to sue for peace with such rapidity and
decision that the war was ended almost before it

had well begun. Denmark paid an indemnity to the Duke of Holstein, and there was no longer a belief that Sweden was weak enough to be plucked. The Czar of Russia, Peter the Great, was in the coalition against Sweden, and Charles turned to him, now that he stood almost single-handed, with a keen relish for his work. His operations against Peter were eminently successful, so that the monarch was compelled to raise the siege of Narva and retire before an inferior force.

Saxony and Poland were next manipulated, with the ease of a master mind. Defeating the Saxon troops near Riga, Courland was occupied, Warsaw was captured without a blow, the Poles renounced the king, who made war on Sweden, and Charles, after many victories, compelled the deposed king to become a consenting party to his own deposition. Peter the Great was again in the field with a superior force, and he was almost ubiquitous in his efforts to counteract Charles, inducing the Diet of Poland to repudiate the king that had been chosen under the patronage of Charles—King Stanislaus—and overrunning some Swedish possessions.

Charles XII. marched into Poland to fight his adversary, but Peter avoided a battle, while harassing the enemy by all means in his power. An attempt on Moscow was a failure, because the intervening country had been converted into a desert, fruitful only in cavalry that could harass and would not fight. An expedition into the Ukraine, in search of promised reinforcements, was a disastrous mistake. The forces sent from Sweden to succor the king were intercepted and defeated, and at length the king himself was wounded and utterly defeated at Pultowa, nearly half his army dead on the field, and his best surviving officers prisoners in the hands of the enemy.

This was the beginning of the end. Charles, wounded, fled into Turkey, where he remained until forcibly expelled by the Sultan, five years later. Upon his return to his own kingdom, he found every indication of weakness that could invite an enemy, nor could even his genius for war regain the advantages that had been lost. When he was killed, by a cannon ball, at Fredrickshall, in Norway, he left for his nation to weep over, besides the fragments of his fame, an impoverished treasury, mutilated territories, an utter loss of prestige, and an incapacity to assert a claim to consideration among the leading powers of Europe. The game of warfare is one from which all parties, even the most successful, rise, if they can rise at all, as losers, and it has been wisely said by one well versed in the science and ethics of government:

> " War is a game which, were their subjects wise,
>   Kings would not play at."

Spain attempted the *role* of conqueror when Charles V. added to the crown of Castile that of Germany;

and, after the emperor, wearied with the march of
life, had retired to a monastery, his son, Philip
II., found his armada shattered, his ports blockaded
or deserted, his people dispirited and idle, and
the nation falling gradually, but not slowly, toward
the tenth-rate power which Alfonso found at the
commencement of his reign.

France began a career of conquest under Louis
XIV., which promised him unbounded glory, and
gratified the insane ambition of the people. A term
of comparative peace during the nonage of the king,
with Richelieu and Mazarin for ministers, with Col-
bert for Minister of Industry and Finance, left
the treasury almost plethoric, and, when victory
perched upon his banner in campaign following campaign, the vain monarch took to himself the honor
that belonged to his subjects' resources. The system of conquest was continued until Europe coa-
lesced against France, and her treasury was exhausted. It was no longer possible to buy victories nor
to win them. Ramilies and Malplaquet told the
same story of utter exhaustion, and then the conqueror, seeing himself deserted by the phantom fortune, cried aloud in his agony of spirit, "Has God
forgotten what I have done for Him?"

There came another era of conquest, and France
once more worshiped military glory. Napoleon was
now the mighty organizer of victory, and the world
has seen no greater since the days of Alexander the

Great. Caesar, who said *"Veni, vidi, vici,"* with perfect truth, for his genius enabled him to come, see
and conquer, had not such nations to contend with
as Napoleon fought with the ragged and shoeless
armies of the republic. Yet the day came when
the wondrous capacity which had made the *sous*
lieutenant, general, the general, first consul, the
consul, emperor; and that *parvenu* emperor, a man
that could convert crowned heads in Europe into a
boat's crew to do him honor, was unable to raise an
army to defend his frontier from invasion, his capital from capture, and himself from an enforced ab-
dication and captivity.

There will come a time, fraught with peril for
this country, when men will esteem conquest so
highly, and the glory of possessions, extended by
force of arms so much, that civilians will see their
liberties imperilled to do honor to military dictat-
ors. In such a time I pray that the sons and daughters of the Scandinavian race in America will remember that the chiefest dangers in wars of conquest are
incurred by the people who supply the soldiers and
cheer on the conquerors. Wars in self defence,
and in defence of liberty, are sacred duties, from
which no patriot dare shrink; but a war of conquest
is a deadly sin.

The death of Charles XII. was the funeral knell
of the greatness of Sweden, but the country remained, and the people, with all the possibilities

for prosperous industries and homes of contentment
in which mainly the triumph of civilization must be
sought.   That nation is happiest in which dynasties
are unknown, or in which the principle of loyalty,
fashions an ideal sovereign incapable of precipitat-
ing wars or making a wreck of freedom. Sweden
had not yet attained that blissful condition, but in
learning the lesson that her less than five millions
of people could not give laws to the globe by mere
force of arms, she was advancing. Territories taken
from the kingdom as the price of peace were appropriated by Hanover, Prussia, Denmark and Russia,
and in 1743, as the penalty for another futile war,
Russia added to her dominions the remainder of
Sweden's provinces east of the Gulf of Bothnia.

Foreign courts dictated the policy that the country should adopt, and the nominal sovereigns of the
land that gave Gustavus Adolphus to Europe were
little more than phantoms. Gustavus III., nephew
of Frederick the Great of Prussia, sick of the turmoil of French and Russian cabals in his own court,
and resolved at all hazards to put an end to the
schemes of the Czar for the enslavement of Sweden,
declared war against the Muscovite in 1771, and the
Peace of Werela vindicated the wisdom of his
course.

The wars of the French Revolution involved constitutional, territorial and dynastic changes which
are of little moment here except as they eventuated

in recognizing Norway as an independent monarchy, with her rights defined and guaranteed by a liberal constitution. Sweden and Norway, joined yet individualized, are prospering in the development of the useful arts beyond all previous records in either land. Manufactories have been multiplied and augmented in power, the busy hum of labor is heard in every village, the fertile land, tickled with the hoe, laughs with more than its accustomed harvests under better methods of husbandry, and the towns teem with a cheerful population wedded to honest labor, which supplies their homes and little ones with food, shelter, clothing, and education, in most respects equal and in some superior to the average of prosperous European nations. Music and the arts generally flourish under the immediate patronage of the royal line and the aristocracies of both countries, so that the names of Scandinavian celebrities girdle the globe with fame, which will endure long after the old era of dynastic wars and tyrannical oppression shall have been forgotten in the better systems of republican federation and popular rule toward which the old nations in Europe are hastening.

CHAPTER XXI.

THE LAND OF THE DANNEBROG.

Denmark—Dan Mykillati—The Dannebrog—Danes and Charlemagne—Queen Thyra's Wall—Canute the Great—Pope Hildebrandt—Esthonian Crusade—Fighting Missionaries—Burgher Representatives—Niels Ebbeson—Queen Margaret—Calmar Union—Lutheran Faith—Ditmarsen Customs—Protestant League—Napoleonic Wars—Modern Liberalism—Loyalty of Love.

But my little ones are not allowed to imagine that the Scandinavian races are confined to Sweden and Norway; it would be unfair to their minds to leave their ideas so stunted and incomplete. Denmark is of the same great family, and has a history that scintillates with splendor, stretching back into the dim uncertainties of the dark ages. The kingdom as it now exists has for its northern boundary the Skager Rack; the Categat northeast and east, with the Baltic and the Sound; on the south the Strait of Femern, the little belt and Schleswig; and on the west the North Sea. The peninsula of Jutland is only part of the kingdom, as the islands of Fuen, Leeland, Laaland, Falster, Langeland, Moen, Samso, Laso, Arro, Bornholm and many of less note are included. The Faroe Islands, Iceland and Greenland and the islands of Santa Cruz, St. Thomas and

23

St. John, in the West Indies, are also Danish possessions that deserve notice. The aggregate of Danish population is less than three million souls, and
that fact fills the mind with wonder as we reflect
upon the part the Danes have played in European
history.

Dan Mykillati, or Dan the Famous, one of the
earliest kings, is said to have given his name to
the country, and to have taught his people many
useful arts; but the dates and events of his reign are
as difficult to fix as the advent of the good time
coming, about which we are accustomed to sing with
vagueness and vigor.

Stoerkodder, the Norse Hercules, was one of his
successors on the throne, but the memories of his
life are as hard to verify as is the descent of the
Dannebrog or ancient battle-standard of Denmark
from heaven, although it would be profane to doubt
that the flag in question did fall from the suggested eminence at the battle of Volmar in Esthonia,
in the thirteenth century, during a crusade against
the heathens.

The figures of a cross and crown were on the
standard, and the workmanship, ascribed to celestial handicraftsmen, was neither more skillful nor
more enduring than could have been obtained in
that age from a nunnery. Twice it was taken in
battle, but its loss on each occasion awakened a
holy frenzy among the troops, so that no enemy

could retain it and live. In the beginning of the sixteenth century there was only a fragment of the precious heritage, but it was treasured as beyond all price. The order of the Dannebrog is the second highest order of knighthood instituted by Denmark, said to have been established in the field at Volmar, in 1219, and to have been restored in the seventeenth century.

Regner Lodbrog and his father, Sigurd Ring, who came some time after the seventh century, following Stoerkodder on the throne after an interval, were also mythical or semi-mythcal heroes surpassing the demi-gods of Greece in the magnitude of their supposed achievements and the desperate valor which they illustrated as the ideal of the nation. We are left to our imaginations mainly to fill the outline that traditions have left us as to the native princes, until the ninth century, when Gorm the Old appears to have reduced the minor chiefs into a recognition of his superiority, so that in the stead of many principalities, with sovereign rights, there was one powerful kingdom. His reign is said to have extended from A. D. 860 to 936, or some time within the dates mentioned.

The Danes, with their swift-rowing galleys, were now the terror of Europe, and they added sails to increase the swiftness with which they could pursue an enemy or descend on hostile coasts. Gorm carried his fierce invaders as far south as Aix la

Chapelle where they plundered the last resting
place of the conqueror Charlemagne, and Gorm was
among the invaders of Paris in 885. In the year
891 Gorm led his forces against Arnulf, afterwards
Emperor of Germany, great grandson of Charlemagne,
the warrior that captured Rome a few years later,
and as might have been expected considering the
disparity of the forces engaged, the Danes suffered an
overwhelming defeat at Louvain.

Thyra, wife of Gorm, was his reprseentative on the
throne while he led his numberless expeditions,
and the fierce woman differed from her liege lord in
only one particular—she favored the Christian faith
while he was in all respects an inveterate Pagan.
The Danne-virke across the Peninsula south of Schleswig, from forty-five to seventy-five feet high, a vast
wall or fortification to protect Denmark from the
Germans during the absence of his fighting men, was
projected and completed by Thyra. She feared no
approaches from the sea coast where the Danes had
established a name that overawed the landbound
nations.

Harold Blue Tooth son of Gorm succeeded him
in 936 and died in battle in 985. By
treachery and daring the king reduced Norway to a
tributary condition for a few years but my native
land soon re-established its independence. Christianity was favored by Thyra mother of Harold and
he with his wife and son Svend or Sweyn were bap-

tized by a monk named Poppa, who succedeed in converting a large number of Danes of all ranks. Richard the Fearless, Duke of Normandy, was an ally of Harold, and the king assisted him largely in several wars with France, which were not without gain to the Danes. Svend or Sweyn, the son of Harold, whose baptism we have mentioned, invaded England in the reign of Ethelred the Unready, and con‐quered a large territory over which he held sovereign power until his death at Gainsbro', in 1014. His infantile baptism did not prevent him from relapsing to paganism when he attained manhood, and death coming upon him suddenly, he ended his career in the faith of his remote ancestors.

Harold and Knud divided their father's possessions, the former taking Denmark as his sovereignty, and the latter England, where he figures largely in history as Canute the Great, having won to himself the whole kingdom after the death of Edmund Ironsides. Mildness and prudence were as characteristic of the man as his integrity, and the Anglo-Saxons learned to be proud of their Danish monarch, whose reign was necessarily more endurable than the elevation of one of their own number, as it did not offend personal jealousies. He was one of the most powerful kings in Europe, and he was distinguished for his literary attainments, being a writer of some merit as well as a patron of minstrels and founder of monasteries. After the death of his

brother he reigned over Denmark as well as in England.   He died in 1036, leaving three sons, Sweyn,
Harold and Hardicanute.

The worship of Odin was abolished in Denmark
in 1018, when Canute became king, and Christianity was established as the national religion.   Sweden and Norway were added to his dominions, and
so were Cumberland—which had been under another
sovereign—and parts of Scotland ; but the eminently
great king was severed from his native land by his
successes, as he preferred England as his residence,
seeing in that country the beauties and advantages
about which Shakespeare enthusiastically wrote :

> "This royal throne of kings, this sceptred isle,
> This earth of majesty, this seat of Mars,
> This other Eden, demi-paradise ;
> This fortress built by nature for herself,
> Against infection and the hand of war,
> This happy breed of men, this little world,
> This precious stone set in the silver sea,
> Which serves it, in the office of a wall
> Or as a moat defensive to a house,
> Against the envy of less happier lands—
> This blessed plot, this earth, this realm, this England."

Canute died when only thirty-six years old, but
he had established a fame of which every Scandinavian must be proud, irrespective of petty divis-
ions and local jealousies, such as we should blush
to foster.

Hardicanute succeeded to the throne of Denmark,
and four years later, upon the death of his brother,

Harold Harefoot, he acceded to the English crown
also, and like his father remained mostly in England until his death, in 1042. Magnus the Good, of
Norway, now reigned over Denmark, under an arrangement made very wisely by Hardicanute, and
the Danes reaped many advantages from the justice
and wisdom of the Norwegian monarch. When
Magnus died he gave the crown of Denmark to
Svend, the nephew of Canute, and that of Norway
to Harald, his own uncle, who tried in vain to defeat the separation, by wars, which were waged at
intervals for seventeen years, until the Norwegian
king desired peace at home to enable him to prosecute a design for the conquest of England.

Harald of Norway was, as we know, slain in battle in that attempt, at Stamford Bridge, in England; his conqueror, Harold, the last of the Saxon
kings of England, was slain soon afterwards by
William the Conqueror's forces from Normandy, at
Hastings; and one year later King Svend of Norway headed the last of the Norse invasions of England in his unsuccessful endeavor to unseat William I.

Svend is said to have been personally a coward,
but he came of a line in which cowardice was unknown, and the story is the less credible when we
consider the dignity and independence of his reign.
The great Pope Gregory, or Hildebrandt, whose
mission it was to exalt the church on the necks of

the prostrate thrones of kings, was a great favorite with Svend to whom he could render signal services from the Holy See; but when that potentate commanded him, under pains and penalties innumerable, to acknowledge himself a vassal of the church, Svend flatly refused, preferring all perils rather than compromise Danish independence. The founder of the royal line that now reigns in Denmark was not a coward in that crisis.

Fourteen sons were left by Svend when he died in 1076, and five of these in succession were kings of Denmark, but their reigns were full of dissension, and, when Niels died, in 1134, there was a time of great domestic trouble, which was terminated by the accession of Valdemar the Great. This prince found the nation impoverished, and without an army, and his first care was to stimulate its industries, so that it could endure the stress of armaments. The Wends and Esthonians were heathen, and Valdemar undertook their conversion by means of the weapon that Christ blamed Peter for using in his defence. His success in war was indisputable, but his power as a missionary rarely endured beyond the day in which he returned his sword to its scabbard. If the faith was not permanently extended by his operations, his dominions were; and his son Knud, or Canute VI., continued in the same course, so that Denmark, as the sturdy henchman of the church—but not its vassal—grew in grace daily.

KRONBURG CASTLE, DENMARK.

Valdemar II., another great king,, son of Valdemar the First, and brother of Canute VI., ascended the throne on the demise of that monarch, in 1202, and became master of nearly all of Northern Germany. The religious war commenced by his father was made a crusade against the Esthonians, with the sanction of the Pope, and his force of sixty thousand troops, with fourteen hundred vessels, were unanswerable arguments. It was during this crusade that the Danneborg was said to have been conferred on the troop by the special favor of heaven, and of course thousands of the Esthonians were baptized; but, unfortunately, the Livonian Knights of the Sword claimed the exclusive right to save the Esthonians from perdition, or to send them thither at the sword's point, and the two sets of missionaries fought like fiends incarnate in the name of God.

Many sanguinary battles were fought between the contending Christian forces, and on almost every occasion the chief advantages were with the troops of Valdemar, so that he returned to Denmark, in 1222-3, at the very height of his power and renown. Valdemar, whose personal prowess was unbounded, was invincible in the field, but his enemies surprised him asleep in his tent on a hunting expedition, gagged and bound him as he lay unarmed and defenceless, and he, with his eldest son, was carried captive into Germany, where he languished a

prisoner, accompanied by his son, in the Castle of
Danneborg, for many years, until a ransom of forty-
five thousand silver marks was paid, completely im-
poverishing Denmark. The price of his liberty
made it impossible for Valdemar to avenge his
wrong upon Count Henry of Schwerin, so he gave
the remainder of his life to his subjects, making
many and great improvmeents in the kingdom.

The first uniform code of laws for Denmark dates
from this era, and so great was its merit that, after
four centuries and a half, the code required amend-
ments only, and was not abolished. Valdemar died
at the age of seventy-one, three days after the code
had been adopted, and his eldest son and fellow-
captive, Valdemar, being dead, the second son, Erik,
came to the throne, in 1241, and reigned for ten
years. Abel, Duke of Schleswig, caused his
brother's murder in 1251, and in that sanguinary
way procured his own accession; but his reign lasted little more than one year before he was slain
by a man that had been wronged by him.

The reign of Abel, who emulated Cain, was rendered remarkable by the first appearance of the
Burgher class in the parliament or Danehof, just
fourteen years earlier than the dates of the first
writs extant in England calling the same class into
the councils of the nation, in what is now known
as the House of Commons, the body that practically governs England. A succession of weak mon-

archs allowed Denmark to fall so low that the
Hanse Towns were able to dictate to that kingdom
the terms upon which the Danes might engage in
fishing, and Danish nobles took advantage of the necessity of an elective sovereign to render themselves
independent of taxation and of kingly power. The
king, striving to vindicate the rights of his position,
was involved in civil wars, and at last driven out
altogether.

Count Gerhard, of Holstein, assisted the rebels,
but established himself upon their shoulders, and
ruled them in the name of his nephew, Valdemar
of Schleswig, with a rod of iron, until he was as-
sassinated by Niels Ebbeson, a Jutlander, in 1340,
when the Germans were driven out of the kingdom. The son of Gerhard took up the task of
avenging his father, and defeated the Danes at
Skanderborg; but after the death of the assassin of
his father, Count Henry was content to retire and
allow the Danes to manage their own affairs, untrammeled by foreign troops. Soon after that
event, and in consequence of very high-handed pro
ceedings on the part of Valdemar Atterdag, the
king, the Hanse Towns were able to compel the
Danes to assent to their having a potential voice in
the election of Danish kings.

The accession of Margaret to the thrones of
Denmark and Norway was a great gain to both kingdoms. She was an able and wise woman, conscious

that the greatness of a people abroad must depend upon security and peace in the workshop and the home. Old foes were conciliated by her womanly tact, and both nobles and people were made her friends. When she had occasion to believe that wrongs were being perpetrated, she went in person to the scene, and by careful inquiry ascertained the appropriate remedy which thereafter she rigidly enforced. Men who had defied the laws with impunity under the rule of her predecessors, found in her integrity and rigor good reasons for hastening to submit and make restitution for the wrongs they had done. She added Sweden to her dominions, and consummated the Calmar act of union, which, had she been followed on the throne by sovereigns of even average ability, would have consolidated the three nations into one great Scandinavian power, able to hold its own against the world, while flourishing in every department of industry and commerce.

Erik of Pomerania, grandson of her sister Ingeborg, the adopted heir of Margaret, was little better than an imbecile, and the persistency of the able queen in her choice of a successor, after she had seen of what poor metal he was made, is the only tarnish upon her reputation as a sovereign.

Erik continued king until 1435, when his tyrannical treatment of the Swedes drove them into rebellion, and he was succesively deposed by the three kingdoms, so that when he returned from the island of Gothland he was not allowed to land in any port, and so died, poor and uncared for, an outcast, in 1459.

The nephew of Erik was chosen his successor by each of the kingdoms, but three years elapsed after his election by Denmark before Sweden and Norway accepted his sway, and he died in 1448, leaving no offspring. Count Christian of Oldenburg, a descendant of the ancient line in Denmark, was now chosen by that nation, and eventually by Norway also, but he was unable to make good his claim to Sweden. He gave the King of Scotland the islands of Shetland and Orkney in lieu of his daughter's dowry, when she married that monarch, but they were little more at the best than barren possessions to Denmark.

Hans, the son of King Christian, succeeded to the crown of Denmark and Norway, but Sweden was deaf to his claims, and the nobles exacted hard terms from him before allowing him to ascend the throne that he did fill. The Lubeck traders and the Hanse Towns, which had grown very powerful and insolent, were chastised by him, so that he was considered a good king. His son, Christian II., conquered Sweden and reunited the three kingdoms under his sovereignty, but his oppressive treatment drove the Swedes into rebellion under the leadership of Gustavus Vasa, whose terrible provocations

and brilliant successes have been already described
in the sketch of Swedish history.   Two years after
that event Christian was deposed by Norway and
Denmark, and his uncle, Frederick, Duke of Holstein, was chosen in his stead as Federick I. The
king reigned only ten years, but during that time
the Lutheran faith was adopted as the national religion.   His son, Christian III., was one of the best
princes known in any age, and during his reign the
Reformation was consummated.   He died in 1559,
and was succeeded by Frederick II.   The free people of Ditmarsen, who had for many years successfully opposed the pretensions of Denmark, were
compelled to submit by this monarch, and the territory that he was able to hand over to his son, Christian IV., in 1588, embraced the seven southern
provinces of Sweden as well as the joint monarchies of Denmark and Norway.   Ditmarsch is now a
part of the Duchy of Holstein known as North and
South Ditmarsch, between the Elbe and the Eider,
an area of about 500 square miles, in which the
people have preserved in a remarkable degree the
manners of old Germany, with the distinctive features of the Teuton, and a collection of laws which
was adopted five centuries and a half ago.

   Christian IV. was born for the distraction of nations.   He commenced his downward career by making war on Sweden, but after two years, hostilities
were abandoned through England's mediation.   In

the thirty years' war he came to the front as chief
of the Protestant League, but was defeated at Lutter and driven out of Germany.   His son made war
on Sweden in the reign of Charles X., and as we have
seen was indebted to England and Holland for protection from the worst consequences of the blunder.

It is unnecessary to recapitulate the later wars
with Sweden; they have been sufficiently described
elsewhere.   The monarchy ceased to be elective
and the hereditary principle was adopted by peaceful revolution in 1607, and in that way the power
of the nobles, so often used to the country's hurt,
was cut down.   The cession to Sweden of the seven
southern provinces reduced the territory of Denmark
in 1660 so that the northern peninsula owed her
no allegiance.   In the Napoleonic wars Denmark
came into conflict with England, and was compelled
by a British fleet under Admiral Lord Nelson to
withdraw from the coalition which menaced the
tyrannical right of search on the high seas claimed
by England, and in 1807, in spite of the strict
neutrality maintained by Denmark, England, acting
upon information that the Danish fleet would be
certainly seized by Napoleon, sent a force to compel
the surrender of that armament into England's
safe-keeping, to be restored at the close of the war.

The Danes refused submission to that tyrannical
demand, but after three days' bombardment of Copenhagen were compelled to allow the transfer; and

two months later England declared war against the
kingdom that she had already crippled and dis-
armed.   Denmark was now for six years an ally of
Napoleon, until the ill-starred expedition to Moscow eventuated in the coalition fatal to the emperor,
and his defeat at Leipzig, whereupon the Danes,
wearied of his arbitrary methods, and overawed by
the allies, were forced into the combination against
the Corsican.

Territorial changes many and various resulted
from the downfall of Napoleon.   Norway was
ceded to Sweden, and compensating territories were
added elsewhere, but the absolutism of the monarchy
remained unchanged until 1848.   At that time a
new wave of free thought in matters of government,
originating in France with Lamartine, Arago, Louis
Blanc and a few other great men of similar tendencies, drove out the citizen king, Louis Phillippe,
who fled under false passports issued to John
Smith, and so left the way clear to establish a republic upon a basis too unstable to be maintained.
The republic having been raised on popular enthusiasm, instead of being securely builded upon virtue
in the nation, terminated in the *coup d' etat* three
years later, and the president for life developed
into an emperor, laid down his authoirty at Sedan,
when he surrendered to Frederick William and
Bismarck.

The wave of freedom disturbed nearly all the

principalities on the continent of Europe, and Frederick VII. of Denmark gave to his people a consti tution which was reasonably concurrent with their instincts. That concession dates from the year 1848, the time of the uprising in Paris under Lamartine. The Schleswig-Holstein difficulty need not be discussed in a child's historic sketch. It used to be said that there was only one man in Europe that fully understood the bearings of that quarrel, and he became insane trying to explain its intricacies to his dearest friend. With such a possibility in the distance, however remote, it will not be wondered at that we do not care to burden the minds of the little ones with such abstruse matter.

Details so dry belong to more pretentious histories, such as may properly be given in celebrating the anniversaries of freedom; but even then I think it well to avoid the tediousness of arithmetic, the dusty pigeon-holes of diplomatists and the pre tenses of dynasties. The glory of the Scandinavian race is the theme upon which my soul runs riot, and that is associated with the increasing freedom secured to Denmark in the constitution of 1866, and to Iceland in the recognition of its constitutional independence, on the occurrence of the millennial anniversary.

24

CHAPTER XXII.

INFANCY AND GROWTH OF PARLIAMENTS.

Race Relations—Anglo-Saxon Liberty—Afghan Ancestors—
Witenagemote—Norman Conquest—House of Commons—John and
Magna Charta—Feudalism—Parliamentary Corruption—John Wyc-
liffe—Puritanism.

The royal family of Denmark is intertwined by
dynastic alliances with almost every crowned head
in Europe, but the king is wise enough to realize
that the permanency of his hold on the sovereignty
must depend upon popular affection, a silken band
which will endure where manacles and chains would
be snapped asunder. The people are the wisdom
and power of nations, as well as the wealth pro-
ducers; when their schools and universities are fully
employed, reducing the best qualities of every
mind, and diffusing sound knowledge through the
land; when their physique and morale assert themselves in stalwart array as armies of defence behind
the frontier when their busy looms and clanging
engines tell of industries well employed in winning
wealth from all sources, then the press will flourish, liberty will rise triumphant above all assaults,
and justice, tempered with mercy, will govern the
globe in the name of the Redeemer.

A SWEDISH WEDDING PROCESSION.

My little ones become enthusiastic, as is their
sire, when I recount the steps by which the courage
of our ancestors builded the liberties of nations;
and I teach them as best I may, that the strength
of a giant deserves no honor unless it is applied to
noble ends. I have sometimes feared that, in my
zeal for the glory of the Scandinavian races, my
children would grow up in the belief that no other
race nor people have done aught for the consolida-
tion of popular freedom; and to guard against that
possible blunder, I like to follow up my Scandinavian sketches by a few brief hints as to the growth
of parliamentary government in England; a tree in
which the Christian world has found fruits and seeds
from which the human race is gathering blessings
at this hour on every continent.

Far back in the dim vista of the past, before our
common ancestors, the Aryans, sent forth their great
migratory hordes from India into Europe—starting
probably from the country now known as Afghan-
istan to us, but called Wilajet or "Mother Country"
by the native tribes—the Scandinavians and the
Teutons generally were one people. Local distinc-
tions established in Europe, as for instance, the
Franks or Freemen—one section of whom overrode
the Gauls, and bestowed their name on France, and
were divided into Salic and Ripurin Franks, by the
accidents of settlement—gave names which in the
ignorance of the earliest historians beclouded the
true origin of the newcomers.

The Franks were known in the reign of Caesar Augustus, which extended from 27 B. C. to 14 A. D., as Bructeri, Chamavi, Amsivarii, Catti, Chassuarii, Sygambri, and by other family and tribal names which had almost entirely merged in the greater cognomens by which they have written their lives into European history, and which were hardly crystallized until two centuries and a half later than the time of Augustus. The unity of Teutonic and Scandinavian mythologies found in the god Odin, Wodin, Wotan, Wuotan, from whom we have the name of Wednesday or Woden's day, has been glanced at already and need not be repeated here, but it is well to establish on a broad and enduring basis the cousinship and common birth of Teutons, Scandinavians, and Anglo-Saxons, the "heirs of all the ages in the foremost files of time," whose deeds have justified the line of Tennyson:

" Better fifty years of Europe, than a cycle of Cathay."

The disintegrating Roman Empire was reinforced with Teuton warriors, until nearly the whole of the armies were Teutonic to a greater or less extent, and when new nations were shaped upon the fragments of lapsed greatness, freedom grew afresh with better conditions and more vigor in Teutonic and Scandinavian States, which found

" So many worlds, so much to do,
So little done, such things to be."

Time does not allow of many details, nor is it desirable to burden the minds of children with dry-as-dust scrapings in the cinder heaps of history, where antiquarians discover suggestive remains; so I content myself with offering to my girls, who are not to be of the blue-stocking persuasion, just a few facts which illustrate the measures in which in other lands besides our own, the free and daring warriors and husbandmen, who established colonies wherever it was possible, addressed themselves without ceasing, though with many and rude rebuffs from privileged classes, to

> "Grasp the skirts of happy chance,
> And breast the blows of circumstance,"

in favor of the freedom which we are all too slowly realizing in this country, in England and in the nations which are specially the home of the Scandinavian people.

The Saxons in England, or rather in Britain, for then the England of to-day was not yet shaped and moulded in the matrix of time, established what was called the Witenagemote, or meeting of the wise, and the leaders of the people, assembling under the shelter of some wide-branching oak, discussed the issues of peace and war, surrounded and listened to by persons of less note, ranged according to their social importance. The lowest rank in the assembly had a voice more or less potential in shaping the decisions of the council, because applause is the breath of life to an orator, and from out of the

crowded audience came sounds of approval or mur-
murs of discontent, when vexed questions of policy
trembled on the verge of decision.

The Witenagemote remained a part of the machinery of government in England, until the time of Edward the Confessor, in the eleventh century, as we
find him sending dignitaries of the church to take
part in the deliberations and expound the sacred,
civil and common law as then understood, on every
question as it arose. Upon his death, Harold,
brother of Edward's wife, by whom the ascetic
king, full of more than monkish strictness, had no
issue, mounted the throne in violation of some
bargain, expressed or implied, between Edward the
Confessor and William of Normandy; and in the
issue of that conflict the sittings of the Witenagemote ceased entirely or became obscured and of
less moment.

It cannot fail to be seen in these few lines that
Canute and his son, Hardicanute, lived and reigned
in England while the Witenagemote was in the
maximum of its power as a national council, and in
that early beginning we find the root of modern
parliamentary government. The Greeks had a saying, that there "were brave men before Agamemnon,"
indicating that the best qualities, and the worst
also, belong to the race and not merely to the individual; and it would be easy for us to find, in
the musty records of the antique time before Christ

was born, traces of institutions somewhat similar
to the Witenagemote; but we are not concerned
here with anything but the development of
modern parliaments, the leaders of which, springing
from the ranks of commerce, as in the case of Wm.
Ewart Gladstone, from the manufacturing class, in
the person of the Quaker John Bright and others or
from the once proscribed race of Jews in the person of Benjamin Disraeli Earl of Beaconsfield

> " Have lived to clutch the golden keys,
> To mould a mighty state's decrees,
> And shape the whisper of the throne."

Feudal institutions had now their full development among the followers of William the Norman
and for nearly three hundred years the Anglo-Saxon tongue was forbidden utterance in law courts of
the kingdom, in petitions to the court of the monarch,
and in parliaments when such bodies convened.
The history of that era is written in the construction of the English language to-day, for the animals
running on the moors and in the fields retain the
Anglo-Saxon names by which their care-takers and
owners designated them, as bull, sheep, and pig, with
many other illustrations that might be given; but
the flesh of the slain animals taken to market for
sale had to be named in Norman French *bœuf*, beef,
mouton, mutton and *porc*, or pork, to tempt the notice of the wealthy conquerors. The parliament or
free speaking council owes its name to the tongue

of the Normans, although the later development of the institution is peculiarly English.

The first meetings after the conquest were probably dependent upon the caprice of the monarch and they were in all likelihood informal assemblages, possessing but little weight, as we find no written records of procedure. Taxes could not be levied without the consent of the people, through their representatives; that is a maxim old as the earliest mention of parliament or Witenagemote, and therefore the necessities of kings would not allow them to overlook the right of the nation to be convened, at intervals more or less brief, when supplies were to be demanded. The king might declare war—that was his prerogative—and the nobles, with their retainers, were bound by their oaths of allegiance to follow him to the field; but unless the military chest was filled by the people there was little chance of a favorable outcome to hostilities. The term "coffers of the State," which we often hear used by gushing orators, had little meaning in those days and never can have much in constitutionally governed countries, as no moneys are ever found in such coffers unless specially ear-marked for set purposes.

It might seem that the rights of a conquered people would be freely trampled under foot by the Normans, and so in fact they were in thousands of instances in all directions, in acts of spoliation and

oppression ; but the parliament was a Norman rendering of the Saxon Witenagemote, in which the
Anglo-Saxon had no immediate recognition.   The
barons were not willing to become mere courtiers
attendant upon the king, and short of absolute rebellion, the parliament, with its concomitant right
of free speech, was their only means for control-
ling the sovereign.   The barons, confronted only by
a king without a standing army, readily asserted
their powers against his, and De Warrene, when
asked to whom he owed the grant of his barony,
pointed to his sword instead of looking at his liege
lord as the grantor.   He was the fair representative
of an imperious class, tyrannical to the people and
rebellious against majesty.

Unless convened in parliament, they could not
and would not grant taxes nor aids of any kind to
the crown; and when convened, they questioned
every proposed outlay, scrutinized and criticised
every act of the monarch, and except on rare occasions, when their vanity had been touched or their
passions roused in favor of some foreign war, they
doled out grants in aid with extremest parsimony.
The kings found that convening parliament was a
proceeding fraught with danger, because it suggested union among the barons against the sovereign
power, and but that they were met by armed men,
ready to enforce at the sword's point the maxim,
"taxation without representation is robbery," there

would have been no parliaments. At first, while
the sovereigns of England were personally rich
with the spoils of the conquest in 1066, so that aids
from the nation were unnecessary, there were but
few assemblies, and they were brief. Later there
were endeavors to dispense with parliamentary
grants, until in the reign of King John, the crown
had become more absolute than is to-day "the Autocrat of all the Russias." The king lorded it over
church and state within his own realm, having
gained the fullest support from the Pope of Rome
by resigning his crown into the hands of a legate of
the holy see, and submitted his neck to the priestly
heel in token of the vassalship in which he consented to wear the emblems of royalty. So strengthened, he never doubted his power to compel the
submission which he did not deserve, and, happily
for England and the world, his designs were defeated.

The Archbishop of Canterbury, Cardinal Stephen
de Langton, was the leading mind on the side of
the barons, the clergy, the freemen, and the commons of England, and he persevered in the struggle
in spite of the positive command of the chief of the
papacy to forbear as against the king, and to pronounce sentence of excommunication against the barons. The battle royal continued with varying fortunes for two years, from 1213 to 1215, and then,
the machinations of Pope Innocent III. to the con-

trary notwithstanding, the barons, armed knights
and yeomen, with an immense array, called "The
Army of God and the Holy Church," entered the
city of London May 24th, and the king fled from
the tower. The result was that Magna Charta
was granted by the king, the document being
signed at Runnymede, and the great charter of the
liberties of all classes has been subscribed times
without number by succeeding sovereigns. Many
of the conditions of that document have been in-
corporated in all the constitutions, national and state,
that have been adopted in this country, and only
the parts that were temporary in essence, relating
to the acts of King John, or to feudal rights since
fallen into disuse, have ceased to possess importance.

The principle which declares taxation without
the consent of the people unjust and oppressive, was
expressly set forth in Magna Charta, and in addition was this passage, of which the great Earl of
Chatham, the friend of America, said in his eloquent and forceful way, "These three words, *'nullus
liber homo,'* have a meaning which interests us all;
they deserve to be remembered, they deserve to be
inculcated in our minds, they are worth all the
classics." Thus runs the clause: "No free man
shall be taken or imprisoned, or disseized of his
freehold, or liberties, or free customs, or be out-
lawed, or exiled, or otherwise destroyed, nor will

we pass upon him, nor condemn him, but by lawful judgment of his peers, or by the law of the land. We will sell to no man, we will not deny nor defer to any man, either right or justice." John tried his utmost, late in his reign, to nullify Magna Charta, and many of his successors have tried to magnify their office at the expense of the people, but the charter is still intact.

The provisos of Magna Charta were all founded upon English traditions which had their origin in the days of the Witenagemote, but the increase of freedom and human rights of which we are conscious arises from our better appreciation of the words *liber homo* or free man. We recognize no man as other than free unless he has been derelict in his duty or is wanting in brain power and must be confined for his own safety and the security of others. For fully half a century after the charter was signed little is known about parliaments, but we may safely assume they were duly convened while the matter was fresh in men's minds.

In the year 1265 writs were issued convening knights, citizens and burgesses to meet in parliament, and this was fourteen years later than the date at which similar writs of summons were issued in Denmark. The fact is important as showing the regularity of parliamentary gowth in different countries and under various names, and it is especially creditable to the Scandinavian race. When the

commons assembled in England at first they met in
the same chambers with the barons and prelates,
and probably that system continued until some time
early in the fifteenth century, when we may imagine
some super-sensitive aristocrat was offended because
the "base mechanicals" dared come

"Betwixt the wind and his nobility,"

and was able to persuade the rest of the barons to
join in asserting their superiority by meeting in another chamber.

Certain it is that before the end of the fifteenth
century the dual-chamber system was in full operation, and the results of that seemingly unimportant
movement have been most favorable to liberty.
Grants of money were made at first by either chamber, with the concurrence of the other, but the barons were not solicitous to give money, and the custom gradually fell into desuetude so far as that
house was concerned. The commons, on the other
hand, although not inclined to be spendthrift, were
willing to support the king in consideration of
favors that the soveregn could extend to the trading and manufacturing communities.

In England as well as on the continent of Europe
sovereigns wisely sought to counterbalance the
feudal aristocracy and their armed retainers by calling to the front the industrial classes or burghers;
and the once dominant lords found themselves just
as important, in the course of time, as the fifth

wheel of a coach. The Anglo Saxon people came once more into prominence, as their language had done after three centuries of endeavor for its suppression. In the one case the mothers and nurses of England proved more powerful than the court and the laws, preserving and developing the forbidden tongue, which has become the vehicle for the finest poetry extant, save the Book of Job, and the grandest philosophy of all the ages, replete with quotable and ever to-be-quoted sentences, such as Tennyson wondrously describes as

> " Jewels five-words long,
> That on the stretched forefinger of all time
> Sparkle forever."

In the other the industrial energy and commercial enterprise of the commons proved more recuperative and persistent than the warlike genius of the barons, knights and esquires, and in the end achieved a victory none the less complete.

Every step made by the commons in assuming control of the purse-strings was made with energy and decision as by men that had come to stay. Quite early in the game, and before "My Lords, spiritual and temporal," saw any significance in the movement, the commons had affirmed the principle that "all money bills must originate in the lower house upon a message from the crown, and may be rejected *in toto*, but cannot be altered by the lords." Before the power couched in that sentence was understood it had been tacitly accepted and endorsed by precedents so that in parliamentary etiquette it was beyond revocation as long as the lower house had power to stand upon its rights.

Commercial and legal acumen in the commons was more than a match for the military vigor of the barons and the dreamy eloquence of the bench of bishops; so we have seen the magnificence of the House of Peers gradually dwindle down into noth· ingness while the aggressive force of the burghers has gradually compressed both sovereign and lords into the proportions and appearance of gilt toys to amuse children withal while the incidence of government with all its welcome responsibilities rests upon the stalwart shoulders of the whole people. Practically, all other things being equal, weight of brain will govern; and the heads of a hundred men engaged in commerce and manufactures, and descended from fathers so engaged, must needs exceed in bulk and value a like number of heads accustomed to elegant idleness and descended from idle parents with similar tastes.

A French philosopher, having sat one night in each chamber of the British parliament, said he found in the commons that one-half the members had small heads and in the lords' house they all had small heads. That describes the actual fact at the time, for nearly one-half of the commons members were younger sons and scions of the aristocracy, with faculties gradually becoming dormant, while the ruling half of that body is made up of the picked manhood of the time. One speech from John Bright stands for more in the house and before the people of England than all the utterances that the Marquis of Hartington stands responsible for or will ever deliver. The brain of Daniel O'Connell weighed as heavy as that of Napoleon Bonaparte. The high moral tone and keen intellect of Gladstone and the incisive clearness and tact of Disraeli have distanced the nobles in their respective parties, and it is a fact well known to all observers that but for new creations by the sovereign, and the faculty for marrrying commoners which the aristocracy of England have developed, the House of Lords would have long since been vacant. But we are crossing the river before we reach the bridge, and that is not good policy; we must just step back a handful of centuries.

After the struggle with John there was no difficulty further as to convening parliaments; the change noted in 1265 meant broadening the base of the institution by calling burgesses by their representatives into the national council, and of course the expenses of members were paid by their constituents, as well as a stated allowance by way of salary. This matter of remuneration pressed so heavily on some of the smaller boroughs that we find them petitioning the king at different times to relieve them from the responsibility.

Centuries later, and before the Reform Bill, which was carried through mainly by Lords Eglinton, Russell and Grey, became a law, there were small boroughs that almost lived on their representatives in the house of commons, who were expected to pay roundly in cash for every vote, and in addition to procure government appointments of a remunerative sort for a little horde of poor relations.

Admiral Lord Cochrane, afterwards Earl of Dundonald, got even with one of the rotten boroughs in a very ingenious way, that deserves mention. There was a regular tariff for the votes of the rank and file, but the general officers in the army of corruption had to be specially considered into the bargain. Lord Cochrane, a brave and liberal officer, was determined to win the seat without paying the wages of sin. General elections occur every seven years or thereabout, but sometimes members become incapacitated to serve, through bankruptcy or insanity, sometimes their seats become vacant from death, or they become politically dead by accepting offices of profit under the crown, and need revival by re-election at the hands of their constituents. There was a vacancy in this way for only one year, the remainder of a term, and Lord Cochrane offered himself as a candidate, premising that he would not pay any man to vote for him.

His meetings were well attended, his speeches
25

were full of eloquent expressions of liberal senti
ment, and his political views *en regle*, but he spoiled
every night's performance by reiterating that he
would pay no man to vote for him. Committees of
expostulation waited upon him, but he was imper-
vious to counsel, and of course he was defeated by
hundreds to one. Only five men voted for Lord
Cochrane and he invited the little band of purists
to dinner after the election. He gave to each man
a letter containing thrice the ordinary *douceur* for a ·
vote, and an expression of his pleasure that there
were some men patriotic enough to cast aside money
considerations in an election. There was of course
no harm in a wealthy man who had not been elected givng presents to his supporters after the event.

Less than a year afterwards, parliament having
expired by effluxion of time, there was a general
election, the members being chosen for seven years,
and Lord Cochrane was besieged every mail with
letters from the men who had not supported him to
come down to the borough and be elected. He began his campaign as before, by saying he would not
pay any man to vote for him, and that was the refrain of every speech, but almost the whole borough
gave the choice in his favor, leaving the old fashioned corruptionist and his money "out in the cold."
The polling day passed as before, and after the
voting a dinner, with a letter for every elector, but
no *douceur*, as the Admiral honored the purity of

their motives, and would not besmirch their newly discovered honesty by an offer of money, which might discredit his election. The disappointed corruptionists groaned, but the member was safe for seven years, and he was too wise to count on a re-election.

In one election for the Borough of Liverpool, in which Mr. Wilberforce was a candidate, the expenses ranged above two million dollars.

Parliaments increased in importance from the time of John until nearly the end of the fifteenth century, when in consequence of the carelessness of the boroughs any person could be sent into the house of commons, and the peers of the realm made it a point to procure the election of their serving men and dependents. This change took place about the same time that the two chamber sittings commenced, and nearly a century and a half elapsed from that time before the lower house regained its status.

Elections were easily manipulated. The writs sent to the sheriff in each shire were by him transmitted to his agents, who acted as returning officers, and they making what arrangements they thought fit as to publicity, would attend at the county court, or at any other hustings, at the appointed time, to receive nominations of candidates. Any person in the secret and possessing the qualification could attend with two friends to propose

and second him, and a few hangers on to make a
show of hands, and the election was usually certain.
Sometimes the sheriffs and their agents, the returning officers, would insert wrong names in the
returned writ, but usually they drummed up ten or
a dozen of the unwashed to carry the pet candidate
by acclamation; and there was but little stir made
in any case however great the malversation.

While the followers of John Wycliffe, known as
the Lollards, were in force, the political and reform·
atory zeal of the translator of the Bible into the ver·
nacular secured more attention to such duties as elec
tions, but after his death, the party being persecut
ed to extinction, every public duty fell into neglect
until the days of the printing press and the con·
summated reformation shed light and warmth on
the body politic. The Wars of the Roses were not
favorable to parliamentary growth, but they were
also very destructive to the aristocracy, as the crusades had been, and the rise of the Puritans, striv·
ing to conform their lives to God's word, gave new
salt to a kingdom that had well nigh lost its savor.
Persecution helped the newly born sect, ridicule
assailed them as precisians or Puritans, without
avail, and perils of burning at the stake for being
found reading the Bible did not in any considerable degree weaken the movement.

Bibles, which had until now been only printed
in the learned languages, having been rendered into

tne vernacular of their respective countries, by Luther in Germany, assisted by Melancthon and his colleagues; and in England by Tyndale, who afterwards sought safety in Holland, there were no insuperable difficulties in the way of smuggling the gospels and the Old Testament into the kingdom, as New York merchants procure contraband silks, and the exponents of free thought felt that they were in a special sense God's people.

Meeting in the darkness of the night, after the sound of the Curfew bell had warned all people to cover or extinguish their fires and lights, the fugitive worshipers, carrying their lives in their hands, listened to the readings and exhortations of some more learned brother, and then with subdued voices, but rejoicing hearts, joined in services of praise and prayer to the Most High. There has been no modern revival like it, for every man and woman that took hold on Christ and lived according to his precepts and example, did so with a full knowledge that spies and traitors were around, dogging their footsteps for opportunities to betray them, Judas like, into the hands of their enemies, who would cause them to seal their witness with their blood. This was a world's revival.

Political vitality was one of the immediate consequences of spiritual light, and immediately after the Puritans rose into notice there began to be an improvement in the composition of parliaments.

The good people were in communication, by means
of trusted agents, with men in high positions all over
the land, and when new members were to be chosen
for the lower house, the conventicle, in an out-house
or barn, became for the time a primary and caucus
without the pernicious intervention of ward bummers. Brethren with special gifts and grace were
importuned to assume the representative power, and
failing success in that way, gentlemen who were
known to be favorable to the cause, although they
had not yet openly embraced it, received the support of the party, who could always muster at the
hustings a sufficient band to outvote the sheriff's
nominees.

CHAPTER XXIII.

PARLIAMENT SUPREME.

Henry VIII.—Queen Elizabeth—Spanish Armada—Cervantes—Shakespeare—Bacon—Cromwell—Hampden—Pym—Eliot—Strafford—John Milton—Revolution 1688—The Two Wesleys.

In the reign of Henry VIII. the house of commons gave so much offence to that imperious monarch by deliberating for a whole day upon one of his demands, that after the grant had been voted he ungraciously told the house that it was well the vote had passed, as otherwise he would have taken a few of their heads to adorn Tower Hill. It was no assemblage of lackeys and dependents that would scrutinize the proposals of Henry VIII. even for a day, for the Tudors wore gauntlets of steel, and seldom cared for silken coverings to disguise their means of operation.

The marriage of Henry VIII. with his brother's widow, Catharine of Aragon, aunt of Charles V., King of Spain and Emperor of Germany, did not result in the birth of a son, and the whole country dreaded civil war, unless a male successor to the throne should be given to the nation, to shut out the possibility of a Scottish succession, through the marriage of Henry's sister Margaret into the Stuart family, reigning in that kingdom. Had a son been born to Henry, he would probably have accepted that fact as an indication of heaven's blessing; but failing that mark of favor, he asked the court of Rome to dissolve the union.

The marriage of Henry with the widow of his brother Arthur, which was arranged when he was only twelve years old, would have been impossible under the canons of the papacy for valid reasons, had not the Pope given special permission; and now, when Henry was at the prime of life, and his Spanish wife, always more dignified than beautiful, was stricken in years, with no offspring but an atrabilious, sickly and unamiable girl, Mary, his conscience tormented him with doubts whether the union had not been cursed of God because he had been married within the forbidden degrees. It was no answer to his scruples to say that there was no consanguinity between the parties; in that age, men bowed down to the ordinances of the church as implicitly as to nature's laws, and the fact that no son had been born was evidence of heaven's displeasure as well as a menace to the continuity of the Tudor line. Parliament was of the same mind with the king.

The pope, appealed to by Henry for relief, promised a divorce, and Cardinal Campeggio was dispatched to England to commence the necessary proceedngs, for Henry was in high favor with Rome, having been honored from the Vatican with the title, *Fidei Defensor*, or Defender of the Faith, because he had written and published under his royal hand a reply to the anti-papal strictures of Martin Luther.

Just there commenced a difficulty which proved ultimately advantageous to England. The nephew of Catharine, Charles V., was answering Luther by hard knocks at the temporal possessions of his princely supporters, and therefore, when he, at the head of the greatest armaments in Europe, wielding the powers of two courts, Spain and Germany, demurred to the divorce as a reflection upon the honor and fair fame of his aunt, it is not to be wondered at that the pope allowed the proceedings of Cardinal Campeggio to be arrested, or at any rate to move so slowly that they might as well have ceased. It is the custom with a certain class of writers to assume that Henry was only a libidinous monarch, seeking the gratification of his passions in the proposed divorce, and even Gray, the poet, ascribes the zeal of the king to his marital designs on Anne Boleyn:

> "When love could teach a monarch to be wise,
> And gospel light first dawned in Bullen's eyes."

We know enough of kings and princes to grasp the fact that when they are viciously disposed, marriages and divorces are among the smallest matters they care for, and it seems as though the green earth spawned panderers to minister to their lusts. Henry sought a legal union from which might be born an heir to England's throne, and if he blundered in the means employed it was a fault of the same class, but more excusable, than that which induced Napoleon to divorce the Empress Josephine and seek an alliance with the house of Austria, although we do not find people alleging lust as the cause of that unhappy union with Maria Louise.

It is unimportant for our sketch of parliamentary development whether Henry was loyal to the nation, and the line of Tudor, or anxious only for carnal pleasure, but in all such matters, it is well to aim at correct impressions, even in the side issues that arise, hence we have been at some pains to investigate the *bona fides* of the king; and as the outcome of our research, the facts so far as they are known, are in the hands of the reader.

Rome played fast and loose on the divorce question until king and parliament were disgusted, and eventually England was severed from the See of Rome to become another papacy with Henry for its head. The divorce was then obtained in the king's own courts. Anne Boleyn was made Queen, and once again a daughter only survived from the marriage. Papal authority was set aside by a parliamentary act setting forth that the Bishop of Rome had no more power in England than any other foreign bishop. This act of 1535 was final on that

WESTMINSTER ABBEY.

question excepting only the brief reign of Queen Mary.

Anne Boleyn, accused of unfaithfulness, on evidence that would not satisfy a Chicago divorce court, was executed in 1536, having been married only three years, and the daughter Elizabeth subsequently reigned. Jane Seymour, Anne of Cleves, Catharine Howard and Catharine Parr were successively married to Henry, and by the third wife he obtained a son to succeed him as Edward VI. Jane Seymour died in 1537, Anne of Cleves was only his wife nominally, Catharine Howard was rightfully accused of infidelity, and put to death, and the widow, Catharine Parr, survived him to marry one of the chief of her former subjects. Parliaments were usually obedient to Henry VIII., but whether that arose from too great deference for the king or from reasonable concurrence in his statesmanlike policy, it would be difficult to determine to the satisfaction of every enquiring mind.

Parliaments became more Puritanical, because the people were becoming thoroughly imbued with the views of the Reformers, but the aristocracy were largely of the old faith, and if the power of the Commons had not been very strong for Henry it may be easily imagined that his lease of power would have been brief. Many of his nobles were able individually to bring more strength into the field than the king, as he had no standing army,

and indeed no armed force whatever, worth naming,
except the *Buffetiers*, since called Beef-eaters, because their peaceful conquests are confined to the
trencher.

Great rebellions arose in Henry's time, the Pilgrimage of Grace, as it was called, being the most
formidable, but the king subdued by tact what he
might have failed to crush by force, and the dangerous nobles who would have welcomed the excommunication of Henry and the declaration that he was under the ban of the Holy See, were severely dealt
with under the law, and laid to rest by the hands
of the executioner.

The claims of the Puritans for an open Bible
were in part conceded under the advice of Thomas
Cranmer, who afterwards, in the reign of Mary,
died an unwilling martyr. The Bible translated by
him or under his direction was under the king's
authority placed in church choirs and porches,
chained to desks easy of access, and the people
were at one time encouraged to read the word;
but later in the reign the right to read the Scrip-
tures was limited to certain classes, excluding ap-
prentices and servants. Henry was not bold enough
to risk free thought in its entirety, but considering
his limitations he was an able monarch and patriot
although he contracted his tendencies towards reform by the maxims of statecraft.

Henry was succeeded by his son, Edward VI.,

under the will of the king, which had been admitted by the parliament as the authority that should determine the succession. Edward was only ten years old when called to the throne in 1547, and he reigned only six years, being but a weakly and ailing boy at the best; but his term of authority, under the protectorship of the Duke of Somerset, his uncle, and subsequently under John Dudley, Earl of Warwick, was favorable to the reformation, and therefore, by reflex action, to the parliament.

Following the precedent of his father, Edward was induced by the Dudleys to make a will, appointing the Lady Jane Grey his successor; and that amiable lady, unfitted by nature to play the part of usurper, for which she was cast by her ambitious father-in-law, the Earl of Warwick, and her husband, Lord Guilford Dudley, reigned like "a mockery king of snow" only twelve days, after which she was consigned to the tower of London by order of Queen Mary, and removed thence only to be beheaded, as were the others implicated.

Mary, familiarly known to Protestant historians and readers as Bloody Mary, did the utmost in her power to win the *sobriquet* that attaches to her name. Reigning in all but five years, religious persecutions in their worst form were confined almost entirely to the last three years, and within that term five hundred persons were put to death for conscience sake, under her orders, besides thousands of others who were subjected to lesser punishments.

The reign of Mary is an era for which English-men may well blush. She was married to Philip II. of Spain, but her husband, after a brief term of residence in England, where he was extremely unpopular, returned to his own country, and could not be tempted back again by the most abject appeals of his wife. So far as such a course was possible, Mary restored England to the fold of St. Peter, but the properties of the chu·ch which were taken by Henry, when the monasteries and nunner-ies were disestablished, had been distributed in so many and such powerful hands that the work of recuperation could not be attempted. Eminent Catholics, and even her husband, Philip II., who never gave up his hope that he might be in some way his wife's successor on the throne of England, tried hard to dissuade the queen from her severities against the Puritans; but her zeal suffered no abate-ment to the end, and it was only by the most ex-traordinary tact and address, that Elizabeth, daugh-ter of Anne Boleyn, survived the daughter of Cath-arine of Aragon by the same father.

Protestants who were lukewarm when Mary and her supporters were dispossessing and doing to death Jane Grey and her manipulators, would have given all that they possessed in this world for an opportunity to reconsider their line of action before the reign of Mary was half over, and on the whole,

considered in that way but in none other, the succession of Mary was advantageous.

The reign of Elizabeth is justly considered the
most illustrious in the annals of England, as within
that term the greatest names in literature became
known to the world. The time will come when the
parsimony of the queen, with other blemishes, chiefly
of selfishness, and what is called statecraft, will
detract largely from the high esteem in which she
has long been held, but, nevertheless, her place in
history will continue to be glorious, because of
such names as Bacon, Shakespeare, Jonson, Spenser, Sydney and others identified with literature,
and such besides as Raleigh, Drake, Frobisher,
Hawkins, and many more that made England mis-
tress of the seas.

When the great queen came to the throne England
was weak and poor, her population altogether was
little more than that of London to-day, and bands
of sturdy beggars could be met in all parts of the
kingdom, willing to enter on any marauding scheme
that promised success without wholesome work.
As then placed, England could hardly have held her
own against any one of the great powers of Europe,
and Elizabeth wisely resolved to secure peace as
long as peace might be possible without absolute
dishonor. She advised parliament to devise means
whereby the sturdy beggars might be set on work,
and she played with dangers that menaced Eng-

land from abroad by allowing every court to believe she could be won in marriage.

Her half sister's widower, Philip II., was very solicitous to win her hand, and she allowed him to amuse himself with hopes and fears until she became strong enough to answer the unwelcome suit more vigorously. The house of Valois was then the ruling dynasty in France, and so continued until after the days of Black Bartholomew, and two members of that contemptible family with Medicean blood in the background, were in succession aspirants for her hand. She listened to numberless proposals of all kinds from nearly every nation in Europe, and even her own ministers could not tell the sinuosities of her foreign policy; but all the time she builded the kingdom over which she reigned, and by all means, including some that an Algerine pirate could have legitimately applauded, filled her treasury.

Open air preaching of the reformed faith near the town cross under a leaden roof in London, was one of her means to govern public opinion; not that she preached, but she dictated the lines of argument and illustration, welding church and state together with mighty blows, which made such preaching acceptable; and then the lesser lights of the church throughout her realm were expected to shape their utterances to the same standard. Royal progresses were made occasionally from castle to castle, and

places of less note were included, the people so
honored being at the end of such visitations much
impoverished in means, and much more enthusiastic
for the royal power than they had been before the
last of the Tudors came that way.

Gratitude, the French say, is a lively sense of
favors to come, and every one of the queen's *pro-
teges* felt sure that some great thing would be done
for the family by her Majesty. Spanish galleons
on their way from South America, were intercepted
by English armaments under Sir Francis Drake and
other such commanders, who made rich prizes of
the golden cargoes and vessels, although the country
was at peace with Spain, and Elizabeth accepted a
lion's share of the spoils, while sturdily denying
all complicity in the offense. Thus the hatred and
contempt for Spanish seamanship, which had long
been latent in English ports, was called out and
strengthened, while every prize towed into harbor
was a means for the enrichment of England's
defences.

The day came when Philip II. of Spain could be
amused with vague promises of consideration no
longer, and in his ports the long threatened Armada
was being made ready, when the brave Devonshire
man, Sir Francis Drake, the circumnavigator of the
globe, second to no man in sailor craft and daring,
swooped down upon the Spanish coast and worked
such destruction that the expedition was postponed

for a year. The invincible Armada came at last,
bringing thumb-screws, racks, boots, and every
ingenious instrument of torture that the Inquisition could suggest as a means for the silencing of
Puritan doubts, combined with the most powerful
armament that Spain had ever sent afloat, under the
command of the most illustrious military men of the
time, and fortified specially with the papal blessing
for the discomfiture of heretics.

The year 1588 will always be memorable among
Englishmen because of the frustration of the designs
of the Spaniard which was then witnessed. There
were one hundred and thirty ships in the Spanish
fleet, some of them of enormous size, under the
command in chief of the Duke of Medina Sidonia,
with two thousand three hundred and forty-one guns
and nineteen thousand soldiers, and they were first
sighted off the English coast one night in August,
1588. Instantly the men on watch signaled from
headland to peak, until the whole coast was a blaze
of watch-fires from Plymouth Hoe to Penzance on
the one side and to Yarmouth on the other, and from
every port there were vessels of all arms crowding
sail to meet the invader. The main fleet, ridicu
lously small by comparison with that of Spain, was
under the command of Lord Howard, of Effingham,
and the queen would not allow to any ship more
ammunition or food than would suffice for two
days.

The progress of the fleet was disputed every mile of the way along the English Channel by ships so small that the Spanish vessels towered above them and could not depress their guns sufficiently to do execution, while every shot from the defending host, fired at point-blank range, raked the lower decks of the Castilians, reducing many of the sea castles to a sinking condition at the first discharge. Fire ships were used with terrible effect by Lord Howard, and the Spaniards must have concluded they had found a coast alive with sea devils.

The strong winds and storms which embarrassed the Spanards upon a hostile shore beyond endurance, just gave to the Puritan descendants of the sea kings of yore a capful of wind with which to manoeuver, so that after discharging a broadside they would 'bout ship and give the foe the benefit of the other set of guns while those first discharged were being sponged out and reloaded. Small vessels, unable to obtain from the royal arsenals more than enough powder, shot and sustenance for two days, made a virtue of their necessities, assailed and captured Spanish vessels of ten times their tonnage, and thus secured the means for further operations against the enemy.

Never was such discomfiture wrought by so small a force since the fall of Goliath before the sling and stone of the boy, David. Yet there was not in either case a miracle; the means employed by intrepid hands were sufficient for the emergency. The fire ships used by Lord Howard were the means of capturing twelve large vessels, and the Duke of Me dina-Sidonia was convinced that he had made a mistake in his calling.

To return by the way of the British Channel was not possible, for the English fleet was being reinforced every hour; there was not a fishing smack left on the beach in any sheltered nook on the rock bound coast of Albion but presently some Puritan crew would arm and man her to fight Spain in the offing, and with a "Yo, heave yo!" that could be heard over the billows, she was run down into the sea to carry her quota of courage to the spot where the battle for the Bible was being fought. Better would it have been for Spain if the Duke had concluded to surrender with all his force, but he dared not for shame.

There was a way out that competent seamen could have made safe around the Orkney Islands, and by that course the Spanish ships were signaled they must return to Spain, abandoning the long contemplated invasion. The coasts of Scotland and Ireland were strewed with wrecks of the great Armada for years afterwards; the chivalry of Spain was destroyed, and that country has never since enjoyed her former status among nations. The warlike enterprise of Spain shrank and withered from that hour; the inquisition, denied conquests elsewhere, settled with a deathly grip upon Spain itself, and the genius of Cervantes, stunted of its fair results, has found no succession in the intellect of that country worthy of the promise of "Don Quixote."

The genius of England was now fairly roused, and the puritanism of the farm house and the coast-line was only on a par with that of London and the large towns. Parliaments were ablaze with love of liberty, and patriotism became the soul of the nation. Elizabeth, having sold injurious monopolies to enrich her treasury, was surrounded in the street by a resolute populace, in deference to whom she revoked the monopolies, but retained the price which the once-favored suitors had paid for the privilege.

The queen died in 1603, and the Scottish succession, so long dreaded, came in the person of James I., who hated liberty, and preached without ceasing, by word and deed, his faith in the divine right of kings to misgovern the world. Parliaments were hateful to him, but, spite of all his kingcraft, he could not dispense with their assistance, and his tyrannical aspirations were daily curbed by a sturdy band of patriots, whose names will never die. Death overtook the master of lying and deceit, and the consequences of his training fell with deadly influence upon his son Charles a few years later. There could be no supplies legally obtained without parliamentary grants, and when the Commons were asked for money, they demanded, first of all, the redress of grievances, with such men as Sir John Eliot, John Pym, John Hampden and Oliver Cromwell to the fore—a band of heroes and statesmen that might raise even Spain to eminence, could their greatness transfuse a race as odors fill the air.

I do not try to tell my children all the story, but the major facts have to be embodied in my narrative. I tell them how many started in the race, and how few reached the goal in that grand struggle for parliamentary rights. Sir John Eliot, as noble a man as ever breathed, and loyal as sunlight, was snatched away from family and friends, by the king's orders, and imprisoned in the Tower of London for having spoken freely and bravely in parliament, as was his duty, and because he could not be prevailed upon to confess himself in the wrong when he knew that he had done right, he was retained as a prisoner in the tower until his death, after which his family were refused even the privilege of his bones for burial.

One man, named Wentworth, was in the patriot band, absoulutly fierce in denouncing the exactions and falsities of Charles; but the king discovered the weak place in the master mind of the statesman, and, ministering to his vanity by titles and preferment at court, the earl of Strafford forgot the principles which as Wentworth he had advocated, or remembered them only to betray the sacred trust in which he had joined so many nobler men. John Pym warned his old associate of the dangerous path that he had entered on, but the course remained unchanged, until he was at last found guilty of treason, and beheaded under a warrant from the royal master to whom he had been too faithful.

John Pym remained in his place, true as the dial to the sun, faithful in counsel, daring in speech as he would have been in act, until the civil war between king and commons had commenced, and then he was stricken down by sickness, and removed by death at the moment when his manly co-operation would have been of the highest importance to his friends and colleagues in the most salutary enterprise of modern time. During the reign of James he suffered imprisonment for having opposed the measures of the government in the commons, but that did not diminish his courage. As lieutenant of the ordnance and as chief of the commission in London, after the flight of the king, the greatness of his possible services was already being shadowed out when death seized him, almost instantaneously. Commencing his parliamentary life a wealthy man, he utterly impoverished himself in the service of the country, and the parliament, after his death, voted fifty thousand dollars to pay his debts.

John Pym confronted James at Newmarket to vindicate the rights of the commons, and either of the

kings would gladly have purchased him with wealth
and honors, but he was above temptation. He drew
up the grand remonstrance denouncing the wrongs
done by Charles, conducted the impeachment of the
Duke of Buckingham, as well as that of his whilom
associate, Strafford, when he proved recreant. In
the short parliament, and afterwards in the long
parliament, as they are respectively called, he was
the leader of the country party, and there was no
man more popular. Could the king have made a
prisoner of him and five colleagues, he believed the
commons could be controlled.

John Hampden, who died of wounds received on
the field at Chalgrove, a Colonel in the revolutionary army, stands out in history as the representative
of patriotism and purity par excellence. He was
of great wealth and related to Oliver Cromwell;
indeed, it is probable that, but for his influence,
Oliver might never have entered parliament. He
sat in the later parliaments of James I., being first
elected in 1621, taking part in the protest against
the proposed marriage of Charles I. to a Spanish
princess, and generally allying himself with the
country party in every movement against the arbitrary encroachments of the crown, although at first
his position was third rate, if not actually obscure.
There were no wondrous abilities in him; like
Washington, he won by moral force, rather than by
intellectual prescience. But, once his qualities be-

came known, none looked upon him from the popular side but to admire.

Hampden was a royalist in the sense of believing
that a king was a necessary part in good government; but, at the same time, he insisted upon all
needful limitations of the royal prerogatives, and
would not allow one cent to be collected by his
majesty without parliamentary authority. When
Charles arbitrarily levied the tax known as ship
money, Hampden fought the imposition in the law
courts, and, although he was defeated by a corrupt
decision on the part of the judges, his action roused
the people to resistance. When the king fled from
London, after having failed to arrest the five members in the House of Commons, in 1642, John Hampden was one of the most active in organizing armed
resistance to the royal authority. At Edgehill and
at Brentford, John Hampden was in command of
the cavalry, and, had he lived, it is very probable
he would have been made commander-in-chief of
the parliamentary forces instead of the earl of Es-
sex; but, at Chalgrove Field, June 17, 1643, in an
affair of cavalry with the fiery Rupert, Hampden was
mortally wounded, and died six days later.

Oliver Cromwell alone remained of that sturdy little band, for Denzil Holles, Sir Harry Vane and
others of that type, were small by comparison with
the leaders. Had the others lived Oliver would
probably have contented himself with a subordinate

position to the end, but as events shaped around
him, he was forced into prominence. He was not
an ornamental member of the Commons, but he
was indefatigable. Slow and hesitating as a speaker, his thoughts always went straight to the goal
and could not be confused. He owed nothing to
the graces and refinement of dress, and, when the
rupture with the king was precipitated by the monarch, he was one of the first to give of his substance, and to gird on his sword in the parliamentary cause. He employed a Dutch general to teach
him the art of war, and then having found the
hired soldiers of the parliament but indifferent
fighters, without an idea of honor and bravery, and
with only a hireling's interest in the quarrel, he began
to recruit his regiment of Ironsides 1,000 strong,
all religious men fighting for God and their native
land.

That act of Cromwell's may be said to have
changed the whole aspect of the war, as he was able
to say of his Ironsides truthfully, when threatening
Louis XIV. of France, that he would march with
them to Paris. "Indeed they have never been beat-
en." Hampden said of Cromwell years before the
civil war commenced: "If we ever come to a breach
with the king, he will be the greatest man in England." He was the commander of the victorious
left wing at Marston Moor, which held its position
when the right had been driven in confusion by

Prince Rupert, and when the impetuous Royalist returned from his brilliant achievement, he found, to his surprise, that Cromwell with the left wing had achieved a glorious victory for the people. In the engagement at Naseby, June, 1645, his command contributed in no small degree to the decisive victory, and his wisdom in administration was equal to his intrepidity in battle; to say more of any man under any circumstances would be superfluous.

The parliament was quite inclined to constitute itself the government instead of the king after Charles had given himself up to the Scotch forces, but Cromwell and the army thought differently. His proceedings in Scotland and in Ireland fastened popular attention upon him, and marked him out as the one man who could save the nation from anarchy. He was, as we might imagine, a man sitting in a carriage, behind a nerveless driver, in just such an emergency as might have cost the lives of all concerned; and without pausing to consider whether such an act might be called usurpation, he quietly assumed the reins, controlled the frightened steeds, reduced their pace to rule, and drove them in safety along the brink of the precipice which otherwise they must have dashed over.

The protectorate of Cromwell made England a first-class power, able to dictate terms to the Pope at Rome, in favor of religious toleration, and to Louis XIV. of France, to compel good faith. John

Milton, the poet, was his secretary and admiring friend. It was the spirit of Cromwell that was in his Ironsides, and without them and him the outcome of the first civil war might have been disastrous to parliamentary government, and civil as well as religious liberty. England has not yet adequately honored its greatest man in the science of government. He deserves to rank, and in the esteem of future ages, will rank side by side with Bacon and Shakespeare, in their respective faculties, as the poet, the philosopher and the statesman-administrator.

When Cromwell died, his noblest son having perished in the civil war, there was no one of his family worthy and able to succeed him. His son Richard, wearied by cabals that his father would have extinguished, resigned the protectorate, to which he was not equal, and in the imminent dread of anarchy the parliament hastily convened for the purpose, called to the throne Charles II., the third in the Stuart line, and in some respects the worst. Parliaments had fallen from their high estate, as congress and all institutions must fall after protracted civil war, and until better conditions have been regained. The gaiety of the court of Charles surrounded wrongs of all kinds with a glitter that was preferred by meretricious thinkers to the sombre excellence of Puritanism; and the tyrannical exactions of James II., brother of Charles, merging into popery,

were necessary to rouse the people to put an end
to the Stuart dynasty.

The daughter of James II., when Duke of York, had
been married to the Prince of Orange, who was
holding together the weaker powers of Europe, to
oppose the designs of the conqueror, Louis XIV.,
of France. William, Prince of Orange, was a thorough Protestant, and came of a trusty race, tried in
the fires of persecution by Spain and the forces under the cruel Duke of Alva, and to him the Protestants of England looked for relief. He would not
take rank, as some hoped he might, as a kind of
prime minister to his wife, who was heir to the
throne failing male descent, so he was made king,
and his wife queen, by act of parliament, after James
II. had fled from the kingdom, overawed by the
general discontent.

The revolution of 1688 was an addendum to the
civil war, and though perforce omitted here, is necessary to a complete narration.

The war in Ireland, corruptions in parliament and
kingdom, treason in army and navy, and claims of
successive Stuarts to the throne, although parliament had limited hereditary rights to Protestants by
express declaratory act, kept the nation in turmoil for
nearly a hundred years, and then better conditions
came slowly but surely, with the open-air preachings and revival services of John Wesley, the founder of the great Methodist church, which now reck-

ons its adherents by millions on this continent and in Europe.

After William and Mary were both dead Queen Anne reigned a few years, plotting more or less to secure the throne at her death for her brother, but her death came suddenly, and the whigs or reform party, destroyed the plans of the slow-moving tories, by proclaiming the Elector of Hanover, George I. King of England. His claim consisted in his being a Protestant by profession and having descended from James I., by a daughter that was married to the Elector Palatine early in the seventeenth century. Parliament, under Walpole, as under many of his predecessors, from the accession of Charles II., was, if possible, more corrupt than a well lobbied congress, but the forces at work in the kingdom, cleansing public morals, prepared the way for better things.

The Church of England was a scandal to the nation, preachings were formal exercises in which thousands of indifferent men engaged for a living, which was often spent in vice and riot.

John Wesley and his brother Charles, and George Whitfield, prepared for that Church, but touched by the Holy Spirit, commenced a series of truly wonderful services, by which their lives were many times imperiled, and under the influences therefrom arising the moral tone of the English people has risen to a standard even higher than that which preceded the birth of Cromwell, or to place it in other words, the tone of mind which in his day belonged only to a few is now slowly becoming the heritage of the whole people. Parliaments could not remain corrupt while churches and the newly expanded press were purifying the Augean stable of the community, so reform bills were demanded and carried, power was broadened at its base by extending the right to vote among the people, and now the parliament of England is the highest and most powerful legislative body that the world has ever seen.

CHAPTER XXIV.

MAY THEIR FAME ENDURE.

Origin of the Book—Singular Vicissitudes—Ballarat Gold Fields
—Wonderful Memory—Sheriff Matson—Olson of Calmar—Olson of
Cambridge—O. Storlee—Foss of Milwaukee—Jas. B. Bradford—
Mr. Willard Merrill—Railroad Enterprise—Commerce and Philan-
thropy—Blundering Preachers—Great Blind Men—Value of Sight—
Summary of Blessings.

_____

> Sweet are the uses of adversity,
> Which, like the toad, ugly and venomous,
> Wears yet a precious jewel in his head;
> And this our life, exempt from public haunt,
> Finds tongues in trees, books in the running brooks,
> Sermons in stones, and good in everything.
> —*Shakespeare.*

> The man that hath no music in himself,
> Nor is not moved with concord of sweet sounds,
> Is fit for treasons, stratagems, and spoils;
> The motions of his spirit are dull as night,
> And his affections dark as Erebus.
> Let no such man be trusted.
> —*Shakespeaere.*

Music was now the daily topic of my discourse,
as well as the delight of my home, and I found in
all my experiences how sweet are the uses of adversity. There had been no sorrow, however dark,
but it had been sanctified to wise purposes, and I
have learned to value sterling friends the better for

having been compelled to test their devotion under circumstances which would have scattered the motes in the sunshine to the four winds of heaven. On one of my visits to Madison, Wisconsin, the capital city of the State, where I had gone in the prosecution of my business and to enjoy the company of my friend Professor Anderson, it was my pleasure to be introduced by him to the Hon. Charles E. Jones, to whom I am indebted for the idea, which until then had never taken form in my mind, of presenting this, my autobiography, to the public.

I afterwards found that Mr. Jones had been for many years in Australia, in which country he has filled the very highest positions as Minister of the Crown in the Colony of Victoria, having been a responsible minister and member of parliament, commissioner of railways, bridges and public works; and also, which to me was far more interesting, having been one of the representatives of the city and gold field of Ballarat in parliament when my father-in-law and my wife's brother were gold miners. Through his kindness I have been enabled to learn many curious facts concerning Mr. Boyer, which otherwise might never have seen the light of day, and to my brother Fred, I am indebted for one incident which deeply impressed my mind at the time and has never lost its significance.

Soon after Fred's arrival on Ballarat he went with
27

his father to attend a great political meeting, in
which the speech of the evening was delivered by
Mr. Jones.   The speech was little better than heath-
en Greek to Fred, as at that time he had not mastered English to any extent, but he was able to
drink in the enthusiasm of the hour and to comprehend some few ringing phrases, with which the orator brought up his audience to fever heat; besides
which, the deep interest evinced by his father
showed him that the occasion was one to be remembered.   At the close of the oration, for the impas-
sioned eloquence to which he had listened was more
than a speech, the old gentleman, although he wore
the rough attire of a miner, was ushered to the
front and introduced to the popular member, and as
the father and son went home together that night
the old man said in the vernacular in which they
usually conversed when alone, "I am more pleased
to have shaken hands with that man than if I had
conversed with the king." Since that time many
opportunities have been afforded me to become acquainted with the sterling qualities of the man to
whom Mr. Boyer referred, and I have found his insight as to character fully justified by my experiences.

In the abandon of friendly intercourse I told some
few incidents of my life, as they have been narrated
here, and to my surprise was encouraged to proceed time after time, until the retentive memory

The Port of Calcutta.

of my friend was fully charged with what he was pleased to call a "lifetime of peaceful adventure." Having mastered the main facts of my career, in the manner indicated, Mr. Jones advised me to offer the volume to the reading public, as a contribution to literature, which could not fall still-born from the press; and notwithstanding all my doubts I was prevailed upon to become an author.

Visiting Chicago from time to time, I found one of the playfellows of my childhood, C. R. Matson, holding the dignified position of justice of the peace in that city, and respected by all classes for the manly integrity with which he discharged the duties of his office. He has since risen to the important position of sheriff of Cook county, and it is not difficult to believe that his manly qualities and his professional acumen, added to an eloquence that never fails, will procure for him yet higher honors at the hands of the people. When we met in Chicago, after many years of separation, it was delightful to find my friend unchanged in all the attributes that pleased me in our earlier companionship, and I have been indebted to him for many signal kindnesses.

The Scandinavian stedfastness, which is exemplified in Sheriff Matson, is winning for our compatriots all through the Northwest an ennobling recognition which must gratify the nationality so honored, while it redounds to the advantage of the whole community. I could not say less of my friend, in justice to what I have realized, but it would be easy to say much more with truth, if it were not for my fear that my language might be supposed too flattering or too partial.

There are a few friends of that period that must be mentioned, and there is no time more apt than the present. In our dealings with men there is an ever-recurring need to judge of character, and where others would have trusted their sight mainly, I have had to supplement the other senses by using the eyes of my friends. I could learn much from the tones of a voice, from the grasp of a hand, from the sound of a footstep, from the mental habits of the persons with whom I conversed, and from the essence of a man's life which surrounds him speaking for him or against him unconsciously every hour of the day; but after all, I have been fain to seek the counsel of my friends almost always before making an important decision in which any dealing with a new acquaintance played a part.

In that way I found myself much beholden to my good friend, P. Olson, of Calmar, Iowa, with whom I first foregathered in Milwaukee, years since, when I was engaged in the broom business. Since that time I have seen him in his home, in the midst of his prosperous enterprises, and in every instance his influence upon my life has been most beneficial. The name has for me a pleasant significance, and

whenever I find an Olson, I am predisposed to discover a friend faithful in counsel and liberal in
deed.   More might be said without approaching the
limits marked by the demonstrated kindness of my
tried friend in Calmar; to say less would be ungrateful.

I have said that the name Olson has a pleasant
significance in my mind, and that fact arises in
part from my contact with Christ. Olson, a merchant of Cambridge, Wisconsin, to whom I shall owe
many substantial acts of kindness as long as I live.
It is easy to repay every business obligation with
interest that makes the advantage mutual; but when
a merchant, whose every hour can be converted into
current coin, steps aside from his business pursuits
for a time to give the advantage of his commercial
insight to one whose claims would be considered
merely nominal by thousands similarly situated,
the heart of the *beneficiare* must be made of unim-
pressionable stuff if he is not moved to express his
appreciation.   I hope the day may come when it
will be in my power to render some service to
Christ. Olson of Cambridge, but until that time ar-
rives I must content myself with these few words of
grateful remembrance.

O. Storlee, of Burlington, Wisconsin, patentee of
the best self-binder in the world, and of many
other useful inventions, is a man so engrossed in
his mechanical pursuits that at the first glance one

would conclude his attention could not be won from
the operations of his workshop, where every known
power in mechanics is represented by appropriate models or diagrams, ready for consultation or
application in working out his own designs for
labor-saving machinery.

Contrary to all such anticipations, I have ever
found Mr. Storlee a sterling friend, who would quit
his work bench without a murmur upon the first
hint of a need for his assistance, as though his time
had no value for either himself or the world which
could not be compensated by the knowledge of a
deed of kindness wisely done. I believe that he is
in the habit of finding rest for his intellectual powers in the cultivation of the higher sentiments and
the moral faculties, and that after such exercises he
returns to his occupation as an inventor like a giant
refreshed.

The value of his many inventions and improvements has been recognized by purchases and royal-
ties, and his fame is established among those best
qualified to scrutinize actual merit, so that I cannot
hope to do him any good by my few weak words of
commendation; but nevertheless there is a satisfaction to myself in the knowledge that I have endeavored to discharge my duty toward one of nature's
noblemen, who has many a time and oft done more
—aye, very much more—than his duty by me.

There was one friend in Milwaukee whom I cannot choose but name, although in his avocation as a handicraftsman John Foss would not seem to challenge recognition. Goldsmith, in his "Deserted Village," comments on his own brother, who was the living entity from whom he borrowed the illustration that has been so often quoted:

> "A man he was to all the country dear,
> And passing rich on forty pounds a year."

Now I would not for one moment compare Milwaukee with "sweet Auburn, loveliest village of the plain," for although lovely beyond all question it is not a village, and its more than two hundred thousand souls, prosperous and increasing, forbid the idea of desertion being applied to the community and the site; but my friend Foss is wonderfully like the dear old vicar in the numberless kindnesses out of small means which have won him the heartiest and deepest appreciation from his surroundings. I have never heard of one instance in which John Foss has failed to respond nobly and readily to a suggestion that he should give his time and means to any worthy purpose, and there are few men who have won more golden opinions from all classes by obedience to the new commandment, "That ye love one another." I have always found him an earnest, trusty friend.

This chapter may seem full of laudation, but in fact the names here mentioned are those of friends in whose praise too much cannot be said.

Happily for me, in my comparatively prosperous days in La Crosse, I became acquainted with a young lawyer full of vim in his profession, and very successful in its practice, then and subsequently a resident of Janesville, Wis. I refer to Mr. Willard Merrill, superintendent of the Northwestern Life Assurance Company, located in Milwaukee, which is doing an amount and class of business that offers the best possible guarantees to the public in these days when so many associations have collapsed. Mr. Merrill has rendered me so many and such signal services that I am utterly at a loss to imagine how some of my enterprises could have progressed without his succoring hand.

The spirit which animated the community of La Crosse during my stay there, and which I hope still endures, seems to well up in every gentleman that formed one of that noble band of citizens wherever I meet them, and to pervade the friends that date from that era. Only in that way can I account for the manifold kindnesses that my family and myself have received from my friend, Mr. Willard Merrill, and his household. Such men win honors in every walk of life, and carve out their own fortunes without apparent effort, as the rose diffuses its fragrance without even willing to scent the morning air. The poet said truly as well as beautifully,

"It is the mind doth make the body rich."

Speaking of Mr. Willard Merrill, and remembering that his family is largely identified with railroad enterprise, I feel bound, on behalf of the needy blind all over this country, to acknowledge the almost innumerable acts of unostentatious kindness that have been extended to the sightless by railroad corporations. It is the custom with a certain type of declamatory writers to denounce railroad companies as extortioners, and monopolists, because, having invested immense capital at great risk in making and operating lines of road which span this continent from Maine to the Golden Gate, and, indeed, in every direction where traffic and travel promise returns, they are not willing to allow their customers to fix for them, beyond appeal, their rates of remuneration.

That kind of criticism is unwise, as well as ungenerous—unwise, because the returns netted by fortunate companies in one direction are certain to induce other investments in feeding and extending lines, which must enhance the value of all property, and by facilitating travel and exchange of commodities multiply indefinitely the wealth of the community. In the ante-railroad history of European countries, partial famines depended not on the absolute failure of the earth's fruitfulness from any cause, but on the absolute, or almost absolute, inability, of the people who possessed food in plenty to transfer their surplus to market. Food was rotting on the ground, or in granaries was being consumed by insects in one district; while in another people were dying of starvation. Roads, when they were made, led by the castles and fastnesses of robber barons, who commanded every practicable ford or bridge over rivers, and took toll, to any extent their greed suggested, from every husbandman and merchant traveling toward market, following

> "The good old rule, the simple plan,
> That he should take that has the power,
> And he should keep who can."

When the rule of the robber barons ceased, the cost of making and maintaining roads still fell, with more or less crushing emphasis, upon the industrial classes, by way of excessive toll on traffic in some countries, and by the *corvée* in France and elsewhere, compelling the peasantry to maintain the highways in good condition to save the gay equipages of the noble proprietors from unnecesaary strain. In England, a local poet in the eighteenth century burst into rhyme, inspired by the badness of the lines of communication, with lines, if possible, still worse, saying:

> "The roads are not passable—
> Not even jackassable."

And royal travelers carried not only arms against highwaymen, but tools for digging their carriages out of deep ruts, from which relays of horses could not otherwise drag them. In Scotland, the want of roads, or their utter badness, completely cut off the highlands from communication during a large

part of every year; and in the lowlands it was difficult, in times of peace, to conduct traffic from one
town to another. General Wade, a military road-
maker, in the eighteenth century undertook the task
of making the main lines of travel rudely passable
—not such roads as we wot of in these days of Mac-
adamized highways and Nicholson pavement—and
again the grateful public broke out in rhymes,
which contained more truth than poesy, as, for instance, in the lines:

"If you had seen those roads before they were made,
You'd cast up your eyes and bless General Wade."

In this country, dentists flourished before the advent of railroads, because the molars of men were
almost shaken from their sockets from the concus-
sion of travel incident to corduroy roads; and persons of delicate frame dared not travel in many districts unless they had conveyances of their own.
Such evils have been minimised, if not removed altogether, by the construction of railroads; and, if it
may seem that the charges are in some instances
excessive, it must be borne in mind that the ties
and ballast of roads will only last a few years at
farthest; that even the best steel rails cannot be relied on under heavy traffic for more than ten years,
and that ten years is the outside computation of the
life of each engine, so that every year, putting accidents out of the question, there has to be provision equivalent to one-tenth the original outlay to

maintain the efficiency of the road and its rolling stock. It is, then, unwise to cut down too rigidly the rates of return that railroad corporations may obtain upon their large and eminently riskful investments.

It is ungenerous, also, to carp at fair returns, or even at large returns for a time, upon outlays of capital which have proved successful, seeing how many millions have been expended in abortive enterprises, meant to exploit the resources of districts which have been too slowly settled afterwards to allow the original investors to recover the bare outlay.

That is a fine and eminently generous injunction, which applies in principle to all ages, although the direct command and illustration were local, "Thou shalt not muzzle the ox that treadeth out the corn." Society can well afford to be liberal in re munerating those who at their own risk have covered the earth with bands of steel upon which commerce can make its circuit, meeting the wants of every class; and favored by which in times of war, when all roads become temporarily the property of the State, the armed forces and *materiel* of the nation can be concentrated on any point that may be menaced with invasion, to launch the vengeance of threatened freedom upon the heads of wrong doers.

I would not make railroad corporations irresponsible and arbitrary if it were in my power to do so,

but I would give them such substantial opportunities for recuperation as must well repay their enterprises where wisely planned, and after that I
would have the State become the proprietor of all
necessary roads, on equitable terms and conditions,
in the interest of every part of the community and
of all industries.

I have diverged somewhat from my first intention, into a discussion of the equities of railroad
enterprises, when it was only my purpose on behalf of all my blind brethren who have been favored
by them, and on my own part more especially, to
thank railroad corporations for free transportation
whenever circumstances have rendered applications
of that kind necessary. The generosity with which
I have been treated inclines me, and I may say
compels me, to speak out of the fulness of my
heart in favor of the management that has so helped
the sightless. They have done this not because the
blind can make returns in any way for kindly treatment, but solely and entirely, as it seems to me,
because our deprivation, appealing to the heart of
the magnates of commerce, has won there an
amount of consideration which money could hardly
repay, and which deserves to be noted and remembered by us all among the good deeds that
make our lives pleasant, whenever occasions may
enable us to do justice to the works of our benefac-
tors.

Kindly feelings toward the blind are not always expressed in such a way as to evoke gratitude from my own class, nor even in such a way as to deserve it, unless very large allowances are made for good intentions to offset maladroit execution.

"He that is stricken blind cannot forget
The precious treasure of his eyesight lost,"

as Shakespeare says; but the less he is able to forget his deprivation, the more irksome does it become to hear himself held up in sermons and addresses as an illustration of the very worst form of affliction that can blight humanity.

As long as intellect remains unimpaired there is a way more or less direct out of every minor trouble, and the blind would find their lot much more endurable if it were not for the well meaning, half informed men in pulpits, blind leaders of the blind, who use the story of Old Bartimaeus as a text whereupon they string unreasoning adjectives and dull platitudes until they have impressed their congregations, beyond hope of reversal, with the idea that a sightless man, if poor, has no refuge but in beggary. That method of reasoning might have had power before medical men, physiologists and teachers began to master the secrets of our being to some extent, and to apply their knowledge wisely to education; but it has force no longer.

The blind man can now learn many handicrafts which raise him at once to the status of a self-sustaining citizen, can study history, philosophy, science, poetry, and some of the arts, including music, with such particularity as to qualify him for the office of the teacher. "My eyes make pictures when they are shut," as Coleridge says in his "Day-Dream," and though it may not be permitted to one man in a hundred generations to rival the mental gifts of Homer,

> "That blind bard, who on the Chian strand,
> By those deep sounds, possessed with inward light,
> Beheld the Iliad and Odyssey
> Rise to the swelling of the voiceful sea,"

yet it is a lesson worth remembeing that two of the greatest poets of all times have been blind men; and in lesser degrees than they, but still in such proportion as to deserve the fullest education, the treasures of intellect that have been vouchsafed to the sightless will amply redeem them from the reproach of mendicancy.

I have listened to the lackadaisical ravings of such preachers and speakers, depreciating the blind under circumstances which would not allow of my replying then and there, until I have found myself vowing that I would some day tell the public, as I now endeavor to do, the injury that is inflicted upon the sightless in the first instance, and upon society at large ultimately, by such reinforcements of prejudice and ignorance acting upon the common mind until the wall of isolation, by which men of ıny class are surrounded, becomes almost impassable. In Chicago first, and afterwards in St. Louis, my applications for employment were met with almost insolent rebuffs, because of the fashion to which I demur, of assuming that blind men are helpless and useless, incapable of giving an equivalent for their daily bread.

"The blind old man of Scio's rocky isle," whose genius led captive the soul of Byron, should be an argument for education and appreciation in those quarters where we have been too long sufferers from a maudlin pity which is to us absolutely revolting. Among the blind there is an ambition to do and attempt all that can be undertaken by the seeing world, and there is a pardonable pride in the exploits of every one of their own class who has widened the bounds to which the endeavors of the sightless have been limited by the tyrant custom, even more than by their infirmities. Our eyes have not been closed in endless night. The mind is still attent within us, capable of seeing with others' senses and looking with a brightness of desire which no depth of affliction will diminish in the living soul, toward

> "The flaming bounds of place and time,
> The living throne, the sapphire blaze,
> Where angels tremble while they gaze."

And the immortal essence is dulled by contact with a mind and body in which the powers of education have been wanting or misapplied.

It is but fair to the blind that those who speak concerning them should say that there are degrees of blindness, in which those who "blind their souls with clay," to use the language of Tennyson, are the most afflicted. We would gladly pray for and receive on bended knees the gift of sight, with souls outpouring fervent gratitude to our Father in heaven, because we then might feast our eyes upon the beauty of this footstool of the Almighty; but we would rather ten thousand times remain shut off from that joy of sense, aye, be severed from communion with the world, than surrender our faith in the mercy and power of the Creator, which is borne in upon us every day through the blessings of which we are conscious, though we are compassed about by darkness as by a wall.

.I shall never look upon the faces of my children, my wife, my friends—as I would gladly do were the power within my reach—until I have left behind me the grave clothes of clay in which we pass through the Valley of the Shadow of Death; but I can shape them all to my mind's eye, full of an ideal beauty, which answers without scar or blemish to the conception of character that has been shaped upon my brain by the circumstances in which we live; and it is not certain that I could really see them with my senses without doing violence in some degree to the pictures already formed of their several well known excellences.

28

We know too well that our chances for gainful employment would be enhanced largely by the added sense, could it be gained, and we do not under-value its worth; but there is no use in crying for the moon. That which is unattainable will not come in answer to our solicitation. It remains only for us to make a virtue of contentment when perseverance could reach no better goal, and to shape our happiness out of a consciousness of the blessings we enjoy rather than waste life in repining.

I was a boy without prospects of life beyond a kind of advanced vegetation, loaded down with a consciousness that I was a burden upon my friends; and a light beamed in upon me, so that I found a school and tutors able and willing to instruct my faculties, until I emerged into the battle of life, a man able to bear some share in the strife of existence. I tasted of the circean cup to which millions have fallen victims, and was already drifting with the current called fashion toward death, when my awakened conscience, fortified by memories of long ago and the forms dearest to my soul, shaped in my dreams a simulacrum of the fiendishness into which men change under the influence of strong drink, and I came out from the contest for mastery strengthened, almost invincible, against the allurements of sense. I was a skeptic rejoicing like a strong man ready to run a race in my capacity to out-manœuvre the less educated and poorly informed in the trick of argumentation, so

that I darkened counsel with words; and in that
moment of my greatest pride in my own strength,
the courage of the flesh, which had sustained me,
passed away, and I was prostrate in supplication at
the foot of that cross where kings in their might are
but as little children, to rise thence full of humble
trust in the divine mercy, having spiritual courage
only through Him in whom we live and move and
have our being.

My life has been checkered by many misfortunes,
but it has not been without joys more numerous
than any pen can recapitulate. My wife and six of
my eight little ones are spared to me, to give me
on this earth a foretaste of Eden until we can respond to the beckoning fingers and the tuneful
voices that call us away to the better land. Under
the blessing of my Redeemer I have no fear but
that I can provide for the training and education
of my children, should my health and strength remain unimpaired; and there is in my mind an abiding confidence that many thousand copies of this
book will be sold with a fair profit, helping the
blind to look out and the seeing to look in, contrib-
uting a little, if it may be, to the prestige, and hence
to the increasing influence of the excellent institutions for the blind, and disseminating in a simple
form the story of the Scandinavian race.

This last thought with me is not the least, for I
love to trace the course of that race which once

ranged the earth at will wherever winds blew and
waters flowed, making themselves masters of destiny for a season by keen swords and keener wit.
Having now after a long probation of sorrow entered
upon a better era, they exercise a commanding influence through simple honesty and courage; and
the continent which was discovered by Erik the
Red, and colonized by his son Leifr, will yet cher-
ish as its greatest pride, the untarnished characters,
the sterling worth and invincible determination of
the Norse-American.

VICTOR GEORGE CAIRNDUFF.
ROSA BELLE.   DAISY.
VIOLET.

CHAPTER XXV.

NOT YET THE END.

Twelve Years—Second Volume—Scarlet Fever—Mrs. McLaren —Children in the Church—A Happy Home—Extensive Travel—W. H. Cairnduff—V. G. Tressler—Col. Geo. R. Clark—We Move to Morgan Park—End of Volume I.

Between progress and digression my narrative has now reached the limit of size allotted to this volume, and there yet remain twelve years crowded full of incident, in which my memory recalls vastly more of joy than of sorrow, but of which as yet my pen or the pen that moves at my dictation has made no note.

It would be a delight to mention here the many new-found friends who have been friends indeed; but chapter after chapter would be required for even that; and so after a few grateful words which I cannot leave unspoken, I will hand the book to you, my readers, indulging the fond hope that some other day I may resume the task which has become a pleasure, and write the second volume of the story of my life.

It may be inconsistent, but it is a trait of nearly all, that the gratitude we feel because the darlings

at our firesides are spared to us, is heightened by
escape from a felt danger of their being snatched
away.   Two of our baby boys left us, and we learned
in time to think of them as bright angels waiting
for us on the other side; but we were not ready to
let our five girls follow them, when four years
ago, in November, December and January of 1885-6,
while we were living in Milwaukee, all were strick-
en very low with scarlet fever.   The hired girl was
at the same time sick.   All this was sad enough,
but the shadow was deepened by our isolation, for,
as is always the case, people, for dread of the disease, feared to come near the house, and it was
difficult to get any assistance even in watching.

During this time we had a friend, Mrs. McLaren,
residing in Milwaukee, who frequently in various
ways ascertained how the children were getting
along, and showed us every possible kindness.
When Christmas came, the children were very sick,
and we were indeed surrounded with gloom.   Santa
Claus had not even been invited, for the loss of a
winter's work had put that mark of hospitality quite
beyond our means.   But we were all surprised, for
Mrs. McLaren wrote us that she had news from
Santa Claus, and that the dolls, pictures, books,
etc, accompanying her note were his gift to our little folks.   Other friends contributed in like manner.

For days before this there had been no change in

the condition of any of the children, and the recovery of all seemed doubtful. We arranged all the presents and took them into the sick room on a table. It was more than medicine, more than watchfulness. It revived them at once, and no relapse followed; and we have ever since felt that, under God's blessing, these friends of ours gave us back our children.

Another epoch in our children's lives so thrills my soul that it must be mentioned here. The history of their Scandinavian ancestry has not been the only class of lessons we have sought to give them. We have told them the old, old story of Jesus and his love; and there came a time, something more than a year ago, when, together with others, four of them, including the twins, Daisy and Violet, then under seven, united with the church on probation. We knew the older ones understood the step they were taking, and as the little ones wished to join also, we saw no cause for preventing them; yet hardly thought the impression they had received would be altogether lasting. All four have, however, been strictly punctual in their attendance at class-meeting and the other meetings of the church, and on the 30th of last June their membership was confirmed, and we feel that they are truly gathered into the fold.

There is no happier home anywhere than ours. No children ever had more devoted care, and of no woman was it ever more grandly true than of their mother that "the heart of her husband doth safely trust in her, so that he shall have no need of spoil." Whatever difficulties, misfortunes and calamities have come to us, she has met all heroically, hopefully. Whether I have come home from any enterprise with a tale of success or of failure, the home has been ever the same bright spot. We have learned from what we have realized together, that "misfortune does not always come to injure," and we are mindful of the motto, "Laugh if you are wise."

Never relaxing our diligence, yet we are not anxious for the future. We moved long ago out of Worry Street in which, indeed, we never took up permanent quarters.

In the earlier part of these twelve years, to which less than twelve pages are allotted, I traveled extensively in various lines of business, in the mining regions of Michigan, and also in the great West, and interesting details could be given of the way I was preserved, and of my escape from many dangers.

In Northern Michigan I met Mr. W. H. Cairnduff, who from the first moment of our acquaintance to the present hour has been one of the grandest in that splendid galaxy of friends that have brightened the pathway for my whole career.

When I met him first he was traveling for his health, and he immediately made it his recreation and his chief pursuit, to apply his extraordinary business ability and unusually bright intellect to my advantage. I wish I might relate minutely how he at once helped and taught me, devoting six months on the first occasion to my work as though it had been his own, and giving me some of the most valuable business points that I have ever been able to get from any one.

Years afterwards we met again. To him they had been years of great prosperity, and to me, of at least partial success; but at the time of our meeting I was probably more discouraged and depressed than at any other period in my whole life. Mr. Cairnduff immediately discovered that he needed a two months' vacation, and proceeded to devote the ensuing two months to my business, and the welfare of my family, as assiduously as he had done the first six months of our acquaintance. This time we traveled in Colorado; but on our return, another consultation between us resulted in plans for my family's removal to the vicinity of Chicago, and the arranging of my business so that I could remain constantly with them.

It was at this time that Mr. Cairnduff introduced me to another friend, Mr. V. G. Tressler, to describe whose excellencies and friendly help, neither the English language nor the Scandinavian contains expressions grand enough. He said he had been praying for years that he might be eyes to the blind; and in fact, having abundant leisure, he has given me more than a year of his time, working as zealously as though his own profit had depended on it; and the prosperity of this, my book, is one of the cherished objects of his care.

Through Mr. Tressler, I became acquainted with Col Geo. R Clark, whose business, to use his own language, is serving the Lord, but who incidentally, to pay expenses, sells real estate. At his suggestion, and through his agency, I took up my residence at Morgan Park, and my two years there have been the best of my life. When the sun shines on us we can more clearly see the loving father's hand than when darkness falls about us, but as I now look back over all the shadows, I clearly trace God's leading, and marvel at his goodness.

My residence near Chicago has been greatly to my advantage, and if that city is so desperately wicked as report would have it, certainly it has never presented to me its roughest side, for I have found in it, in proportion to its population, a greater number of eminently good people than I ever found anywhere else. Of these, Col. Clark from whom we bought our home is one. He has given more than twelve years of work gratuitously to the holding of religious meetings at Garden City Mission, open every night as well as Sundays, and through his work thousands have been saved from a life of sin. Labors like this will not be wthout reward, for

"they that be wise shall shine as the brightness of
the firmament. and they that turn many to righteousness, as the stars for ever and ever."

"Past labors are pleasant," and though I have
worked severely, I enjoy in the retrospect the labor
expended on this volume, which I cannot better
close than with the words of England's laureate,

> " Howe'r it be it seems to me
> 'Tis only noble to be good,
> True hearts are more than coronets,
> And simple faith than Norman blood."

www.ingramcontent.com/pod-product-compliance
Lightning Source LLC
Chambersburg PA
CBHW032015110726
47901CB00004B/1100